HUNTING MIDNIGHT

"Sets the standards on erotica-meets-paranormal . . . Will have you making a wish for a man with a little wolf in him."
—*Rendezvous*

"Amazing . . . Red-hot to the wall." —*The Best Reviews*

"A roller-coaster ride of hot passion, danger, magick, and true love." —*Historical Romance Club*

CATCHING MIDNIGHT

"A marvelously gripping mix of passion, sensuality, paranormal settings, betrayal, and triumph . . . Dazzling . . . A sensual feast." —*Midwest Book Review*

"Holly has outdone herself in this erotic tale . . . A must read." —*Affaire de Coeur*

"A wonderfully passionate read." —*Escape to Romance*

ALL U CAN EAT

"Amazing! . . . A must read. There are no excuses for missing out on this book." —*Romance Junkies*

"The sensuality level is out of this world . . . It's light-hearted, deliciously naughty, and simply perfect fun."
—*All About Romance*

THE DEMON'S DAUGHTER

"A sensually erotic novel, and one of Ms. Holly's most entertaining."
　　　　　　　　　　　　　　　—*The Best Reviews*

"Thoroughly engrossing . . . An exceptional book . . . A must-have for fans of more erotic romance." 　　—*Booklist*

STRANGE ATTRACTIONS

"A sizzling, erotic romance . . . Readers will enjoy this wild tale."
　　　　　　　　　　　　　　　—*The Best Reviews*

"A different kind of erotic story." 　　—*Sensual Romance*

PERSONAL ASSETS

"For a sensual and sweeping examination of contemporary relationships, with the extra zing of some very hot erotic writing, you can't do better than *Personal Assets*."
　　　　　　　　　　　　　　　—*Reviews by Celia*

BEYOND SEDUCTION

"Holly brings a level of sensuality to her storytelling that may shock the uninitiated . . . [A] combination of heady sexuality and intriguing characterization."
　　　　　　　　　　　　　　　—*Publishers Weekly*

"Emma Holly once again pens an unforgettably erotic love story." 　　　　　　　　　　—*Affaire de Coeur*

Books by Emma Holly

Upyr Books

The Fitz Clare Chronicles

BREAKING MIDNIGHT
KISSING MIDNIGHT

COURTING MIDNIGHT
HOT BLOODED
(with Christine Feehan, Maggie Shayne, and Angela Knight)
HUNTING MIDNIGHT
CATCHING MIDNIGHT
FANTASY
(with Christine Feehan, Sabrina Jeffries, and Elda Minger)

Tales of the Demon World

DEMON'S FIRE
BEYOND THE DARK
(with Angela Knight, Lora Leigh, and Diane Whiteside)
DEMON'S DELIGHT
(with MaryJanice Davidson, Vickie Taylor, and Catherine Spangler)
PRINCE OF ICE
HOT SPELL
(with Lora Leigh, Shiloh Walker, and Meljean Brook)
THE DEMON'S DAUGHTER

BEYOND SEDUCTION
BEYOND INNOCENCE

ALL U CAN EAT
FAIRYVILLE
STRANGE ATTRACTIONS
PERSONAL ASSETS

Anthologies

HEAT OF THE NIGHT
MIDNIGHT DESIRE
BEYOND DESIRE

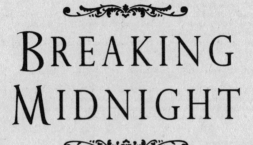

BREAKING
MIDNIGHT

EMMA HOLLY

BERKLEY SENSATION, NEW YORK

THE BERKLEY PUBLISHING GROUP
Published by the Penguin Group
Penguin Group (USA) Inc.
375 Hudson Street, New York, New York 10014, USA
Penguin Group (Canada), 90 Eglinton Avenue East, Suite 700, Toronto, Ontario M4P 2Y3, Canada
(a division of Pearson Penguin Canada Inc.)
Penguin Books Ltd., 80 Strand, London WC2R 0RL, England
Penguin Group Ireland, 25 St. Stephen's Green, Dublin 2, Ireland (a division of Penguin Books Ltd.)
Penguin Group (Australia), 250 Camberwell Road, Camberwell, Victoria 3124, Australia
(a division of Pearson Australia Group Pty. Ltd.)
Penguin Books India Pvt. Ltd., 11 Community Centre, Panchsheel Park, New Delhi—110 017, India
Penguin Group (NZ), 67 Apollo Drive, Rosedale, North Shore 0632, New Zealand
(a division of Pearson New Zealand Ltd.)
Penguin Books (South Africa) (Pty.) Ltd., 24 Sturdee Avenue, Rosebank, Johannesburg 2196,
South Africa

Penguin Books Ltd., Registered Offices: 80 Strand, London WC2R 0RL, England

This is a work of fiction. Names, characters, places, and incidents either are the product of the author's imagination or are used fictitiously, and any resemblance to actual persons, living or dead, business establishments, events, or locales is entirely coincidental. The publisher does not have any control over and does not assume any responsibility for author or third-party websites or their content.

BREAKING MIDNIGHT

A Berkley Sensation Book / published by arrangement with the author

PRINTING HISTORY
Berkley Sensation mass-market edition / July 2009

Copyright © 2009 by Emma Holly.
Cover photos: "Couple" copyright © Masterfile; "Archway" copyright © Jupiter Images.
Cover design by Lesley Worrell.
Interior text design by Laura K. Corless.

ISBN: 978-0-425-22867-8

BERKLEY® SENSATION
Berkley Sensation Books are published by The Berkley Publishing Group,
a division of Penguin Group (USA) Inc.,
375 Hudson Street, New York, New York 10014.
BERKLEY® SENSATION and the "B" design are trademarks of Penguin Group (USA) Inc.

PRINTED IN THE UNITED STATES OF AMERICA

10 9 8 7 6 5 4 3 2 1

To all my readers,
for joining me on the ride.

Somewhere in Europe,
December 24, 1933

Edmund Fitz Clare woke to a darkness so complete he might have been struck blind. He lay naked on his back on a flat steel surface, his immortal limbs as stiff as stone, his belly grinding with hunger. His inability to see—when normally the dimmest light sufficed—inspired a twinge of fear he could not repress: a primitive terror of helplessness. Though he tried to raise a glow in his aura, no illumination came, a sure sign that he was as weakened as he felt. He struggled not to panic, but to take in his surroundings in other ways.

He needed all the information he could gather if he was going to get out of here. That he'd best get out, and soon, was crystal clear to him.

The place in which he'd rather pointlessly opened his eyes was cold, damp, and smelled of moldering stone. The cold didn't make him shiver; he was a vampire, after all, and he didn't need to be warm. Nonetheless, the chill was unpleasant. It seemed to worsen the pain in his head, the radiating spears of torment he could hardly think around.

He had the unsettling impression that he'd lost a good bit of time.

He'd been shot, hadn't he?

The question inspired a curious relief. He distinctly remembered being shot—and with iron rounds, the one metal his kind was weakened by. He'd been standing on Hampstead Heath, squaring off with . . . with two young *upyr*, one male and one female. They'd wanted him to kill Nim Wei, the queen of all the city-dwelling vampires. The pair had been rebelling against her rule and had hoped to use Edmund as a stalking horse. When that plan failed, they'd lain in wait for him in the park and had fired on him with machine guns.

What he couldn't remember was what he'd been doing on the heath in the first place.

His fists clenched with frustration, which was when he noticed his wrists and ankles were shackled—by iron, unfortunately. Chains attached to the cuffs, and probably to the table, allowed each limb a few inches of play. Edmund wrenched against the heavy links, his heart rate rocketing as instincts from another species kicked in. He had a wolf's soul inside him, but with this metal touching him, he wouldn't be able to take its form. Indeed, all his vampire powers were inhibited.

That realization spurred him to fight harder against his confinement, which increased his blood flow, which caused the pain between his temples to surge to sledgehammer blows. He had to force himself to calm, breath by breath, muscle by muscle, until the agony eased enough to let him think again. He was all right; trapped, apparently, and not at full strength, but not in imminent danger. Perhaps he'd been shot in the head. Perhaps one of the rounds was still there. Maybe that was why his thoughts had turned to pudding. His body couldn't push out iron the way it would other poisonous substances.

Edmund wondered how long he'd survive with a bullet

inside his skull. Were master vampires vulnerable to brain damage?

That thought was another puzzle piece. Edmund was a master vampire now, an *elder*, as his race called it. He remembered what had triggered the chain of events that led him here, with a flood of relief profound enough to leave him limp. Auriclus, the founder of Edmund's line, had walked into the sun. When he died, his power had been portioned out among his followers, and Edmund's share had pushed him to the next level of potency. He'd been afraid . . . Here his mind stalled again. He'd been afraid of *something* related to his new status. He'd been running away from it when he blundered into his attackers' trap.

He shifted uncomfortably on his cold steel bed, trying to piece the fragments into a sensible whole. He went back to the part he knew: that the sudden increase in power had been too much for him, that it had flared out of his control. He'd feared he might harm someone. He'd been worried about humans, hadn't he? Humans he loved? *Upyr* could love humans, couldn't they?

Threads of fire seared his brain as synapses reconnected, but this time he didn't back off from his attempt. He saw flashes. Faces. Two young human males, one dark, one fair, their arms slung protectively around a blonde girl-woman.

Daddy, she exclaimed, laughing at him. *How could you forget me?*

Time folded back. He saw the girl-woman as a child, no more than four or five years old. Her tiny, warm hand curled around his as real as night. She was alone in the world. They were all alone, and he was saving them. This trio of humans was his family now.

Edmund's eyes were hot, his heart aching.

You've done a good job with them, said another, infinitely dear voice. *You let them all be just who they are.*

He cried out, unable to keep the hoarse sound inside.

Estelle. Like magic, his beloved's name shuffled the cards of his life into their proper place. Sally and Ben and Graham were his family, all of them orphaned in the last Great War. Edmund had been passing for human when he adopted them, working as a professor of history at a nearby university. Estelle Berenger was Sally's friend. Edmund had been in love with her almost since he'd met her when she was fifteen. He'd saved her from being killed by a lightning bolt by leaping between her and the strike in his wolf form. The incident had left her different, as if a bit of his immortal nature had shot into her cells with the energy. She was still mortal, but she had gifts . . . strengths no mortal ever bore.

Estelle was also his fiancée. A moan broke in Edmund's throat as that awareness returned; joy and sorrow mixed like bitter herbs in wine. He and Estelle had just announced their engagement to his family. Edmund had been making love to her, had bitten her for the first time, when Auriclus's power had slammed into him. Estelle had lit up in the backwash, the very blood in her veins glowing like white fire. Edmund hadn't known the secret of the change before he so summarily became an elder, hadn't known his aura and not his blood was the key. When he finally found out the truth, he didn't have the know-how to shut it off. Edmund had thought he was going to make Estelle a vampire, and maybe his family, too, without them having a chance to say yes or no.

Edmund's branch of the *upyr*, the shapechangers Auriclus had founded millennia ago, didn't believe in changing anyone against their will. *That* was why Edmund had fled to Hampstead Heath, to take himself and his new elder powers too far away to influence his loved ones. He'd wanted to protect them.

Which was how he'd gotten himself shot, shanghaied, and chained to a steel table.

Oh, Estelle, he thought ruefully. *How I wish I'd simply stayed with you.*

He only had a moment for the regret.

Another vampire had entered the space he was in. Edmund heard the faintest footfall, sensed the slightest shift in the air. He tried to read the *upyr*'s mind, but found only a blank spot where it should have been. Bereft of any means to defend himself, every muscle in his body coiled.

"So," said a deep male voice. The shadow of a German accent gave the word a clean, crisp edge. "You're back with us again. I'd begun to wonder if Li-Hua and I had done too much damage."

"Frank," Edmund gasped, the name rising to the surface unexpectedly.

"And lucid," said his visitor. "That's good to know. Hit the lights, darling."

The order confused Edmund, until he realized another *upyr* must have come in. Frank's female partner, he presumed.

She, it seemed, was amenable to being told what to do. The aforementioned lights exploded in a blaze of brilliant white, blinding him in a whole new way. They were the sort of lights cinema people used, a whacking great bank of them supported by a braced metal pole. When Edmund's eyes stopped tearing, he saw he was in a large, windowless cell, its walls lined with blocks of granite. Mold streaked the stones' chiseled surfaces, the source of the mustiness he'd smelled earlier. He craned his head to see more. The table on which he lay was straight out of a morgue, complete with drains along the sides to let fluids run conveniently out.

The vampire, Frank, smiled at him. Edmund hadn't caught more than a glimpse of him before the shooting started. Dressed in a dark, double-breasted suit, Frank was very tall, very muscular, and very Teutonic—precisely the sort of male *der Führer* swooned over. His fair hair fell in waves to his warrior shoulders, while his face could have graced a Renaissance painting. His fangs had run out, making his smile a somewhat less-angelic sight. Given that the *upyr* was fingering a scalpel in his long white hand, Edmund didn't think he was in for a tea party.

"Tell me when you're ready for me to roll the film," Li-Hua said.

She was a lovely Oriental woman, as slight and feminine as her partner was masculine. She was dressed in baggy black trousers and a thick fisherman's sweater. The bright red kerchief tied around her neck added to her bohemian flair. The lights taken care of, she bent to the eyepiece of a motion picture camera on a tripod. Her assurance as she aimed and focused told Edmund she'd done this before.

"Why are you recording this?" he asked. His throat was hoarse from disuse, causing him to wonder yet again how long he'd been at this pair's mercy.

Frank stepped closer. "For fun and profit, of course."

"Profit?" Edmund rasped.

Though he would rather have shown no reaction, he jerked when Frank spread the hand that didn't hold the scalpel across the hollow of his bare belly. As soon as the vampire touched him, Edmund became aware that he could *feel* the bullets inside him, could sense them striving to overcome his recuperative powers. The projectiles were cold, gray things, deadening the flesh around them. There weren't as many as Edmund expected, mere dozens rather than hundreds. Also unexpected was that the skin of Frank's palm was warm, his long, blunt fingers buzzing with a fine tremor.

Clearly, Frank was looking forward to cutting into him.

"You've no idea how fascinating it is to watch an elder heal," he said dreamily. "Your body has been trying to push those bullets to the surface since you were shot. At first I had to slice quite deep to give them a channel out, but now it barely takes an inch or two."

"How long have I been here?" Edmund demanded, suppressing his shudder at Frank's obvious regret. "Where have you taken me?"

"I was most concerned about your head wound," the other man continued, ignoring him. "If Li-Hua or I had a lump of iron in our brain, we'd be drooling wrecks—and never mind the state we'd be in if we hadn't fed in as long as you. You, however, master vampire marvel that you are, are recovering like a trooper. Honestly, I couldn't be more pleased or proud."

"Where *am* I?" Edmund insisted. The younger vampire wasn't trying to avoid his gaze. Taking his chance, Edmund tried to push his will at him, to force him to answer. It wasn't as easy to thrall vampires as humans, but a master should have had the power. Regrettably, Edmund's attempt accomplished only an intensification of the torture in his head. As soon as he released the effort, clammy pink blood-sweat rolled into his eyes.

Frank appeared more amused than offended.

"I don't think I ought to tell you," he said coyly. "In your current state, I don't believe you could pass a telepathic message to anyone, but I'd really rather not take the chance."

It might not have been helpful, but Edmund's temper broke.

"Oh, *do* struggle," Frank approved, as Edmund thrashed and growled in his chains. "I'll enjoy this so much better if you fight. So will my beloved, for that matter."

"I'll kill you," Edmund swore through his teeth. His fangs were sharp now, his bloodlust rising with his rage. The flexible steel table made a sound like thunder as he writhed. "If I have to claw my way out of the grave to do it, I'll kill you both."

"We don't want you in the grave," Frank chided. "We want you hale and hearty and in full possession of your elder power."

Edmund gave his shackles a tug that had the chain smoking on his palms. If he'd been in wolf form, he would have torn out Frank's throat.

"You're insane," he panted, forced by the excruciating pain of holding the iron to unclamp his grip. "You've no idea who you're dealing with."

"Neither do you," Frank said, all playfulness gone. "You will soon, though, once we get on with this experiment." He turned to his companion, gesturing for her to turn the crank that started the film.

When the blade cut into his belly, Edmund didn't bother to restrain his scream.

London, Christmas Eve

Christmas wasn't Christmas without Edmund.

That was the thought Estelle couldn't banish, though she did her best to shed her tears out of sight from Edmund's family.

His home in London had been decorated just as always. The fire was crackling; the cider mulled. In honor of the holiday, Edmund's ubiquitous stacks of books and periodicals had been shoved against the baseboards. Thanks to their housekeeper, Mrs. Mackie, plates of fresh-baked sweets turned the air homey. Sally hadn't let her older brothers evade a single Fitz Clare tradition, no matter how disheartened their adoptive father's absence made them all.

"We *need* to be merry," Sally had insisted. "Daddy would want us to. For Estelle's sake, if nothing else."

The guilty looks Graham and Ben shot at Estelle had almost caused her to laugh. Edmund's youngest had never needed muscle to get her way. Thanks to her skill at manipulation, the Fitz Clare library-parlor was swagged with greenery and stuffed to bursting in one corner with a fat, twelve-foot fir. Presents were heaped beneath it, the messiest—ironically enough—courtesy of Sally.

They'd each bought a gift for Edmund. Just in case.

Robin Fitz Clare, Edmund's son from his long-ago human life, had just finished crawling under the branches to tuck his offerings into the pile. Probably feeling Estelle's eyes on him, he sat back on his heels and grinned across the room at her. His presence was new this year, and Estelle was deeply pleased by it. Robin was an admirable man for someone who wasn't a man at all: humorous, loyal, ready to do what he thought was right, irrespective of his own comfort. Estelle had sensed his essential goodness the moment she laid eyes on him, which she probably wouldn't have done if Edmund's mysterious abduction hadn't thrown them together.

The silver lining was bittersweet. The professor had been gone for weeks, with no clue as to where he'd been taken other than it had been in a dark, unmarked motor van.

But that wasn't what Estelle wanted to dwell on tonight. This was the season for counting one's blessings. Robin's exotic golden vampire beauty—which he didn't trouble to hide inside the house—added a literal glow to what might otherwise have been glum proceedings. Estelle had to wonder if his choice was deliberate. On the surface, Edmund's son seemed simple and good natured. Underneath, he struck her as a person who thought things through.

He'd been looking out for them ever since his father disappeared, quietly placing himself between them and possible danger. Though Robin had his own life to live, his own . . . needs to see to, it was he who went to London's *upyr* queen to discover if she had psychically sensed any more about his father's kidnapping, he who made sure the Fitz Clares had the funds they needed to keep the house running, he who walked Estelle home from her job at Har-

rods every night after the sun had set—though the last
might have been to prevent Graham from escorting her.

She lowered her head to hide an unavoidable smile.
Estelle sincerely doubted Graham would act on or even
mention his attraction to her again; he was too cut up about
the part he'd played in Edmund being caught. Robin, however, seemed unable *not* to defend his father's interests.

"I'm glad we're together tonight," Estelle said, grateful
for every scrap of appreciation she could feel. "I remember
coming to this house as a girl and thinking how miraculous it was that people really could be happy this time of
year."

"Your parents were prats," Sally said, her customary
bluntness in full force. "Scrooge before the ghosts visited."

"We're glad you're with us now," Ben put in. "You
always brighten our spirits."

"Here, here," Graham said, lifting his cup of mulled
cider.

His cheer was forced, but he was trying. Sally sat on the
rug beside him, her soft blonde curls resting on his knee.
Despite her youth and occasional selfishness, no one could
have been more sensitive to her brother's misery. In the
aftermath of Edmund's disappearance, she'd refused to let
Graham pull away from the family. Estelle knew Edmund
would have loved his daughter all the more for it.

Now Sally sighed wistfully. "Daddy gives the best
presents."

"The perfect presents," Ben agreed.

Robin surprised them all by snorting out a laugh. "He
can read your minds, loves. He knows exactly what you
want."

"He wouldn't!" Sally exclaimed, defending him.

Robin's grin was too bright to be human. "He would,
Sunshine, when it comes to picking the right gifts."

"But not about other things. Daddy respects our privacy."

Graham patted her slim shoulder. "Of course he does."

His reassurance didn't take. Sally's cheeks were prettily flushed, her sweet blue eyes worried. Estelle concluded Sally must be concerned about her precious daddy sussing out some secret. Before Estelle could soothe her, Ben reached from the sofa to squeeze her arm.

"Graham's right," he said, soft but firm. "The professor isn't a snoop."

"Or not much of one," Robin muttered humorously beneath his breath.

Estelle's funny ear, the one the lightning had charged with Edmund's power, caught the words. She must have reacted, because Robin's gaze shifted to hers. His face was serious but kind.

"Your gifts are getting stronger, aren't they?"

An invisible shiver ran down her spine. He'd spoken so quietly Estelle was certain no one but she had heard. His guess was spot on. Her gifts *had* been getting stronger. When Edmund's energy had swelled that last, fateful night, it must have given her a second dose of whatever the lightning had transferred. In truth, she'd scared herself a time or two since he'd been gone, though for his family's sake she hadn't mentioned it. Luckily, Robin didn't seem to require an answer. He held her gaze, nodded at some private thought, and then smiled at the rest of them.

"You could open *my* presents," he said. "Since I won't be here Christmas Day."

Sally blinked at him until her confusion cleared. "Oh, right. You'd burn up."

Robin laughed and ruffled her curls. "Not quite, Sunshine. More like turn as red as a lobster or nod off between every word."

"Then you should open ours," Sally said. "So you can dream about them tomorrow."

Robin actually blushed, the color bright on his pale, pale skin. He must have fed before he came to them.

Seeing it, Sally crowed with laughter. "You *are* a silly vampire if you thought we wouldn't get you gifts!"

"I didn't want to presume— Really? You purchased gifts for me?"

Sally dissolved into amusement just as a knock sounded on the door.

"I'll get it," Estelle said, not wanting to disturb the others.

She couldn't keep her jaw from dropping when she saw who'd arrived. The tiny vampire queen of London stood on the stoop, wrapped in a long black fur like Snow White's rival from the fairy tale. Edmund's former lover, the person they'd initially thought was plotting to harm him, held a steaming dish between her alabaster hands, apparently not bothered by its temperature—or the strong brandy fumes. Her expression, which was really *no* expression, didn't twitch despite Estelle gawping.

"May I come in?" she asked, smooth as cream. "I don't want this pudding to get cold."

Estelle moved numbly back to make way. "You brought us a Christmas pudding?"

"I was told it's traditional. I ran from the bakeshop to ensure that it would stay hot." Considering she could run at least as fast as a speeding train, the vampire wasn't trying to make this out to be a hardship. She stepped into the entry where not so long ago she and Robin had engaged in epic battle. Her cool, dark gaze slid over the repaired walls. "I see you managed to patch the plaster."

"Yes," Estelle said. "Graham and Ben are quite handy."

"Graham and Ben are Edmund's sons."

"Yes."

She and Nim Wei stared at each other. The vampire queen was so exquisite it was hard to imagine the human Edmund had been not wanting to be bound to her forever.

"Pudding," Nim Wei reminded, holding it out.

Estelle took the container gingerly by its handles, though

her funny right hand barely felt the heat. "I'll just . . . nip into the kitchen and get plates." She glanced unsurely at the parlor door. "Would you like to say hello to the others in the meantime?"

"I would," Nim Wei said. "Thank you."

Hope prodded Estelle to speak as the *upyr* reached the threshold. "Nim Wei?"

The beautiful vampire turned, her mink hood fallen back to bare equally luxuriant straight black hair. Estelle tried to swallow her nervousness. "Have you come because you've heard something about Edmund?"

Nim Wei's expression took on a new shade of gravity.

"No," she said. "I've put the word out to those underlings whom I trust, so I have ears to the ground around the world. I regret to say, however, that I have not learned anything useful."

Estelle hadn't known the queen was doing more than mentally seeking Edmund. Her practicality impressed her, though it did suggest Nim Wei's powers had limits.

Estelle mulled that over as she ran her errand. When she returned to the parlor with a serving trolley and plates, Graham was standing next to Nim Wei by the mantelpiece. Since Robin was chatting quietly with Ben and Sally on the sofa, Estelle assumed their tête-à-tête was safe. Even though, at six foot and some inches, Graham towered above his companion and had to bend his neck considerably, Estelle knew the queen could snap him like a twig. He seemed calm enough beside her, maybe even a bit less glum. Graham might not be dashing or silver-tongued, but he was very courteous.

Oddly, his looks didn't fade into the background next to the *upyr*'s. His was an honest, ordinary handsomeness, composed of plain brown hair and clean, bluff features. Somehow, Nim Wei's more extravagant beauty underscored how pleasant ordinary could be.

"I was apologizing to Nim Wei," he said. "For mistaking my handler for her."

Graham's handler at MI5 had tasked him to spy on Edmund, thus exposing the professor as a vampire. She'd pretended to be Nim Wei so that Edmund's old amour would get the blame for the betrayal. She'd also turned out to be behind Edmund's abduction.

"I see," Estelle said, noting that Nim Wei's smooth expression remained unchanged. She was so still that Estelle jumped when her perfect red mouth opened. The movement seemed as strange as if a doll had proposed to speak, almost dizzying.

"And I," announced the queen, "assured Graham I did not hold him responsible for what he'd done while under my enemy's influence."

Don't stare at her so much, Robin's voice murmured in her head. *The queen is powerful enough that she could hypnotize a human with little more than her beauty.*

Estelle wondered if she'd been trying to.

Robin startled her by answering. *I don't know, but even if she's on our side, I think we're better safe than sorry.*

Somehow intuiting the exchange, Nim Wei's head turned slowly from Estelle to Robin. She frowned as her eyes fixed on Edmund's son.

He smiled innocently.

"Your majesty," Graham said. "As it's Christmas, I wonder if you'd be willing to accept a token of our esteem."

The interruption was adept. Nothing in Graham's manner said he was either toadying or trying to distract the queen from Robin. In a flash, Estelle saw why Britain's foremost intelligence agency would want to recruit him. Graham seemed so genuine, so forthright, that even a vampire would not suspect him of subterfuge. Nim Wei's eyes were round when she looked up at him.

"You wish to give me a gift? You didn't even know I was coming."

Graham smiled gently, then bent to extract a bottle-shaped package from beneath the tree. "We bought this for the professor. In case he returned. But you've been so helpful I'm sure he'd want you to have it. Robin tells me you can drink wine, and this is our father's favorite French claret. Hopefully you'll enjoy it, too."

Nim Wei accepted the gaily wrapped bottle, curling silver bow and all. Seeming slightly stunned to be holding it, she turned it between her hands. "Thank you . . . I . . . That's very kind of you."

"Let's have pudding!" Sally exclaimed, her own genius for interruption less studied than her brother's. "I smell so much brandy in the batter, I think we can get drunk on that!"

Naturally, Sally's portion held the traditional silver threepence, though Ben teased she ought to hand her luck to him to pay off her outstanding debts. Nim Wei slipped out during the laughter, waving Estelle back to her seat when she would have seen her to the door.

She must find us very odd, Estelle mused. *Very foreign.*

It occurred to her that some of Nim Wei's stiffness might have been due to feeling awkward among the tightly knit and sometimes boisterous Fitz Clares. Estelle remembered her own time on the fringes of their circle, the yearning that could fill her when she was with them—though they'd never purposefully excluded her. Certainly, it couldn't be easy for a supernaturally powerful leader to experience anything of the sort. Queens were supposed to rule, no matter what.

Most of the time, Penelope Anderson—Pen to her friends—did what her father asked. Sure, she knew how to talk her way around him, but if Arnold Anderson truly put his foot down, Pen toed the line.

They were all each other had, after all. Mother hadn't been a part of their lives since "retiring" to her family's Charleston plantation when Pen was ten. *My health*, she'd said in her languid drawl as her childhood servants fussed over her. *Delicate constitutions weren't meant to keep up with you two*. The way she'd put it made it sound like people who wanted to get out of bed and do things had something wrong with them. Why Mother married Daddy in the first place, Pen didn't know.

Well, she did know, actually. Daddy was handsome and forceful, and he'd swept Mother off her feet. Maybe Livonia Peachtree hadn't been so languid when she was eighteen. Maybe it was only when she had Daddy *and* Pen shooting off their rockets that her nerves had failed.

Pen grimaced at the distinguished black door before her, its painted panels shining in the streetlights, the wreath that hung from it tasteful. Small, plain pinecones nestled among the needles, joined by a single cranberry velvet bow. It was a veddy British wreath, one that would whisper "Merry Christmas" rather than shout.

Pen's attempt to assert her national superiority didn't quite succeed. Her spine was tight, her hands clenched determinedly around her long cashmere coat's lapels. Daddy had forbidden her to come here from the hotel—and after all her best arguments. He'd said Graham Fitz Clare had gotten himself into murky waters, and he wouldn't have his daughter floundering in after him. Pen had asked him to come with her, but he'd refused.

He's in a deeper mess than I can get him out of, Pen, he'd said. *It's beyond my reach*—something Pen didn't for a moment believe.

Daddy was a powerful international industrialist. He had friends in every branch of government, right up to the president. It simply wasn't possible for him to be helpless.

Then again, even Arnold Anderson had to be wrong sometimes.

Before her courage could fail her, she reached through the wreath and rapped the brass knocker.

She smoothed her hair while she waited, a nervous

gesture she would have squelched if she could. Her bob was auburn—with a little help from her hairdresser, to whom she also owed her stylish waves.

You look fine, she snapped silently to herself. *Stop fussing.*

The door opened at last, laughter and the scent of cookies gusting out with the warmer interior air. The laughter surprised her; embarrassed her, actually. This was a family holiday, and she was an intruder. She shouldn't expect the Fitz Clares to faint with gratitude for her visit simply because their father had gone missing.

"Good evening," said the woman who'd come to the entryway. "Can I help you?"

She was gorgeous, was Pen's first thought. Cheekbones like slabs of cream set off a mouth kissed to rosy fullness by a kind creator. Any movie star in the land would have shed blood—their own or others—to claim her glowing, thick-lashed gray eyes. The woman was taller than Pen, though Pen wasn't short, and a good deal more generously curved. Pen knew she herself was attractive. Men chased her all the time, even without knowing how rich her father was. This, however, was a woman who could steal male hearts on the strength of her looks alone. The faint red scar that rayed around her right eye would be no more hindrance to that than a beauty mark.

"I'm Pen Anderson," she said, belatedly finding her tongue. "Graham works for my father."

"Oh," said the woman, casting an anxious and hardly flattering glance back over her shoulder. Pen caught a glimpse of a warmly lit and very cluttered library. It was from there the sounds of merriment came. The woman looked back at Pen, seeming no surer of what she ought to do with her uninvited guest. "I'll . . . see if Graham is available. Perhaps you'd care to wait here?"

She wouldn't, but, "Thank you," Pen said and pulled off her gloves.

The woman increased her sense of having overstepped the bounds by shutting the library door behind her.

Thankfully, Graham didn't keep her waiting, though his first words were less than welcoming. "What are you doing here, Pen?"

He looked different from the last time she'd seen him. Older. Not thin, but somehow filling up less space. Shadows darkened the hollows beneath his eyes. Graham had never been what she'd call jolly, but the face he showed her now was somber. An inexplicable little heat bloomed between her legs, one she'd only felt a time or two for him.

"Father was worried," she said, willing her blush not to rise. This wasn't exactly a lie. Her father *was* worried. He simply wasn't intending to get involved.

"I don't work for your father anymore."

"He wouldn't have fired you," she said. "Not for going AWOL for a few days. He understands it's hard to concentrate on work when things happen in your family."

"He didn't have to fire me. I gave notice."

"Graham." Stymied, she shoved her gloves in one pocket and laid her hands on his big forearms. "Let us help you find your father. Let me. You know how good I am at talking people into doing things for me. I have—" She hesitated, uncertain how much to reveal. "I have connections even Daddy doesn't know about."

Graham looked into her eyes, longer than she could remember him doing before, despite how many times her father had invited his protégé to join them for dinner. Graham wasn't flirting, not by a long shot. His gaze was haunted, and Pen had the impression he wasn't truly seeing her.

"There's nothing you can do," he said at last, dully. "There's nothing anyone can do."

"That can't be true. There's *always* something one can try."

Graham shook her hold away. "Go home, Pen. This isn't your business."

A second man stuck his head outside the library door, one whose good looks—unlike Graham's—were immediately obvious. "Everything tickety-boo out here?"

"Everything's fine," Graham said dourly. "My former boss's daughter popped over to wish us a happy holiday."

"Well then." The man flashed a winsome grin. Though she'd never met him, Pen suspected this was Graham's younger brother, Ben. "Happy holiday to you as well."

Graham ignored him.

"Go home," he repeated softly, leaving Pen with little choice but to comply.

She was on the stoop, back in the cold night air, when she heard the brothers speaking through the imperfectly shut front door.

"There's a woman who could pop your cork," Ben remarked, to which Graham responded with a snort.

"She's a harridan. And a brat. And she'd probably poke a man's heart out with those skinny ribs of hers."

Pen gasped at the sting of hurt that stabbed through her. The strength of the pang surprised her. Graham was no crush of hers. He was, as even her British friends insisted, a damned-dull dog. But he'd always been kind to her, always respectful and courteous. Her father believed him a paragon.

And now she knew what that paragon thought of her.

She forced herself to continue down the steps to her Duesenberg, to open the door to the smart red speedster as quietly as she could. It didn't matter what Graham thought. He certainly wouldn't be the first to call her spoiled. Pen had loads of friends, but she was aware she wasn't universally adored. As her father liked to say, no person worth knowing was.

So what if, when she occasionally imagined being married, it was Graham's dependable face and form that swam into her mind. That was merely the effect of propinquity and her father admiring him so much. It was only natural if Pen's subconscious wanted to please her daddy with her selection.

She wasn't in love with Graham Fitz Clare. She wasn't even close.

She repeated that to herself as she shoved her Duesenberg into gear.

Bedford Square

Ben was worried about Graham. He'd always been the quietest of the Fitz Clare siblings, but up until lately he'd never been morose. Hoping to talk to him without the girls overhearing, Ben sought him out in the kitchen where he'd gone to clear the pudding plates.

He found him in the scullery with his sleeves rolled up, the tap to Mrs. Mackie's deep washing-up sink running full out. The housekeeper would be gone for the next few days, home with her family. A single bulb shone from a socket above the old-fashioned basin, its glare throwing the weariness of Graham's features into sharp relief. Not a shred of the cheer he'd forced earlier remained. Graham was watching the heating water run over his big, square hands. He turned when Ben said his name, seeming to shake off his blankness with an effort.

"Girls all right?" he asked.

"The girls are fine. They're saying good night to Robin. It's you I'm worried about."

Graham picked up a plate and began washing. His face was grim, his motions too precise to be natural. "No need to worry about me. I'm not the one who was abducted for Lord knows what reason."

"Graham . . ."

"They say he's not dead. Estelle and Robin and even that vampire queen. They say they'd 'sense' it if he was. But I'm thinking, wherever he is, he's not having a damned picnic."

Graham set the clean plate in the drainboard, took a cup, and began to scrub it under the water. His movements were jerky now, his cheeks grown flushed. Ben wanted to beg his brother not to punish himself this way, but didn't know the words to soothe him.

"It's not your fault Edmund was taken."

Graham snorted derisively. "A perfect stranger told me the man who'd raised me was evil, and I believed her."

"She thralled you to believe her."

"I dragged our father out of his bed. I held him in the sun until his skin blistered, for no better reason than to prove I knew what he was. Hell, I half wanted the woman he loved to be mine instead."

"*Half* wanted, Graham. That's not the same as—"

With a wordless roar, Graham threw the china cup he'd been washing against the wall. It struck so hard it seemed to explode. Then his whole body sagged.

"Fuck," he said, panting at the brief exertion. "Fuck, fuck, fuck."

"Graham—"

Graham held up his hands to stave off Ben touching him. "I'm all right. You don't need to cosset me like Sally does. I'm simply tired of not being able to *do* anything."

"It's not your fault," Ben repeated helplessly.

"Right." Graham sighed and rubbed his forehead. "It only feels like it is."

* * *

In the end, Ben didn't have much choice except to leave Graham to his demons. Feeling as exhausted as if *he'd* blown up, he trudged up the stairs to his room.

Christ, what a Christmas this was turning out to be. Ben appreciated Sally's intention not to let them wallow around the clock, but he'd be glad when this holiday was over.

Graham had one thing dead right. Not being able to take action to help their father was sodding hell.

His heart gave a wrench of another sort when he found Sally in his room. She sat on his bed in her soft knit frock, her back propped on the iron head rails, her slender, stockinged calves curled under her bottom as if she were a child. She practically was a child. Only seventeen to Ben's twenty-two. Her cheeks were rosy, her eyes big and serious. The fingers of one hand were playing nervously with her toes. She was ridiculously pretty sitting there like that, a sweet confection of femininity. For better or worse, Ben had never met another girl he liked looking at quite so much. Nothing felt as right as when Sally was near him.

Or as wrong, for that matter.

"Is Graham all right?" she asked.

He didn't have the energy to lie. "I don't know."

"Do you think I should go to him?" She was already getting up.

"No," he said. "Not this time."

"I hate this," she said. "I hate that Daddy still isn't here."

She scooted down the mattress on her knees, and though he didn't mean to, he walked to her and took her hands. Her palms were hot, their silky skin slightly damp. Chills streaked through him as the color on her cheeks deepened. Spurred by these little signs of her excitement, his cock was stirring fast enough to notice, thickening, rising, until the shameful lust that had tortured him nearly half his life was only seconds from sinking its claws in him.

Her gaze locked on his with a jolt he felt.

"I hate this, too," she whispered. Her fingers squeezed his, their power to arouse him taking his breath away. "I hate that we can't comfort each other the way we want. We're not really brother and sister. Not truly."

Her words were all it took for his erection to reach full rigidity, to begin to pound and ache like it would kill him.

"I can't risk the family knowing what we've done," he said—or maybe begged—hoarsely. "Not on top of everything else."

Her fingertips slid around his wrists, under the cuffs of his cotton shirt. A shiver he couldn't control vibrated down his tailbone, straight to the swollen knob of his cock. A tiny jet of fluid spurted out its hole. He didn't have the fortitude to pull back when she stretched up to brush her mouth over his.

"Shut the door," she said against his now buzzing lips. He had to fight not to lick them. She tasted minty, like tooth polish. "We can be quiet. None of them has to know."

The groan that wanted to roll from him branded that a lie. If she'd been trying to be seductive, he might have resisted, but her simple vulnerability wreaked havoc on his good judgment. Her eyes were pleading, sparkling on the verge of tears.

"We haven't been together since Daddy disappeared. I can't sit still for thinking of you. I can't sleep for the dreams it brings. My body hurts to have you in it again. The things I feel for you aren't going away."

"Sally." His hand lifted of its own volition to stroke her face.

"Close the door," she urged, nuzzling his palm. "Close it now."

He was so stiff, it was a wonder that he could walk. He

managed, though, and shut them alone together of his own free will.

She grinned at him as he returned, joy welling up in spite of everything. She rubbed her hands in anticipation along her thighs. "I want you so much, I don't know which part of you to touch first."

He pulled his navy sweater-vest over his head, too over-heated to leave it on a second longer.

"Is that a hint?" she teased.

"I'm hot," he said, attacking his shirt buttons next. "You get near me, and I start to burn."

He didn't get any cooler when she wriggled her frock upward. Her breasts were bare beneath the pale green knit, their nipples flushed and pulling tight. Excitement arced through his penis, though his racing heart was still finding blood to pump. She wasn't big, but her high little tits had always done it for him, a red flag waved in front of a rutting bull. He wet his lips at the way her bosom jiggled when she threw her garment across the room. Her blonde curls were tousled, her mouth swollen. She ran her hands up her torso, rubbing them around and over her darkened nipples as if they itched.

Another tiny spurt of fluid jetted from his prick.

"Finish undressing," he rasped. "I don't think I can wait.

"Just the panties," he corrected when she started to unfasten her lacy white garter belt. "I fucking love the look of you in that."

She blushed, but did what he asked with mesmerizing slowness. Dressed as she was, she must have known they might end up here. He didn't know how to be sorry. When she was done, the garters framed her golden thatch like a French postcard.

That kicked him back into motion, but it wasn't easy to wrench off his own clothes when he couldn't tear his eyes from her. As it was, he nearly fell over yanking off his socks. His erection didn't waver, just bounced up and down at his groin like it was pneumatic. He wanted to be in her, wanted to fuck her until neither of them could stand. He felt like he was turning into an animal.

"Stay," she said once he was naked.

"I can't stay, Sally. I need you now."

"Stay." She came off the bed toward him, grabbing the back of his plain wooden desk chair along the way. "Put your right foot on this."

She spun the seat around for him. He looked at it, then at her. She was breathing harder than she'd been before, more obviously aroused. His chest felt tight with his excitement. "You want my foot up there?"

"Please, Ben. I want to see all of you."

He did it. He couldn't not. She stepped into the space he'd made and cupped his balls.

"Oh, God," he said, abruptly so close to coming the little hairs on his arms stood up. He gulped for breath and tried to rein his responses. "Sally . . ."

She went on tiptoe, lifted her face, and he simply had to take her mouth in a deep, wet kiss. They moaned down each other's throats. She tasted so good, like heaven, like coming home after having been away for years. He pushed his tongue deep between her lips, sucked her, nipped her, lost his breath in feeling her respond just as hungrily. Every time he kissed her, she seemed to get better at kissing back. She was a genius now—a spine-melting, tongue-stroking cock torturer of a genius.

She pulled free long before he was ready.

"I want to do this," she panted. "Don't stop me."

His brain wasn't working fast enough to stop her, or to guess what she intended. She was kneeling on his hard floorboards, running her hands up and down the backs of his naked legs. Shivers wracked him as she ruffled the fine gold hair.

"I love your legs," she praised. "They're almost as pretty as a girl's."

"Er, thanks?" he laughed—until he lost his power to speak in a startled gasp. She'd tipped her head to the side and had taken one of his testicles into her mouth, laving and sucking it at the same time. He tried to say her name, but all that came out was a breathless grunt. Her fingers stroked the tendon at the top of his inner thigh, the one he'd made stand out by propping his foot on the chair. Hardly able not to, he stretched that tendon more and thrust his hips forward, wanting to expose all of himself to her. He couldn't believe how good what she was doing felt. His hair wasn't just standing up now, it was standing up in waves.

"You're going to make me come," he finally managed to warn her.

"Good," she said and switched to the pulsing testicle on the other side.

He held on by the skin of his teeth, reduced to digging his nails into his palms before she finished stimulating his ball sac. When she took his shaft into her mouth, tears of tormented pleasure squeezed from his eyes. Her little tongue was licking him all over, her suction strong enough to send bolts of feeling shooting up his spine.

"Don't," he gasped as she ran the pointed tip over his throbbing crest. "That's too much. I want to be inside you."

She removed her mouth, though her hand still gripped him beneath the head. She squeezed hard enough to make his pulse go wild.

"You're leaking," she said.

He looked down at her, at himself, red and swollen trapped in her hand. Her tongue curled out to strafe up the now steady trickle of pre-ejaculate. The sight was unbelievably intimate. Her mouth. His glans. Her throat moving as she swallowed the taste of him. A thrill no force on earth could have stopped shuddered up his vertebrae.

"On the bed," he said, his voice turned to sandpaper. "No arguing. Just do it."

She did it, moving awkwardly but not delaying.

"Spread your legs for me."

She spread them, her sex pink and swollen and glistening wet. Ben's breath rushed out of him. She was his. He could take her. The allure of that was primitive and strong. He grabbed her thighs and buried his mouth between.

Her whimpers made his cock hurt, the way she thrust up her pelvis and grabbed his head. Her hard little clit was beating like a miniature drum.

"Ben," she whispered, grinding her pussy against his mouth. "Oh, God, Ben, *please.*"

He licked her until she writhed with longing, until her nails pricked his shoulders and her breath came in desperate gasps. Then he sucked her tender bud between his teeth and pulled.

Her body arched off the bed in an instantaneous orgasm. True to her earlier promise, she was silent except for her fight for air, but she came and came and came until he thought two minutes must have passed. He knew without being told that she had not pleasured herself since they'd last made love. No woman climaxed like this unless they'd been waiting.

The knowledge was a goad his agonized arousal hardly required.

If she'd abstained, that made two of them.

"Enough," she sighed, going limp at last. "I want *you*, Ben. I want your cock inside my pussy."

Christ, she wound him up when she talked like that, when she said "cock" and "pussy" and "I want you." He couldn't do a bloody thing but obey. He crawled over her, his muscles tight and shaking, his distended penis as hard as an iron bar.

She lifted her knees in welcome.

"In me," she said, her slumbrous eyes holding his. "Slide it in nice and slow."

"You're killing me," he swore, but he slid his dick in

slowly—with a long, luxuriating moan. Lord, pressing into her was beyond good. She was velvet around him, creamy and warm and tight. He almost felt too thick for her, too hard and brutish, but she took him as if their different bodies had been born to fit. When he reached his end, and hers, her arms came sweetly around his back.

"I love you," she said as she hugged him. "No matter what, I love you."

Her declaration brought tears to his eyes, hot and pricking. He stroked her curls from her damp forehead.

"I love you," he said, more huskily than she had. "No matter what."

She smiled at him, and the dream he'd been dreaming since before he knew what it meant came true for him again. His hips began to push and withdraw, slowly at first and then harder when she begged him to. They didn't just make love, they fucked, too much need and energy in the movements to use the sweeter word. When they kissed each other, it was hungry. When they sighed, it held deep relief. Ben felt like he'd been waiting longer to spill than a mere few weeks. When he came, the rush of it hot and violent, his body was too greedy to soften.

Not that he wanted it to soften. He sensed she'd join him again the next time.

"You *are* good," she said, a little purr in it, her hips rotating back at him as smoothly as his were.

He nipped her lip, then jerked when she tugged his nipples hard enough to raise an echo of his recent orgasm. His cock thumped helplessly inside her.

"Ooh," she teased, feeling it. "You liked that."

"Did I?" he teased back. He was glowing from his climax, made daring by the knowledge that his skill pleased her. He stuck his finger in his mouth, got it wet, and wriggled it beneath her bum.

"What are you— Oh!" She jumped as he pushed his fingertip just inside her back orifice. Her eyes widened.

"I'm fingering you," he said. "And I'm going to keep doing it, rubbing over and over these nice, rich nerves, until both of us blast off again."

"Ben," she squeaked, her body twisting at the new sensations. "You shouldn't— That makes me—" She closed her eyes and groaned softly.

"Makes you feel dirty?" he suggested, beginning to pump his cock into her harder. "Makes you feel pleasure in places you think you shouldn't be able to?"

Her hands clutched tighter on his sweating back.

"Yes," she said, so delightfully susceptible, so innocently wanton that his whole groin ached. "Keep doing that. Keep doing that to me."

He hadn't expected quite that much encouragement. His body went into overdrive. He pounded into her like a drive shaft on a big lorry, pleasure surging, balls drawing up, every stroke so good it was hard to bear. The way her pussy clenched made him gasp for air. Both their thrusts were so desperate their bodies slapped noisily. He could only pray Graham hadn't returned to his room, because he was damned if he could ease up. He needed this like he needed breath, like he needed his heart to pound. Sally was mewling, pleading, her skin flushing all over as he worked his finger into her faster. She came a second before he did, gushing over him as she'd only done once before. He covered her mouth with his to muffle her ecstatic cry, but was too wrenched by ecstasy himself to actually kiss her.

He was coming like a damned freight train. He almost shouted at the power of it. Spunk shot from his penis in long, squeezed bursts—so hard, so copious, it felt like he hadn't emptied his balls since the day he'd had his first hard-on. By the time he finished, his seed was running warm from her, around his slowly softening erection.

Shit, he thought, keeping the curse to himself so he wouldn't scare her. He'd forgotten to pull out again. For that matter, he'd forgotten to use the condoms he'd made a special point of stocking up on, despite vowing to himself that he wasn't going to take her anymore. Jesus, Mary, and Joseph. What an idiot he was.

Blissfully unaware of his thoughts, Sally's touch was sliding gently up and down his back, her lashes resting like fans on her sex-flushed cheeks.

"I love it when you come," she said sleepily. "I love how your muscles tighten and you shove in hard."

Ben didn't know whether to laugh or cry. She loved it when he shoved in hard—as if he could help himself, as if anything but pouring himself deep inside her had ever felt this right.

If he lived to be a hundred, he'd never understand how that could be.

Nim Wei stood, unseen and unsuspected, in the darkened mews behind Edmund's home. Motorcars sheltered in what had been stables not long ago—or not long ago to her. The world changed in the blink of an *upyr*'s eye, humans coming and going as swiftly as butterflies. It was stupid to get attached to them, stupid even to be interested. The Fitz Clares weren't her business, and they certainly were no Victorian Christmas card. Even now she heard two of Edmund's adopted children, the younger boy and the girl, having at each other like crazed rabbits.

Pagan or not, she knew that wasn't what being thy brother's keeper meant.

Go home, she told herself. *There's nothing here for you*.

Her feet ignored this sensible advice. Given the tug the Fitz Clares were exerting, she had to wonder if some small part of her psyche wanted to be adored the way Edmund was.

The cellar door creaked open to issue a tall male shape, one that trudged up the concrete steps and into the mews with her. A match flared, lighting the face her immortal eyes had already recognized: Graham Fitz Clare, sneaking a cigarette. She fingered the bottle of claret that hung heavily in her mink's pocket. He'd treated her considerately, in spite of all that must have weighed on his mind. Perhaps there *was* more she could do for him.

"Filthy habit," she observed, coming forward out of the shadows so he could see her. "But if you don't want the full handful of decades you've been allotted, do puff away."

Graham looked at her, then threw the gasper down and ground it out with his shoe. "Your majesty."

She liked the natural way he said that, as if *your majesty* were her proper name.

"I've been thinking," she said. "If you really want to help your father, you'd have more power to do so as one of us."

Graham's mouth fell open as she walked to him. Another man as big and physical as he was might have looked stupid with that expression, but Graham's intelligence shone too keenly from his features.

"It isn't an offer I make casually," she added. "I'm very selective about the humans I transform."

Impulse had her laying her hands lightly on his chest. He'd donned no coat, and his muscles were warm and solid beneath his clothes. His heart beat faster at the contact, though he betrayed no outward sign of it. Nim Wei gave him points for control. He was no open book, but she was a strong mind reader, and this close she could sense him remembering Li-Hua. Images of being bitten by the vampiress flickered through his mind, especially of the traitor fellating his cock before her fangs sank in. Li-Hua had drunk his blood to deepen her thrall, but he'd enjoyed that tangle of pain and bliss—and now felt ashamed for it.

Nim Wei had as little use for regrets as she did for not pursuing her desires.

"You'll enjoy being bitten even more with me," she said,

letting enough throatiness into her voice to be audible. "*I* think you're an attractive and healthy male. *I'd* take my time demonstrating that."

Graham closed his mouth and swallowed.

"Nim Wei." His big hands surrounded hers, warming them pleasantly. "Might I . . . have some time to consider your kind offer?"

She didn't need to give him time. She knew his answer the moment he gently lifted her touch from him. If his eyes hadn't been tight with pain, if he hadn't been unaware himself that his decision was already made, she might have lashed out at him.

He wanted to be changed, with a mix of fear and desperation that was ripping him apart. Becoming a vampire would alter his life irrevocably, and it would certainly shock his family. He was remarkably, even admirably, free of the usual desire to live forever, but he was ready to do anything—anything at all—that could save Edmund.

He simply wasn't ready for the person who changed him to be her. Like his father before him, he didn't trust her more ruthless nature not to infect his. He didn't trust her not to turn him into a monster.

She stepped back from him, unable to say a word. She saw she'd been correct before.

There was indeed nothing here for her.

Estelle hesitated at the open door to Edmund's bedroom. All was quiet on the third story, the house beneath her dark, the great city around them still.

She'd put off coming up the stairs as long as she could.

She'd been spending nights with Edmund's family, rather than at her flat, more and more often. It was easier on his children, not seeing this room empty. Tonight, she knew it was harder on her. Though there was no logic in the belief, she'd truly thought he'd be home for Christmas. He'd have known how much it meant to them. If he'd been able, he'd have escaped whatever fix he was in.

Her hands were clenched together between her breasts, worry fighting with the urge to pray. She dropped her arms and released her breath, then stepped inside the silent room. She'd been praying since he'd disappeared. Heaven had to know all her requests by now.

The covers to Edmund's heavy four-poster bed were turned down. Despite her mood, Estelle smiled at the fresh bouquet Mrs. Mackie had set on the little side table with the drawer. White lilies with sprigs of holly spilled from the vase, sweet and simple like Edmund preferred. Estelle suspected the Fitz Clares' housekeeper had shed her own tears for her employer.

A small sob threatened to close her throat, surprising her with how close her storm of grief was looming. Estelle choked it back and forced herself to wash up and change into sleeping clothes. She chose Edmund's rather than her own, his cool, slick pajamas still smelling faintly of his woodsy scent. Whatever else the last burst of his energy had done to her, as long as she wore these garments regularly, she seemed just as able as he'd been to keep the silk from wrinkling.

Her final act before lying down was to open the bedside drawer and retrieve the box that contained her extravagant, Russian-style engagement ring. An old jeweler friend of Edmund's had sold it to him one midnight. She slid it on her finger with the sense that they were connecting again. All day she shared Edmund—and missed Edmund—with his family. Now, with his pledge sparkling on her hand, he felt like he belonged to her once more.

She slid beneath the sheets with a sigh that ached, hugging the second pillow to her breast as if it were him.

Edmund, she thought, unable to resist one prayer. *Please be all right. Please come back to me.*

* * *

Edmund was alone again in the dark. The male vampire, Frank, had cut the remaining bullets out of him—with the exception of the one in his head. Though the gashes had sealed themselves, his muscles quivered uncontrollably in the aftermath, shocked by the pain they'd been assaulted with for the last few hours. That pain had excited his captors enough that they'd taken a break to couple forcefully against the wall of his cell, driving each other to a number of long, gasping orgasms. Their writhing dance had been unexpectedly beautiful, stirring a dim but unmistakable response in him. Edmund supposed he was glad he wasn't too weakened to feel desire, and gladder yet that the poisonous iron had been removed, but his body felt incredibly raw inside. He wasn't certain how much more damage he could have healed.

He also wasn't certain how much longer he could stand the hunger he was suffering from. Had he been able to break his chains, he would have killed Frank simply to feed, whether it helped him escape or not. That didn't bode well for future clear thinking, though it was hard to strategize when he had no idea what the pair planned for him.

He didn't even know what day it was.

He tried to reach out with his *upyr* senses. Frank and Li-Hua couldn't be in this place alone. It felt big to him, a massive weight above his subterranean cell. Chances were, they had associates. Other vampires, or perhaps humans. Surely one of them had a mind—and knowledge—that he'd be able to use.

The headache his efforts inspired was not as bad as before, but the result hadn't changed. He read no more of the minds around him than if he'd been a powerless mortal.

Estelle, he thought, unable to keep his thoughts from her. *I swear I'm trying.*

And then, for one miraculous second, he caught a

glimpse of her. She was curled up in his bed, tears trickling down her face as her mental guards fell with exhaustion. She was even more beautiful than he remembered, so warm, so dear, he thought his heart would crack with the love he felt. His ring glinted on her finger, the diamond as true and flawless as he wished he could be to her.

The picture slipped away as quickly as it had come, but he didn't think he'd imagined it. His imagination wouldn't have put her in his room, though he was grateful for his family's sake. Estelle might not be much older than his children, but hers was a steady soul. She could comfort people just by being near them. He only wished she had someone to comfort her.

I love you, he thought. *Lord, I love you.*

A huge wave of weariness washed over him. Wherever he was, dawn was drawing closer—not arrived yet, but near enough that in his current state he couldn't remain awake. He sank, a cold stone dropping through dark waters.

He didn't often dream, so he was surprised that one came to him. When he woke to sleep, snow stretched in a vast field around him, sparkling with diamond brightness under the sun. He winced and shielded his face, but the rays weren't burning him. Intrigued, he turned in a circle. Immense alpine mountains ringed the plain of white, some of their crags too steep for the snow to cling. They seemed to tower above his smallness like slumbering gods.

"Edmund," Estelle's voice said from behind him. "Where are we?"

He spun to her, his heart leaping up with joy. His gaze ran over her hungrily. She was naked just like he was, and Estelle naked was a sight to see. "I don't know where we are. Why aren't you holding me?"

She smiled and opened her arms.

He didn't seem to move, he simply seemed to be wrapped in her embrace. The kiss they shared was delicious: wet, deep, so real he felt an erection rise urgently.

Happily, she was urgent, too.

"I want you," she groaned. "I've missed you so much."

He felt himself falling back into the snow. She fell with him, the heat and cling of her pussy driving magically down on him as they hit. The drift beneath them was like a pillow, icy but wonderful. Too eager to wait, he took her waist and urged her into motion. He was hard as diamonds, thick and throbbing inside her. She rode his aching length like a goddess, and although he knew he was dreaming, he also sensed he was going to come in truth. His groin had that sort of weight, that sort of gathering pressure. Needing release more than he had known, he ran his hands up her body and over her breasts, their gorgeous silken weight causing him to groan.

She was a gift no *upyr* could deserve.

"Hurry," he said. "I want to come before we wake up."

She hurried and tightened and gasped for breath like she needed the orgasm as much as him. Her wetness ran down him, practically steaming, and increasing with every stroke. Her nails dug into his shoulders. Her face twisted with strain.

"Bite me," she pleaded. "You look hungry."

She had no idea. He pulled her down and plunged his fangs into her neck. Ecstasy exploded in his taste buds. Unlike when he'd bitten her in real life, he felt no hesitation, no fear for her as he drank her blood—just an incredible, uninhibited sensual enjoyment of doing what his nature drove him to. He began to climax and didn't stop: coming with his mouth, coming with his penis, coming with his skin itself as he held her close to him and fed. He knew his sleeping body would be ejaculating, too. Her blood was light running down his throat, a golden wine more potent than sunshine.

"Yes," she moaned, her head flung back, her climax joining his fervently. "Oh, Edmund, *yes*."

* * *

Estelle jerked awake to the echo of her own soft cry. Edmund's room was dark, empty of anyone but her. She realized her sex was clenching strongly in orgasm. She was peaking that very instant, as if Edmund's cock were thrusting inside her. A quick, embarrassed heat rose into her cheeks, a far cry from her recent—if imaginary— abandonment. Edmund's pillow was between her legs. Even now, she squeezed her pelvis over it.

The spasms ended as she gasped and stopped.

She'd never had a climax in her sleep before.

Hardly knowing what to make of this one, she sat up and pressed a hand to her pounding heart. Her neck throbbed where she'd dreamed Edmund had bitten it. She felt shaky and light-headed—as if it had been too long since her last meal. At once, her stomach growled in agreement. She wasn't hungry; she was starving. No doubt the idea of Edmund being denied sustenance had put the thought in her head, but whatever the reason, she was going to have to sneak downstairs to quiet her pangs.

As empty as her belly felt, she hoped Mrs. Mackie had prepared a roast before she'd gone.

White's

Graham wished he felt more relief that Christmas Day wasn't as eventful as Christmas Eve. Neither of his siblings were bowls of mirth, and Estelle was downright distracted, murmuring about odd dreams when asked what was troubling her. Like a group of sleepwalkers, they opened presents and ate breakfast. After that, Estelle returned to her flat—leaving the house at Bedford Square with the deflated emptiness only a finished holiday could bring.

Despite his being glad it was over, the intervening hours until sunset dragged. Graham had already spent too much time alone with his thoughts. He was almost certain he'd misstepped when he hadn't immediately accepted the vampire queen's offer to change him. Her face had been stiff and cool as she backed away. Admittedly, vampire faces often looked like that, but Graham thought he'd registered a difference. A human with her expression would have been hiding hurt.

The question was, had Nim Wei taken sufficient insult to withdraw her aid from their father's search? Graham's ignorance of vampire culture left him at sea as to how to undo the damage—or even if it was wise to try.

Though such thoughts were poor company, he had to wait for dusk to visit White's. As he'd only recently discovered, the professor's favorite haunt was not a gentleman's club for academics, but a secret vampire hotel. As soon as it seemed late enough, Graham borrowed Edmund's car and drove to Piccadilly, parking the Minerva just off the Mall and walking to St. James Street.

Being behind the wheel, where their absent father normally sat, had been deucedly depressing.

Graham's pulse picked up as he approached the three-story building, making him feel more awake than he had all day. Maybe his old handler at MI5 had been right. Maybe he did have a latent fondness for danger.

With its discreet plaque and slightly dusty bow window, White's looked just as stuffily elegant as the area's other clubs. Nothing about its brick and marble facade suggested supernatural creatures resided here—unless one found undrawn drapes suspicious. Robin had informed Graham that White's was named for its owner, Lucius White, the oldest living *upyr* in the world—the same master vampire who had transformed Robin and Edmund. Only he could have established what amounted to a hostel for shapechangers in the heart of Nim Wei's capitol. Though Lucius was not—according to Robin—political, he believed that ceding London entirely to the blood-drinking broods could marginalize the shapechangers. Age-old agreements had given Nim Wei's line the cities as their playground, but in this modern age, shapechangers couldn't afford to hide away in wild places.

For one thing, there weren't enough of those places left. The human world left footprints everywhere.

In acknowledgment of this, White's was a neutral zone, where curious shapechanging vampires could dip their toes into the river of city life. Robin had warned Graham that mostly pack leaders came, and they could be hot tempered. If Graham ever needed to reach him here, Robin advised him to be polite.

Polite Graham thought he could manage, though whether he could simulate the vampire version of good manners remained to be seen.

He rang the bell, a soft, bright chime that echoed in the space within. The ensuing wait gave him time to admire the glossy finish on the paneled door. No decorations marked that it was Christmas, so perhaps some of the resident vampires had religious antipathies. Unless they did, crosses and the like didn't bother them, just one of the misconceptions Graham had been obliged to shed after he met Robin. With some embarrassment, he remembered once arranging to meet Li-Hua, his ersatz handler, in St. Paul's. She'd had no fear of the Christian god, and their surroundings hadn't hampered her a bit from playing him like a puppet.

Shifting his weight uncomfortably, Graham wondered if he'd come too early. The sun was still reflecting a few red glimmers off the Georgian windowpanes.

The door opened without warning.

"No solicitors," said the tall, slender man behind it. He was dressed like a butler, but his face was pure aristocrat, down to the probably useless monocle he'd screwed into his right eye. Though his glamour was in place, his features were too regular to be human. Graham tried not to show that he'd noticed the vampire's waistcoat was misbuttoned. Apparently, he *had* woken someone.

"I've come to call on Robin Fitz Clare," he said in a firm but mild-mannered tone. "I'm Graham Fitz Clare. I believe Robin left my name with your staff."

"Ha!" said the butler for no reason Graham could discern, though the *upyr* did step back to allow him in.

As soon as the door was shut, the house fell utterly silent, as if the civilized world's greatest city were no longer rumbling outside. Graham could hear his own breathing but little else. If the residents of White's were up and moving, they weren't causing floorboards to creak. Graham couldn't smell anything, either: not food, not people, not the normal mustiness of an old building. The dust he'd seen on the window was restricted to the outside. Inside, everything was spotless: the damask on the walls unfaded, the carpets colorful and plush—all seemingly untouched by age.

Which was appropriate, Graham supposed.

Though he couldn't know what being a wolf was like, he knew in that moment how it felt to venture into a territory not his own.

"This way," the butler said, leading him up a curving marble staircase with an ornate filigree brass rail. Halfway up, Graham's escort looked back at him over his shoulder, flashing a grin that exposed two unnaturally sharp incisors. "You're early for a visit. Our guests haven't had breakfast yet."

Graham suppressed a shiver with an act of will. He suspected he didn't want to know how it would be served. "I'll be more considerate next time."

"Ha!" the butler said again. Luckily, the bark of sound didn't seem angry.

They proceeded down a corridor whose dark doors were closed. At the last threshold, the butler stopped.

"These are Fitz Clare's rooms," he said, giving the raised mahogany panel a nice, sharp rap. As they waited for a response, he leaned close enough to let Graham feel him sniffing his neck. "*Do* enjoy your visit with the new master."

This time, Graham's instinctive shiver couldn't be repressed. The butler grinned, seeming pleased he'd been able to frighten him. Clearly, the pleasure was more than cerebral; his fangs were extending over his lower lip, looking white and shiny and sharp. His monocle glittered crazily. Unable to help himself, Graham froze like a rabbit before a snake. The folding knife he'd put in his pocket now seemed useless. He wasn't sure what his strategy ought to be if he was attacked. Would the other guests be drawn like sharks if his blood was spilled?

"Stevens." Robin's voice came sternly from the silently opened door. Graham fought not to sag with relief. "I'll thank you not to tease my guest."

"Spoilsport." Stevens pouted, though he did move away.

Warily, Graham watched the butler glide down the corridor. Somewhat to his dismay, Robin watched him. Graham would rather his weakness weren't on display.

"Sorry about that," Robin said, gesturing Graham into his sitting room. In the twilight, it was hard to tell, but Graham thought it was decorated in blue and brown. "We don't get many human visitors. And Stevens is Lucius's manager, so he isn't happy about me suddenly outranking him. I gather this is important."

Robin looked sleepy, so Graham belatedly hoped he would think it was.

"It's about Nim Wei," he said as Robin turned on the lights and closed the door. "I'm afraid I've put my foot in it."

Robin plunked into a sky blue chair that could have graced a museum for dead French kings. Indeed, all the furnishings looked historical, including the heavy brown velvet drapes. Seeming immune to the splendor that surrounded him, Robin rubbed his face. Whatever the vampire equivalent of a morning person was, Edmund's son wasn't one. Though his clothes weren't rumpled, he wore the same casual evening garb he'd had on the night before. For all Graham knew, he'd slept in it. Vampires didn't crease things as far as he could tell.

"Go on," Robin prompted, his hands dropping wearily to his thighs. "I know I don't look sprightly, but I'm listening."

Deciding he oughtn't put it off any longer, Graham

shared what had happened between him and London's *upyr* queen.

"I wanted to accept her offer," he finished. "I've been thinking I wouldn't feel so ruddy useless if I had extra power to act. I just couldn't say yes to her. My gut kept telling me there'd be strings attached. Unfortunately, I'm relatively certain my hesitation insulted her."

"Probably," Robin said, then let out a sigh. "Don't kick yourself over this. Your father insulted Nim Wei first. She wanted to change Edmund, too. He turned her down and had Lucius do the deed instead."

"Do you think he would . . ." Graham rubbed his jaw, unaccustomed to being on ground this uncertain. "I know you *upyr* don't accept anyone who asks, but do you think Lucius White would change me?"

"He might, if he were here. He and his wife went on a 'walkabout' in Australia. I don't have the faintest how to contact them." Robin pinned Graham with a long, measuring stare, one that told him more lay beneath his jovial front than he usually let on. Graham knew not to fidget under the perusal. "I could change you myself if I were convinced it was a good idea. Your father isn't the only one who became an elder when Auriclus shared his power."

It seemed best not to say anything to that. Robin wasn't the type to be swayed by other people's arguments. Still looking at Graham, he pushed back in his gilded chair and stretched out his legs. "Your father would probably kill me."

"Not really," Graham said, which inspired a snort from Robin.

"No, not really. But this isn't a club you can resign from after you've joined. Your life would never be normal again. And we shapechangers aren't all as decent as your father. Some of us are neck sniffers."

Graham colored up at having his thoughts divined. "That butler was a shapechanger?"

"Yes," Robin said. "Everyone at White's is. Our founder would have preferred it if all of us only ate as wolves, but the truth is most *upyr* have a taste for blood—whether they belong to his line or Nim Wei's. Biting humans is our nature. If you become one of us, that nature will be yours as well."

"I understand." Graham held Robin's eyes as steadily as he could, determined to pass this test. He might not be sure he wanted to join this odd community, but he knew his redemption hung in the balance. He *had* to do this. It was the only way he saw to be of true assistance to his father.

Robin blinked and steepled his fingertips.

"As it happens," he said, "I had an interesting meeting after I left your home last night. Someone from the British government contacted me. It seems that X Section is in shambles, what with Edmund gone and your real handler dead. This . . . individual asked me if I'd be willing to step in temporarily. Make sure nothing happens to the other agents they have in play. I'm inclined to accept, if only to hear what news concerning Edmund might fall into human hands. If I made that commitment, however, and we found out where Edmund is, it might be difficult for *me* to go rescue him."

Seeing where this was going, Graham's heart pumped faster. "You could send me," he said, trying not to sound breathless. "And I'd be much more useful if I were as strong as you."

Robin smiled gently. "You'd be as strong as I could make you, which is more than most of Nim Wei's get can say. Rumor has it she doesn't like to sire competitors. Make no mistake, though, this won't be a cakewalk. You'll need training, Graham, maybe months of it, or your strength will be as useful as a cannon in the hands of a four-year-old."

"I'll do whatever it takes."

"I don't doubt that." Robin's eyes turned sad. "I wish you didn't want to do this, Graham. I wish I weren't willing to

let you. If I didn't fear you'd turn to Nim Wei instead . . ."
He trailed off and shook his head. "You're very young to be
making this choice."

"I don't think my . . . *our* father can wait for me to get
older." *And I need to do this*, Graham added silently.

Robin seemed to have a knack for peering into his head,
stronger even than Edmund's. "That's what troubles me
most," he said.

Despite his words, Robin rose with the air of having
made a decision. When he removed his dinner jacket and
tossed it, folded, over the chair, Graham knew his impression was on target.

"Now?" he asked in spite of wanting to seem ready.

"We may as well," Robin answered. "We don't know
when we'll have to move to help your father, and I want to
give you all the training I can squeeze in."

Graham hadn't thought about what the process of trans-
forming him would involve. Perhaps he hadn't wanted to.
Jacket gone, Robin stepped to a midnight blue brocade
couch and sat.

"How will you—" Graham said, then stopped as his
throat closed up.

Robin's grin slanted up his face.

"No," he said to Graham's unspoken question. "I imagine Nim Wei implied that changing you required sex. She'd
love to get her hands on a healthy specimen like you, all
the more so because it would twit Edmund. As it happens,
though, the change doesn't work that way. You will, however, have to come over here."

Graham came like a Frenchman to a guillotine.

"Sit," Robin said, patting the cushion beside him. "I
want to get a closer look at the mark Nim Wei's imperson-
ator laid on you."

"It's still there?" Graham asked, startled, as he lowered
himself stiffly.

Robin took his jaw and turned it to the side. Graham

suspected whatever he was examining wouldn't show up in a mirror. "It is. I could feel it as a sort of fog when I was reading you."

Graham told himself not to flinch as Robin leaned closer. Having the other man's head that near to his neck, feeling him begin to breathe as the scent of mortal blood had its predictable effect, was almost as unnerving as the butler's proximity had been.

Chances were Robin hadn't broken his fast, either.

When Robin straightened, his hand remained on Graham's shoulder. "I don't think I can remove it. The first bite a human receives can have a lasting influence, and that woman, Li-Hua's mark went deep. I could mute what she's done—drown it out, if you will—if I put my bite over hers. Truthfully, I'm not sure I can change you if I don't overrule her claim."

Which meant Robin didn't have a choice not to drink from him.

Graham wanted to squirm but forced himself not to. He remembered how pleasurable Li-Hua's bite had been, like an orgasm that exploded straight out his nerves. He noticed Robin was holding his lips slightly rolled together, as if his fangs had lengthened and he was hiding them.

"I'm not—" Graham said, though his groin was tingling softly in betrayal. His hands clenched atop his thighs. Lord, how his old friend, Cecil, who'd had an unrequited crush on Graham, would enjoy seeing him hoisted on this particular petard. "Men don't attract me."

Robin squeezed his arm reassuringly. "I know, Graham. Try to think of being bitten as comparable to a skilled massage. No matter who the hands belong to, you can't help if it feels nice."

"That's what makes me nervous," Graham confessed.

Robin's breath snorted out his nose. "Look on the bright side. Once I feed from you, we'll both be more relaxed."

"All right," Graham said, screwing his eyes shut so he could pretend to be invisible. "I'm ready."

Robin gave his arm a pat and leaned in. Graham had an instant to register the other's quickened breathing, and then Robin's fangs sank in with a sharp, bright pain. The pain didn't bother him as it should have. Graham found he'd developed a taste for this shining, sensual knife edge. Forewarned, he braced for Robin's first feeding pull.

The ecstasy of that was better than he'd feared, maybe because Robin was more powerful than Li-Hua. Graham moaned, unable to contain the sound as Robin drank from him. His hands found Robin's back and clutched him in a panic he couldn't like at all. He remembered the day, toward the end of the last Great War, when he'd learned his parents had been killed. His sense of being alone in the world, with no one to care for him, had branded his young spirit. Edmund had saved Graham, but he'd never erased his wariness of clinging. He didn't want to cling now, didn't want to need anyone that deeply.

Shh, Robin soothed deep inside his mind, rocking him, coaxing him not to fight the building waves of bliss. His lips were stone wrapped in silk, more arousing than Graham wanted to admit. *You're all right, Graham. I promise you, you're all right.*

More than thought crossed the bond the bite was forming. Robin's confidence was unmistakable, the strong affection he felt for his father's adopted son. The pleasure of this act didn't threaten him. Over the centuries since he'd been changed, Robin had seen every weakness—willing or unwilling—that human flesh could be heir to. He didn't judge Graham for his reaction; he just wanted him to open the door for what they had to do.

Graham was as limp as warm taffy when he pulled back.

"Look at me," Robin said.

Graham looked at him, woozy from the strong erotic buzzing that ran through him. He didn't know when it had happened, but Robin was holding him sprawled across his lap, a strange position for a man as big as Graham. Robin's normally pale cheeks were ruddy, and light rayed out from his head as if a halo surrounded it. His eyes were the same rich blue as Edmund's. They weren't trying to thrall him, but they were very beautiful.

I could never have eyes like that, Graham thought wistfully.

Robin's expression flickered before it went still again.

"Edmund wasn't the father to me that he was to you," Robin said aloud. "Not when he was human. He was a bit of a shit, actually. I've watched him change himself, trait by trait, year by year, until he became the person he wanted to be. I learned to admire him a great deal for that. You, though, you and Sally and Ben, gave our father the chance to respect himself. Being there for you healed him as nothing else could have."

Graham felt his eyes burn and spill over. The last of his defenses washed away with the tears, with the love for the professor he and Robin shared. Robin's glow flared like an exploding star. Graham saw nothing but that brilliant light, felt nothing but a delicious fire that sparkled with infinitesimal diamonds of sweet, cool ice. Robin flowed into him with those diamonds, and so did the universe. The sense of peace Graham felt was indescribable. He saw his many mistakes meant nothing, saw that the Power that made him, that made everyone, had no concept of failure. He was worthy. He was loved. He was wholly and forever safe. He didn't need to do anything to deserve this. He'd earned it just by existing.

And then the sensation of his own body snapped back to him. He was solid again, a being with bones and skin and barriers to intrusion. He reached for the peace, to pull it to him again, but it was gone like a once-heard fragment of a heartbreaking song. He was plain old Graham. No more. No less.

Or maybe not.

When he tried to stand, he fell to his knees.

He wasn't weak, he was overwhelmed. Every color he saw was more saturated, every tactile sensation more detailed. The carpet seemed to pulse beneath his hands as he kneaded it. When Robin spoke, his voice was as layered and enthralling as the world's finest symphony.

"All right then," he said with a casualness that staggered Graham. Hadn't the universe just stood on its head? "According to the memories I inherited from Auriclus, this is the bit where I'm supposed to compel you to forget what we've done. I'll admit I don't see the point. You can't change anyone until—and if—you turn elder."

Graham looked up at him and was dazzled. Robin's unglamoured skin sparkled with rainbow hues. Graham could happily have stared at him for the next ten years.

"Ah," Robin said. "It's been so long since I was changed, I forgot this part. I should probably leave you alone with your sensory overload."

"Wait." Graham caught his shirtsleeve, his hand flashing out almost too fast too track. Hungers throbbed inside him: for food, for sex, for stimulation of every sort. They felt good to him, but also quite urgent.

"I'll bring you a drink," Robin assured him, reading his confusion. "And a female, if the other guests are up and willing."

The mention of a female was welcome for more cause than one. Beautiful or not, Robin wasn't a person Graham wanted to be easing any of his hungers with. Likely Graham should have thanked the *upyr* for his consideration, but the feel of his own body distracted him. He realized he could count his pulse, could hear his most sensitive tissues stiffen as blood surged into his cock. The weave of his undershorts was a hot torment. Defenseless against the impulse, he tightened his buttocks to make the cotton move over him.

As that pleasure stole his breath, he saw he hadn't truly

known what lust was. Now his desires were big enough to drown the world, leaving little room for embarrassment—or rational thought, for that matter. Though Graham had never understood men who strutted, this burst of male strength inside him demanded it. He could have fucked a regiment of women and still been hard.

"I won't be long," Robin said, and shut the door behind him.

Graham barely heard him. His skin was pulsing, his nerves crackling like live wires.

I'm one of them now, he thought. *I'm going to be like this all the time*.

When the glass of blood Robin returned with came to him warm, Graham didn't question where he'd gotten it.

Tottenham Court Mansions

⚜

It was only ten in the evening, and Estelle's bed was calling to her.

Edmund had made love to her in her flat many times. Presumably, their mingled energies lingered. She thought this might help her dream about him again, but was it pathetic to want it to?

She'd postponed answering that question while she ate a heartier dinner than usual. Sally's eight o'clock 'phone call had also taken up some time. Evidently, Graham had sent a note round to Bedford Square, saying he and Robin were on an intelligence-gathering trip and wouldn't be in touch for a few days. Sally had seemed determined to find that suspicious, but Estelle had no energy for new worries. If Graham was with Robin, he'd be all right—no matter what they really were doing.

Her attempt to occupy herself with a book was a complete washout.

Her body wanted him with her and didn't damn well care if he was only a fantasy. Giving up, Estelle took a bath and drank a small glass of wine. With a sense of anticipation that shouldn't have been conducive to sleep, she folded down her sheets and slid in. Closing her eyes, she said his name to herself.

This might be foolish, but she was going to try.

When she woke to sleep, she stood in a long underground corridor, its damp, rough stone dungeonlike. She couldn't conceive why she'd conjured it. She also wondered why she'd forgotten to wear clothes.

Was this tunnel a Freudian symbol for her frustrated sexual desires?

Shrugging, she walked toward a distant electric light. She'd been naked in dreams before, though she was glad her undressed body didn't feel the cold. The atmosphere was so dank a circle of mist surrounded the shadeless bulb. Estelle reached it sooner than she could have in real life. The light marked a leprous steel door with heavy rivets and a barred window set in it. Estelle was tall enough that she didn't have to stand on her toes to peer through.

Behind the door she found Edmund.

Despite the hour, her beloved slept—and the slumber was not his usual diurnal unconsciousness. His natural glow was dim: an anemic flicker of luminescence around his limbs. Also uncharacteristic was that his chest rose and fell with breathing. He was naked, his stark white body shackled and chained to a steel table. To Estelle, he looked beautiful but too thin, as if the energy that powered him had started to consume his flesh. Faint red lines marked his skin in patterns she couldn't make sense of. The marks appeared to be scars, but she couldn't think what would have left them. Edmund had the power to heal anything.

I want to be in that room, she thought. *I want to be with him.*

The cell door had been solid when she leaned against it to look inside. It melted around her as she stepped forward, tingling over her skin but not stopping her.

She looked behind her in wonder, then thought: *I want a blanket for him.*

A thick one appeared, already folded over her arm. The wool was a muted silver color, as soft as it was substantial. She could pet it and feel the texture of its fibers. She regretted that people couldn't remember dreams this vividly after they woke up. While they were going on, they truly were magical. She went to Edmund and pulled the blanket over him. She hoped it would warm him, but she didn't know the rules of this encounter. Aching for him, despite his questionable reality, she laid her hand on his sleeping face. His waving golden hair spilled around his head.

"No," he said with a shudder. "Don't cut into me again."

"Edmund," she said. "It's Estelle."

His eyelids struggled open, their irises flaring. "Estelle?"

An instant later, his fangs ran out full length. He turned his head away in shame. "Oh, God, Estelle, I'm so hungry."

"I know," she soothed, climbing over him onto the table. "It's all right. I'm hungry for you, too."

He couldn't touch her; his wrists were trapped by the iron cuffs. Instead, his hips bucked up at her where she straddled him. Maybe this was why she'd left off her pajamas. Her nipples tightened as his gaze slid from her breasts to the triangle of curls between her legs. He licked his lips, then the shining length of his incisors. His teeth weren't the only sign of his arousal. His erection lifted, tenting the wool in a steady rise. When he spoke, he was hoarse.

"Come under the blanket," he said. "I don't care if you are a dream."

She didn't care, either. As conveniently as it had materialized, the blanket reappeared over both of them, a gentle mantle of privacy. Their impromptu shelter was lit by his inner glow. Estelle bent to his chest, kissing and licking the first red mark she saw. As luck would have it, it bisected his right nipple. She formed her lips close around that and gave a pull.

Apparently, in his current state, her sucking the little bead was a powerful stimulation. He made a strangled sound as his spine bowed off the steel table.

"Estelle," he gasped. "Do that again."

She'd been warm already, but his plea tightened her sex as if a firm, hot fist were clenching around it. Creamy liquid overflowed her folds, tickling as it trickled down. The sensation seemed far too real for a simple dream. She licked a second score mark, this one crossing his pectoral, and thrilled to his deep, rough moan.

"Are you sure this is what you want?" she asked throatily. "Maybe you'd prefer to feed from me first."

"Lick me," he insisted, his body writhing under her. "Lick me all over. I'll want to bite you when I spend, when I can't bear waiting anymore."

Heat flashed feverlike over her body. She knew what his kind enjoyed: that drinking and coming were their ultimate pleasures, each exponentially sweeter when they were combined. She licked him, slowly, lovingly, over his chest and ribs, across his hollowed belly and his restlessly shifting hips. His skin was velvet poured over his perfect form, a sheer delight to run her hands over. The odd red marks continued down his legs. She didn't kiss all of them, just the ones on his inner thighs. His muscles there looked like they were carved, his craving for release bunching them. As she teased higher, he sprawled his thighs as much as the chains allowed. His balls—tight now with arousal— glowed as if they had coals inside.

She feathered her nails over the contours of the contracted sac, reveling in the involuntary jerking of its skin. Even in sleep she remembered the fascinating creases and seams of him. The slight dip that curved between his testicles called irresistibly to her fingertips.

"Higher," he said as she explored it, the order harsh. "Suck my cock."

It didn't matter that he was telling her what to do. Estelle felt absolutely, intensely free. She could perform any act she pleased on him. Peculiar though it was, this was her dream, her fantasy. She ceased caressing his balls to steady his thick, hard shaft between her thumb and fingers. Then she simply had to pause to admire: the taut, satiny skin; the dark, pulsing veins; the mushroomed shape that was so intrinsically aggressive. This organ had been designed to thrust inside her, to give any woman pleasure. His foreskin, which she supposed had been less exotic when he was mortal, was fully retracted over his penis's flaring rim.

She hadn't forgotten how sensitive he was where it normally covered him.

Then again, just being a vampire made him sensitive.

Smiling to herself, she used her second hand to push the delicate sheath back over his bulging knob. The skin of both was unbelievably soft, despite the firmness they contained. Happily, his foreskin had sufficient play to be twisted from side to side over his crest. Edmund groaned and throbbed in her hand, his hips surging up for more rubbing on this rewarding spot. The clear fluid his slit was leaking made her plaything glide beautifully.

"Oh, God," Edmund said once he'd caught his breath.

A nicer woman would have wished his chains away. Instead, thinking her imagination had been very clever to tie him down, she decided it would be good to put her mouth around him while her fingers played.

Edmund rewarded her by coming, a hot burst of fluid he cut short with some act of will she hadn't known him capable of.

"Not yet," he snarled through teeth that sounded like they were gritted. "I'm not coming until I'm in your pussy and I can feed."

Estelle had sympathy for his wishes, but this was her show, and she wanted to experience his orgasm as intimately as possible—without her own distracting her. With a hum she didn't really mean to soothe him, she sucked him deeper and harder. She put her tongue and cheeks to work as if she'd never known what shyness was.

Up and down his shaft she pulled with her lips, licking firmly around the head and flicking into the hole. He twitched for her and gasped and fought against coming with all his strength. When he begged her to stop, she didn't. She knew neither of them truly wanted that.

His restraint wasn't up to its usual level. Like her, he'd grown used to frequent and rewarding sex. He succumbed in minutes, gulping desperately for air a second before his release burst free. This time he couldn't stop his pleasure. This time he shot long and hard.

When he finished jerking, she slithered up his chained body, her sex positively pounding with unmet needs. Loving how alive she felt, she kissed the musky taste of his ejaculation into his eager mouth. His chest felt so good beneath her breasts that she had to rub her nipples there. Widening her knees was an even wiser choice. Like a magnet, the opening to her sex found the head of him. Edmund thought that was inspiring, too. With a gasp and a heave of his entire body, he nicked her lip with his fangs. She was wet and pulsing, but she didn't take him yet, just held him poised for entry.

He was still rock hard, of course. One climax was never enough for him.

"Estelle," he said. "For God's sake, get on with it."

Knowing it would tease him, she stroked her neck, then watched from inches away as his nostrils flared. "In my dream, I smell really good."

He laughed, a little shakily. "In *my* dream, you do as well."

She took pity on him then, and on herself. His eyes held hers as she pushed her pelvis down his shaft, their glow burning hotter as he was engulfed. Their heads were still close together. His tongue swept out to heal the cut he'd made in her lip—though not before enjoying a taste of her.

"I was afraid that first orgasm would wake me up."

"Not yet," she purred, because in her dream state it seemed as if she could enforce her word. "You're not waking up until I'm done with you."

His hips cocked up at her, into her, increasing his penetration. His eyes closed briefly with the intensity of his pleasure. When they opened, they were aflame. "This is so good, Estelle."

"Wait," she said, her voice gone languorous with the heat and stretch of him. "It gets better."

It did get better. Everything in her soared as she rode him, as he angled his hips so his thrusts hit the sweetest places inside of her, places where her nerves were screaming for more pressure. Her clitoris stood out like a little barb, as sensitive as if he'd been rubbing it, so hot she half expected it to glow. Somehow, he managed to tug it with each stroke. His thickness helped him do this, the way it dragged her skin back and forth, but even so, his sexual dexterity astonished her. She was rising as fast as if his hands were free. Even bound, he was incredible at this. And he wasn't holding back the way he so often did. He was doing what he needed, *taking* what he needed.

More, she heard him urge in her head. *Estelle, I have to have more.*

Growls came from his throat as he thrust with ever-greater force, knowing no matter what he did he couldn't hurt her in a dream. His supernatural strength felt glorious to her, his long, thick maleness pumping at high speed. The rise of her sensations was equally speedy. Her fingers dug into his steely biceps as she came with a deep and lengthy shudder of ecstasy.

Her inner contractions detonated his. Edmund grunted and shoved to his limit inside of her, his cock swelling one more marvelous fraction. Even as he groaned out his climax, his other hunger peaked—its demands no longer possible to deny. His head whipped off the strange metal table, and his fangs struck her neck, making her *his* captive. His lips clung to her, his cheeks hollowing strongly. Bliss swept out in hot, sweet floods from the place he pulled.

This was what her body had been craving since he'd disappeared, not just carnal knowledge but complete union. She knew control of the encounter had passed to him, but she surrendered without a qualm. His ragged moans satisfied her need to give all she had to him. Nothing could be better than the sea of pleasure that was crashing over both of them. With all her heart, she dove into it.

She wasn't prepared for him to stiffen and pull away. As she stared at him in surprise, he licked her scarlet blood from his lips.

"They're coming," he said.

"No one's coming," she objected, snuggling down with her cheek to his shoulder. Maybe if she held him, he'd begin again. "It's my dream, and I didn't invite guests."

"Estelle." His sharpened tone brought her head up reluctantly. "You know very well this isn't a normal dream, nor is it only *your* dream. We have a chance here—" His eyes cut away as he listened to something she could not hear. "I need you to try to read them. I need you to see if you can discover where they're holding me."

"How can I do that? You're the one with the vampire powers."

"You got yourself here, Estelle. You dream-walked. If you try, you might be able to do more."

"*You* try."

"I can't, Estelle. They left a bullet in my head."

That shocked her to breathlessness, but he didn't give her time for questions. "Now," he said. "They're almost here. You need to focus."

Focus on what? she wondered, left clueless.

"You came in from the passage," he said. "Go back there."

She didn't want to, but his will seemed to compel her. Though she'd been solid, now she floated backward like a ghost, through the leprous steel door into the musty stone corridor. Two figures were moving down it in her direction—vampires to judge by their smooth, pale skin—one male and one female. Their hard white hands held a third figure between them, a human boy, maybe seventeen, who was wearing a stained apron. The boy was walking but just barely. Every few steps he stumbled, forcing the other two to catch his elbows.

They stopped in front of Edmund's cell.

Estelle shivered with a dread she could not control. Dream or not, she knew this was bad.

The boy's eyes were as glassy as if he were drugged. He wasn't fighting the hold the vampires had on him. Indeed, he barely seemed aware of where he was.

Though she shrank back, neither vampire gave any evidence of seeing her.

"Are you sure this is a good idea?" the female asked. She was Oriental and petite.

"I'm sure," said her much taller blond companion. He had what sounded like a German accent. "Our guest should be hungry enough by now to drain this one."

"But what if his strength returns?"

"The iron will hold him. I wouldn't put you in danger, my pear blossom."

The female vampire didn't argue, though she still appeared skeptical. They struggled to open the door without letting their unsteady burden drop. Estelle realized she'd better make her attempt if she was going to. The noise the vampires were making seemed destined to wake Edmund, and—whatever he'd meant by dream-walking—Estelle didn't fool herself that she could do it unless he helped.

Where are you? she thought at the woman, judging her the weaker of the two.

The female vampire's perfect little forehead creased. "Did you hear that, Frank? I think the bastard's trying to read me."

"You're blocking him, aren't you?"

"Of course I am!" the female vampire snapped. "I think he's doing it in his sleep."

"That can't be. I left the bullet in his head specifically to prevent that possibility."

His reasoning didn't impress his partner. She reached up to bang on the metal door, raising a clangor fists that small shouldn't have been able to create.

"Wake up," she yelled through the barred window. "You in there, wake up now!"

Back in her London bedroom, Estelle shuddered and obeyed.

She made a sound of disgust as fear-sweat prickled over her. This wasn't how she would have chosen her fantasy to end. Then she laid her hand on her belly. Once again, dreaming about Edmund had convinced her stomach that it was empty.

The sensation of having fed didn't last beyond Edmund waking up. Estelle had passed him some of her energy, but only enough to keep his body from slipping into a protective coma, not enough to repair his depleted state. His hunger was just as bad as before, a grinding pain in his belly.

The noise that accompanied his return to consciousness suggested Estelle had been discovered trying to read Li-Hua. To ask her to attempt it had probably been a waste of time. Estelle had no experience in such things. But that was the problem with trying to accomplish things in a dream. Sleeping minds didn't function logically.

Li-Hua's banging ceased as the cell door clanged open. She and Frank filled the opening, their hands occupied in holding a sagging male human under the arms. He was young, gangly, not a child but not yet grown into a man—Sally's age or thereabouts. Edmund's stomach clenched with alarm.

"You're awake then," Li-Hua said. "Glad to see it."

Edmund couldn't tear his gaze from the kitchen boy—or more precisely, from his sluggish jugular pulse. He smelled sickly sweet, like he'd been drugged, but it hardly mattered. He was food. Enough to return Edmund to his former strength. Assuming he'd be allowed to drink all of him.

His fangs shot out painfully at the thought, harder even than they had for Estelle. His throat burned with hunger, each beat of his heart sending an ache of longing thudding through his veins.

"Looks juicy, doesn't he?" Frank observed.

"Give him to me," Edmund growled in a voice that would never be mistaken for human.

Frank stepped forward, still holding his side of the human up. Then he stopped and chuckled. "That was excellent, Fitz Clare. I stand warned that you still have a bit of your power to thrall. Aren't I lucky it's not enough? You'll get your meal when we think you should."

"What do you want from me?"

Frank smiled and propelled the boy toward him, his big hand shoving the center of the human's back. His victim stumbled, arms wheeling. Even drugged, he didn't want to fall. His poorly coordinated hands caught the side of the table Edmund was chained to. This saved him from sprawling over Edmund's chest, but only just. The boy's arms trembled. He didn't have the strength to push himself upright again. His frightened eyes were less than a foot away.

Edmund suspected he resembled the boy's worst nightmare.

"Don't," the boy whispered, slurring it. "Don't bite me."

"Oh, tut-tut," Frank said with mock sympathy. "You'll enjoy it. Even better than you enjoyed what my blossom did to you in the scullery."

The boy shook his head, a terrified little jerk he seemed to hope only Edmund would see. "Please don't kill me, sir."

Edmund closed his eyes and groaned. He knew he could kill the boy. In fact, it seemed likely. Normally, an *upyr* couldn't consume a life-threatening volume of blood, but he'd been starved too long, and he was precious short of self-control. His immortal body's drive for self-preservation could simply take over and force him to. His muscles strained as the scent of the boy's blood rose. It was a cloud he could not escape, its intensity increasing as the boy's heart pumped faster in panic. This was not a beneficial development. Edmund's wolf couldn't help associating the response with prey.

"Yummy," Frank said like an advert on the wireless.

Sensing the heightened danger, the boy was struggling to push away from the table, his palms slipping on the metal with sweat and weakness. Frank settled that by clamping his hand over the back of the boy's neck, forcing him down until his throat was smashed against Edmund's mouth.

Edmund's mind went black.

He heard himself say *no* from a great distance. His hands were burning, clenched tight around the links of the iron chain. The pain cleared his thoughts slightly.

"No," he repeated more clearly, wrenching his head to the side, away from the hellish temptation. "Thank you, but I'd rather not."

"Jesus," Li-Hua murmured. "Look what he's done to his hands."

Edmund knew they were raw. They felt wet against the iron, as if he'd gripped so hard his skin was bleeding.

"Fine." Frank jerked the boy impatiently away. "We'll try this again when you're hungrier."

Edmund was breathing too hard to answer. He watched Li-Hua catch the boy when Frank thrust him at her. The human's arms came around her to steady himself. Li-Hua helped him find his footing, her tiny size making the embrace appear ungainly. Spindles of gold glowed in her dark eyes as she studied Edmund around the boy's shoulder. Her gaze was calm but curious.

"He'll die anyway, you know," she said.

Edmund imagined this would happen not long after they left his cell.

"Not by my hand," he responded.

The kitchen boy's mournful moan rendered this a very flimsy victory.

Café Royal

"Graham!" Robin pitched his voice to carry through his old friend Vanessa's door. To his annoyance, the thumping and moaning that was going on behind it drowned him out handily.

"Oh, yes," crooned Vanessa's seductive tones. "Bite me right *there*."

Robin tapped his foot, whistled at the ceiling, then pounded the side of his fist into the wood. Night had fallen hours ago. No one could accuse him of being overly impatient.

"Graham! I thought you wanted to learn to hunt for yourself."

It seemed Graham could hear him, after all. The creaking of the bedsprings paused, then sped up precipitously. Graham was racing to a quick finish. More *ohs* and *yeses* rang into the air, not all of them Vanessa's. Their crescendo was a loud tandem groan, followed by the sound of bodies collapsing onto a mattress. Then silence reigned.

"Some time this decade," Robin suggested.

To his surprise, it was Vanessa who opened the door. A vibrant tangerine silk robe draped her tall, curvy form, which she leaned against the door frame as if she were in need of support. Robin sincerely doubted she was. His old friend's expression was that of a cat who had swallowed quite a few canaries. Given her similarity in body type to Estelle, Robin had known his friend would flip Graham's switches. That she was equally delighted was a lucky happenstance. She tossed her wavy, wheat blonde hair behind her shoulder.

"Darling," she said, sotto voce, "how can I *ever* repay you for asking me to help out this nice young man?"

"Don't break him?"

Vanessa's laugh was throaty. "I very much doubt I could. His powers of recovery are as formidable as his appetite."

"He's new to all this," Robin cautioned, somewhat alarmed by her attitude.

"Yes, he is," Vanessa agreed with no diminution of her humor. Her tongue curled out to lick her upper lip. "Happily, he's also a quick learner."

Graham spared him being the recipient of more details by squeezing past Vanessa and out the door.

"Sorry," he said to Robin. "We got caught up."

His grin of apology was boyish—or it would have been if his fangs hadn't been out. He wasn't more than half dressed—his trousers not yet fastened, his shirt dangling by the collar from his hand. Robin mentally rolled his eyes as the lovers exchanged a long, tonguey kiss goodbye.

"You're really going to let me hunt?" Graham asked, once he'd managed to disentangle himself. As they strode swiftly down the passage toward Robin's room, he made short work of pulling on and buttoning his shirt. Robin was glad Graham didn't appear to be falling for Vanessa. Robin's old friend was no romantic. A sexual fascination was the only kind he could recommend.

"I am," Robin said. "Your glamour has gotten good enough to go out in public *with my guidance*."

Graham didn't miss his emphasis. "Right," he said, and tried to look trustworthy.

"Pull in your fangs," Robin reminded him, feeling a headache begin to bloom. This wholehearted enthusiasm was not what he'd expected when he'd changed Graham.

"Sorry." Graham grimaced as he forced his incisors up. "I was thinking about Vanessa."

"Well, don't think about her in front of humans, at least not until you've gotten one of them alone."

Graham made a soft, low noise—possibly involuntary—which said the idea of hunting was just as appealing as his memories of his bed partner. Pretending not to hear it, Robin ducked into his room and retrieved their dinner jackets and coats. He handed Graham's long herringbone tweed to him.

"The idea is to blend," he said. "Don't walk too fast. Always damp your glow. Don't leave off your outer garments even if the cold doesn't bother you. You don't want to alarm your quarry. You want them to be at ease."

Graham shook his head. "That's so strange. Thinking of humans as *them*."

It was bound to get stranger the first time he fed from one—not that the warning would help. Some experiences one simply had to have for oneself.

Robin kept these thoughts unvoiced as he and Graham exited White's front door. Out on the stoop, the night was frosty but clear. Graham hesitated, then slowly and deliberately pulled on his gloves.

"Where are we going?" he asked.

Robin gave him points for trying not to sound too eager. A human probably would have missed the pent-up vibrance behind his words.

"Not far." Trusting Graham to follow, he trotted down the steps and turned right on St. James Street. "You might practice breathing while you have the chance. Humans don't always notice when you forget, but it reassures them if you remember. After a while, drawing air into your lungs will feel as normal as ever."

"Right-o," Graham said, doing his best to breathe in and out the way he used to . . . without thinking about it.

Robin was glad they were walking slowly. It took a few attempts before his pupil looked anything but bizarre. The remainder of their journey passed quietly while he tried to recapture the hang of it.

"Here we are," Robin said. They'd reached the Café Royal's brightly lit Regent Street facade. Eight floors tall and bursting at the seams with music and laughter, the famous gathering spot for bohemians was no cellar pub. Though it wasn't as wild as it had been in the days of Oscar Wilde and his louche salons, visitors were as apt to meet a lord here as an artist. Robin knew it would suit their aims.

"Here?" Graham said, sounding unconvinced.

"Here," Robin confirmed. "Predators follow the herd, and there's no better place to catch a meal than at a watering hole."

This was not the most sensitive choice of words. Graham turned to regard him with dawning horror. Though he'd been looking forward to hunting, it was clear he hadn't considered its implications in full.

"Most of them will be drunk," Robin explained. "And likely the sort of people who pride themselves on being originals. Even if they notice something queer about you, they may shrug it off. They'll be too busy aspiring to be queer themselves."

Graham blinked and kept his mouth tightly shut. Robin thought it just as well some of his student's eagerness had worn off.

A gentle mental push to the maître d' got them a table in a corner of the Domino room, though this required displacing a trio of diners less persuasive than himself. The

Royal was always crowded—as were many of the establishments Robin liked to frequent. Add to that the fact that it was New Year's Eve, and tables here were worth their weight in gold. Robin had learned to think of this nudging out of humans as survival of the fittest, a philosophy he decided not to share with Graham.

He glanced at Graham as the boy carefully lowered his impressive form into a rather froufrou chair. The change enabled humans to fulfill whatever ideal blueprint their genes contained. They remained themselves, only perfected. Now Edmund's eldest had to be a handspan beyond six foot and Lord knew how many stone—all of which was hard-packed muscle. Robin felt a flicker of pride at the job he'd done. Graham made a magnificent beast of an *upyr*, like a hero from an ancient tale. Give him a sword and an attacking dragon, and he'd look perfectly at home.

At the moment, the hero seemed a trifle dazed by his surroundings, though this probably had more to do with the colorful ceiling frescoes and their effect on his *upyr* sight than any intimidation he felt at the café's glamorous clientele. To human eyes, the Royal was all candlelight and romance, its ornate Victorian splendors lost mostly to shadow. To Robin and Graham, for whom the space was nearly as bright as day, it was plaster candy whipped into a gorgeous, high-ceilinged fantasy.

Countless white balloons bobbed in a net above them, awaiting midnight for their release.

"I forgot," Graham said, glancing up at them. "I hope—"

He closed his mouth, but Robin knew what he was thinking. Graham hoped his family wouldn't find his absence at New Year's Eve too unforgivable an offense.

When the waiter wended his way to them through the reveling crowd, Robin eschewed champagne (which they couldn't drink; something to do with the bubbles) to order a bottle of red wine and a plate of starters that neither of them would eat. He left the Bordeaux untouched until he spotted a likely target for Graham's first outing.

"There," he said, nodding toward a plump young woman who sat alone at a tiny table by the wainscoted wall, nursing a cloudy glass of absinthe. "She's by herself, and her clothes didn't cost her much. The waiters don't know her, so she's not a regular. She might be trying to turn artist's model. You see the way she's scanning the room? She's probably hoping to spot someone famous and have them buy her a drink. Barring that, she'd be grateful if anyone noticed her tonight."

"She's pretty," Graham said.

The hint of wistfulness in his observation had Robin huffing out a laugh. Graham widened his eyes in question. He had no idea what a specimen of manhood he had become.

"She's not too pretty for you, my friend. Even with your glamour up, you aren't the simply pleasant-looking man you used to be. Walk over there, Graham. Meet her eyes and see what happens."

"Just meet her eyes?"

"Trust me, Graham, she'll handle any chatting up that's required."

Graham could not believe how easy picking up the woman was. He was used to females smiling vaguely and ignoring him in favor of more dashing examples of his gender. This one lit up from head to toe when he approached her—literally lit up; he could see her human energy flaring as her gaze slid over him from head to toe.

If he'd had the blood to blush, he would have.

"Well," she'd said. "You look man enough to buy a girl a drink."

That drink had turned to two, and then she'd suggested—

without any prompting on his part—that he might be man
enough to walk her back to her flat. As Robin promised,
she'd supplied virtually all the conversation, though Graham had to admit he didn't hear much of it. All along the
way as they strolled, Graham was conscious of Robin following a distance behind them. The vampire's oversight
might have been irritating but for the fact that Graham was
utterly unsettled by the state he was in. He was salivating at
his companion's smell, his own heart racing at the audible
pound of hers. He didn't want to bed her, he wanted to tap
her vein. His hands were trembling with hunger, his fangs
too sharp to hide from any but the most besotted eyes.
From the way the woman was hanging on his arm and bat-
ting her lashes, she was besotted enough.

With some dismay, Graham realized he didn't recall her
name.

When Robin's voice intruded in his head, it was embar-
rassingly welcome.

Turn her into this park, he said. *If you enter the building
where she lives, you'll increase the chances someone will
see you.*

Graham nodded, unable as yet to send psychic messages
reliably. From the way the back of his neck was prickling,
Robin was reading him anyhow.

"Here?" The woman gave a breathy, flirtatious laugh as
Graham guided her through the small square's gate. The
iron latch stung his fingers, but he ignored the discomfort.
The woman's plump little hands were sliding up his arm
again. He'd never buttoned his coat after leaving the café,
and her generous breasts pressed into his side. "You *are* an
eager boy."

"I want you to myself," he said.

He kissed her because she expected it, lifting her up
because she was too short to easily bend down to. Her
mouth tasted deliciously of her humanity, flavored with
an overlay of absinthe. Absinthe, however, wasn't what he

thirsted for. As he kissed her, Graham's head began to buzz with hunger, as if an electric current had seized his brain. Barely thinking, he found a tree and pushed her spine into it. Though he loved the give of her curves beneath the pressure, he was conscious of the need not to crush. Robin had already warned him about that. Fortunately, the force he used was fine. The woman undulated against him, her limbs twining around him like a vine.

"Lord," she groaned, her pelvis grinding against his belly. She seemed to have left her modesty at the bottom of her absinthe glass. The hem of her dress was rucked to her waist. "No man ever made me feel this way before."

He didn't know if she meant it and wasn't sure he cared. His fangs throbbed like they were trying to tear from his gums. The woman couldn't help but notice it.

"What's wrong with your teeth?" she broke from the kiss to ask.

Bite her now, came Robin's insistent voice. *You're going to lose control if you wait longer.*

Something in him tried not to listen, tried to deny his strange new urges. He couldn't do it. His fist gripped the woman's hair, pulling back her head. The gesture satisfied a need he hadn't known he had. Her throat was bared for him, helpless, the strong, quick pulse beating out a potent seduction.

"What are you doing?" she asked a second before he struck.

His teeth made a sound he knew he'd never forget, different from biting Vanessa, whose flesh was not so tender and vulnerable.

He moaned, pulling instantly. Richness flooded his mouth. He'd found the human woman's vein, his instincts stronger than his resistance. He'd tried cocaine once, under the supervision of Martin Walser, his old MI5 mentor. Walser had wanted him to experience what it was like to function while mentally impaired. That drug was not as powerful as this woman's blood. Drinking from a living human being rather than a glass was an orgasm for his whole body, soft as velvet, penetrating as a sword.

No wonder Auriclus's line couldn't be convinced to eat only as wolves.

He drank and swallowed and drank again, hearing the woman cry out but not registering at first that she was trying to squirm closer. She was coming, her underthings wet and sticky where she bucked against him.

"Oh, God," she moaned. "Oh, God, don't stop."

Abruptly, he was terrified that he could not. He wanted more and more, and his jaw was locked on her throat like it had a mind of his own. Had he taken too much already? Was he going to drink her down? Her head was lolling, and his mouth still wanted to pull. A sweat like ice popped out beneath his arms. He was going to kill this stranger before he could stop himself.

A hand curled gently around the back of his neck.

"Shh," someone said. It was Robin's voice. He was standing behind Graham now, beneath the bare, winter limbs of the chestnut tree he'd shoved the woman up against. "You're not going to kill her. She's simply limp with pleasure. Calm yourself. You can let her go if you want to."

He did want to. He did. He knew he'd had enough to constitute a meal. The hinge of his jaw clicked as he forced its muscles to relax. Jesus, Mary, and Joseph, he was turning into a snake.

And then he let her go, let his victim settle onto her feet with his hands gripping her elbows to hold her up. Graham was nearly as wobbly. His body shook the same as if he were ill.

The woman's eyes were closed, moving like a dreamer's behind her lids.

"Her bite has started to heal," Robin said, "But you need to finish the process. Imagine your energy flowing into her like a golden light as you lick her wound."

Graham obeyed, shuddering at how good the last bit of blood tasted. When he forced himself to push back, the woman's neck was unmarked.

"Good," Robin said. "Now let me have her. You're in no state to test your thralling skills tonight."

Graham was glad Robin didn't try to remove her immediately. It took a moment for him to throw off his instinctive possessiveness. He imagined animals felt this sense of ownership toward prey they'd caught, an insight that did no favors for his jangled nerves.

"I've got her," Robin said, easing her gently out of Graham's grip.

Though Graham had been the one to bite her, Robin had no trouble taking control—perhaps because he was a master now. He thralled her just like vampires did in novels, shaking her a little to wake her up and instructing her to look deeply into his eyes.

You're well, my dear, he soothed in his mind-voice. *You're relaxed and perfectly safe. You drank too much at the Royal and had a cab drive you home. You'll remember nothing about me or this other man when you wake up. You never met us. We're a dream that's fading even now.*

Graham let Robin walk the addled woman across the street to her flat. He remained in the empty square, cross-legged on the cold grass, his head hanging in his hands.

With perfect, ironic timing, thousands of church bells began to chime. Evidently, the stroke of midnight had arrived. Between the peals, Londoners could be heard cheering.

Well, Graham thought. *Happy buggered 1934.*

Graham's new, black mood left Robin nonplused. He supposed Graham's shock was due to being changed before he'd had a chance to thoroughly consider what being a vampire meant. Robin had been in his sixties when he turned *upyr*, an old man for his century. While Robin's youth had been returned to him, his inexperience had not. He'd also had the benefit of watching his father undergo the transformation, and his uncle, Aimery.

Compared to him, Graham was a baby to either race.

Not sure what to say, he sat beside Graham on the icy grass. His huge *upyr* body was radiating heat from his meal, but he didn't appear to appreciate what a nice thing this was. He looked sidelong at Robin like his favorite pet had died.

"How does my father live with this?"

That Robin could answer. "Graham, your father is—and was—a different man from you. This part was never so hard for him."

"But I'm thinking of them as food!"

"They are food. Even after you take your wolf soul, you'll crave the taste of them."

Robin had shared this truth as gently as he could, but Graham said, "I don't know if I'll be able to bear that."

"My friend, you don't have a choice. We are what we are. For your own sake, you need to make peace with that."

"I don't even remember that woman's name!"

"You gave her pleasure," Robin pointed out. "And for a while, once she recovers from her temporary swoon, she'll be stronger than she was before. That's the gift our bite brings humans."

"A gift she didn't ask for."

"She didn't say no." Hoping to reassure him, Robin patted his knee. "Our line's traditions forbid us from drinking if we're refused."

"That woman didn't know there was something to refuse."

Robin ventured a crooked smile. "Every system has its loopholes . . . but I see you're not amused. Look at it this way: How many people in this world feel so conflicted about satisfying their natural desires that they can't savor a lovely act like sex? Your desire to drink human blood is just as natural. You may choose not to indulge it, but you can't make it go away. Even our sainted founder didn't manage that."

Graham rubbed his face up and down. Robin squeezed his shoulder.

"It's your choice, Graham. For myself, I don't see how fighting what I am, how *hating* what I am, would help anyone."

Graham still didn't answer, but Robin sensed him mulling this over.

"Come," he said, hopping to his feet. "We'll run home, and you can spend the rest of the night with Vanessa. She'll like biting you even better now that you've fed. Tomorrow night, I'll help you break the news to your family."

"Oh, Lord," Graham groaned, but Robin decided any response was better than glum silence.

Bedford Square

Vanessa was, well, dead to the world when Graham woke in her bed at first dark. Over the course of this last week, he'd learned that being second-generation get to the most powerful vampire in existence had advantages: early waking being one of them. He stood over Vanessa, reminding himself that he, too, looked like a marble statue when he slept. His skin would be as cold as hers, his chest as motionless.

Sighing, he slipped out of her room to find Robin. At least he didn't have to worry about snoring now.

"Right on time," Robin said, seeming startled. No doubt he'd expected Graham to drag his feet tonight.

"Rather get it over with," he said brusquely.

They hired a cab, though they didn't need one to travel fast.

"If you want to pass for human," Robin said, "you need to keep up human habits."

Graham found he couldn't answer. His throat was too constricted to speak. In his longing to help his father, he hadn't realized how difficult it would be to tell his family what he'd done. Though it was cowardly, he spent the cab ride to Bedford Square tightening up his glamour. If his siblings could see him as his same old self, if only at first, maybe this would be easier.

Sally was coming down the stairs as Graham let himself and Robin in with his key.

"Graham!" she exclaimed with the unstudied delight that was so characteristic of her nature. Also characteristic was her punching his chest a second later. "You are so naughty, going away like that and making us worry!"

Graham rubbed the spot on his breastbone that didn't hurt. "Good to see you, too, Sally."

"Well, come in," she said, waving for them to. "Hullo, Robin. The others are in the parlor. I'm sure they'll want to hear what you found out on your 'information gathering' trip."

Graham's heart lurched at her mention of *others. Others* suggested more than Ben. *Others* suggested Estelle. Deuce take it. He wasn't ready to tell her.

In his consternation, he must have let his glamour waver. As luck would have it, Sally turned back to him just then. Her brow furrowed first, her rosebud mouth pulling into a baffled moue.

"Graham," she said slowly, "are you wearing lifts in your shoes?"

Estelle came to the open parlor door. She seemed more beautiful than ever, sexier than any screen goddess. Though he wished it were otherwise, Graham's vampire vision could only find new perfections in her appearance. Her aura glowed somewhere between a vampire's and a human's, its patterns less organized than Vanessa's but more so than Sally's.

Her scent, on the other hand, her wild and spicy, mouth-watering scent, exerted an attraction he wasn't certain he could resist. She smelled of home and comfort, but—most of all—of forbidden desires. Estelle was the prize he wasn't allowed to chase. Graham began to breathe as he'd struggled to just the other day. Though he fought to control his glamour, his gums pulsed dangerously.

Naturally, Estelle was the first to guess what was wrong.

"Graham?" she said. The question in her voice was like a vise pulling around his ribs. She pressed her hands together before her mouth. "Oh, Lord, Graham, what have you done?"

"Graham's done something?" Ben had joined Estelle at the library-parlor door. When he looked at Graham, all he could say was, "Bloody hell."

Graham lost his nerve and reached behind him for the door handle.

"No!" Estelle was beside him in an instant, her right hand clamped around his left wrist. To his amazement, he was unable to break her hold. He'd known Edmund's energy had changed her in various ways, but not that she was strong enough to restrain him. He tugged harder, wanting to be sure he wasn't imagining it, but Estelle's grip on him was secure.

He raised his brows, silently indicating Sally and Ben. Did they know she could do this? Estelle shook her head, a motion so small he doubted anyone but a vampire would have noticed it. The gesture clearly asked him not to tell.

The knowledge that she was also keeping secrets didn't allay his guilt.

"No running," she said aloud, softly. As her big gray eyes looked pleadingly up at him, they were as lustrous as sunlit gems—almost as lustrous as an *upyr*'s. "Edmund would still be with us if he hadn't run."

"I'm sorry," he said, the words choking out. "I had to do something."

"I understand," Estelle said. "We *all* do."

Her addendum was as stern as any mother could have

made it, despite her being only a few months older than Graham.

Ben smiled at her implied scold. "I understand," he said to Graham. "I think you're a nutter, but I understand."

"Well, I don't," Sally said. "Oh, I get that you're a vampire, but how are you going to help Daddy if you have to sleep all day?"

"The people who captured Father are vampires, too. My being one evens the playing field."

"But what if—"

Robin cut her off by hugging her shoulders with his arm. Now that Graham knew the control it took, he was impressed by Robin's gentleness. "Why don't we go into the parlor? We can talk about what this means. Graham is going to need your support in order to make the most of his advantage."

"He'll have it," Sally said darkly, her tone warning him he'd better prepare to pay for the privilege.

They were playing a waiting game.

That's what Estelle thought hours later as she sat in the window seat in Edmund's bedroom, her fingers pressed to the chilly glass. The mews behind the house were dark, leaving her reflection clear. She wondered idly what sort of windows Edmund had grown up with. Arrow slits, she supposed. She found she could picture him in a castle. He'd told her once that he'd fought to defend his family and his estates.

She hoped he was fighting for himself now.

Her hand fell to her thigh, clad in his paisley silk pajama bottoms and a modest wraparound cotton robe. She was afraid to climb into his bed. Ever since the night she'd seen him tied to a table, her dreams had come in confusing fragments—unpleasant enough to wake her up. In them, she'd *been* Edmund, and someone had been trying to make her bite a human being. She'd both wanted to and dreaded it. If she fell asleep here rather than at her flat, she feared more of the same. Edmund's presence was stronger in his own home.

She didn't want to dream about him suffering.

She thought of Graham instead. There had been wet eyes all around during Robin's discussion. Well, except for Robin, who couldn't be expected to share their shock at seeing Graham so altered.

It was hard to describe the changes. His face remained Graham's face—same square jaw, same honest features— but now the way they combined was strangely arresting. His hair, which had been an ordinary if healthy brown, gleamed with shades of russet and gold—and this was *with* his glamour in place. He was handsome, in the way only very masculine men can be. Estelle couldn't say whether he was taller, as Sally thought, but he certainly gave that impression. Emotionally, he seemed uncertain, worried that his family wouldn't accept his choice. Physically, his confidence couldn't have been more transformed. Graham might not have been aware of it, but he stood and moved like Robin and Edmund did, like men who could command themselves, like men who could pretty much handle anything.

Given that this was so, it had surprised her—probably as much as it had Graham—that she'd been able to hold him at the door.

She had to wonder just how strong she'd become. Had she underestimated the latest spate of changes she'd experienced at Edmund's hand? Were the vivid dreams she'd been having more than phantasms of her lonely mind?

If they were, she had no business avoiding them.

She didn't have time to ponder that idea, because a tap sounded on the door. "Come in," she said, and Graham entered.

He didn't step any closer than a foot inside the threshold. As if he'd forgotten what Edmund's room looked like, his gaze ran around the walls. When his attention settled on her, he seemed cautious. "Not going home tonight?"

Estelle shook her head. "Not tonight. You know Sally likes it when I'm here."

He dropped his eyes. She knew he liked having her here as well, though his reasons weren't as simple as Sally's. Though he stood quite across the room, her funny right ear, the one the lightning had run through, heard his heart rate pick up to human speed. That happened to Edmund, too, when he was nervous.

"Estelle," he said, "do *you* judge me for making this choice?"

She didn't judge him, she worried. He was more sensitive than any of them had understood. She only prayed he could be happy in this new life.

"How can I judge you?" she said. "I'm in love with your father."

He met her look. His eyes were glowing, just a little, glimpses of pure gold shimmering under the brown. Their soulful beauty almost stole her breath. "We're all grateful for that, Estelle. We're all glad you're here with us."

Her smile was an extension of the warmth welling helplessly in her heart. Lord, she loved this boy Edmund had raised. She knew Graham meant what he said. She also knew it was hard for him.

"Thank you, Graham. For what it's worth—" She hesitated, then said what she'd been trying not to admit. "I'm glad you made the choice you did. I feel as if Edmund has a better chance of being rescued now."

Her praise brought the faintest tinge of red into his cheeks, but his color wasn't all that changed. His fangs were lengthening. She could see the tips beginning to jut over his lower lip. It seemed the change in his heart rate had been due to more than nervousness. "Thank you, Estelle. I . . . I'll just wish you good night then."

He left in a burst of unnatural speed, probably too disconcerted by his hunger's rise to control his velocity.

"Good night," Estelle whispered . . . and wondered if he would hear.

Somewhere in Europe

❧

Following Estelle's aborted attempt to read Li-Hua's mind, Edmund was assigned a daytime guard, an *upyr* named Durand who favored black combat fatigues without insignia. Frank called him *Captain* Durand, which suggested there might be others under his command. Adding up his name and looks, Edmund deduced a mix of French and Italian ancestry. Durand was tall and lean. His eyes and hair (which he wore in a thick, long braid) were close to pure black. Though his features were refined, his skin had once been so swarthy that even as a vampire it was olive. His jaw seemed to bear the shadow of a beard he no longer had. Durand's accent was Swiss, which might or might not have been a clue to Edmund's whereabouts.

Durand himself seemed unlikely to provide the answer. The guard was not a talker, his job being to ensure Edmund didn't do anything "tricky"—as Li-Hua put it—while he was asleep. Every hour on the hour while the sun was up, Durand would poke Edmund with the tip of his army knife. This important duty required that Durand stay awake himself.

Clearly, he was one of the rare *upyr* who had cultivated the ability. Just as clear was his reliance on the prop of human drugs to help him out. Though sunshine was no worry in this prison, today his eyes glittered in the light that spilled through the barred cell window from the single bulb in the corridor. His inky irises appeared to vibrate with the cocaine's false energy.

Because he'd just woken Edmund by stabbing his thigh hard enough to bleed, Edmund was not inclined to be friendly.

"*Upyr* can become addicted," he pointed out. "It takes longer than it does for humans, but I've seen it happen, especially since the doses we have to use are high."

Durand cocked one dark brow at him. "I'm sure I'm grateful for your concern."

This was the first hint of humor Edmund had heard from him, and the longest string of words.

"I'm not going to kill them, you know," he said. "Those humans your bosses keep bringing here."

Durand turned his gaze to the wall. "You think you won't." He paused, then jerked one shoulder before continuing. "In any case, what does it matter? Frank and Li-Hua are killing them anyway."

Edmund studied the man's sharp profile. Durand's lips were thin, the set of them faintly disapproving. Was there a chink here he could widen?

"They can't be killing all the humans. They're servants, and you can take it from someone who's had them, they're not as easy to replace as you'd think. Or do you suppose Li-Hua wants to sweep the floors herself?"

Durand's mouth twitched on the side Edmund could see. He covered the tiny indicator of amusement with an equally tiny frown.

"You should sleep," he said. "You have fifty minutes until I stab you again. An *upyr* as weak as you can't afford to stay awake all day."

"What do they want from me?" Edmund asked, daring to put the barest mental push behind the question. His temples throbbed, but he ignored the pain. "Are they hoping I'll change those humans into *upyr* if I drain them? Are they assuming my guilt would force me to it? Do they believe this would gain them some advantage?"

Edmund hadn't known he had enough strength for any thrall of his to be noticed, but Durand narrowed his eyes at him.

"Master or not, you won't thrall me, Fitz Clare. I am not a child."

Which implied he might be thinking his employers were.

"Why do you work for them?" Edmund demanded. "Swiss mercenaries have a tradition of honorable service. I'd have thought there wasn't gold enough in the world to make a man like you their creature."

Durand returned his stare to the wall. "I am not a man. Neither are you."

"We're always men. No matter how long we've been *upyr*, no matter what drove us to be changed, we can't erase the fact that we were once human."

He gave Durand time to tighten his lips over that, then added even more softly: "We're in your homeland, aren't we? In Switzerland where you were born. That's why my words are getting through to you. Here in this place, you remember who you used to be."

Durand rewarded him with a glare. "Sleep," he ordered. "Or I will poke you every half hour instead."

Edmund didn't have the resources to rebel. He'd accomplished all he could for now, little as it was. He closed his eyes and immediately felt himself sinking. The bullet in his head was like a chip of ice, one that stubbornly refused to melt. There wasn't much he could do while it was in there—other than make stab-in-the-dark guesses. He wished Estelle would dream-walk to him again. He

hadn't sensed her—or not clearly—since the night Frank
and Li-Hua had presented him with his first victim. He
didn't know if Durand's disruptions were keeping her
away, or if Estelle hadn't figured out what she'd done. Possibly, the explanation was no more complicated than that
she was sleeping when he was awake. Whatever the reason,
fighting this struggle alone was wearing him down.

He didn't want to turn killer, not even to save himself.

An idea came to him, a glimmer in the fog. Auriclus
had passed on more than power when he'd killed himself,
he's also bequeathed knowledge—odd packets of this and
that, which Edmund had tucked away in his mind's cor-
ners. Surely one of those tidbits would help him now. The
elder had to have known a few tricks that didn't require
much physical energy.

One fact was obvious: If Estelle couldn't come to him,
he'd have to find a way to reach her.

Frank hadn't arrived when Durand's shift was up. Though
the sun was setting, Fitz Clare didn't stir, too exhausted
by his ordeal to rouse at the normal waking hour for their
kind. Durand felt much the same. He waited ten minutes,
then locked the cell door behind himself. The precautions
his employers were taking with Fitz Clare weren't unrea-
sonable. Holding a master vampire captive was a bit like
sitting on a bomb and praying it wouldn't blow up beneath
your ass. Durand approved of making hard decisions to
achieve hard goals. He'd been doing it all his life, including
his human one. He was simply tired of doing it tonight.

Sadly, rest wasn't destined to be his yet. Li-Hua was
waiting for him outside the room he'd chosen for himself
after agreeing to their contract. It was at the top of the fortress's highest tower, its windows allowing him to observe
the approaches to their stronghold—while also being set
apart from where the others slept.

Captain or not, Durand was fond of his solitude.

"Did Fitz Clare talk to you?" Li-Hua asked.

Durand rubbed a prickling at the back of his neck. It was probably just Li-Hua, trying to read how loyal he was. But she could try all she wanted. He was as good at blocking intrusions as she was, and he had more practice.

"Fitz Clare always talks to me," he said.

"We want his secrets," she pressed.

"He's close to breaking," Durand said. "A week. Two at the most. This resistance you and Frank are seeing is his final burst. He only seems stronger because he's desperate. I've seen it happen with prisoners before."

Li-Hua paced a two-step distance up and down the corridor, her delicate white fingers worrying her lips. Her lithe little body was dressed in black tonight, and the snugness of her trousers around her curvy bottom made him think she might be trying other means than money to bind him to her cause. If she were, she probably had Frank's permission. As to that, Frank would probably want to watch.

Li-Hua spun on her heel at his nearly inaudible private snort.

"We don't want him *too* weak," she said.

"If Fitz Clare drains a victim to the point of death, he won't be. He *has* figured out you want him to change the humans, though I don't believe he knows why."

Li-Hua frowned, then waved her hand in dismissal. "It doesn't take a genius to figure out that much."

"Are you sure you can learn what you want just by watching him?"

"Frank is sure." Li-Hua stopped pacing and met his gaze head-on. "There *can't* be that much more to it than we know. Drain a human, return the blood before his heart stops beating, watch him writhe in pain while he transforms. The document Frank acquired is clear on those steps."

The document Frank acquired was an obscure fourteenth-century manuscript, copied and illuminated by a human monk named Kenelm. If the bawdy pictures the monk had hidden in the margins were any indication, Brother Kenelm had had a problem with boredom. Durand wanted to believe the text could be trusted, but he wasn't convinced.

Just because something was old didn't mean it was true.

"Master *upyr* have an extra puzzle piece," Li-Hua said. "Some secret key they only share among themselves. Whatever it is, we'll be able to catch it when we film him in action."

Though Durand didn't say a word, his expression must have been skeptical.

"You have as much at stake as we do," she reminded him. "You're almost as old as Fitz Clare. If anyone but Nim Wei had made you, you'd be a master now yourself."

Durand knew it took more than age to make a master. He also knew she was likely right. He'd always been among the strongest of their kind.

"I remember why I'm here," he said.

"See that you don't forget." Li-Hua began to walk away and then turned. "I want you to drill the others twice as long tonight. Frank and I haven't been impressed with their performance."

Frank and she had unrealistic expectations about a lot of things.

"I'll need a few hours' sleep," he said. "I'll start again when I'm fresh."

Anger flashed across Li-Hua's face a second before she nodded. Even she knew he couldn't function around the clock. More to the point, neither she nor Frank knew anything about whipping untried soldiers into shape.

"Very well," she said. "We appreciate your dedication to your job."

He nodded in return and stepped into his chamber's privacy. He hadn't been lying; he did need sleep, but he needed something else even more.

This part of the building had never been finished by its architect. Like the dungeon, its walls and floors were simple mortared stone. Durand strode across it to the window that faced west, where his body knew the sun had set. He threw back the heavy drapes and opened the shutters. Outside, rank after rank of snowcapped mountains formed a dark, frozen sea, a visual hosanna to the Almighty. As always, Durand checked the trails and passes. Satisfied that they were empty of threats, he retrieved the iron knife he'd stashed in the embrasure. The weapon was as old as he was, but because he used it so often, it had never rusted or dulled.

With quick, practical motions, and using only his left hand, he opened the buttons of his black military shirt. The back of his neck still hummed, but no doubt that was the product of weariness. Li-Hua was no longer near enough to read him. He pressed the blade to his bare breastbone, the iron a dull, cold burn. The hilt had been wrapped in leather so he could hold it without shaking.

This is for Michael, he thought, drawing the first shallow score down his skin. *For Philippe, for Charles, for Hans, for William, and for Matthaus.*

He honored each of his fallen brothers with a dripping line of blood. The scars previous cuts had left, each at different stages of healing, formed an upraised sunburst on his chest. He drew a breath, tightened his grip, and—as he had every night for the last four hundred and seventy years—plunged the blade straight through the center of the marks. As iron cracked bone with the forceful thrust, he saw the faces of his slaughtered friends—his only friends—as they'd been when they were alive. His love rose like a tidal wave, drowning out for one fraction of a second the desert of his loneliness. He held in his cry and pushed the knife harder.

The tip didn't pierce his heart, but it came damned close.

* * *

Jesus!"

The oath exploded from Estelle as she jerked awake in Edmund's bed. She had to touch her chest to make sure it wasn't bleeding, had to flex and open her fingers to uncramp them from a knife she had never held.

She looked toward the window. The angle of the light said it was almost sunset. Dimly, she recalled someone carrying her here from the window seat where she'd been debating whether or not to fall asleep. For Graham's sake, she hoped the person who had carried her had been Ben.

She sat up and pushed her tousled hair from her face. Why was she dreaming she was a stranger? Had Edmund been trying to read this man, this Captain Durand, and somehow their wires got crossed? Were such things even possible?

Unable to answer, she slipped from the bed and pulled her robe more tightly around her. The dream had been very real. Not particularly useful as far as rescuing Edmund went, but real. Wherever he was, night had already fallen. She recalled the moment when Durand had looked out his window at the mountains. There had been mountains in her first dream of Edmund, too. She wished she could identify them, but one snowy peak looked the same as any other to her. What had Durand called them? A hosanna to the Almighty?

He'd also claimed Edmund was close to breaking.

Realizing she'd been standing in one spot, staring at nothing, Estelle shook herself and padded to Edmund's bathroom. There she splashed her face with water over the pedestal sink, then studied her wan reflection in the oval mirror. Her legs were so shaky she had to brace on the basin to remain upright.

For a moment, she didn't notice the figure behind her reflection, standing white against the steel blue tile. When she did see it, it took another moment for her to recognize who it was; he was so strained and thin compared to the man she knew. The closeness with which his skin clung to his beautiful bones made her heart ache.

"Edmund," she breathed, shaking even harder.

"Don't turn around," he warned. "I'm sorry to scare you. I'm not really here. It's an old spell Auriclus knew, a ritual to project an image to a loved one. You can only see me in the mirror."

"Are you all right?"

"I am." His smile was heartbreaking, sad and loving at the same time. "But I don't know how long I have. My captors haven't been leaving me undisturbed for long. Estelle, I think I'm in Switzerland. I know that isn't terribly specific, but if you came here, if we were physically closer, I think it would be easier to communicate. I'm afraid I can't get through to anyone else."

"I'll come," she said without hesitation, and Edmund gave her that smile again.

"I don't want you to endanger yourself. I want you to bring help." He grimaced, his image flickering like a faulty reel of film. "I'm sorry, love. Robin will know what to—"

And then he was gone.

A hanging second passed, after which Estelle burst into a storm of tears. Edmund had been here. She was awake. So the dreams were real, and he was in Switzerland, somewhere with a lot of mountains. It was progress, finally, but it was also horrible. Edmund wasn't well. She could tell he wasn't well at all.

She forced herself to sit and drink a glass of cool water. She had to calm before she spoke to the others. The last thing she wanted was to panic them.

It's too soon, Graham," Robin said. "You haven't had enough training. I'll have to go to Switzerland instead."

He and the rest of the family were gathered in Edmund's bedroom. Estelle found this awkward in more ways than one, but they'd all wanted to look at the spot where she'd "seen" Edmund. To her surprise, no one had accused her of imagining his visit.

Or maybe it wasn't surprising. Once you'd seen two vampires fight at super speed in your entryway, maybe you could believe anything.

"You can't go," Graham said to Robin. "You promised to look after X Section."

Graham sat shoulder to shoulder with Ben on the window seat, which left the bed to Sally and Estelle. Robin prowled back and forth along the carpet, his energy too wound up to be contained. Though she knew everyone's attention was on other things, Estelle couldn't help wishing she'd had time to straighten the covers before they'd all tramped in.

Everyone except Graham and Robin wore pajamas. The two *upyr* were dressed for the beginning of their "day."

"You're not ready," Robin said, a growl in it. "You can't even find a meal by yourself. You could have hurt that woman you bit last night."

"Graham bit a woman?" Sally gasped.

"Shh." Ben reached out to squeeze her knee.

"You told me I was doing well," Graham retorted accusingly.

"For your first time, yes! But how are you going to negotiate a train journey across Europe? It's true you're powerful compared with most newborns, but you're not equipped to play human for days on end, much less to function while the sun is up."

"I'd get my own compartment. I'd lock the door."

"And what happens when a conductor comes to punch your ticket? Will you wake up or lie like a corpse?" Robin shoved both hands through his golden hair. He was so upset the waves actually stayed mussed. "It's not only your safety you'd be risking. It's the life of every *upyr* everywhere. The general population mustn't know about us. The humans' stakes would be sharpened before you reached Paris."

Graham's truculent expression was so *him* it made Estelle smile. When he opened his mouth to argue, she broke in.

"I have to go," she said. "And that's not open to debate. Thus far, I'm the only person Edmund has been able to contact. We're going to need to narrow down where in Switzerland he is."

Sally planted her fists on her hips. "If Estelle goes, I go. I'll be able to distract conductors better than she can." While everyone gaped, Edmund's youngest drew a deep, bracing breath, perhaps unconsciously showing off the assets with which she intended to mesmerize railway personnel. "Graham can bite me if he's hungry."

"*Sally*," Ben and Graham said in unified dismay.

"Actually . . ." Robin rubbed his chin as he looked from Sally to Estelle. "Feeding from one of you might prove workable, although Estelle—if she would permit it—would be the best candidate. Edmund's energy has changed her most. If she's careful to eat well, that should compensate her for the blood loss. To be honest, at this point I don't know if Graham *could* hurt her, even if he lost control."

Graham came as close to turning red as a vampire was able to.

"I'd be willing," Estelle said after a slight hesitation. She had a feeling that, no matter how logical this solution was, Edmund wasn't going to like it. His territorial instincts wouldn't allow him to. Nor could Estelle blame him. The act of feeding was intimate. Given her druthers, Estelle wouldn't have shared it with anyone but him.

As if she understood, Sally curled her hand around Estelle's and squeezed.

"So we'll all go," Ben said. "I can look out for the girls while Graham is sleeping, kick him awake when he needs to be, and help him rescue the professor once we know where he is."

Though Ben sounded matter-of-fact, his palms were rubbing up and down his thighs. Apparently, Estelle wasn't the only one who was feeling daunted by this task. An ordinary life simply didn't prepare one for rescuing vampires from each other.

"None of you should be going," Graham said dourly.

"We have to," Ben countered. "I know you want to do this, Graham. I know you need to. But you can't do it without us. There's just no earthly way it would work."

"Bugger." Graham's favorite curse was reassuring. It said he was feeling more like himself. He pushed to his feet, heaving a resigned sigh. "I'll make reservations for all of us to Zurich. We'll decide where to go from there."

"First class," Sally piped up. "We'll need private sleeping cars."

"First class," Graham agreed with a rueful smile. He reached down to ruffle his sister's curls, then simply stared at her with tears welling in his eyes. Estelle had never seen such naked love in his face. "If anything happens to one of you . . ."

"Nothing will," Sally said. "We'll find Daddy, and we'll be fine."

Graham's emotions didn't permit speech. He nodded sharply and left the room.

Victoria Station

London's third-busiest railway station was its usual grubby, sulfurous-smelling self.

If anyone had asked, Ben would have said he preferred being in control at the wheel of a motorcar. He could have driven them to the night ferry to Calais, but Graham had booked their passage out of London on the train. Also without consulting him, Graham and Estelle were overseeing the tagging of their hastily packed trunks. Left without useful tasks, Ben cooled his heels with Sally on the sooty concrete of Platform 2. The line of cream and chocolate Pullman cars had already pulled in, their crisply uniformed staff moving here and there to help passengers. Ben had his hands shoved firmly in his coat pockets, his sole defense against the temptation to touch Sally. They were alone together with no one paying them any mind, a circumstance he'd been trying to avoid since the last time they'd succumbed to their mutual lust.

Though they stood half a foot apart, and Sally was well swaddled by her long fox-fur coat, Ben could have sworn he felt her ripe little body radiating heat. The current that connected them couldn't be turned off by their consciences. Ben's cock was bumping up against his trousers at the power of it, his erection all the more insistent at having been denied what it wanted most. He didn't need to look at Sally to know she felt the same. Her soft cheeks would be flushed, her tempting mouth swollen. He loved her mouth. Loved kissing it. Loved feeling it brush over his chest and prick . . .

"I wish you weren't coming," he said glumly.

She didn't turn to him any more than he had to her. Instead, her gaze stayed on the windows of the dining car. "You know I have to come. Estelle can't travel with you and Graham alone. And you'd worry if I stayed here. Robin will be too busy with his spy stuff to look out for me."

"I don't know if I can stand it," Ben confessed in an undertone. The toe of his shoe edged toward her. "I want to be with you, pretty much all the time."

Sally shuffled closer and snuck her hand into his coat pocket. When he gripped her fingers in the hidden space, the sensation of intertwining them was so intense, so longed for, that it felt like a sexual act.

"I know," she said, her voice as husky as his had been. "We'll just have to be extra good."

Her thumb was rubbing a tormenting circle in the cup of his palm. No doubt she meant to be soothing, but every nerve ending in the tip of his penis tingled crazily. Somehow he didn't think being "extra good" included this. Enjoying her touch all the same, he rocked uneasily on his heels, then yanked their hands apart as Graham and Estelle approached.

"We're set," Estelle said, her manner as practical as ever, though she seemed slightly disarrayed. If Ben had ever needed proof that she was steady, this situation with the professor was providing it. "Our baggage is stowed, and two adjoining coupés have been assigned to us."

Graham handed out the boarding passes without speaking. He looked pale to Ben, not sickly but tense and pinched around the mouth. His eyes were brighter than they should have been, with little gleams of gold shining in the brown. He was like a wire with too much electricity forced through it. The effect was hypnotizing, the changes from the Graham he knew. Ben had to force himself not to stare.

He still couldn't believe his brother was a vampire.

"You all right?" he asked as they fell into step.

It was a sign of Graham's distraction that this question didn't annoy him. "I'll be fine as soon as we get inside."

They found their compartments with the help of a white-gloved steward. True to his word, Graham had not stinted on their accommodations, which were indeed first class. Sally cooed over the glossy marquetry, called Graham a dear, dear man, and then insisted on examining both tiny washrooms before deciding which coupé should be hers and Estelle's. They were exactly the same as far as Ben could tell, as clever as they were compact. While Sally dithered, Graham stood like a statue in the passageway, not rolling his eyes even once. It was as if he'd fallen asleep on his feet with his eyes open, and it looked queerer than Graham could have imagined. Ben had to nudge him into motion through the door Sally left to them.

"Sorry," Graham said, belatedly realizing what he'd done. "I'm still getting used to watching everything I do."

He didn't look like he was watching it any better now. His pallor was increasing, his skin beginning to shimmer like moonlit stone. Ben shut the compartment door, deciding he would mention this if someone came knocking.

"Sit," he said instead. "I'm going to get a crick looking up at you."

Graham sat on the banquette sofa and clutched his knees. The seat could be converted into two bunks, but Ben didn't think they'd bother with that tonight. Graham certainly didn't look as if he would rest—explode with impatience, maybe, but not rest.

"When do we pull out?" he asked.

"Thirty minutes, thereabouts."

Graham nodded and looked whiter. His hands were glowing on his dark trousers. Ben felt his chest constrict.

"Graham . . ."

Before Ben could warn him he'd lost his glamour, Graham jumped to his feet. "I don't think I can wait. I think you need to call her here."

"*Her?* You mean Estelle?"

Graham nodded, his lips rolled together over his teeth. "Robin warned me not to wait too long. If I'm too hungry, I might hurt her."

This was more than Ben could hear comfortably.

"I'll get her now," he said.

Graham caught his sleeve as he touched the door handle. "You come back, too. I don't want to be alone with her."

Ben suspected the problem was the opposite.

"I'll come back," he said, at which Graham sagged like a pierced balloon and sat down again. Sweat broke out beneath Ben's arms. What the devil was he going to do if Estelle weren't available, or—worse—if she'd changed her mind?

Fortunately, he bumped into her coming out of her and Sally's compartment. She squeaked the door shut behind her in the narrow corridor.

"Is he okay?" she asked.

Ben shook his head, both relieved and sorry not to see Sally. He spoke so only Estelle could hear. "He says he needs to, er, have a bite. Robin warned him not to wait too long."

Ben had an urge to apologize, but Estelle's reaction was businesslike.

"All right," she said. "I'll go straight in."

"He asked me to stay while you were with him."

Her eyes flicked to his, held, and then looked away. "All right," she repeated, reaching for the door handle.

Graham leaped to his feet as soon as she came in. "I'm sorry, Estelle. I—"

"No," Estelle cut him off. "We already agreed to this." She looked around the little cabin. "Do you want to do it sitting or standing up?"

Graham looked at her and then at the banquette sofa. Clearly, he was thinking about doing a different "it" than Estelle had meant. A little flush washed into her cheeks as she recognized what she'd said.

"We'll sit," she said more gently.

She took the corner of the couch where it met the window, pulling down the shade before she tugged Graham by the hand next to her. Her gray traveling outfit was as close to prim as a voluptuous shape like hers allowed, its jacket buttoned, its skirt smoothed neatly over her knees. She and Graham resembled awkward strangers on the sidelines of a dance—or they did until Graham started breathing faster and staring at her neck.

"Estelle," he said pleadingly.

The yearning in his voice had Ben's hands fisting. He'd backed up against the closed compartment door, the fancy inlaid wood blocking more retreat. He could see Graham didn't want to make the first move.

Estelle gave him a small understanding smile. She undid the single button on her blouse's white collar. "Sooner started, sooner finished," she said.

Graham's Adam's apple bobbed. He took her shoulders between his two big hands and bent to her neck. He inhaled once, hovering, his eyeteeth gleaming white and long as his lips pulled back.

Ben was unable to look away: a rabbit whose burrow-mate was about to be prey.

Graham's fangs made a soft punching noise into Estelle's flesh.

The sound broke Ben's paralysis. He flinched, struggling not to voice the oaths he was swearing silently in his mind.

Estelle stiffened, but that was all. Graham's hold had tightened on her upper arms, unconsciously kneading them. Ben didn't think Graham had started drinking yet. His lips were locked to her neck, but his body remained tight, his breath chuffing in and out in his fight with himself. Then, as if he realized he truly couldn't hold off, his cheeks sucked in for his first mouthful. Estelle's eyelids screwed shut, almost but not quite as if she were in pain.

Graham's rumbling groan of pleasure stood the hairs on Ben's arms on end.

Ben's brother was aroused. Only his upper body was twisted toward Estelle. His knees were splayed to face away from her. Thus exposed, the hump straining in his trousers looked big enough for two men. Graham's haunches shifted at the discomfort this huge erection caused, his lower body wanting to turn more intimately to his partner even as his conscience forbid it.

A much more mournful sound broke from his steadily swallowing throat.

"It's all right," Estelle said, her eyes still closed, still tense. Her hand rose to pet his hair. "I know you have to do this."

Her tenderness might not have been a good idea. Graham moaned again and gripped the back of her head. He was changing the angle of her body, giving himself better access to his feeding point. Estelle gasped, but did not protest. Her position was now so awkward, Graham had to slide one arm around her waist or let her fall to the floor. His strength made the contortion look easy, but Ben knew he must be working to control himself. He and Estelle were both being careful of each other—not to move too close, not to touch the wrong things—and still the essentially erotic nature of what they were doing could not be denied. The two of them were like some old-time painting of a virile god ravishing a lush maiden.

Unable to keep his own blood from heating, Ben

clenched his jaw and turned his gaze determinedly to a wall panel. The idea that Graham might have to bite Sally made him want to stab his brother with a sharp object. He'd give Graham his own vein ten times over before he'd permit that.

To his relief, Graham broke free before long. He lifted Estelle's body back into the seat. The whole thing hadn't lasted more than five minutes.

"Okay," Graham huffed out, seemingly as much for his benefit as Estelle's. "That's enough. I'll . . . I'll just heal the bite mark now."

He closed his eyes and ran his tongue across the two little wounds. Apparently, this was pleasant for him. He exhaled hard and then pushed away. He was glowing like a big electric bulb, but even as Ben watched, he tamped down the radiance. Though his lips weren't bloody, he drew the back of his hand over them. Seeing as he was conspicuously still aroused, Ben didn't think disgust inspired the gesture.

Estelle pushed carefully out of the corner of the banquette. She was almost steady when she reached her feet. She put out her hands, palms outward, to forestall Graham from helping her. Estelle was a born peacemaker, but for once, she didn't seem to have words to say.

It was Graham who filled the silence.

"I tasted him," he said, sliding forward on the seat to look up at her. His face was strange, both cautious and very moved: reverent, Ben could have said. "When I drank from you, I felt the mark Edmund left."

Estelle appeared as if she were about to speak, but in the end she just shook her head. She leaned down to Graham, her hand coming to his shoulder to support her weight. She pressed a gentle kiss to his brow.

"It's fine," she said. "Let me know when you need me again."

She squeezed Ben's arm as she left. He saw the troubled

expression she wasn't showing Graham. What happened here had shaken her.

Never again, he promised himself. *I don't care if Graham begs. I am never being witness to this again.*

As soon as she was gone, Graham collapsed in his seat. His head was back, and his eyes were closed. Despite these signs of weariness, he looked a damned sight better than he had before—relaxed for the first time that night. His glamour was in place, so there was no more whiter-than-white glimmer. He could have passed for normal if Ben hadn't known him before.

His lips twitched over some cause for amusement Ben must have missed.

"Well," Graham said on a gust of air. "Wasn't that ducky?"

"Not to mention slightly oedipal."

Graham snorted at Ben's stab at humor. His head came up, and his eyes opened. Sharp as ever, they read Ben's awkwardness with no trouble. "I suppose I should be glad I stopped without help. Look, I'm sorry to have put you through that. And sorry that *sorry* seems to be my new favorite word." He cocked his head at the door, his grin sheepish but winsome—the old Graham, plus a spark of something more. "There's a bar on this train, I hear. I could buy us both a drink, and we can find out what it takes for vampires to get sozzled."

"As long as you don't start lighting up like a firefly. I don't have a sack to throw over you."

"Ha ha," said Graham, which—oddly enough—was exactly what he would have said when he was human.

"You can drink then?" Ben asked as they worked their way down the corridor. A female passenger gave Graham wide eyes as they turned sideways to pass her. His shoulders were almost too wide to fit the normal way.

"Only red wine," Graham said, seeming not to have

noticed the woman's admiring stare. "Or clear water. If there's any single malt, it's going down your gullet."

Ben thought about what he'd seen between Graham and Estelle, and what he'd felt while he'd watched.

"Not a problem," he said.

Estelle returned to the next compartment, where Sally had curled up on the burgundy velvet banquette. Despite all that was going on, Edmund's daughter was sleeping as peacefully as a four-year-old who'd been kept up past her bedtime. Above her hip, a golden crown had been embroidered onto the seat back. AOE said the crest's curling letters: Arlberg Orient Express. The monogram seemed appropriate for the princess Sally was. Estelle tucked a throw around her and took the single swiveling armchair for herself. The chair had to be tiny to fit the space. Equally tiny was the half-moon table beneath the window, with its shirred and fringed red lamp. Sitting next to it, Estelle felt like a grown-up visiting a child's playhouse.

A long whistle sounded, signaling departure. As the train lurched into motion, she pressed her hands to her trembling mouth.

She wasn't going to cry because her body had betrayed her by taking pleasure in Graham's bite. Any vampire had the power to make her enjoy that. According to Edmund, the skill was part of how the species survived; victims who struggled might endanger them. And Graham was someone she cared about. Feeding him *hadn't* been the same as feeding Edmund. Her connection to the professor was so much deeper, so much more a meeting of souls. What she'd experienced with Graham couldn't compare to it.

So she didn't cry as the train clacked along the tracks over the darkened Thames. She simply prayed that Edmund wouldn't find out and be hurt.

Paris

Graham Fitz Clare caught Pen flat-footed by spiriting his family out of London in the middle of the night. The message from her informant at Thomas Cook didn't reach her at the hotel until the following morning. Fortunately, the booking agent was able to tell her that the Fitz Clares would be stopping for the day in Paris and had reserved a room. Pen had to scramble (and tell her father a few creative lies about a sudden urge to buy French couture) but she was able to recoup lost time with a hop to the Continent on an aeroplane. The inconvenience to her schedule seemed small to her. Everything she'd dug up about Graham's father since Christmas Eve, when Graham so rudely told her to mind her own, had whetted her interest.

Most intriguing was that his father didn't seem to have a past. Edmund Fitz Clare had simply appeared in London thirty years ago. Once there, he'd obtained a position at the university, wrote a popular book on the rise and fall of civilizations, and generally set about being recognized as a brilliant scholarly mind. She could find no employment history, no record of his supposed schooling at Oxford (which was mentioned in his dust jackets) or how he'd made his money. This last was significant. Though his books sold well, the income from his writing and teaching absolutely did not account for his net worth, which her man at Lloyd's gauged at upward of ten million pounds. The adoption records for his children were sketchy, the hours he worked as a professor laughable. When Fitz Clare lectured, the hall was packed. When he didn't, no one batted an eye.

Incomplete though the profile was, it made Pen wish she'd met him. Graham's father must be quite the Svengali to pull off all that.

Pen's best bet was that his current identity was manufactured, that he'd escaped—or got his start in—criminal enterprise. Chances were, some former shady associates were behind his abduction. Graham was bound to be shocked once he learned the truth, but Pen couldn't help that. No one should expect their father to be perfect. From the occasional personal information Graham let drop, she knew Edmund loved his son. As far as she was concerned, that was reason enough to do everything she could to help him.

Most definitely, she'd be more help to the senior Fitz Clare than Graham. Graham had been a private secretary, for goodness sake. The gravest danger he'd faced was ensuring her father's luggage didn't get misplaced while they were traveling. The fact that he'd brought his family with him on this rescue mission merely proved her point—though she held out some hope for his brother, Ben. Her brief glimpse of him at Christmas had suggested he was a man who wouldn't balk at skulduggery. Graham, by contrast, was a Boy Scout when it came to following the rules. He'd probably hamstring his brother out of doing what good he could.

By the time Pen got herself and her baggage to the appropriate departure platform at Gare de l'Est, she was feeling positively virtuous about sticking her nose into Fitz Clare affairs.

Since the objects of her munificence seemed not to have arrived, she allowed herself the pleasure of taking in her surroundings. Though Pen loved the speed of flying, she couldn't entirely resist the romance of the rails. The line of mirror-bright royal blue wagon-lits seemed to stretch forever, their touches of gold decoration like braid on a uniform. A clatter of feverish preparation issued from the galleys. Guests in fancy dress were being ushered to a gourmet meal in the dining car. Out over Paris, the sun had begun to set, the lengthening shadows tinged now with blue. Pen could see this because the departure platform was covered but not enclosed, with slots for multiple trains to pull beneath the glass and metal roof. Farther down the tracks, nearer to her train's snaking tail, windows were molten with orange flame.

It occurred to her that Paris's east station would have been a marvelous setting for a tryst—exotic, evocative, men and women shoved together into close quarters. A grin tugged her mouth at the incongruity of the idea. She was meeting Graham here, and anyone less loverlike she could scarcely imagine.

Despite her amusement, she didn't lose track of the sights and sounds around her. Since picking up her new . . . hobby, she guessed she'd call it, she'd schooled herself to remain alert without seeming to. She heard the Fitz Clares approach before she saw them.

When she did see them, they presented an unusual picture. Graham Fitz Clare, all six foot and some inches of him, was being supported between his brother, Ben, and the same gorgeous Amazon who'd opened the door to Pen in Bedford Square. Even with their assistance, Graham was stumbling down the platform stairs on India rubber legs, barely able to keep his eyes open.

"Christ," swore his brother as his footing slipped. "Would you *try* to wake up? You're a blinking baby elephant."

"Let me take more of his weight," said the woman. "It's my right arm I've got around his waist."

The woman tightened her arm as she spoke, which did seem to bolster Graham. Pen's eyebrows shot up at that. She wouldn't have guessed this curvaceous female had that much strength. She must have been training as a lady wrestler in her spare time.

Behind this singular trio, Graham's petit four of a little sister skipped lightly down the stairs with her blonde curls bouncing under a blue beret. Someone—probably her father—had spent a fortune on her long, banded fox-fur coat. A fur like that would keep her warm in Siberia.

"We're almost there, Graham," Sally chirped. "Soon you'll be all the way out of that nasty sun."

Because this was true—if a strange thing to say—Pen judged it time to lift the curtain on her opening act.

"Heavens," she said, stepping hesitantly into the path the Fitz Clares would have to travel to the first-class cars. "Can it be—?" She let her hand flatten on her breast. "Why, Graham, fancy meeting you here!"

The others' eyes came to her before Graham's did. None of them looked pleased to see her.

"It's Miss Anderson," the gorgeous Amazon said after a brief, stunned pause. "The daughter of Graham's old boss."

When Graham's head slowly lifted, his skin was as flushed as if he'd been drinking—the answer perhaps to why he was finding sunshine so onerous. Though Pen disapproved of imbibing so much one ended up hungover, an odd shock vibrated through her as his gaze found hers. Beneath the shadow of his fedora, his eyes seemed different, simultaneously sleepy and piercing. She broke the connection, then couldn't help noticing that the shoulders he'd draped around his companions looked broad enough to climb on.

Evidently, in the past little while of not seeing him,

she'd forgotten what a substantial, square-jawed specimen of maleness he was.

"It's Pen," she said in response to the Amazon, ruthlessly squelching any evidence of her thoughts. "Only people who don't know me call me Miss Anderson."

"What are you doing here?" Graham asked.

"Well, that's not very friendly," she laughed, affecting a bit of the Southern flutter her invalid mother was so fond of. Pen would have preferred not to have an accent at all, it being a reminder of a childhood with a woman she did not respect. Still, it had its uses, especially when it came to disarming men. "I'm on a shopping trip to Zurich. Father's birthday is coming up. You know how he loves watches."

"Zurich."

The steel that had entered Graham's voice seemed to help him stand on his own. He unwound his arms from his companions' necks and shook his coat sleeves down. Pen's heart began to thump harder. She was tallish herself—rangy, she liked to say—but in the years she'd known Graham, she couldn't recall him looming over her like this. He seemed new to her, a big, dangerous stranger. It took an effort to respond the way she'd planned.

"Don't tell me you're going to Zurich, too! How delightful. I've been longing for company on the trip."

"That's funny," said his sister. "I usually bring friends *with* me when I travel."

Pen gave her a sharper look than she'd expended on her before. Graham's fluffy little sister was pursing her rosebud mouth, all femininity and innocence. Innocence notwithstanding, she had her hands wrapped around Ben's arm as if *he* needed protection from Pen's presence.

"Alas," Pen said, calculating this together at lightning speed, "none of my usual shopping *compagne* were free to come."

Graham interrupted whatever sugared barb his sister

was set to deliver. "You," he said, pointing at Pen with one blunt finger. "Over there, with me."

She wouldn't normally have obeyed, but it was in her interest to get this over with. She allowed him to guide her by the elbow toward one of the tall green columns that held up the arched glass roof. His grip was firmer than she expected. She had to take a few double steps to keep from being pulled off her feet. Pen had been with boisterous bed partners, men who'd just as soon play polo as kiss a girl. None of them had ever dragged her along like this. If they had, maybe they wouldn't have ended up on her discard pile. What Graham was doing sent the most peculiar flush tingling up her legs.

"Now," he said once they were out of earshot and in the shadow of the next train. "What are you really doing here?"

Pen yanked her arm away. "I told you: I'm shopping for my father."

"And I told you to stay out of our affairs."

"Would that be because you're doing such a bang-up job of handling them yourself? Look at you, Graham. I understand you're upset. I care about my father, too. But it's barely five in the evening, and you're almost too drunk to walk."

Pen had always liked Graham's plain brown eyes. They looked kind, she thought, and had thick lashes. Now they seemed to shoot sparks at her with fury. He'd taken hold of her arms again, his fingers digging into her muscles through her cashmere coat. Struggling would have been a sign of weakness, so Pen ignored the pinch of discomfort. If he thought his anger could intimidate her, he had another think coming. She lifted her chin and met his glare.

"I paid for my ticket. I've as much right to ride this train as anyone. Anyway, if you didn't want me to know you were off to rescue your father, you should have used a different travel agency from the one you always book Daddy through."

To Pen's absolute amazement, Graham's growl of irritation dampened her panties. His teeth were gritted when he responded.

"My family and I are taking a holiday. A respite from what's happened. It's nothing to do with the professor. You should know better than to hare off on wild chases after people you barely know."

She'd give Graham this: He was a surprisingly convincing liar. Everything he'd said seemed genuine—so genuine, in fact, that she experienced a rare moment of self-doubt.

"You need to go home," he went on, his concentration of will so fierce she could almost feel it pressing on her forehead. "It couldn't be more inappropriate for you to interfere in this."

"Who's interfering? I'm looking for a special gift for my father."

Graham released his hold on her so abruptly she stumbled back. His glower was impressive. "Your father should have spanked you more often when you were a girl."

"My father never spanked me. But maybe you imagine *you* could make up for that."

The challenge was out before she could call it back, precisely the sort of man-woman gauntlet she never tossed at Graham. He stared at her with his jaw hanging, his big chest going in and out with surprise. Something about the movement affected her. He was just so *big*, so thick and muscular. His weight would trap a woman, would press her down and not let her up. Pen felt her nipples tighten inside her clothes, the contraction quick and unmistakable. That reaction was succeeded by a second gush of warm, silky liquid between her legs. Pen wasn't prone to blushing, but the blood that caused one rose hot and unwelcome into her face.

Graham began breathing harder for reasons other than surprise. Her only logical conclusion was that he'd guessed that she was aroused.

He clapped his mouth shut as if something terrible were going to come out of it otherwise. The gleam in his eyes brightened dangerously. She remembered him calling her a harridan to his brother, saying she'd poke a man's heart out with her "skinny" ribs. The flush in her cheeks threatened to catch fire with embarrassment. Pride was all that kept her gaze from dropping.

So what if Graham knew he'd attracted her? So what if she didn't particularly attract him back? No doubt that busty Amazon goddess who hung around his family was more his type. She refused to let it matter. Pen Anderson didn't play poor thing for anyone.

"Pen," Graham said, his tone turning conciliatory. "This is stupid. There's no reason for you to travel all this way just to—"

Though it went against everything she'd trained herself out of doing, Pen's temper took over.

"Don't you pity me," she said, and shot her arm out to punch his chest.

He caught her fist before it reached him, his reflexes so fast she gasped. "Who said anything about pity?"

He honestly seemed perplexed. She struggled stupidly for a moment to regain control of her hand, but his muscles might as well have been made of steel. She couldn't budge him at all.

"Let go of me," she ground out.

He looked to where he held her as if surprised to find her fist caught in his. His fingers uncurled slowly. "Pen . . ."

She stalked past him, her face truly searing now. "We both need to go in now. They're calling the *all aboard*."

They weren't, as it happened, but she was sure they would soon enough.

* * *

Graham followed his brother into their compartment, his brain still fuzzy from having been forced outside before nightfall. *Sundrunk*, Robin had called it when he warned him. The phenomenon was more powerful than the wine he'd had with Ben last night. The effect of that had faded almost as soon as the alcohol hit his stomach. Sadly, any interest he might have felt in these discoveries couldn't occupy his mind.

A certain obstinate American was monopolizing his thoughts.

The sensation of the sun finally slipping under the horizon was a relief he barely registered. Graham didn't know which annoyed him most: that Pen was shoving herself into this in clear defiance of his wishes, that she believed Edmund's disappearance had driven him to drink, or that she seemed to think there was something *she* could do that he could not. Condescension was no stranger to Pen's nature, but this truly took the prize!

His teeth were grinding as he wrenched off his unneeded coat.

Yes, Pen had spent a lifetime telling other people, including her friends, what to do, and, yes, most of them obeyed. But just because the world jumped when her industrialist father snapped his fingers didn't mean it would do the same for her. Even if it had, that didn't qualify her for rescuing supernatural creatures from mysterious plots.

Graham stopped himself just in time before he tore the compartment's tiny closet door off its hinges. With more care—if not more calmness—he eased it open and hung his coat inside.

What he wouldn't give to show Pen the truth of what he was for five sweet minutes! He'd felt a shadow of that satisfaction when he'd gripped her arms. She'd reacted to that, all right. Not like he was her father's pet, but like he was a man. He'd smelled her excitement, had seen it in her rising flush. He couldn't recall seeing her blush for any of the guffawing college boys who were perpetually making up to her.

And then her blush had spurred him to react himself.

Her blood had done it. She'd smelled so blasted good, and he hadn't eaten anything this evening. Not that eating had been foremost in his mind. When her cheeks went pink, his cock had thickened up so fast it should have made him dizzy. The thing was still twitching in his trousers, just waiting for him to think too hard about her again. Something nicked the inside of his cheek, and he realized his fangs were down.

"Damn it," he muttered to himself, his hand flat on the glossy finish of the marquetry wall. This was the last thing he needed before he had to call Estelle.

"Graham . . ." said Ben.

"I know," Graham snapped. "I'll get my glamour back up."

"It *is* up," Ben said. "Mostly." He held his coat, waiting for Graham to move aside enough for him to put it away. "I was going to say you need to get rid of that woman."

Sighing, Graham took Ben's coat from him, opened the closet, and slipped it onto a chained hanger. "I swear, I didn't invite her. She just showed up. She's got this idiotic notion that we can't save the professor without her help."

"Can't you use your vampire thrall on her?"

"I tried, but apparently it isn't very good yet. I'm not sure she felt it at all. Look, I'll talk to her again. Maybe I can be ruder. Really insult her this time."

Ben's amusement snorted out his nose. "Sorry, Graham. I don't think rudeness is one of your vampire powers."

"I've been rude to her before," Graham said.

The guilt that crossed his face made Ben laugh again. He sat on the slim banquette. "Maybe I should talk to her."

"No," Graham said, hastily enough that Ben's eyes

widened. Possibly Ben could make more headway with her than him. Ben was the one with experience, the one women swooned over. All the same, Graham was reluctant to hand this off. "Pen's my problem. I'll take care of her."

Ben drew a breath, then thought better of whatever he'd meant to say. He rubbed his palms up and down his thighs. "Do you want me to call Estelle now or wait until we pull out?"

Graham registered Ben's unease, seeing just how obviously he didn't want anything to do with Graham and Estelle's arrangement. Graham's brother was good to be game, but this really wasn't his responsibility. Like everything else that was royally buggered up right now, it was Graham's.

Restraining the sigh that wanted to gust from him required a considerable portion of his vampire strength.

"Thanks," Graham said, "but Estelle and Sally made reservations in the dining car." His smile twisted. "It wouldn't be fair to keep them from eating so I can. I'll talk to her myself later."

"You're sure?"

"I'm sure. Why don't you join them? I'll close my eyes and rest here a bit."

Ben rose and slapped his shoulder. "It's too bad you haven't taken your wolf soul yet. We could bring you the leftovers."

Graham laughed and slapped him back. "Go," he said. "I'll be fine."

He would be fine. As long as he kept all thoughts of Pen or Estelle far away from him.

Dressing for dinner was de rigueur for first class, so Pen shook out her best war togs. Her pale, ankle-length green satin was stylish without being showy: modest in the front and low in the back. Though her breasts were next to nonexistent beneath the bosom's drape, the flowing bias cut made the most of her slender height. Slipping into a pair of matching three-inch heels increased the willowy effect, as did her endless strand of pink South Sea pearls. *They* were showy, no question, but Pen had discovered it rarely hurt to let people know you came from money. When you appeared rich, you could always speak modestly. With a swipe of lipstick and a dash of rouge, she looked every inch the toast of New York she was; not the most beautiful Bright Young Thing, but certainly among the most spirited.

"All right, Pen," she murmured to her reflection. "Into the fray with you."

Given how well her last conversation with Graham had gone, it was no surprise that her palms were sweating as she moved between the little tables in the dining car. What did surprise was her disappointment at not finding Graham with his family. The seat beside the Amazon goddess was empty.

"Well," she said to the goddess, who was facing Pen and thus saw her first. "We meet again."

The goddess looked startled but not angry. Before she could decide she should be, Pen smiled and held out her hand. "I don't think crashing your Christmas Eve party counts as a proper introduction. I'm Pen Anderson."

"Estelle Berenger," her target said, bemused. The shake she gave Pen's hand was unusually firm for a woman. "This is—" She looked unsurely at her tablemates. "These are Graham's siblings, Ben and Sally."

Ben gave her a nod, while Sally stared coolly. Pen could see the members of this audience weren't going to be pushovers.

"Look," she said, judging a bit of frankness might serve, "I don't know how much Graham told you about me—"

"Nothing at all," Sally interjected, and crossed her arms.

"Right," said Pen. "Well, he wouldn't. We're not best

chums or anything like that, but my father's very fond of Graham, and I really think I might be able to help."

"We're on holiday," Ben said. "How can you help with that?"

A gleam of amusement entered Estelle's rather amazing lambent gray eyes. The expression performed magic on her already lovely face. She wasn't wearing a speck of makeup, but apart from the faint red scar that rayed like a spider around one eye, her skin was as smooth as cream. Her pillowy, flushed mouth made even Pen think of kissing it. The idea that Graham was around this vision on a daily basis caused Pen's stomach to clench. Men like Graham were supposed to have plain love interests.

The goddess blinked and rubbed her right earlobe. Her sudden grin was as unexpected as it was blinding.

"I'm the professor's fiancée," she said.

"Oh." Pen's mind took a moment to rearrange itself. "Forgive me. I assumed—"

But she couldn't admit what she'd been assuming. That would have been even more awkward. Good Lord, though! Professor Fitz Clare must be a charmer to bag a woman as young and beautiful as Estelle.

"Won't you join us?" Estelle asked. "Graham is indisposed at the moment, and we have an extra place. I'm sure you'd rather not eat alone."

Pen got the distinct impression that Sally had just kicked Estelle beneath the table. Ben, too, was staring at Estelle as if their family friend were a few bricks short of a load. Luckily for Pen, she hadn't come here to be sensitive.

"That's very kind of you," she accepted. "I'd welcome the opportunity to get to know you all better."

Dinner with the Fitz Clares was an experience. The amount of laughter they shared took Pen aback. In their situation, she doubted she'd have been able to prevent her worry from swallowing her. But they had a shorthand when they spoke to each other, teases and jokes only they knew the punch lines to. They weren't clever like Pen's friends were, but she found herself unexpectedly jealous of Graham for being a member of this close circle. The Fitz Clares could count on each other through thick and thin. Pen wasn't certain the same was true of her set.

It was the professor's fiancée, Estelle, who tried to make her feel welcome, asking her about her father and their world travels. She even coaxed Pen into talking about fashion, not because she was interested, but because her friend, Sally, was. For whatever reason, she seemed to want the others to warm to her.

"Your father knows a lot of powerful people," Estelle observed, her fork poised over the second dessert Ben had slid to her. Estelle wasn't pudgy, by any means, but from the amount she ate she must have had a hollow leg. "I can't imagine sitting down to dinner with the queen."

"Well, it was Roosevelt," Pen said. "Not royalty. Americans aren't as fussy about that kind of thing. Daddy has heaps of friends in the government. Industry is important to the whole country."

Industry was important to the people who made Pen's hobby possible—not that she was going to talk about that.

"Americans aren't as fussy about a lot of things," Sally said pointedly.

"Such as good manners?" Estelle said silkily back.

This was too much for Sally's control. "Don't be scolding me! She pushed her way in here with some stupid story about shopping. Even you can't believe she's on the same train as us by coincidence. Graham told her to mind her own business, and she ignored him!"

"Sally—"

"She's right," Pen said softly, interrupting Estelle. "I am being pushy, but only because I sincerely think I can help. I have contacts, Sally, my father's and my own. Suppose they could help your father out of the trouble he's in. Do you honestly want to risk shutting me out?"

"You don't have the first idea about it," Sally said, her curls trembling with anger. "Your stupid contacts can't help with this."

"Maybe if you told me what you knew about your father's situation . . ."

"Stop being a buttinsky!" Sally exclaimed.

Ben cracked up. "A buttinsky?"

"It's a word," his sister huffed. "I read it somewhere."

"Maybe we could talk about this later," Pen suggested. She dabbed her mouth with her napkin and rose. "Thank you for being as tolerant of me as you were."

She tried not to show that the back of her neck was prickling with self-consciousness as she walked away. Apparently, the effort added a little extra something to her normal stride.

"Stop staring at her bum," she heard Sally snap, to which Ben—like males of every country and every age— innocently responded, "*What?*"

Why were you so nice to her?" Sally complained. "Her and her '*compagne*' and 'Mah daddy had dinnuh with the president.' She's the enemy."

Sally's unerring mimicry of Pen's slightly Southern accent made Estelle want to smile. "I *asked* her about her father, and she's *not* the enemy."

Ben exchanged a look with Sally. With Pen's disappearance, he and his sister had relaxed together, shoulder to shoulder, on their side of the table. "Actually, she sort of is. I mean, we can't afford to have her hanging around while Graham is trying to find his sea legs. What if he flashes his fangs at her?"

"I think she likes him," Estelle said.

"Oh, pull the other one," Ben scoffed. "Girls like her eat men like Graham for breakfast."

"Maybe the old Graham. I'm not sure she'd make an easy meal of him now. Anyway, I . . . caught a little of her thoughts with my funny ear."

"Ugh." Sally wrinkled her nose. "That is *so* unnerving. Who wants to know what people are thinking? Your arm being super strong seems much more fun to me. Just imagine who you could arm wrestle!"

Estelle had to smile at Sally's attitude. Ever since Edmund had "appeared" in her bathroom, and she'd had to be more forthcoming about the effect his energy had had on her, Estelle had worried about the others' reactions to her freakishness. She saw now she shouldn't have. To Ben and Sally, her gifts were merely one more oddity among the rest.

"I can't read people the way Edmund does," she assured Sally. "Only now and then. The important thing is, Pen's not lying about wanting to help Edmund."

"That doesn't mean she can," Ben put in.

"Maybe not." Estelle looked down at her empty pudding plate and wondered where the sweet had gone. Being a snack for vampires certainly perked up one's appetite. That reminder sobered her mood. She lifted her gaze to Ben, suspecting that—of the two of them—he'd be the likeliest to catch her meaning. "I simply think it wouldn't be a bad idea for Graham to have a distraction. We can be extra careful about what we say in front of Pen."

Ben's eyes were too understanding. Estelle turned her own aside.

"She's still a buttinsky," Sally grumped.

What she was was an attractive woman who shared a trait or two with Sally.

"You're right," Estelle said aloud. "But with luck she'll be a useful one."

The Orient Express

          ✦◆✦

Pen returned to her compartment, which had been converted to its sleeping configuration while she ate dinner. She was hoping a few deep breaths would restore her usual sangfroid. She wasn't used to people treating her with Sally's open hostility, though she told herself she could handle it. She aspired to be of true service to her country, and not just a hobbyist. That being so, and considering what was happening in the world these days, she would have to grow a thicker skin. The thought inspired the tug of a smile. Sally would probably say her skin was plenty thick enough.

Feeling better, Pen used her tiny washroom and freshened her makeup. This train would reach Zurich before the next day passed. She couldn't sit on her duff if she expected to get the skinny from the Fitz Clares in these hard-to-escape confines.

She ignored the fact that her heart was fluttering as she stepped back into the swaying passageway. Nerves wouldn't harm her. Nerves would just keep her sharp.

Some distance away, a piano was playing in the bar car,

the Gershwin tune loud and bouncy to compete with the guests' laughter. Pen hoped Graham wasn't there. He'd be hard to pump for information in all that noise. On the other hand, if he *had* turned to drink lately, liquor would likely loosen his tongue. Deciding this was a good—though perhaps not commendable—strategy, she nabbed a bottle of champagne from a steward who was passing with an ice bucket, trading it for a large franc note from her beaded purse.

"Young love," she said by way of explanation, at which the startled steward laughed.

She was swinging the bottle by her hip, dancing a bit to the drifting bursts of the piano, when she spotted Graham coming out of his compartment.

He was wearing dinner dress: boiled white shirt, black jacket, white fringed scarf around his lapels. She'd seen him in formal clothes before, of course. Her father had included him many times in social events, and he'd always looked perfectly acceptable. *Acceptable* wasn't how he appeared tonight. Pen had never seen him so effortlessly confident. He dwarfed the corridor with his size, yet not a single seam of his garments betrayed a strain. His clothes fit him as if conforming to his frame were a privilege. Whoever his new tailor was, Pen couldn't help but silently applaud.

Graham hadn't seen her yet. He was turned toward the door adjacent to his, contemplating it. Her breath caught in her throat as he rubbed his chin, her fingers nearly slipping on the champagne bottle's dewy neck. There was something in his profile that killed her greeting before it could emerge.

He looked as if his heart were breaking, as if he longed for something he was never going to deserve. It was an expression Pen wouldn't have thought to see on his face. Graham's heart was supposed to be as stolid as the rest of him.

Maybe she hadn't been so far off in pegging Estelle as his love interest.

Possibly she made some sound, because Graham's head jerked around to her. His eyes widened a second before narrowing in anger.

"Pen," he said, his displeasure painfully apparent.

Ignoring the twinge of hurt, she held up the champagne as a peace offering. "Are you really indisposed, or could I tempt you with a glass of this?"

"I don't drink champagne," he said, the words grating out. His gaze ran up and down her slim evening gown, his mouth tightening with an emotion she couldn't identify. She knew the pale green satin clung to her faithfully, but she supposed that didn't ring any chimes for him. "Have you seen my family?"

"When I left them, they were sitting over coffee and dessert."

His face flickered at that. Maybe he thought they shouldn't be enjoying themselves without him. Then again, maybe he was mad at her.

"When you *left them* . . . Damn it, Pen. Why were you with them? Why can't you leave this alone?"

"I just want to talk to you. We've done that before— pleasantly."

"Sure we have. Whenever you wanted to impress your father by being nice to his protégé."

His scorn scraped her rawer than she expected, perhaps because it was—just a bit—deserved.

"I like you, Graham," she said. They weren't far apart. Two careful strides brought her close enough to rest the chilled bottle of Vouvray against his chest. Something happened to his heart when her hand met his starched shirt-front. It jumped—once, hard—as if it had only started beating that moment. The feel of the strange convulsion pushed her own blood quicker through her veins.

His eyes searched hers, the light in them hard. He was looking down on her as few men were tall enough to do.

"You like me," he repeated skeptically.

The swaying of the train jostled them closer, causing their thighs to brush. Pen fought to keep her voice steady.

"Of course I do. Why wouldn't I?"

The train took a curve, and his hands came to her elbows to steady her. She had to wonder if he was paying attention to what he was doing, because his fingers started caressing her through her sleeves. Simple though the contact was, the slow, circling squeeze had heat swelling in her groin: forceful tingles of sensation that tugged nerves inside and out. She was wet in moments, spilling over with readiness. The scent betrayed her. His nostrils flared an instant before she felt a sudden lifting and shifting behind his fly. He was getting hard, faster than she had ever known a man to do. The evidence suggested that he was—as her friend Coretta liked to say—*verra* well hung. Her knees gave way without warning, obliging him to hold her up with the grip he had on her arms.

Pen's throat made a soft, involuntary noise, a mix of protest and plea. She could only pray he had not heard it.

"I'll tell you what I think," he said, bending close enough for his breath to stir the auburn waves she'd tucked behind her ear. "I think you're so determined to elbow your way into my family's private business that you'd do anything to trick me into trusting you."

Chills chased down her spine at his angry words. The Vouvray bottle thunked to the carpet, luckily without breaking. Pen was so breathless, she could barely get out a response.

"I think," she managed to say, "that you'd be better off *letting* me trick you instead of mooning like a puppy after your own father's fiancée."

She had no other description than that Graham went white, so white her eyes were fooled for a moment into thinking he was glowing.

"You go too far," he said in that stiff, tight way British men excelled at.

"Do I?" Finding her feet at last, she slid her hands up his heaving chest. His heart was really pounding, almost as hard as hers. "I think maybe you're wishing I'd go farther."

It took standing on tiptoe for her satin-draped pelvis to slither over his erection. She'd thought she was prepared, but his size shocked her. He was so big there, so thick and hard, that she nearly lost her nerve. Graham made a growling noise and threw the door behind him open.

She didn't have a chance for second thoughts, or even to catch her breath. His big, hard hand had grabbed the scruff of her neck and was shoving her into his room ahead of him, forcing her to move or fall. She heard the door slam shut behind them, felt a thick, steely arm wrap around her waist to lift her up. The compartment spun around her as she gave a little shriek. Graham was dropping onto the banquette with her stretched facedown across his lap. Satin hissed up her legs. She remembered too late that she wasn't wearing a full complement of underthings—just garters and stockings. She hadn't wanted to spoil the line of her gown.

"No!" she gasped, abruptly furious.

And then his hand rang stingingly on her bare buttocks. His palm was broad enough to sear fire into both her cheeks.

"Want to play with me, do you?" he demanded, spanking her twice more in quick succession. "*You* want to play with *me*!"

"No, Graham," she pleaded, trying to wriggle away from the continuing fiery blows. "It's not like that!"

But it was no use to struggle; he simply held her trapped by the neck with his other hand. She couldn't believe it. He was spanking her just as she'd inadvertently dared him to earlier, as if she were anyone. Her face was smashed against the blue velvet seat while her bottom grew hotter and hotter.

It also grew strangely sensitive. The pain he was inflicting performed a peculiar alchemy inside of her, her body coming fully awake for the first time since she'd been born. She should have been screaming for help, but her throat didn't want to open enough for that. Instead, part of her wanted to push her buttocks up into his palm, to make him hit her harder.

If that wasn't odd enough, the prodigy of a cock that was bumping into her stomach did not subside with his exertions. Impossibly, it was growing bigger and harder.

Any sensible woman would have been frightened by a drill that huge.

"All these years," he growled, his hand going *wham-wham-wham* as steadily as a machine. His breath was coming in great huffs. "Daddy's little darling, doling out the pats like I was a dog. Do you think I *cared*? Do you think you were *ever* the sort of woman I wanted? You don't know how to be nice to a man. Hell, you don't know how to be nice to anyone. Estelle is ten times the woman you are. I'm better off mooning after her."

"Graham—" was all she could whimper.

Her bottom was blazing, creamy fluid running in hot trickles from her pulsing sex. It felt like she had a second heart in there, like if he just hit her a little harder, she was going to have an orgasm. Pen never came that easily. Despite a number of attentive lovers, most of the time Pen didn't come at all. As to that, she had a hard time coming by herself. Driven beyond pride or sense, she writhed and let out a groan.

"Christ," Graham said, his blows stopping. His voice was tight and amazed in the sudden quiet. "You want this. This is turning you on. I can smell you like a cat in heat."

"You want it, too," she panted. "Or do you think that monster in your trousers grew by accident? Why don't you shove it in me, Graham? Why don't you give us both what we want?"

Pen struggled to get her hand where it would do some

good, whether on him or herself she couldn't have said right then.

"Stop," he barked, and she did.

They both knew then that he was in control, and that she wanted him to be. The revelation was humiliating, but also weirdly erotic. His big, hard palm slipped over the curves his spanking had turned to fire. The heat of his hand hurt just a bit. Her pulse went crazy, anticipation accelerating it. His touch slid lower, between her trembling thighs. They were slender, no barrier for him at all. The blunt tip of his longest finger forged through her sticky, swollen folds. His nail was smooth, not ragged like some men's were. She moaned and thrust her hips up at him. The invitation was sufficient. His finger slid inside her creaming vagina, all the way in, all the way up, the digit as thick as some men's penises. He worked it in and out with mesmerizing gentleness.

The sound of her extreme wetness should have embarrassed her.

"Oh, God," she said, so desperate for release she could hardly think. "Oh, God, please."

"Do you want my cock?" he asked hoarsely. "Or do you want this?"

"Both," she groaned, twisting her body around his intrusion. "Everything."

He lifted her from him with an ease and swiftness that pointed up how very strong he was. Annoyed that his lovely finger wasn't in her now, she wobbled on her feet and kicked off her high-heeled shoes. The sound of them tumbling across the floor had his eyes firing. His lips were rolled together, his expression grim. If not for the massive ridge arching against the trap of his trousers, she'd have thought he didn't want her at all.

"Take that off," he rasped, nodding at her gown. "Unless you want me to rip it."

She pulled the slinky satin over her head, too aware of

what her body looked like without it, of how different it must be from the women he preferred. When she was bare but for her white stockings and garters, he closed his hands on her waist. She stood between his big outspread thighs, trembling with excitement and worry. He looked at every inch of her, the way men will when they have you naked for the first time, as if savoring a new toy. She didn't want him to see her insecurity over his reaction, but it must have been blazoned on her face.

"You're pretty enough," he said, his fingers tightening beneath her lowermost ribs. "Pretty enough for anyone."

She huffed breathlessly. "Why, Graham, don't overwhelm me with compliments."

He stopped her nervous laughter by leaning forward and latching his mouth around one diamond-hard nipple. All she could do then was clutch his head and try not to moan as his flicking tongue sent her to heaven. Each pull of his cheeks inspired an ache that reverberated low in her sex. It made her want other kisses from him, even more personal. Through a haze of pleasure, she felt him ripping off his bow tie, heard him tearing down his zipper . . .

He groaned with relief as the cloth parted.

"Yes," she gasped, her neck like taffy, her control over herself destroyed. "Pull out your cock. That's the part of you I want."

He tore his mouth from her and pushed her to her knees on the soft carpet. His legs splayed wide around her, a prison she had no desire to escape.

"Take it then," he said, a harsh rasp of sound. "Take my cock in your hands and suck the head right now."

"You just want me on my knees to you."

"Yes," he said. "After all these years, that's exactly what I want!"

His face looked as strange as she imagined hers did, a kind of crazed exaltation tightening its muscles. This

moment wasn't one that came into many people's lives—
to live out a fantasy you hadn't even known you had. The
sound of his ragged respiration sped her own. Her eyes
fell to his lap as if dragged there. He'd already pulled his
trousers open, and his great, thick cock was on display—
waiting eagerly for her to do as he'd asked. She couldn't
believe how tall it was standing, like a soldier rising from
the rounds of his balls. The sheer size of the organ made
her glad he'd only asked her to take the head, and then that
thought made her lick her lips. Lord, what would he feel
like forging into her sex? His skin was paler here than she
expected, closer to white marble than pink flesh. Against
that pallid backdrop, the veins that fed his hardness formed
a tracery of blue. She swallowed as a tiny drop of fluid
squeezed from the central slit.

"Do it," he ordered in a voice like sandpaper.

She did it. She grasped his shaft and pulled the head
toward her lips.

His hands closed hard on her shoulders as the softness
of her mouth surrounded the pulsing crest. His groan came
out like he was fighting it. His cock felt so sleek, so hot and
vital, that she laved it like sweet candy. That he liked just
fine. He gasped for air before he could speak again.

"Oh, yes," he praised once he was able to, his fingers
kneading her shoulders, his buttocks tightening to push
his pelvis avariciously up at her. "Oh, God, the way your
tongue feels going around . . . Give me more of that. Suck
me. Lick me. Oh, God, Pen, *bite me there.*"

Despite her arousal, his request shocked her. He didn't
let her pull back as she would have, but caught her head in
his hands to keep her where she was. His hold was both
gentle and immovable. When she rolled her gaze up, his
bulbous crest still pulsing in her mouth, his eyes were like
a glass of whiskey set before a fire. They smoldered, but
not with fury. The secrets in them hypnotized her. Who'd
have thought Graham wanted things like this?

For that matter, who'd have thought she did?

"Bite me," he repeated more steadily, convincing her he meant it. "Use your teeth on my cock."

She didn't want to hurt him, but she couldn't seem to resist. His utter sureness cast a spell on her. She pressed her teeth into his most vulnerable flesh, beneath the rim where his head swelled out. The yearning rumble of his sexual groan titillated her. This was power of the most basic sort: woman over man, lust over intellect. His cock jerked like he might be coming, but nothing spurted out. His shaft was firmer than she'd anticipated; he didn't flinch in the least at her teeth's pressure. She bit him harder and suckled at the same time.

This was what he'd been waiting for, this edge of pain mixed with his pleasure. He shuddered as if a strong electric current were running through his whole body.

"Pen," he cried out hoarsely.

The sound raked up her clitoris and made it throb. As much as she was enjoying having him at her mercy, she couldn't wait for her release anymore. She was too certain that it would be good. More excited than she had any experience tolerating, she pulled back and lifted her gaze to him.

"I want you in me," she said, her voice as dark and foreign as his had been. "I want you shoved between my legs and on top of me."

He stared at her, maybe trying to read the truth in her eyes, or maybe just struck speechless. She smoothed both thumbs up his twitching shaft. She mustn't have bit him as hard as she'd thought. She'd left no marks on him that she could see.

"Make me come," she said. "There aren't many men who've done that, and I want you to."

He sucked in a breath at her honesty. A second later, his expression took on a determination that delighted her. Here was the trustworthy Graham she knew. If he promised, she knew he would deliver.

"I will," he said, and swiftly tore off his nice jacket. "As many times as you want."

He knew they'd both lost their minds, but it hardly mattered. He wanted in her, up her, his body urging him to do it now.

Her confession that she hadn't come with many men made him crazy. Perhaps before it would have alarmed him. What did he know about pleasing women who needed to be handled with extra skill? Now, however, he thought he could give her what she was hoping for. He had new strengths, new observational powers. In a hundred subtle ways, he could tell when a woman liked what he was doing.

He could count her heartbeats as he lowered her to the carpet and crawled over her. There wasn't much space on the floor of the compartment, but Graham was ready to use it all.

"Graham," Pen purred, her hands sliding down his shirt to caress his cock.

Her touch was pure, sweet torture on his newly sensitive vampire nerves. From testicles to tip she stroked and measured him. His fangs strained in his gums, fully down and throbbing. He should have called Estelle when Ben suggested it earlier. Hungry as he was, he didn't dare bite Pen. He was too likely to drink too deeply. Even if he didn't, he doubted he could thrall the memory from her afterward. The smart choice would be to stop now before it was too late. The last thing they needed was Pen discovering his secret.

His human *and* vampire libidos ordered him to screw being smart.

"Come to me," she crooned, her endless legs rising up his sides. "Come inside me. Use your weight to press me down."

He wanted that enough to tremble. Wanted to crush her sleek, lean body and her burning little bum. His handprints were on her skin, his personal brand on those tight, round globes. He didn't know how he'd missed the charms of slender women up until now. Pen's slimness was exciting, like a long, lithe eel squirming under him. Her hands undid the buttons of his shirt, racing down them to bare his chest to her breasts. Her greed made him feel like his mind was slipping some crucial rein. He gasped when her hips cocked up to press his erection between them. It was fortunate he didn't really need oxygen. When she began to roll her silky, creamy petals up and down his shaft, his lungs tried to stop functioning.

"I don't know how long we have," he burst out reluctantly. "Ben could return any time."

"You better hurry then. I want my orgasm now."

Her hands were on either side of his face, tugging him toward a kiss. He wanted it, but knew he'd better not let her feel what had been happening in his mouth.

"Wait," he said and reached between their bodies to shift his cock into position for entry. That distracted her handily. She gasped at the feel of his pounding crest wedged in her opening.

"You push," she said, though she already was. "I want to feel you shoving it in."

He got a good, firm hold on the adorable halves of her arse and did as she asked. Even with both of them pushing, even with her body creaming from the way his grip stung her paddled bottom, it took a good two minutes of squirming and cursing for his cock to penetrate to the end of her. His prick was simply too fat and long to go in faster.

"Oh, Lord," she breathed as her body wriggled fiercely to keep him there, to drive him farther if it were possible. With her eyes squeezed shut from the pleasure, her spine arched hard. "Graham, I need to—I'm going to touch myself now."

He nearly lost his glamour at the unearthly surge of arousal these words inspired. Wasn't it enough that she gloved him in living heat? That her muscles flickered like fingers on his supersensitive cock? She was going to masturbate in front of him as well?

"You don't . . . want me to do it?" he managed to choke out.

She shook her head, her fingers already squeezing between them. Like a special torture for the sexually needy, he felt them on his abdomen and then the root of his pounding cock. "It's better if I do it. I need this too much, and it's hard for me. Please . . . you move now. You move inside of me."

He moved, testing her readiness. Finding his path liberally oiled, he shifted to genuine thrusting, then was reduced to grunting as her first orgasm clamped her channel around him. She flung her head back, but Graham barely saw. The sensation of compression on his cock was incredible. Her pussy was so sweet, so juicy and tight and hot. That heat was gold to his body now, no longer taken for granted or commonplace. He shoved her hand aside, needing to pleasure her himself. The pad of his finger found the slippery swell of her clitoris. His vampire brain remembered how she'd been rubbing it, down to the smallest nuance of speed and rotation. His finger moved exactly as hers had—except with a bit more force.

To his delight, she groaned and bucked and bit the bare meat of his shoulder as she came again.

"Harder," she pleaded when she could speak. "Graham, really fuck me now."

Just finding his pace himself, he thanked God for women and their fondness for more than one orgasm. The only danger seemed that he'd take Pen too much at her word. He'd had no practice restraining his strength with Vanessa. She was a vampire, too, and could not be hurt. The fact that Pen could be injured was an aphrodisiac too powerful for him to deny. Ashamed of himself but totally incapable of stopping, Graham dug the fingers of his free hand into the rug, trying to expend his rising tension that way.

"More," Pen demanded, her slender pelvis snapping up at him. "Graham, don't hold back on me!"

Her hands had slid under his open shirt, her nails scoring the sweating skin of his back. The scent of blood exploded in his head.

"Graham," she growled, because he was still trying to fight his natural urges. She grabbed him by the ears and pulled him closer. "Fuck me all the way."

"I can't," he gasped even as his hips pumped faster. He licked his teeth, hoping she couldn't see. He couldn't use all his strength on her. If he did, he wouldn't just hurt her, he'd rock the bloody sleeper car off the rails.

He tried to work her clit more cleverly with his hand, to give her what she wanted in a different way. He squeezed it between two fingers and rolled. All he got for his efforts was her teeth sinking into his earlobe.

Or not exactly all. His cock jerked at the sting of that, stiffening to the edge of pain. It seemed control of her wasn't all he'd craved. Just as it had for Li-Hua, his body thrilled to being hurt in return. This was the sexual nature he'd been born with, heightened now by being turned *upyr*. His head felt like it was suddenly filled with light. Something was happening to him, something that made every cell in his body strain for release.

He was sensing Pen's emotions.

She didn't simply want to be fucked with abandon, she needed it. All her life she'd been yearning. For love, for adventure, for experiences that were *big*. The peaks she'd enjoyed tonight—though they were sweet to her—couldn't fulfill desires of that magnitude. She wanted to climb mountains, and he'd given her foothills.

"Oh, God," he moaned, knowing precisely the Everest he could offer her.

She caught him by surprise by kicking forcefully off the floor and rolling him under her. His head smacked into the wall, but—apart from taking a second to shake the ringing clear—this didn't trouble either one of them.

Pen was riding him like a bronco from one of her American rodeos, not the least bit worried about hurting him. She was so gorgeous he lost his breath.

"I'll say what's hard enough," she growled.

He steadied her by the waist, awed by her wildness, swept away by her lust. Her little breasts were bouncing on her narrow ribs, mere swells of rounded flesh with nipples as red and pointed as raspberries. The spare muscles of her stomach demanded that his thumbs reach to caress them. He couldn't shake his awareness of the needs that were driving her, and that awareness made his own held-off climax rise like a storm boiling. She took his hands from her sides and locked their fingers together tight, forcing him to support her gyrations with the strength of his arms. Her pussy was a flame licking over him, the violence of her thrusts impossible to resist. All his varied excitements seemed to gather in a ball at once. His testicles lurched upward with imminence.

"Pen," he gasped, knowing he had seconds until he went.

She flung her body down on him, their arms spread to either side.

"I want to feel your heart," she cried. "I want to feel it beating against mine when you go over."

He groaned as the tornado that was his climax burst through its walls. Her neck was too close, too tempting. His lips peeled back, his fangs aching. His cock began to spurt the instant he bit down.

Everest, he thought and sealed his lips to her neck.

Drawing his first mouthful did it for Pen. She stiffened like a board and then let out a true scream of ecstasy. With their emotions linked, her pleasure roared over his. She tasted so good, so *right*. His sense of victory was unprecedented: that he could give her these pleasures, that *he* could. His ejaculation fountained harder, creating a glare like fuses popping in his brain. Nothing mattered but her, nothing but staying in this place of perfect carnal amity. He rolled her beautiful body beneath his again, pulling at her vein, crashing things to the floor, slamming into her like a madman while she clung to him desperately.

She liked him above her, overpowering her, as much as he relished being there.

Yes, said her thoughts, reaching him in words for the first time. *Oh, yes, oh, yes, oh, yes!*

Even though he'd had his orgasm, and had it extremely well, his body let loose again in synchrony with hers. It still wasn't enough. He wanted more and more of her. He kept straight on fucking her until the door opened.

Sodding hell, he thought and drew his fangs out reluctantly. His hips stopped thrusting a second later. They didn't want to. They wanted to keep going. He rested his forehead on the floor beside her, where her gingery hair foamed out in waves. He closed his eyes in self-defense. He was pretty certain he didn't want to see who'd come in.

Pen seemed not to realize there was anyone to see. Dazed, she pressed her hand reflexively to her neck wounds. "Graham," she said, heat beating off her in waves. "Why is your skin glowing?"

"Yes, indeed," Ben said scathingly. "Why don't you explain that to all of us?"

Wagons-Lits No. 2,205

❧

Pen eyed Graham warily from the opposite end of the small compartment. This had to be the strangest postcoital interlude she'd ever experienced—not to mention the most crowded.

Ben and Estelle sat on the blue banquette, with Sally on the floor between them. Sally had rescued the champagne bottle from the corridor and was picking at its foil cork cover. Near them, Graham leaned—or maybe *loomed* was a better term—in front of the coat closet. This left the single armchair by the window to Pen, an isolation she was very cognizant of.

At least she wasn't naked anymore. Graham had gotten the better deal on that front. Because he'd barely undressed, he hadn't had to yank his crumpled clothes back on in front of witnesses. Only his bow tie lay on the carpet, along with two dog-eared novels, Pen's high-heeled shoes, the red shade to the table lamp, and a monogrammed marble ashtray that had split in two. Long, ragged tears stood out in the rug, as if a furious animal had clawed it. As far as Pen knew, Graham had ripped them while in his throes.

Little though she wanted that knowledge to affect her, she couldn't avoid squirming in her chair. It wasn't fair that a man like Graham had been able to do what he did to her. She'd told him things she'd sworn she'd never tell anyone, for no better reason than wanting a ride on his champion cock. For goodness sake, she'd masturbated with him inside her! And this was *after* he'd declared he'd be better off mooning over Estelle, who was—and she quoted—"ten times the woman" Pen was. She must have been insane to have sex with him. That or desperate for the most stupendous orgasm of her life.

Her body still shimmered from the strength of it, from the way satisfaction had exploded through every nerve. Did other people climax like that? If they did, why weren't they copulating all the time? Pen was lucky if she had half a dozen orgasms in the course of an entire year, and they'd never been on the order of what she'd felt with Graham. Clearly, unbeknownst to her, she liked her lovemaking rough, or how else could she explain her reaction to Graham gnawing on her neck?

The toothmarks still hurt, but she refused to put her fingers there. She forced herself to pay attention to the others.

The undercurrents between the Fitz Clares were eccentric, to say the least. Graham's family was a little too concerned about what he'd done with Pen, and too unconcerned about the aspects of the situation that would have troubled most relatives. The possible damage to Pen's reputation—not that she thought it mattered in this day and age—hadn't been mentioned once.

"You were shaking the train," Ben was saying to his brother. "Shaking. The. Train. We heard Pen screaming two cars away. Is this what you call convincing her to go home?"

Pen winced as Estelle laid a calming hand on Ben's bunched forearm. She supposed her orgasmic cry had been pretty loud.

"What's the point in apologizing?" Graham returned wearily. "We both know 'I'm sorry' doesn't change a thing."

"At least he *wasn't* killing her," Sally put in.

Only Estelle smiled at that, her head turned toward her lap to hide the curving of her generous lips.

"No, he wasn't killing her," Ben agreed. "He was just fucking her nearly to death."

"Hey!" said Pen, preferring that everyone remember she was still there. "I'm fine." She was fine, she told herself. Mortified, maybe, confused and a trifle bruised, but she couldn't honestly complain about those souvenirs. She'd enjoyed getting them, after all. "Apart from the biting, Graham only did as I asked."

"Ah, the *biting*," Ben said with an emphasis she could not fathom.

Ignoring him, Pen turned in her chair until her knees faced Graham. "I admit, I wouldn't mind you explaining that. I mean, your teeth were . . ." *Long as an animal's?* her mind suggested. *Sharp as knives?* And he'd drunk from her. She knew she hadn't imagined that. Her hand crept toward the wounds she'd sworn she wouldn't touch. "You left a real pair of holes."

"It's nothing," Graham said, shooting a hard look at his brother. "A bad habit."

"It's more than that, Graham. You—" She lowered her voice and tried to speak exclusively to him. "You drank my blood. Do you have a mental condition? Is that why your family's so concerned for you?"

She'd tried not to sound like she was judging him, but he crossed his arms all the same. His brows were beetled together above his nose. "If I have a mental condition, you must as well. Or did I dream you screamed with pleasure when I fed from you?"

Her mouth had fallen open at the sensual threat in his voice, and it took an effort to close it. Her skin began to pulse with the memories he'd stirred up, memories she hadn't known she had. His lips moving silkily on her neck. His tongue lapping at the blood. His teeth like burning steel sunk into her flesh. Her body heated and grew wet, fevered for another chance to join with him. There had been a bond between them when he bit her, more than simple—or even twisted—pleasure could account for.

She admitted—strictly to herself—that she wouldn't have minded exploring that bond again . . . preferably in a locked hotel room.

"Christ," Graham said, his head wrenching away, his hand snapping up to cover his mouth.

It was like he knew what she was thinking.

"He does know," Estelle said. "Or he senses it. But it's not disgust that makes him turn away."

Graham stared at Estelle as if she'd slapped him. Chills crashed over Pen in waves. Estelle had not just said that. Or if she had, it was a coincidence. She couldn't read Pen's mind any more than Graham could.

"You may as well tell her," Estelle said to Graham. "She's a bright woman. She's going to put the pieces together soon."

"You're saying he's—" Pen swallowed, watching Graham: the pale perfection of his skin, the way he covered his mouth as if he wanted to hide something. Seen as he was tonight, he was like a creature from a story, beautiful and doomed. Snippets of Bram Stoker novels came back to her. She remembered how the sun had reddened his face, how he'd barely been able to stay awake. She couldn't deny he was different than he'd been before, but still what Estelle was suggesting was ridiculous. "You can't be implying he's a vampire. You can't expect me to believe vampires are real!"

"They're real," Sally said, surprisingly gentle for her. "My daddy is a vampire, too. Not the rest of us. Well, except for Estelle. She is a little bit of one."

Pen flopped back in the chair with her head spinning, aware of all of them watching her. None of them were denying Estelle and Sally's words. Not Graham. Not Ben, who—of them all—most seemed to want this hidden. Crazy though Estelle's claim was, it made sense. It would explain, if not everything, quite a lot.

"I have to see," she said, springing forward again. She turned earnestly to Graham. "Show me your fangs, and I'll believe you."

"I'm not sure I want you to believe me," Graham said sadly.

She came to her stockinged feet and walked to him. "Show me, Graham. You can trust me with the truth."

He didn't stop her when she reached for his face, so familiar and yet so changed. She pulled his upper lip back on either side with her thumbs. His incisors weren't as long as she remembered, but they were longer than normal teeth—normal human teeth anyway. They resembled tiger teeth: white and curving and sharp. She couldn't repress a shiver as she examined them. His lips were soft, his gums smooth and hard. Around the roots of his incisors, the skin seemed inflamed. Curious, she stroked it from side to side.

Graham caught his breath as his fangs jutted longer in quick surges.

Her gaze darted to his haunted and haunting eyes. Golden lights flickered in their depths, their thick frame of lashes like deep brown mink. The effect wasn't an illusion. The glimmers were really there.

I made love to this man, she thought. *His body was inside mine. Even now, my blood is in his.*

"Pen," he said on a barely audible breath of air. Attraction vibrated between them. She knew without having to look that he was hard again.

"For God's sake," said his brother. "Could you please not do that in front of us?"

Pen snatched back her hands and blushed as hotly as if she'd been caught touching lower things. To judge by Graham's reaction, what she'd done wasn't terribly different.

"So . . . you're a vampire," she said, fighting back the heat in her cheeks. "And your father's a vampire. And—" Her hands flew to her mouth as a few more pieces dropped into place. "Other vampires must have kidnapped him! Is there a war? Did you become a vampire so you could fight?"

"Pen." Graham steadied her shoulders between his hands, a welcome hint of laughter as he said her name. "There isn't a war. Or there isn't yet. But you can see why I didn't want you involved in this. Rescuing my father isn't a job for civilians."

"But you have to let me help! I know your secret now. And don't even think about pulling that look-into-my-eyes-and-forget-everything rot with me. I can be just as useful as I would have been when I thought your father was a criminal."

Graham's jaw was the one that was dropping now. "You still want to help?"

"Of course I do. I mean, your father is still your father. He's still a person, more or less. Becoming a vampire doesn't seem to have turned you into an infernal being. Lordy." Pen clutched her aching head. "I can't believe I'm saying these things, but—trust me—I mean them."

"I—" Graham spluttered, reminding her of the Graham of old. He drew straighter. "Pen, I'm sorry, we can't accept your kind offer."

"Pen could stay with Sally and me," Estelle said, causing both of them to turn in surprise. "You can't thrall away what she knows, after all. You're still too young an *upyr* for that. Maybe Robin can do the job when this is over. In the meantime, someone has to keep an eye on her. Make sure she doesn't spill the beans to the world."

"I wouldn't!" Pen said, offended, though a second later she realized just how interested the people she secretly worked for would be in these developments.

"I wouldn't," she repeated more staunchly.

Estelle offered her one of her mysterious Mona Lisa smiles. Sally had called her a "little bit" of a vampire. While Pen couldn't guess what that meant, she also couldn't deny that it might be true.

"We may as well pretend you'd blab," Estelle said. "I don't know how else to convince the men to let you come along for the ride."

Pen held her gaze, trying to read what was going on behind it. Unfortunately, she didn't have the knack for snooping that Estelle seemed to.

"Well, good then," she said, abandoning the attempt. "I'm on the team. Tell me everything that's happened up until now, and we'll get to work."

"Oh, boy," Ben responded. The roll of his clear green eyes wasn't remotely flattering.

Pooh," Sally said when she and Ben were finally alone in the corridor.

Estelle and her new best friend had gone off to "talk," taking the lovely bottle of Vouvray with them. Graham remained in his and Ben's compartment, repairing the damage his and Pen's wild vampire sex had caused. Sally had taken one look at the long rips in the carpet and slapped her sewing kit into his hand. Graham had accepted it without a murmur, not cajoling her to use it as most men would have.

That had disappointed Sally. Her temper being what it was, she would have welcomed an excuse to fight.

"Estelle is right," she sighed. "Pen has taken a shine to Graham."

Ben squeezed her shoulders sympathetically, his hands deliciously strong and warm. "She won't keep his interest long. Graham likes his women softer than Pen Anderson."

"Ha," Sally scoffed. "Given how our luck is running, she'll end up our sister-in-law. I swear, if my life gets any more awful, I'm going to lay down and cry."

She'd meant Ben to laugh, but she supposed her joke cut a bit too close to the bone. He pulled her to his chest instead, wrapping her wonderfully in his arms. Sally said what she knew they were both thinking.

"If Pen comes with us to save Daddy, you and I will have even less chance to be alone."

Ben kissed the top of her head. "We're alone now."

They were, but not very. Pen and Graham had underscored the dangers of forgetting how close the rest of the world was.

"I love you," Sally whispered into Ben's collarbone. "Forever and ever."

His hold on her tightened until she could feel his heart thundering beneath her cheek. There was fear in the sound, and lust, and a million more emotions she knew swirled inside her as well. One of his hands was cradling her head closer, cherishing her without a word. She loved what his body said about his feelings, but she didn't protest when he kissed her curls and let go.

Even Sally had to grow up sometime.

Estelle led Pen to the farthest pair of facing armchairs in the empty observation car. The windows were overlarge, allowing passengers to enjoy the spectacular alpine views. At the moment, the landscape they rolled by was dark, the train tracks cutting through ever-steeper slopes as they progressed northeastward across Europe. No one else was interested in staring out these windows now, and the small shaded sconces on the walls were lit. Hoping for just this sort of isolation, Estelle had brought the abandoned champagne with her—somewhat to Sally's dismay.

Pen looked far more rakish drinking from the bottle than Estelle would have, but Estelle supposed a crowd as smart as hers thought nothing of such things. Even with the practice she must have had, the American was a trifle squiffy by the time Estelle finished spelling out what was what. Since Estelle had caught a wisp of Pen's intention to get Graham drunk, she didn't feel a bit guilty.

Estelle might want Pen on this trip for her own reasons, but that didn't mean she'd play fast and loose with the Fitz Clares' safety. They were her family now, and she put them first. The tipsier Pen became, the more Estelle was able to read from her—and the easier it was to picture Pen as the stylish party girl she must have been in her own milieu. The bottle sat on the floor now, no more than swallows left. Pen's thoughts remained vague, but her emotions lapped through Estelle in intermittent waves.

That she was attracted to Graham was clear. Also unmistakable was that this made her uneasy. Estelle wasn't a hundred percent convinced of the girl's trustworthiness. Something was tugging Pen in two directions, but what it was Estelle couldn't tell.

Interestingly, Pen was most stupefied by the revelation that Graham was a spy.

"Graham's MI5," she repeated, her slender fingers toying with the sheer silk scarf she'd thrown around her neck to hide Graham's bite marks. "You're certain. He didn't just make that up."

"Edmund said Graham was the kind of recruit they look for. Educated. Pleasant manners. Loyal to his country, but not particularly political. MI5 prefers that its agents fade into the background."

Pen pulled a face. "I don't think that's going to work for him anymore."

"Maybe not, but supposedly he'll get better at his glamour. I gather it was Graham's association with your father that first drew him to the agency's attention. They reckoned he'd meet persons of interest traveling with an important international industrialist."

Lot of that going around, Pen's mind muttered.

"It's a good thing you decided to trust me," Pen said aloud. "I do have contacts in Switzerland. Not in the government. Not even nice people, to be truthful. Still, they're useful sorts for dirty jobs."

"I'd be interested to hear how you met them," Estelle said.

"Oh, college boys. That sort of thing." Pen waved her hand airily. "You never know where old boyfriends will end up."

"Or new ones," Estelle suggested with a little smile.

Pen's blush was faint, but—to Estelle's sharp eyes—not invisible. Pen patted the folds of her scarf as if to assure herself that the silk still concealed what she was thinking so hard about.

"Graham can heal those marks," Estelle pointed out. "I'm sure he'd welcome the chance to redress a little of what he did to you. Our Graham has a finely honed sense of justice—maybe too finely honed."

Pen's gaze met Estelle's directly. "I want you to know Graham didn't force me tonight. Nothing about what happened was nonconsensual."

Estelle felt her smile broaden. Sally would kill her for thinking it, but—oh—she could like this girl. "Thank you for setting the record straight."

"Well, I know you Brits value playing fair." Pen pushed unsteadily from her chair. "And now I think I'd better get back to my compartment before my feet forget how to take me there."

Estelle watched her weave down the center of the car with an odd sense of wistfulness. Pen and Graham were just starting the dance she and Edmund spun to. Estelle couldn't predict where their version of it would end, but seeing Pen simultaneously hope for and resist romance made Estelle feel old.

Actually, seeing Pen and Graham together made her feel widowed.

Estelle caught her breath in horror at the traitorous thought. She wasn't widowed. Not even close. Edmund was out there, and they were going to save him. Otherwise, what was any of this for?

Switzerland

The girl Frank and Li-Hua brought to Edmund's cell could not have been older than thirteen. She struggled between the vampires, lurching this way and that while their hold on her didn't move at all. She seemed most intent on increasing the distance between her and Edmund, who—in his present, starved-down state—must have seemed a great deal more horrific than the breathtaking creatures who'd dragged her here. As she stared at him, openmouthed, her eyes were so wide with fear they showed their whites all around. Despite her shivers of fright and cold, her body had the healthy plumpness of a well-cared-for child.

Someone who loved her had braided her hair into two fair plaits.

Edmund's hands curled into fists as his fangs stretched viciously from his gums. She was a child, the ultimate innocent, and yet if the chains hadn't trapped his wrists, he was certain he'd have reached for her. The girl smelled as fresh as a spring meadow, the beat of life inside her strong. Every convulsion of her heart seemed to sing to him, every whoosh of her warm, young blood. Unable to ignore the lure of her vitality, Edmund couldn't contain a groan.

Li-Hua smiled as if he'd given her a present. "We didn't drug her like the others. We thought you might enjoy a lively one for a change."

The girl let out a thin, terrified wail.

Edmund couldn't speak, couldn't rip his gaze from her. She seemed no more able to look away from him, gaunt and monstrous on the steel surgical table. His mouth was pooling with saliva, his veins aching with hunger. He could actually feel them, like wires of need burning through his flesh. He looked helplessly at Durand. The mercenary stood by the barred cell door in a state of relaxed readiness. His hands were clasped before him, one hand gripping the other's wrist, his expression just as blank as could be. Though his eyes slid briefly to Edmund, they didn't show that he cared one way or another about what was going on. When they flicked away, Edmund felt his last thread of hope unravel.

He didn't have the strength to reach mentally for Estelle, even assuming she could be reached. His one dream of her since projecting his image into her mirror had been troubling, to say the least. In it, a male *upyr* had been biting her—and she'd been enjoying it. Chances were it wasn't a true vision. Edmund could dream his fears the same as anyone. Estelle deserved his trust. She was not a woman who broke vows. Knowing this hadn't kept his heart from plummeting, and it didn't shore up his spirits now. If what little help Estelle had to give him wasn't enough . . . If he called her to him, and still drank this girl's life down . . .

Edmund didn't think he could bear to have Estelle witness that.

"She's too young," he said to Li-Hua, surprising himself by speaking at all. He hadn't known he was going to, and he wasn't sure what he was aiming at. His voice was strange, rusty from disuse. He tried again for the hell of it. "Bring someone older tomorrow night."

"You don't give the orders here," Frank said.

The girl must have sensed her fate was being decided. She began to murmur frantically under her breath. Edmund didn't know the particular German dialect she spoke, but he recognized a prayer when he heard one. Frank didn't spare her even a glance. His attention was fastened hawk-like on Edmund. Edmund endeavored to pull his thoughts together a little more.

"Let her go," he said. "Return her safely to her family. If that one"—he jerked his head toward Durand—"swears you've complied, I'll do whatever you want."

"No!" Li-Hua protested as Frank's lips parted to respond. "If Fitz Clare is that close to breaking, we should push harder now."

"A girl like that will be missed if she disappears," Edmund said.

Li-Hua's face turned ugly. "She doesn't have to *disappear*. You can change her, and she'll be fine."

Edmund closed his eyes, wearier than if his years numbered in the millions. The girl wouldn't be fine. She'd be a creature she didn't understand and hadn't asked to become.

"I won't change her," he said, knowing this one urge he could control. "If I drain her, I'll let her die and go to her God."

Li-Hua's curse was a snarl of fury that filled the cell. Durand broke into it.

"Let Fitz Clare have his way." His voice was cool and smooth, rationality personified. "You've broken him. One more night won't matter to your schedule."

"It matters if Frank and I say it matters," Li-Hua snapped.

Frank laid a calming hand on her shoulder. The pair exchanged a look above their weeping victim's head, no doubt concerning the importance of keeping their cocon-spirator mollified.

"Fine," Li-Hua said. "But don't blame me if tomorrow evening comes and we still can't make him do what we want."

"That won't happen," Durand assured her. "This is the last of Fitz Clare's fight."

Edmund turned his face away from them to the wall, shame coursing through him like hot acid. He knew what Durand said was true. He'd saved this girl so he could kill another. Gained a night only to lose his soul.

Help me, he thought to a deity he rarely asked for anything. He'd taken the best life had to offer. It seemed both presumptuous and ungrateful to pray for more. Now, though, he had no choice but to beg assistance. His own resources were exhausted. *Please, God, find some way to help me.*

He sensed no answer, which—everything considered— hardly surprised him. Frank and Li-Hua exited with the girl. For whatever reason, she viewed their departure as cause for alarm.

"*Halt die Klappe!*" Frank bit out as her whimpers rose. *Shut your mouth.* Though his German was different from hers, the girl understood. She fell silent as abruptly as if she'd been slapped. Edmund heard only her feet, stumbling and scuffing, as they dragged her down the underground passageway. When that sound also faded, Durand spoke.

"They'll take her home," he said. "Frank will thrall her memory from her, and she'll be safe. They know better than to break their word to me."

"Well, bully for you," Edmund panted, his strength not up to speaking normally. "You let them bring her here in the first place, and you'll let them bring the person they choose tomorrow night. And when I, inevitably, kill whoever it is, you can live with your role in that on your conscience for the rest of your immortal life."

Durand's breath sucked sharply into his lungs. Big, bad mercenary that he was, he couldn't have been accustomed to being spoken to this way. Edmund braced himself for the hot, sharp prick of Durand's army knife, but it didn't come.

"I have no reason to love humans," Durand said.

Edmund doubted anyone but himself could have heard Durand's underlying defensiveness, the hint of stiffness beneath his calm. Edmund couldn't have said whether simple anger or something more strategic goaded him to push at it.

"That girl is guiltless. Whatever you think you gain by working with Frank and Li-Hua, you can't deny that involving her was unjustified."

"I have sworn an oath," Durand said.

"To a pair of murderers!" Edmund's head swum from the effort it took to inhale deeply enough to shout. "Christ, man, if you have the smallest shred of decency, just kill me now and end this."

"Is that what you want?" Durand asked seriously.

Edmund's heart stuttered in his chest. *Was* that what he wanted? He'd spoken in passion, but maybe he'd spoken the truth. Was Estelle bringing Robin to rescue him? Would they find him in time? And if they didn't, could Edmund face Estelle and his family carrying the knowledge that he'd taken innocent lives? He didn't fool himself that Frank and Li-Hua would be satisfied with a single trial. They wanted the secret of the change; he'd worked out that much. That he couldn't give it to them hardly mattered. They'd let the bodies pile plenty high while they tried.

Was one victim too many, or should he wait to throw himself at death?

How tired did a person have to be before he was entitled to give up?

The bullet Frank had left in his skull throbbed mockingly. *Weak*, it jeered. *Edmund Fitz Clare is weak*. Hadn't his father said so when he was human? Hadn't he held Aimery up as the stronger of his sons? Edmund admitted his own questions sickened him. No amount of suffering could entitle him to sacrifice even one human. Death ought to be what he wanted, but—God—he wasn't ready to go.

His throat was tight, its tissues raw. "I don't want more mortals to die," he forced out.

Durand's black gaze bored into his. Edmund didn't know if the mercenary heard the evasion in his answer, and could not have sworn if he wanted him to. He held his breath while gears seemed to tick-tick-tick behind Durand's eyes.

"I cannot kill you," Durand said at last. "I would be forsworn. I will, however, leave you the means to find your way to death yourself."

He pulled a knife Edmund hadn't seen before from the back of his black military trousers. Though the edge was honed, the blade was a dull, dark color. The hilt was wrapped in leather and stamped with what appeared to be a family crest. Given that it was an *upyr*'s possession and would not age, the knife was probably older than it looked.

"The blade is iron," Durand said, turning it back and forth. His own eyes followed the movement as if coolly contemplating the weapon's charms. "It should be long enough to nick your heart muscle. If you want to pierce a chamber, you'll have to blow the breath out of your lungs and shove very hard. I expect your life will end quickly then. Even elders die from wounds like that."

Satisfied that Edmund had heard him, he laid the knife on the steel table, just beyond the tips of Edmund's left fingers.

"Are you right-handed?" Durand asked.

"Yes," Edmund said faintly.

Edmund's brows had risen in disbelief at his guard's actions, but Durand seemed not to notice. The mercenary nodded and walked around the foot of the table. When he reached its middle, he drew a key out of his pocket. He slid it into the lock for the iron band that cuffed Edmund's wrist. A moment later, Edmund's right hand was free. To his dismay, he was unable to lift his arm.

He understood then why Durand had placed the knife where he did. With his one free arm refusing to move, Edmund had no hope of stretching across his body to use the weapon against Durand.

"You will have to tell your blood where to go," Durand said. "To return the circulation to those muscles."

This seemed to be a process the mercenary was familiar with. He must have been held prisoner himself, once upon a time. His tone was staggeringly casual.

"How long can you give me?" Edmund asked hoarsely.

Durand thought. "An hour," he said. "If you haven't killed yourself by then, you will never see this knife—or my mercy—ever again."

Zurich

Graham thought he might be getting the hang of this vampire stuff. Though it had been morning when their train pulled in—and blinding bright with it—he'd made it from the railway station to the hotel under his own steam.

True, the Hotel Schweizerhof was only across the street, and, yes, as soon as he'd reached the room he and Ben were sharing, he'd toppled like a tree. He'd *remembered* doing it, however, remembered the sparkling, snow-clad city and the broad avenue, remembered the Schweizerhof's neoclassic marble facade and Sally's coos of interest at the nearby luxury shops.

So what if he'd woken again at sunset to discover he'd toppled to the floor rather than the bed? Progress wasn't the sort of thing a person ought to cavil at. He didn't have a crick at least, and he wasn't burned. Someone had been kind enough to tuck a pillow under his head and pull a blanket over him.

Graham found himself hoping the someone wasn't either Estelle or Pen.

There was no way of telling, because he'd returned to consciousness in an empty room. Ben had scribbled a note (which Graham didn't have to turn on the light to read) letting Graham know where he and the others had gone to eat.

The reminder of dinner, and the difference in what that now meant for him, darkened Graham's mood. In a million ways, large and small, he had set himself apart from those he loved.

"Tough," he said aloud to the gloomy silk-papered walls.

He flicked the lights on defiantly. He would do as Robin advised. He'd keep up his human habits. He'd cling to his human heart. No matter what, he didn't have to lose everything he was.

The room's telephone was a luxury Graham was grateful for. He used it now to have the switchboard dial London. When Robin answered, the older vampire sounded much more alert than Graham. Using oblique language, in case the hotel operators were nosy, Graham informed him they had arrived and asked if there'd been news about Edmund. Robin confessed there had not. Edmund's captors weren't showing up in the sights of any of MI5's intelligence networks—including the exotic ones. He tried to soothe Graham by reassuring him there wasn't bad news, but this seemed stingy comfort to him.

He rung off no happier than when he'd lifted the receiver.

It seemed his only recourse was to wait for Estelle to have another of her dreams. Restless, he rose from the spindly French-style desk he'd sat at to make his call. The curtained window was a single stride away. Their rooms were on the hotel's north side, overlooking the Bahnhofstrasse and, farther on, the frozen Limmat River's quay. Graham had always had sharp eyes, probably thanks to growing up absorbing Edmund's energy. Even so, he'd never seen anything like the scene that spread before him when he pulled aside the draperies.

Most of Zurich's residents rode the trams, but a few long cars passed slowly along the streets, their headlights sweeping the lower levels of the old buildings—bankers, perhaps, being chauffeured home after a day of stacking up gold coins. Even better illumination came from above. The moon had risen. Coupled with Graham's vampire vision, it turned the snow-covered city into a breath-stealing, fantastical landscape, so rich in detail and color that his heart beat faster at its sheer, preposterous beauty.

If money was the world's blood, a child could see its streams ran generously here.

A memory separated from the jumble of his morning exit from the train station. As soon as they'd stepped into the cold sunshine, Estelle's pulse had quickened like his was now, as if being here, in the same country as Edmund, made a difference that she could feel. Her head had come up like a hunter's, her senses on alert. Clearly, she thought their chances of finding him were better here. The least Graham could do was try to believe the same.

A knock on the door brought him out of his reverie.

He knew who it was before he opened it. His visitor's heart had its own distinct music.

"Pen," he said. His greeting was softer than he meant it to be. He reminded himself he ought to be wary, for both their sakes. The last thing they needed was a repeat of their madness back on the train, regardless of how pleasurable that had been.

He braced a bent arm on the door frame to block her from coming in.

"Graham," Pen returned. She wore a smart traveling suit, the very latest fashion in cobalt blue. The fit was perfect on her slender frame, and the color brought out the russet in her auburn hair. Her mouth, which was wide and mobile, was quirked in the slightly condescending smile with which she regarded most men she knew. Not her father, of course; him she respected.

She lifted her brows as Graham continued to stand and stare.

"I thought you might be hungry," she prompted.

Her words were an erotic lash. Graham's body readied itself for sex and feeding as if it didn't have a second to spare.

"You shouldn't be offering to do this," he said stiffly, in every sense of the word, trying to speak clearly around his fangs. "You haven't had time to recover yet from last night."

Pen shrugged and gave her neck what he was sure was a deliberate stroke with one finger. The wounds he'd left the previous night remained, half hidden by the drape of her expensive scarf. Graham fought a shiver of arousal.

"I feel fine," she said, that infuriating smirk still hovering around her mouth. "Slept like a baby. Ate a big lunch. As long as I'm intruding on your family's business, I might as well be useful."

Graham licked his teeth before he could stop himself. Despite her flippancy, her scent was rising, her body heat warming it. Criminy, she smelled delicious, the slightest whiff of her making his mouth water. The pulse beneath her two small bruise marks beat hard enough to see. He felt a drop of pre-come squeeze from his cock, the sudden wetness a tiny kiss of sensation.

"I don't think—" He cleared his throat and forced his eyes up to hers. They were a lovely whiskey color, slanted slightly like a cat's. Graham wasn't sure he'd ever noticed that before. "Pen, I don't think I could restrict myself to just feeding. In fact, I'm relatively certain I'd push for more."

Pen pursed her lips in amusement and ducked beneath his arm through the narrow space he'd left at the door. "What makes you think 'more' isn't exactly what I've come for?"

"Pen—"

She shut the door firmly behind her. "For heaven's sake, Graham, could you try to remember we're adults and that this isn't the last century?"

"Just because *I* take this sort of thing seriously—"

He stopped. His hands had closed on her shoulders, and the feel of her so warm and close and fragrant made him forget what he'd meant to say. He wanted to fuck her again, wanted to bite her and drink. Her face lifted for the kiss he was already leaning in for. His body was so hard and tense he was trembling.

"Yes," Pen murmured, her eyes half closed. "Let me taste you again."

"I share this room," he groaned out reluctantly.

"You shared the other. This time we'll wedge a chair under the door."

He couldn't resist her. Maybe he'd never really wanted to. He let her go, but only to leap at vampire speed to the desk and return with her proposed privacy measure. It didn't take a second to brace it beneath the knob.

"Oh, my." She pressed her hand to her heart as her hair settled from the breeze he'd stirred up. "Please don't do everything that fast."

She made him laugh, and somehow that seemed more dangerous than all the other things she did to him. He remembered how she'd stroked the base of his fangs when she was confirming he was a vampire, how she'd caught her breath in a gasp when they'd jerked longer. *Your father is still your father,* she'd said, *and becoming a vampire doesn't seem to have turned you into an infernal being.*

If he'd been that loyal when he'd discovered the truth about Edmund, none of them would be risking their lives now.

Still waiting for his response, Pen planted her hands on her boyish hips. He wouldn't have guessed the pose could look so sexy.

"Well?" she prompted, her eyes gleaming teasingly. "Where's my kiss?"

"How can you not be afraid?"

"Of you?" Pen snorted. "Please."

And then it was all right, because this was the Pen he knew. He growled and grabbed her and dove into her mouth, tongue first. Still not frightened, she moaned and dug her fingers into his scalp. She could kiss, Pen could, full out, no shyness, her tongue a sleek wet dagger battling with his.

"Lick my teeth," he said, tearing free, unable to keep the demand inside.

She didn't just lick them, she sucked, as if his fangs were two little cocks. When her tongue rubbed the base of one, Graham shuddered from head to toe. He didn't cut her, but the restraint that took increased the excitement of what she was doing. For all her experience, Vanessa hadn't kissed him this fucking well. Graham rumbled with pleasure at each pull of Pen's lips and tongue, his cock swelling to the utmost limits of its skin.

"Oh, God," she said. "I love hearing you make those noises. I love knowing how ready you are."

She tore her own clothes off, then gasped when he removed his at super speed. She seemed to like seeing him naked.

"Now that's what I call a picture," she purred, stepping back so her eyes could drink in every inch of him.

To him, at least half those inches felt like they were bouncing at his groin.

He let her push him onto the bed, let her climb over him and run her hands like a blind woman up his chest. She cooed admiringly at the feel of him.

"Your skin is velvet," she marveled, her strong, molding passes making his pectoral muscles hum. Her grip continued testingly down his arms. "And your biceps are hard as steel."

"That's not all that's hard as steel," he said and knocked his hips up at hers.

His aching tip bumped her labia. She was wet there, silky and swollen. She smiled and took his shaft into her slender, warm-fingered hand. Human heat rushed into him at her touch.

"Thick," she said, pulling her fist upward. "Thick and long and hard."

Hot, spangled pleasure dragged a groan from him. She bent until her wavy auburn hair brushed his face.

"Take me," she said. "Make me feel like you did last night."

His blood thundered at her words. He rolled her underneath him on the bed. Being on top was like the last time, except they were both naked. The slide of her skin on his was a gift to make him dizzy. Pen's endless legs rose to either side of his hips as her hands slid slowly down his spine. When she gripped his buttocks, her fingertips digging in, he couldn't hold back a grunt of urgency.

She had no idea how much he wanted to ravage her.

"You're sure?" he said, his voice gone rough. "You want me to bite you, too?"

He was looking straight into her eyes. He saw her pupils dilate with excitement a second before she nodded. Given this dual assurance, he began to ease his cock into her tightness. The first slight shove had her heart speeding.

That was a thrill he didn't think any male could tire of.

He was almost sorry when her neck arched with pleasure and her eyes slid shut. Sadly, ordering her to look at him seemed too intimate. She'd made it clear she wasn't doing this for romance. He watched her instead—the flush that swept up her breasts, the hard, tight pebbling of her red nipples. Goose bumps broke across her shoulders when he forged in the final inch.

"Lordy," she breathed, squirming around him. "You are hung like a damn stallion."

"Does it hurt?" he asked even as he met her wriggling with a push of his own.

Pen's breath caught in her throat. "Only as much as I want it to."

They were speaking in whispers, their gazes locked once more. Graham felt a rush of sultry wetness around his embedded cock. Pen ran her tongue around her kiss-swollen lips. Graham shuddered deep inside. Aroused almost beyond bearing, it was hard for him to get his next question out.

"Do you want me to bite you now or at the end?"

"The end," she said, so breathless he could hardly hear her. "Fuck me hard and only bite me when you can't stand to wait."

He asked for no more permissions, but gave her what she'd demanded. It was very like their first encounter—in roughness, in wildness—except this time was better. Graham knew what Pen liked, what she needed, and she knew she was going to get it. With that confidence to bolster them, she was even less inhibited than she'd been before. She let him take charge of pleasuring her, and didn't hold back in urging him on. Each time she came, she seemed to want the next peak more. Graham restrained his climax as long as he could, but mostly so he could revel in tormenting her.

Both of them craved the pleasure that came from him biting her.

He'd noticed her accent grew more Southern as her impatience rose. She was drawling now, her vowels honeyed. Unfortunately for his control, the sound had the same effect on him as the scent of blood.

"Please, Graham," she finally begged, her nails scoring down his back. "Please, Graham, now."

He yanked her hands off him, fisting their fingers together and stretching out her arms. He didn't have to tell her she was his prisoner; her body knew that all by itself, knew and responded. Her pussy tightened around his thrusts, her eyes nearly rolling back.

"Oh, God," she said, high and shaking. "Oh, *God*."

His upper spine seemed to arch him down to her by itself, the already forceful driving of his hips speeding up. He worried for a moment that he was fucking her too hard, but her neck stretched for him, her breath moaning in longing. Her veins were distended from exertion, the sight so sexy to his new nature that it unnerved him. He didn't think he could have held off to save either of their lives. His balls felt ready to explode.

"Don't scream," he warned a heartbeat before his fangs plunged in.

She didn't scream. She moaned like a lonely boat in a fog at sea. Her fingers squeezed his until her knuckles cracked, their strength a match for the abrupt fury of her orgasm. Not wanting her to hurt herself, Graham let go. The way her arms immediately slapped around his torso startled him, but he didn't mind. They clung to each other as he pulled heaven from her vein, arms wrapped tight, pelvises jammed together, senses rocked by a bliss so huge it was frightening. Nothing could penetrate it but their own ecstasy, nothing but their mutual groans of greed. His ejaculation burst anew with each swallow, sucked from his prick by her contractions. The sharpness of the pleasure astonished him, the continued force and intensity. He didn't count how many times it happened, but the glow the repeated peaks shot through him was very sweet. They spread out and finally settled like warm, spiced wine.

Pen sighed like she was sorry when he pulled both his penetrations free.

This time he healed her bite marks, kissing and licking the wounds while sending his energy into her. Pen gave a tiny start, then relaxed again.

"Oh!" she said. "That tingles."

Her voice was sleepy, her body limp. He pulled her unresisting on top of him. She felt softer lying against him than he'd dreamed she could. The sensation was so pleasant he couldn't seem to stop running his hand up and down her back. Her head fit perfectly into the hollow of his shoulder. This, he thought, was a far superior way to finish lovemaking.

"You okay?" he asked. "Not too weak or dizzy?"

"Mmm," was her reassuring, if not informative response.

"We should skip tomorrow. Give you a chance to recover."

Now her hum of answer was a tad grumpy.

He wondered if he could go without feeding for a day. He appeared not to be in danger of taking too much from her. Twice now he'd stopped without a struggle. He wished he'd asked Robin how often he could drink from a single human who hadn't been unnaturally strengthened like Estelle.

He shifted atop the covers. He knew he'd rather not feed from his father's fiancée a second time. Then again, taking Pen exclusively didn't strike him as entirely comfortable, either—and not only because that might compromise her health.

As if she felt him thinking, Pen propped her chin on her forearm and looked at him. "You know, Graham, you're better at sex than I expected you to be."

Graham huffed out a laugh. "Just for that, I should tell you *you're* exactly as I expected."

"You didn't think I'd be good in bed?"

He'd thought she'd know a lot of tricks, that she'd be skilled but not open. Considering what she'd said about having trouble coming, maybe he hadn't been far off. An orgasm was a moment of vulnerability, a surrender to sensation in another person's company. He suspected Pen wasn't especially fond of that.

The smile that tugged his lips irritated her.

"Answer me," she ordered, shoving his shoulder.

"I'm just wondering why I'm the first man to have shown you so much pleasure."

Pen's whole face tightened: eyes, mouth, even her aristocratic little nostrils pinched. She pushed off him and began to hunt for her clothes.

"I knew I shouldn't have told you that. Honestly, Graham, don't you know the meaning of discretion?"

"I can't be the first man who's asked. Or didn't you let the others know you weren't satisfied?"

"My personal life is none of your business."

Her tone was as crisp as her motions—no Southern belle showing now. She'd yanked her panties up her long, long legs and was currently buttoning her blouse. Graham remained where he was, watching her transform into her old self. Only the intensity of the color flying in her cheeks suggested she was the same passionate woman who had come apart in his arms.

It occurred to him that someone, somewhere, had taught her she needed to guard herself like this. The swiftness with which his fingers curled into fists didn't put him at ease. He wanted to sock whoever it had been, a gesture he sincerely doubted Pen would appreciate.

"You're a vampire," Pen said, as if responding to some retort of his. "Of course you can pleasure me."

Graham sighed inwardly. God forbid she should think him naturally competent.

"You're crooked," he said, nodding at her buttons.

Pen pulled a face and threw his shirt at him.

Pen was little more than an itch prickling in Graham's veins by the time Ben returned from dinner.

He shot Graham a look as he hung up his overcoat and jacket. When he shut their shared closet, the smell of snow and cold diminished but didn't disappear. Ben's skin held the scents as much as his clothes, the perfume of a night—and a city—Graham had yet to explore.

Was this what other vampires felt when they traveled,

this sense that each new place had the potential to be a feast? Graham shifted in the overstuffed armchair, his eyes turning to the snow-festooned world outside. His discomfort with his change in status was diminishing. He was getting used to the thought of feeding on human beings.

He wondered what it said about him that this was happening so soon.

"So." Ben plopped into the armchair opposite his. His creased but clean white shirt set off one of his ever-present sweater-vests. With his tousled hair and lazy, athletic pose, he resembled one of the college boys Sally was continually pestering him to become.

As to that, he resembled one of the college boys who was continually dancing attendance on Pen.

"So," Graham said back to him.

"You and the boss's daughter."

"Former boss," Graham corrected, ignoring Ben's invitation to be forthcoming. Permanently former boss was what it was looking like, unless Arnold Anderson wanted to stop using his assistant when the sun was up.

"I guess you two reached an understanding. Sally and I heard thumping in the room when we first came back."

"Hell," Graham said. "Sorry about that."

Ben waved his apology away. "It's all right. Sally and I took a walk. It was nice to be out in the quiet and talk."

"It's not all right. Sally's too young to be hearing things like that."

"Sally probably knows as much about sex as either of us."

"She's seventeen," Graham said, aghast.

Ben pressed his lips together, his expression twisted by some emotion Graham couldn't read. "Eighteen next month."

"Still . . ." Graham leaned back in the upholstered chair. He considered Ben's troubled face. "You and she haven't been fighting as much lately. I guess she's finally growing up."

Ben frowned at a piece of lint on his trousers. He

brushed it off, then shook his head as if to reject whatever thought had just run through it. Watching him, Graham experienced a twinge of alarm.

"Is something wrong with Sally?"

"No," Ben said. "Sally's fine."

"I know she doesn't exactly like Pen."

"She understands, and so do I. You turning to Pen is better than—"

He stopped, because they both knew what it was better than: Graham feeding on Estelle and enjoying it a bit too much.

"I think she's nervous," Ben blurted. "Estelle, I mean. Because of this dreaming about Edmund thing. That's a lot of pressure to put on falling asleep."

"She'll come through. Estelle always does."

"Yes, she does." Ben rubbed his thighs up and down. Graham supposed Ben found the topic of Estelle as sticky as he did.

"Pen means well," he said, though in truth he wondered if she did. Her casual dismissal of his pre-vampire bed skills still rankled.

Ben sank back, chuckling. "That's the Graham we know and love—fair to everyone."

"Hardly. When it counted most, I wasn't fair at all."

"Graham." Ben's manner was reproving. "You did the best you could when you found out what our father was. You did what you thought was right."

Graham was rising, unwilling to have this conversation yet again. Being careful not to use too much force, he squeezed his brother's tense shoulder.

"I'm going out. I think I should feed a second time tonight."

"By yourself?"

"I have to do it eventually. I don't think it will be a problem. I'm not very hungry. I'll look for a drunk. Someone who'll think they imagined what happened if my thrall falls flat." He thought this through and nodded to himself. "I want to skip tomorrow night. I don't want to wear Pen out."

Ben popped to his feet. "I can come. Or you could . . . feed from me instead."

His hesitation spoke louder than his words. Graham fought not to show how touched he was. That would only make Ben uncomfortable.

"I need to do this. Need to show myself I can handle my new life."

When Ben's eyes remained worried, Graham placed his hand gently on his arm. "Don't forget how strong I am now. Or how cautious I've always been. Inexperience is probably my biggest weakness to overcome. All of you protecting me isn't going to help with that."

"You're not the only one who's made mistakes."

Ben's unexpected intensity gave Graham pause.

"Maybe not," he said after a hesitation. "But I'm the one whose responsibility it is to set this particular mistake to rights."

Switzerland

Precious minutes passed while Edmund commanded his arm to wake. It seemed forever before he was able to stretch across his torso for Durand's knife. The moment he grasped its leather hilt, energy flooded him.

The effect told him Durand had used this knife *a lot*. His aura had infused it until it had become what humans would have called a power object. The possibilities that suggested caused Edmund's sluggish blood to move faster.

A blade like this could be turned to more than suicide.

Edmund gasped at the idea that came to him then. It was mad, and probably fatal, something only the very desperate would have tried. If he failed and somehow managed to survive, Frank and Li-Hua's vengeance would know no bounds—no matter how their violence might offend Durand.

If he succeeded, though, if he pulled off this crazy thing, he might have a chance to escape this prison with his soul intact.

He tested the fingers that had so recently prickled back

to life. He knew he wasn't ready to kill himself, but for a chance to be free, to be reunited with those he loved, he was positively willing to risk death.

Do it then, he ordered himself. *You don't know how long this will take.*

Buoyed and not wanting the surge of hope to have time to fade, he searched inside his head for the last bullet.

In moments, he knew where it was to the millimeter, a squashed lump of coldness in the soft tissues of his brain. He lifted the knife from where he'd rested it on his chest. His grip was sweating, and he ordered it to stop. He placed the tip three-quarters of an inch beneath his right temple.

Slow, he cautioned as the toxic metal started to burn his skin.

He wanted to thrust as shallowly as possible, just enough to create a path for his natural healing power to push the flattened projectile out. He reminded himself this knife would not affect him like a normal blade. There would be pain, probably a whacking great deal of it, and possibly increased weakness from bleeding. He would have to ignore both. Absolute precision would be crucial. Head wounds didn't kill *upyr* as easily as those to the heart, but with an iron knife, even a master could be slain.

A prayer formed without his willing it. For strength. For life. He filled his lungs with the musty air of his cell.

Then he pushed inward until the knife crackled through his skull.

The pain was blinding. With it came an odd disorientation to his thoughts. Colors swirled in the darkness, scents and music that weren't there. Someone laughed—his wife, Claris, he thought—as blood ran thick and cool into his hair.

Daddy! Robin cried in alarm, the voice of a human boy.

He stood in the arched stone doorway to Edmund's old study in Bridesmere, watching his father stab himself in the

head. The stained glass window with the Fitz Clare crest
threw shards of jewel-like color across the floor. Blood
plopped onto his fat account ledgers, making the numbers
run. Robin was just a towheaded child, skinny as a rail in
his navy doublet and knobby-kneed black hose. Edmund
had let him down too many times in the past. He couldn't
add this injury to the rest, couldn't make his own son watch
him top himself.

Then he remembered. Robin was all grown-up, and
this was a hallucination. The knife must have wakened
and mixed up some memory. Edmund grunted and pushed
harder.

He gained another inch and the bullet moved, rocking
in its cage of flesh as if it were sentient. Sweat poured off
him in agony. He couldn't see anymore. He didn't know if
he'd screwed his eyes shut or just gone blind. He didn't dare
remove the knife. The wound could close and trap the spent
slug again. He could hear the thing shifting now, like boot
soles sliding on wet gravel. His hand began to tremble, his
breath to pant. He wanted to scream but didn't know how
far off Durand had withdrawn.

He called on the power the guard had left in the blade,
willing it to steady him.

Come on, he thought to the bullet. *You* want *to get out
of me.*

If he'd had anything in his belly, the sensation of the
bullet squirming from him would have made him throw up.
Instead, he simply shuddered as it clinked onto the table's
surgical-style drain and rolled.

The instant it was safe to do so, he yanked the knife so
frantically from his head he lost his grip on it. It clattered
to the floor a second after the bullet.

Jesu, he thought, his heart too tired to race in panic.
Please let me not have damaged my brain.

He couldn't tell if he had. His thoughts were tangled,
and he was frighteningly weak, his body trembling in slow

motion. He couldn't see. Wetness pooled beneath his head, the slowly closing stab wound still trickling. He couldn't afford the blood loss. He thought he was passing out . . .

He didn't know how long it was until he came to himself, but when he did, he could see again—more than see. Despite his physical weakness, his mind was clear. The obscuring veils he'd been trying to perceive through were gone.

With them torn away, he could feel Estelle's presence. Relief poured through him in a golden balm. He was whole again, filled up, learning only then how this brave young woman completed him. Her consciousness was not distinct, but it felt real, like a gentle blanket on his shivering soul. He sensed that she was dreaming and not lucid, her thoughts too confused to communicate usefully with him.

Don't worry, love, he thought to her. *I can do what I need to now.*

Schloss Oberbad

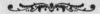

Frank and Li-Hua had suites for both day and night in their mountain fortress. Naturally, the rooms in which they slept were underground and windowless. The rooms in which they whiled away their waking hours, however, lacked nothing in luxury.

Switzerland's mad duke Wilhelm had commissioned this residence in the latter half of the last century. Wilhelm was fond of architecture, especially the ostentatious sort. This particular fortress was an ode to the glories of a Middle Ages that never was. He spent a sizeable chunk of his fortune on the thing—hence the "mad" appellation laid upon him by worried heirs. Despite his relatives' irritation, he created a castle to end all castles from imported stone and exotic wood and a veritable sea of gold enamel work. He died after living in his magnum opus for a mere three months, possibly murdered by those same frustrated heirs. If so, they hadn't profited long from their crime. Fifty years later, the family was dead broke, enabling Frank—who'd had literal lifetimes to amass his ill-gotten gains—to pick it up for a relative song.

The family's lawyers—whose heads were, manifestly, made of cement—had resisted him thralling the asking price lower.

Garish though the castle was, it was no sugar-candy construction. Its fortifications were solid, its views both useful and sublime. Frank thought it would make a lovely base of operations for his future kingdom, the one he and Li-Hua were risking everything to found.

Frank didn't ask too much, he thought. His queen, some adoring subjects, perhaps a designation as a principality like Liechtenstein. Switzerland was already split into cantons. He didn't see why the Lower Engadin shouldn't become his, no more than he accepted that the old guard among the *upyr* should always have everything their way. Relative youngsters like Frank were just as fit to rule. Certainly, he and Li-Hua were better suited to grasping the complexities of the modern world.

It was a well-worn train of thought, and it had him pacing their sitting room, past the rich Wagnerian murals and the wall of stained glass windows. The famous German composer had been another of the duke's obsessions, one Frank did not share. Depictions of Wagner's operas were plastered around the house. For as much attention as Frank was paying, Parsifal's eternal quest for the grail, which supplied the theme for this room, might as well have been the adventures of a pack of pigs.

His beloved offered no distraction. Li-Hua was dressing, a process that sometimes took longer than it ought, considering how swiftly she was capable of moving. Frank wished he felt more confident of their progress. Fitz Clare was too damn stubborn, and too much relied on him. Being forced to take that stupid girl back to her village had been the last straw for him. If Fitz Clare didn't crack soon, Durand was going to owe him.

Frank stopped in front of a large tigerwood armoire and blew out his breath. He was far too agitated for their evening plans.

Of a mind to change that, he gripped the bronze guilt pulls to reveal a padded velvet interior. The cabinet housed his prized Stradivarius, stolen of course, though that hardly mattered now. Its true owner had long since returned to dust. It was Frank's energy, Frank's love, that had preserved this instrument in its pristine state. With an inward sigh he couldn't quite repress, he tucked his jaw into the chin rest and poised the bow.

Stravinski's Violin Concerto in D burst from the strings, called out by the infinitely sensitive movements of Frank's fingers. To ensure his concentration, he played it at double speed. Frank could have joined any orchestra in the world—Berlin, Paris, what have you—but he would never be a soloist. Technically, every chord was perfect, even Stravinski's peculiar D to A stretch. Emotionally, Frank's performance was always flawed. True virtuosity depended on quirks of imagination he did not possess. To his everlasting regret, he had just enough depth of spirit to know that particular summit would remain forever unscaled by him.

Becoming a vampire had made him better, but it could not make him the best.

He let the final notes of the capriccio fall away, their bittersweet beauty lingering in his ears.

"You should have told me you were going to play," Li-Hua said from the door between the sitting and dressing room. "I would have joined you."

Her black concert grand gleamed in the room's corner. *She* was a virtuoso. Had been even when she was human, though as a female she'd been a rarity. Their queen had forbidden her from playing in public after she was changed. Nim Wei had feared Li-Hua's unnatural skill would expose *upyr*kind to humans and thought she had the right to decide that question for all of them.

The reminder of what they were fighting for felt timely.

"You're too kind, darling," Frank said, "and very beautiful tonight."

She was perpetually beautiful to him: a perfect, ruthless flower of femininity. Her faintly military red wool suit could have been sewn onto her lithe body, her every curve demanding worship, her tight black leather gloves provocative enough to elicit shivers of attraction. How Durand could resist her Frank didn't know, but he supposed it was just as well. Durand had precisely the cold self-command his pear blossom loved.

"You need your charm," she said with a saucy, half-hidden smile. "Your thoughts are clear as spring water."

At times like this, Frank appreciated her humor. They could be marked for death by either of the *upyr*'s hidebound leaders for what they were about to do.

Li-Hua blurred to the table where he'd set down his pocket watch. Its works concealed a few tiny pieces of iron covered in her blood, her "charm" for sharing her knack for not being read with him.

"Buck up," she said, pressing the cool, engraved silver into his palm. She curled his fingers over it. " 'Faint heart never won fair maiden.' Keep your guard up, and we'll be fine."

Frank kissed her hand. "What would I do without you?"

"Be hellishly bored and horny."

He laughed at her way with slang. "Very well," he said. "Let's go bag ourselves a Nazi."

Their quarry was every bit as prompt as Frank expected; he was German, after all. They met him on the opposite slope of their valley in a crowded restaurant, one of many that had opened in this developing spa town. At a table not far away, the mayor was eating with his family, all of them—baby included—wearing matching snowflake sweaters. The sweaters disturbed Frank, but not the *Bürgermeister*'s proximity. He meant to be seen and known here . . . just not for what he was.

Commander Teudt of the *Ahnenerbe*, the innocuously named Department of Ancestral Heritage, rose from his chair at Li-Hua's approach. He bowed stiffly, his expression tugged between awe at her flagrant beauty and disapproval over her participation in what he must have thought was men's business. Frank had observed similar reactions in modern German males before. His countrymen seemed unable to reconcile their view of women as either Madonnas or whores.

Frank was glad he had no such blind spot. As a child of the Renaissance, when many women had guided great families, he didn't underestimate the female of his species.

"Heil Hitler," Teudt said by way of greeting.

His accompanying salute was sketchy—as Frank imagined it would *not* have been in his homeland. Most Swiss tended to look askance at such gestures. Probably for similar reasons, Teudt's storklike frame was clothed in a black double-breasted suit and not a party uniform, though Frank noticed a pin with two small lightning *sig* runes shining on his lapel. The Nazis' occult bureau hadn't been absorbed by the SS yet, but Frank suspected this was only a matter of time. *Der Führer* was too fond of controlling everything around him to leave that group of obsessives on their own for long.

"Right," Frank said in response to Teudt's party-approved hail.

The omission earned him a frown he didn't mind at all. However useful Germany's present administration might be to his goals, he saw no purpose in letting them believe he'd be their puppet. He pulled Li-Hua's chair out, then sat himself.

"You know I don't like meeting this openly," Teudt said primly.

Frank leaned back in his seat and smiled. He knew the noise of the other diners gave them the privacy they required, and Teudt was too nervous for him to pay the complaint real mind. Even as the Nazi tried to look authoritative, his little round spectacles betrayed his shakes by flashing in the light.

"We've nothing to hide," Frank said. "Nothing could be more natural than my having dinner with a countryman."

Teudt jumped as Li-Hua's toes found his ankle under the table. Perspiration glittered on his brow as both his fear and arousal rose. The Nazi pushed his sliding spectacles up his nose.

"We viewed your footage of the vampire healing," he said in an undertone. "My colleagues and I found it suggestive."

"Only suggestive?" Frank inquired.

"Every moviegoer knows the cinema can lie."

"True," Frank agreed, "but I know of no director who creates effects that good. More to the point, you insult me and my partner by implying we would fabricate evidence."

Teudt's glance flicked to Li-Hua. His lips thinned in a manner he probably thought was stern. "We need more of a demonstration than you've given us, if we are to know the stories of your kind are true. We want your subject to change a human into what you are."

Frank ordered his pulse not to accelerate. "Do you now?"

"Yes," Teudt said. His hands were flat on the table, the skin around his nails gone white. "You're asking for a lot of money, and you're asking for it in gold."

"Of course I am. Everyone knows the reichsmark isn't worth the paper it's printed on these days."

"A temporary situation, which has been improving, thanks to our *Führer*."

"I'm sure," Frank agreed, "but I'm not changing my demands. Only consider what my product could be worth to you. Men of your choosing turned into warriors of unimaginable strength and power, the ideal of the *Übermensch* pushed to new limits. Impervious to injury. Silent as the grave. Your *Führer* is ambitious, and rightly so. Don't you think he'd find a use for such assassins?"

"The usefulness of your proposed 'product' is not in question. Your ability to deliver is."

Li-Hua had peeled off her long black gloves. Now she reached across the table to slide her pale, slim fingers over their quarry's hand. When Teudt flushed the color of a brick, she smiled. "Haven't we given you, of all people, sufficient reason to believe in us?"

"That you are what you say, yes," Teudt rasped. The tip of his tongue wet his nonexistent upper lip as he remembered how she'd done that. Li-Hua had popped his cork, over and over until he'd fainted, with no more contact than her teeth sinking into his neck.

Neither she nor Frank had wanted to fuck him.

"You want to trust us," she crooned, putting her thrall in it. "It would give you pleasure to please us."

"Stop that," Teudt snapped, a hint of shrillness in his voice. He gripped the crucifix he was wearing beneath his shirt. The blood Li-Hua had taken from him should have strengthened her influence, but the antique cross was surprisingly—and annoyingly—effective. Since neither Frank nor she had any fear of ritual objects, Frank concluded that one of their kind's elders must have spelled it at some point.

Braced by his victory, Teudt pulled himself straighter. "We cannot do business if you are going to try these tricks. As I said, I do not doubt what you are, only that you can"— he waved his hand in a vague circle—"supply more of the same. Until you establish that to our satisfaction, I am not authorized to release funds. You have one week to provide us a record of a transformation. After that, my colleagues have instructed me to break off talks. The *Ahnenerbe* is not going to waste its resources chasing wild gooses."

The waiter arrived with menus, but Teudt was rising and waved him off.

"One week," he said, his officiousness its own form of dignity. "Do not contact me without results."

"Prissy bastard," Li-Hua muttered as Teudt left. She'd turned in her chair to watch him, her elbow slung over its rungs. "If we didn't need that gold . . ."

"Yes," Frank agreed. "If we didn't need that gold, you and I would both enjoy killing him."

It was simply their bad luck that founding kingdoms was so pricey.

Still trembling, Otto Teudt stopped to catch his breath on the stone-flagged terrace that would be this restaurant's *Biergarten* come summer. His heart was in his throat, throbbing like a bite of fear he could not swallow. Striving to recover, he smoothed his mouse brown hair beneath its brilliantine. His ears were colder than they should have been. He'd left his hat in the restaurant but was damned if he'd return for it.

He'd had enough of monsters for one night.

Teudt was a mystic by nature, a scholar dedicated to unearthing the Fatherland's glorious past. These vampires were too solid for him, too coarse and unpredictable. For his own sake, he hoped they didn't meet his deadline. He wasn't convinced the Reich could trust them.

On the other hand, he couldn't help wondering what it would be like to be one of them. To have that power, that beauty, that stupefying lack of fear. If half their gifts had been his, Teudt would have risen even faster through the party's ranks.

His anxiety receded in contemplating that. It was with pleasure that he gazed across the steep alpine valley. A few lights burned in the village, but the fortress on the tallest

summit outshone them all. The windows of Frank Hauptmann's snowcapped fairytale castle glowed like the gold
the vampire was so intent on piling up.

Teudt imagined himself living there, *der Führer*'s man
in Switzerland. The Reich wouldn't need Hauptmann once
they knew his secrets. Teudt had heard Duke Wilhelm's
former library was impressive: a treasure trove of old Ger-
manic manuscripts. Teudt could return to his true calling
and leave this liaising nonsense to someone else.

Realizing Hauptmann and the woman might be coming out any time—because *they* weren't going to eat, were
they?—he shook himself from his fantasies. As he strode
away, he assured himself he moved with purpose and not
alarm.

Better not to become a meal for vampires a second time.
Teudt didn't trust anything that felt that good.

Estelle jackknifed up in bed, her system inundated with
exhilaration and urgency. Nazis were after Edmund, and
he'd performed surgery on his own head. Had he seen what
she did through Otto Teudt's eyes? Had he removed that
bullet so he could build a bridge for her to dream-walk
over? The amount of faith that would imply startled her.
Edmund believed in her.

"I know where he is," she said.

"Know where who is?" Sally grumbled sleepily. The
beds in their room were small, but Sally's curled-up kitten
posture made hers look big. When Estelle's words registered, she sat up. She pressed her hands to her stomach.
"You mean you know where Daddy is?"

"He's in the town of Schloss Oberbad, in the famous
castle—the one the crazy duke who loved Wagner's operas
built."

"Castle Lohengrin? Like they put in tourist bro-
chures?"

"Yes!" Estelle bounced on her mattress. "It was night, of course, but I saw it as clear as day."

"Wow," Sally breathed. "We know where he is. We have to tell Ben and Graham. We have to book seats on the first train out."

"We have to be careful," Estelle reminded.

"I know," Sally said, then flung herself out of bed to embrace Estelle. Her hold was tight enough to make her squeak. "We know where he is! Oh, God, Estelle, this is good!"

Estelle eyes pricked as she hugged Edmund's daughter back. She couldn't speak, neither of her fears nor her hopes. With Sally so happy, they didn't seem important.

Then, probably because Sally was trying so hard to conceal the thought, something slipped from her mind to Estelle's that changed everything.

Cursing silently, Durand lowered his field glasses. He was in his tower, doing a quick survey of the valley while waiting for Fitz Clare to decide if he wanted to live or die. The moon that hung in the star-flecked sky was as good as a searchlight to his *upyr* eyes. He'd had no trouble recognizing Otto Teudt standing on the terrace of the restaurant opposite. The supposed scholar popped up in the papers periodically, spouting off his theories that the Aryans had been civilization's true founders. Teudt was a crank with important friends, all the more dangerous because he drew no distinction between wishful thinking and rational study. Teudt would accept one strange thing that was true, then bury it beneath a hundred that were not.

And he was Frank and Li-Hua's foreign contact, the "highly placed German" they were hoping to do business with. No wonder they hadn't wanted to divulge his name to Durand. Durand understood necessity sometimes made for odd bedfellows, but if his employers thought they could control Teudt and his cronies, they were out of their ever-living minds. Some people thought the Nazis and Hitler were comical. Durand had lived long enough to experience, firsthand, the lengths human fanatics would go to.

Add to that the likelihood that one or another of Fitz Clare's powerful connections would eventually ferret out where he was, and Durand saw he was going to have to increase his already extensive precautions. This brilliant—if risky—plan was beginning to look like a disaster waiting to explode. Durand found himself hoping Fitz Clare had succeeded in killing himself. The loss of their captive on his watch would be awkward, but it would put an end to Frank and Li-Hua's dangerous gamble.

Not that Durand was holding his breath.

"Fuck," he said, momentarily letting out his frustration.

"Sir?" said the vampire standing patiently by the door to his turret room.

Durand looked at the man. He was almost succeeding in standing at attention. *Upyr*kind didn't make ideal soldiers; few among them liked following orders or hard work. Those who'd signed on for Frank and Li-Hua's little revolution weren't especially different. Fortunately, Durand's current companion had taken to training better than some.

"I want to double our watch on the rail station and passes," Durand said. "The minute anyone spots any of the faces in the file I distributed, they are to notify me, personally, without delay."

"Yes, sir," said his adjutant. "Who do you want me to pull off drills?"

Durand gave him names, older *upyr* who could remain alert for at least a few daytime hours. He wished he had sufficient personnel for twenty-four-hour rotations, but he was doing the best he could. They had a few local human servants who could fill the holes. If there was anything Durand could do to stop it, this assignment wouldn't end in failure.

He stayed where he was, by the window, until he heard his aide's quick footsteps descend and leave the tower. It was time to check on Fitz Clare's status—more than time, probably.

Durand wasn't optimistic that their prisoner had chosen sensibly.

The Oberbad Hotel

The trip out of Zurich was very different from the trip in. Gone were the sybaritic luxuries of the Orient Express. They rode the same trains ordinary Swiss people used, though they were able to reserve a sitting car to themselves. Graham was wedged in the corner farthest from the window, sitting up but sleeping like a stone. They'd covered him with a hat and blanket—not only to protect him but to hide the unnatural gleam of his skin. Keeping up glamours required consciousness, and Graham was thoroughly out. Pen sat next to him, calmly reading the international *Tribune*. She ensured the swaying train didn't tip him over by periodically leaning into him.

That Graham wasn't perceptibly breathing, they simply had to hope no train personnel would see.

They were on the final leg of their journey, from St. Moritz to Schloss Oberbad. Presumably the scenery was spectacular, but the shades were drawn to shut out daylight. Estelle could only *hear* the wheels clacking through tunnels or over high bridges. More troubling, she couldn't sense Edmund any more than she had since she'd woken up from her dream of him.

She told herself this was because the sun had risen. Likely, he was weak as well as asleep. One couldn't perform brain surgery on oneself without recovery time. In spite of her worries, she couldn't help smiling at how strange her life had become. As much as she liked her job, racing across Europe to rescue her vampire fiancé from a Nazi plot was a far and interesting cry from typing letters at Harrods.

"Not long now," Ben said as the echo of the train indicated they were crossing another gorge.

Ben sat next to Pen and Graham, across from Sally and Estelle. Sally was sleeping again, curled up with her head in Estelle's lap.

"No, not long," Estelle agreed, attempting to soothe her nerves by petting Sally's soft blonde curls.

Ben watched the motion as if it soothed him, too. Estelle closed her eyes for a moment, painfully aware of Sally's youth. She was a child, but if the fear Estelle had read from her was founded, she wasn't going to be able to remain one long. Though Estelle could not presently name the boys in her set of friends, Sally must have been more serious about one of them than they'd known. She hoped Ben wouldn't put whoever it was in the hospital. Despite their differences, he'd always been protective of Sally.

"Is she all right?" Ben asked, seeing the anxiety in Estelle's face.

"Fine," Estelle said, then let out a little sigh. Sally would consider this a betrayal, but Estelle couldn't risk her or her unborn child's safety. If that cost her Sally's trust, so be it. She met Ben's waiting gaze. "I want to talk to you and Graham alone later."

Ben's eyebrows rose just as Pen glanced up from her newspaper. Wisely, he asked nothing.

"As you like," he said, and smoothed his corduroy trousers.

To everyone's relief, Graham stirred shortly before their arrival. Dusk had fallen, the sky a deepening aqua behind the window shades. Though he'd roused, Graham was still sleepy as they disembarked. Ben had to elbow him in reminder to pull up his glamour.

It was a piece of good fortune that there weren't many eyes to see them. The station at Schloss Oberbad was small: a simple open platform with a tiny stacked-stone building butting up to it. What the station lacked in grandeur, the surrounding mountains compensated for. They were massive, their snow-caked peaks lost in wispy clouds. The last of the sunset had painted the vapors gold. Beneath them, a village as pretty as a postcard climbed either slope of the valley they had chugged into. Most of the village buildings were old and quaint, their smoothly plastered fronts decorated with the colorful murals residents called sgraffiti.

It was hard to believe this picturesque Swiss hamlet harbored anything more dangerous than hot cocoa addicts.

Sobered by the realization that it did, Estelle took in the scenery as the porters retrieved their trunks and piled them onto a rolling cart. Horse-drawn sleighs were lined up on the other side of the station, suggesting the streets weren't navigable by auto. Estelle suspected Ben wouldn't be pleased by that.

"We've been spotted," Pen said in an undertone behind her.

Naturally, Estelle looked around. She saw nothing except an ordinary station crowd: bundled-up locals, a few tourists carrying skis. Graham must have seen something different, because he nodded.

"The young man with the dog," he said, low and casual back to Pen. "And possibly the old man in the knitted cap."

"I missed the young one," Pen said, annoyed.

"He'd have been a vampire. Gone now, I'm afraid. Too quick to track."

"Hmph," said Pen, regarding him. Then she shrugged. "May as well resign ourselves, I suppose. We were never going to make a stealthy entrance with this lot. At least we know we're in the right place if we're being watched."

"And if they don't know we know we've been spotted . . ."

"Exactly," Pen agreed—which was clear as mud to Estelle.

She did know she didn't like being referred to as "this lot," as though she and Ben and Sally were some sort of baggage that would slow Pen down. Had she forgotten it was Estelle's dreams—which apparently Pen still doubted—that had gotten them this far? Pointing that out was tempting, but probably not productive. As long as Graham was getting on with Pen—and he seemed to be—the American's presence was useful. She reminded herself that she liked Pen in general. Keeping the peace was more important than a momentary prick to her pride.

"Our sleigh is ready," Sally said, interrupting her internal bristling. She rolled her eyes at Estelle, demonstrating that she, too, thought Pen was being a pill. It was childish, but Estelle immediately felt better.

They all piled into the loaded sleigh. Pen and Graham seemed to have more voltage running through them than before. Evidently, being spied on excited them. Pen's sharp cheeks and nose were pinker than the cold could account for, and Graham's brown eyes were distinctly bright. When Sally complained that she was freezing, Ben wrapped her close in a big blanket. For herself, Estelle wasn't sure how she felt. Relieved that they were here, perhaps, but unsure of what would come. It didn't help that where they were didn't seem quite real. Apart from their time in Zurich, which hadn't been too unlike London, Estelle had never traveled out of the British Isles. The driver clucked to his big horses differently than drivers did at home, and the signs seemed to be in everything but English. Graham could read them; he had a knack for languages, but to Estelle they were mysterious. Pen, it seemed, was fluent in the local *Schwyzerdütsch*, for she was soon chatting animatedly with their driver.

Estelle probably felt as humble as the American could have wished by the time they reached the spanking new, multistory Oberbad Hotel.

There all went smoothly under Graham's direction—at least until Sally stepped down from the sleigh and fainted in Ben's arms.

Oh, hell, Estelle thought. To her dismay, she wasn't close enough. Pen got to Sally before she could.

Ben looked positively stricken as he held his limp sister.

"She's all right," Pen soothed. Looking like she'd done it before, she crouched down to administer a few light slaps to Sally's now chalky cheeks. "It's probably the altitude. Some people need more time to adjust to it."

Her treatment was effective. Sally's eyes flickered behind their lids. When they opened and cleared, Estelle knew the terror that filled them had nothing to do with their height above sea level. Sally's fear for her future had been confirmed.

"It's all right," Estelle said as Sally's hand instinctively covered the middle button of her fox-fur coat. "You fainted, but you're all right."

Sally looked to Ben, who stroked her tousled hair from her face.

"You're all right, sweetheart," he confirmed. "Graham will get our rooms, and you can lie down."

Sally blinked and sat up on the cold pavement. The hotel staff were fluttering around them, asking if the little *Fräulein* needed anything.

"Oh, boy," Sally said, color flooding her cheeks again. "Sorry about that!"

* * *

Ben joined Graham in the corridor outside their rooms. Estelle and the hotel's doctor were with Sally and had shooed him out. Though the paneled door told him nothing, Ben couldn't stop looking back at it.

Not being in there, holding Sally's hand, was nearly killing him.

"She'll be fine," Graham said with the slightest edge of impatience. "Sally looks like a cream puff, but you and I know how tough she is."

It was because Ben knew this that he was worried.

"You're going out," he said, belatedly noting Graham's dark peacoat and treaded boots. A black knit cap covered his brown hair. He looked different, like a villager, slightly shabby and prepared for bad weather.

"Reconnaissance," Graham said. "I want to look over the castle's defenses. See if I can discover exactly where Father is being held."

"You want me to come with you?"

Graham shook his head. "Stay with the girls. If I'm not back by sunrise, you'll know where I've been. And for God's sake, don't tell Pen what I'm doing. I don't want to hurt your feelings, but I can move a lot quieter and quicker without either of your help."

"Trust me, my feelings are fine. Just—" Ben paused to choose his words. "Don't take chances, Graham. It won't help anyone if you end up in trouble."

"I won't. Tonight I'm only getting the lay of the land." Graham grinned, a startling flash of bright white teeth. "I'll save the chances for later on."

Ben was glad Graham's dourness had lifted, but this wolfish humor was not the alternate he would have picked. "I mean it, Graham. Be careful."

Graham's smile softened. "You be careful, too, Ben.

The professor's kidnappers know we're here. I don't want any of you leaving the hotel, or going anywhere alone. Lock Pen in her room if you have to."

Ben snorted. "I thought that was your job."

"Hardly." Graham let out a breath that might have been regret. "I'll be back. Probably in a few hours."

Ben watched him stride away down the carpeted corridor, his movements quick and confident despite his size. Had his brother walked like that before? Had Ben simply not noticed?

"Blast," Estelle said, coming into the hall and closing the door behind her. "I wanted to talk to Graham, too."

Ben's blood pressure shot up dizzyingly. "Is something wrong with Sally? Is this about what you hinted at on the train?"

Estelle's expression twisted in a way that didn't reassure. "Sally is—" She stopped and started again. "I want you to try not to be upset. I know how protective you are of her. Things like this happen sometimes, and families simply have to pull together and get through it."

"Please, Estelle. Just tell me what's going on."

"I think— Ben, I don't believe Sally fainted because of the altitude. The doctor could confirm it, but I'm relatively certain she's pregnant."

Ben's face went icy as the blood drained from it.

"Please don't judge her," Estelle pleaded. "You know how she loves attention. One of those boys who trail after her like puppies must have talked her into being intimate."

"One of those boys . . ." Ben's voice came out as weak as if he were the one with altitude sickness. Estelle's words were fading in and out. If Sally was pregnant, he knew too well who the father was. Sally had never been with anyone but him. He knew that as surely as he knew the Alps were tall.

A baby. He rubbed the cleft in his chin. He and Sally were going to have a child. Emotions surged inside him. He was hot and cold, not knowing what he felt—except that he really wished he could hold her in his arms right now.

This was going to change everything.

"The important thing is to telephone Robin," Estelle was saying. "I know he has his own responsibilities after taking over X Section, but someone has to come and bring Sally home. It isn't only her safety we'd be laying on the line."

Ben stared at Estelle as if he'd never seen her before. "Robin," he repeated.

"Do you want me to ring him?" Estelle offered. "I can, but I'd really rather stay with Sally."

Ben forced his mind to tick over. "I'll call. You stay. Graham doesn't want us to separate."

"I'll go find Pen then," Estelle said. "I imagine Graham would prefer we kept our eyes on her as well."

As soon as the doctor left, Sally threw off the bedcovers. She was fine now, all better, and she had to get out of this stifling room before she ran out of air.

Estelle knew.

Sally had read it in her eyes the moment she recovered from her faint. Estelle's sureness had cemented Sally's. She was pregnant. Not late. Not thrown off her normal cycle by the stress of missing her father. It didn't matter that she hadn't gotten sick or puffy like other women did. All her life, she'd been as healthy as a horse. The few times she'd tried to squirm out of school by playing sick, her father hadn't believed it. He'd simply smiled his gentle smile and asked what was wrong. *Maybe if you tell me, you'll feel better.* She always had. The professor had a way of listening as if no one's problems mattered more to him. Nothing was too childish to tell him, and he'd never, ever acted disappointed in her.

She didn't see how he could fail to be disappointed now.

She'd betrayed his trust—and with a man to whom he'd given every bit as much as he'd given her.

She muttered a curse as she tugged on her heavy coat. She was going to think this through. Her father wasn't here to help, but she could still take a shot at it. Somehow, she would find the strength to face this.

She ducked down the stairway. Her face was tear stained, and she didn't want the boy who operated the lift to see. Across the lobby, where she emerged, a long wall of French doors stretched. Behind them, a stony terrace looked out on tall mountains. No doubt crowded during the day, the terrace was empty now. Sally hurried across the lobby before any of the hotel's well-meaning staff saw who she was and asked questions. It was too much to hope that they'd forgotten her grand entrance.

Her breath gusted out in relief when she reached the fancy formed-cement balustrade on the terrace's farther side. Soft moon shadows picked out the crags and precipices of the huge mountains. Isolated ski runs seemed lost among dark patches: outcrops of granite too steep for snow to cling to. These were not friendly mountains, but they had a peace to them that slowly stole into Sally. Finally, she understood why Estelle had wanted her own flat. Sometimes being alone was heaven.

She wasn't truly alone, of course. For the next eight months she'd always have company.

The smile that curved her lips took her by complete surprise. She was going to have a child. Ben's child. If she could ignore everything else, she had to admit that made her happy. Ben would be a wonderful father, the very best a baby could have. She imagined him rocking it in his arms, little dimpled hands reaching for his hair, little feet kicking. She would like caring for a child. Loving it. Being as good to it as the professor had been to her. The responsibility didn't frighten her. Perhaps it should have, but she thought—just maybe—she'd been born to be a mother.

Her eyes burned with tears she didn't try to hold back, her gloved hands tightening on the icy cement rail. She was glad about this. That might be crazy, but she was glad.

And then an arm snaked around her throat from behind.

For a second she thought it was Ben's arm, that he was angry she'd gone outside by herself. When it tightened and began to choke her, she revised the assumption.

Rage exploded inside her like a star gone nova. This had to be one of the villains who'd taken her father. Lifted off her feet, she kicked violently back and caught a pair of shins. She knew the blows were harder than any she'd inflicted in her worst tantrum, but the man who held her didn't cry out or stagger.

That really made her go wild, flailing and kicking and growling behind her teeth like an animal. No one was going to hurt her or her baby.

"Oh, please struggle," said a laughing voice by her ear, slightly accented. "I love it when your kind do that."

Sally had her right glove off. Without an instant's hesitation, she jabbed her fingers backward into her captor's eye. Her aim was perfect.

"*Madre de díos,*" he swore, as something squished viciously.

Well, then, Sally thought. His accent was Spanish.

Her nails had gone so deep the vampire had to yank them out. This loosened his hold on her neck, giving her a chance to breathe. Sally filled her lungs and shrieked like a banshee. The sound was louder than even she expected it to be, ricocheting off the wall of mountains in front of her. Surely someone would hear it and come.

"Shut up," the Spanish vampire ordered, cuffing her head hard enough to set her ears ringing.

He dropped her as he did so, and Sally fell dizzied to her knees. Her attacker had one hand cupped over his injured eye, but he wasn't what she'd call disabled. She started when a second vampire swung like a shadow over the railing and landed crouched. The shadow impression was no accident. Both her attackers wore mottled gray and black. Snug black balaclavas covered everything but their eyes.

"*You* grab her," said the first one. "She's a hellcat."

There seemed no point in running. The vampires would be too fast. Forced to rely on her remaining weapon, Sally stopped panting and screamed again.

The first scream reached Estelle in Pen's room. She'd been trying to convince the American to join Sally and her for supper, if only to keep her inside. Pen was dressed as if she'd intended to go out, in trim brown trousers and a man's dark peacoat.

Estelle forgot all her persuasions when the shriek split the air.

"Sally," she murmured.

"What about her?" Pen asked in confusion.

Concluding she'd heard the sound with her funny ear, Estelle ran to the window and threw its latch. "There! On the terrace. Sally's being attacked!"

With the casement open, Sally's next set of screams was audible to them both.

"Find Ben," Estelle ordered, dashing for the door.

She should have known Pen wouldn't listen. Not daring to wait for the lift, Estelle slammed down the nearest stairwell. Pen followed directly behind her. Though Estelle's legs were longer, and probably a bit stronger due to Edmund's influence, Pen kept pace with her noisy gallop down the enclosed steps.

Estelle felt quite envious of Pen's trousers.

"I can fight," Pen assured her. "By the time we find Ben, she could be gone."

Estelle's mind filled with curses she didn't have breath

to say. They had to get there in time. Sally's well-being was more precious than ever.

When they reached the terrace, they saw the desk staff had heard the ruckus and were trying to rescue Sally. They were struggling with the vampires, but not making much headway. To Estelle, it looked like the vampires were pretending not to be as strong as they were, perhaps under orders not to expose their true nature. There were four attackers now, instead of the two she'd seen initially. One held Sally under his arm, big furry coat and all, and was trying to climb with her over the terrace rail. Sally's struggles weren't making it easy, but soon enough he'd have to succeed.

Pen appeared to reach the same conclusion. With a cry like a bird of prey, she picked up a chair and rushed him. The fellow looked around at the noise, but didn't let his wriggling burden go. Free to charge as she pleased, Pen smashed the chair over his head with so much force that it broke apart. This caused the man to drop Sally but not to fall over. His glare as he faced Pen was like two flames shining out from his black headgear.

He called Pen something that sounded like *puta*.

God help us, Estelle thought, and jumped into the fray herself.

She quickly discovered it was better if she didn't think. Thanks to Edmund, her muscles had memories her mind knew nothing about. Her right fist sent a vampire sailing into a wall, the impact on his skull sufficient to knock him out. She ran to Sally, catching her arm and helping her up. Pen stunned them both by spinning on the ball of one foot, shooting her leg out backward, and kicking a vampire in the gut. Not only did the blow double him over, it also threw his body over the balustrade.

"Hit that one!" Pen shouted while Estelle gaped. "That uppercut of yours is ferocious!"

Estelle used it on the vampire Pen had pointed out.

Dazed, he stumbled into the cement railing, which began to crack. Seeing the opportunity and inspired by Pen's example, Sally grabbed his legs and helped Estelle tumble him over it. The final vampire standing took one look at his comrades and vaulted voluntarily into the gulf. That left the man Estelle had knocked out earlier to be disposed of.

Wincing at the sight of the hotel's staff, all five of whom were now laid out, Estelle hefted the remaining vampire over her shoulder. He weighed a ton, more than a human his size would have. Because he'd begun to moan, she decided she'd better hurry. Grunting with exertion, she dropped him off the terrace, too. Pebbles and stones rattled down the scarp after him. He landed hard, with a thunk like a flour sack. Estelle could just make out his shape in the moonlit shadows at the bottom of the gorge. Even though she had firsthand knowledge of vampire powers, she was amazed at how little time it took for him to groan, push up on his hands and knees, and run jerkily away.

That he was fleeing rather than climbing up to attack again filled her with relief. She was especially glad the desk staff were unconscious. If they were lucky, the hotel employees wouldn't remember much of the melee. Estelle was pretty sure being set upon by the undead could get you kicked out of most hotels.

"Wow," Pen panted. She'd tottered to Estelle's side and was leaning over the railing shoulder to shoulder with her. "That fall should have killed them. Those vampires are something else."

Estelle thought Pen was something else as well. The woman's nose was trickling blood like it might be broken, her left eye swollen shut and swiftly purpling. Her peacoat had been ripped open, and one leg of her trim brown trousers was shredded up to her thigh. She looked a wreck compared to Sally, who—despite being the object of the attack—barely had a bruise. Possibly, growing up around Edmund's energy had worked some magic on her, which made what Pen had accomplished all the more impressive.

Pen had fought off two superstrong, supernatural creatures with strictly human fighting skills.

"Here," Sally said, holding up a handful of snow. "You'll want to chill your nose before it swells."

Pen tipped her head back and pressed the snow to her face. "Shoot," she said. "I'm going to be irritated if this is broken."

Estelle and Sally exchanged a glance at this relatively mild reaction. They'd both expected the heiress to exhibit more vanity.

"Pen," Estelle said, "where the flaming hell did you learn to fight like that?"

Pen evaded her eyes by dropping the first scoop of snow and gathering a second one. "Old boyfriend. Lieutenant in the Marines."

Estelle believed that as much as she believed Edmund's captors weren't going to try again, but Sally interrupted before she could press for a straight answer.

"Eww," she said, frowning at her hand. "I think I have vampire eyeball under my nails!"

Ben woke on the floor of a broom closet. His knees were shoved up to ensure he'd fit, and a lump the size of a goose egg throbbed behind his head. He'd been on his way to ring Robin on the lobby 'phone when an unseen assailant had laid him out.

"Crap," he said, using the doorknob to regain his feet. The closet spun sickeningly around him, but he didn't wait for it to stop before he stumbled into the open. If he'd been attacked, chances were the girls had been, too. He needed to get to them.

As it turned out, his heart had thundered into overdrive for no reason. He found the girls sitting in the lobby with the hotel's extravagantly mustachioed manager. He was apologizing profusely, assuring them Schloss Oberbad was *not* a hotbed of criminal activity.

"It is tourists," he declared. "Crazy foreign tourists who don't know how to behave. The little *Fräulein* said she heard one of those scoundrels speaking Spanish, and that is proof."

The "little *Fräulein*" was Sally. She had the same supremely innocent look on her face that she always had when she told lies, so sweet and wide-eyed you'd think her mouth wouldn't melt butter.

Ben decided this wasn't a good time to share where he'd woken up.

"Ben!" she cried, as soon as she spotted him. She ran to him and hugged him, which was welcome, considering. Her enthusiasm, however, wasn't all joy at his presence.

"Don't ask questions," she whispered as he hugged her back. "We'll explain everything later."

This was when he registered the shocking state Pen was in.

"We're certain it's not your fault," she was saying to the manager, her tone somehow conveying the opposite. Her Southern accent had thickened, until more than a whiff of magnolias perfumed her words. She might look as though she'd been in a brawl, but she was every inch Arnold Anderson's hard-to-please daughter. "I assure you, we've no desire to sue or any silliness like that. No matter if those scoundrels were disguised, I'm convinced they weren't guests of *your* fine establishment."

The manager blanched at that suggestion. "I could call the *Polizei*," he offered unsurely.

"You could," Pen agreed. She leaned back and crossed her rather torn-up trouser legs. "I don't think *we* want all that fuss, but if you believe it would help catch whoever it was . . ."

"I'm sure it was only thieves," Estelle soothed, seemingly more for the manager's sake than Pen's. "They probably took one look at Sally's coat and assumed she was dripping jewels."

"Of course," said the manager. "And if the little *Fräulein* or any of you would care to use our hotel safe . . ."

Pen rose smoothly, drawing the others to their feet with her. "That's very kind of you, Herr Basel. I think we'll just return to our rooms now and let you know later if we need help."

Graham caught up to them as they all filed into Pen's rooms. Back from his reconnaissance, he looked flustered and a bit windblown. Ben had yet to receive a decent explanation of the attack. The girls had been too busy congratulating themselves on what a good team they'd made.

"What's going on?" Graham asked. "The manager practically bowed to me as I came in."

He did a double take when he caught sight of Pen's battered face.

"Good Lord, Pen," he burst out. "Can't I leave you alone for ten minutes?"

"Oh, pardon me," she retorted. "I thought you'd be grateful if I helped save your little sister from a bunch of fiends!"

You have to go home," Ben said to Sally, caught between fury and pleading.

They were still in Pen's rooms, though Pen and Estelle had left to see if the hotel doctor could tape Pen's nose. She'd refused Graham's offer to try to heal it, reasoning that the hotel staff had already seen the damage, and having it magically disappear would be suspicious. His aid rejected, Graham leaned against the wall with his big arms crossed. The news that Sally was pregnant hadn't gone down well, and she hadn't yet revealed who the father was. Graham looked every bit as disgusted with her female stubbornness

as Ben was—not that either of their disapproval budged
Sally. The angrier they got, the more truculently her little
lower lip pushed out.

"I am *not* leaving you," she said.

"Sally, please," Ben begged. "Didn't you listen to
Estelle's stories of what she saw in her dream? Those vampires tried to abduct you because they're convinced that if
the professor drained you to the point of death, he'd change
you into what he is. He'd do it to save your life. They think
you're his weakness."

Sally sat up straighter in the sleek Danish-style armchair. "My child is not going to grow up"—*without a
father*, Ben could almost see her thinking—"believing her
mother is a coward. Anyway, I've proven I can take care of
myself."

"Oh, really? Would that be because you can scream at
twice the volume of anyone else?"

"You're his weakness, too," Sally said tartly. "Or do you
honestly believe the professor doesn't love you as much as
me?"

"You're a girl." Ben ignored the burn that threatened
behind his eyes. "He's more protective of you."

"*You're* more protective of me. *He* loves us all the same."
She rose so she could grip his arms, her hold so tight she
had to feel him trembling. "I love my baby, Ben. Probably
more than you might believe. But everything in me, every
instinct I have, tells me staying here is what I should do.
Daddy needs all of us to save him."

Despite his efforts, Ben's tears slipped free. "You said
her."

"What?"

His voice was completely choked, even after he cleared
his throat. He spoke quietly so only she could hear. "You
called our baby a her."

Sally's cheeks flushed the color of a rose. "Well, I wasn't
thinking. For all I know, it's a he."

"*Our baby?*" Graham repeated, pushing off from the wall.

Ben's heart stuttered. He'd forgotten Graham's hearing was extra sharp. His brother gave him a long, cool stare—which he was even better at now that he was a vampire—then shook his head. Ben couldn't help but think he didn't seem entirely surprised. Disappointed, maybe, but not surprised.

"Don't tell, Graham," Sally pleaded, clutching Ben's arms harder. "I don't want anyone to know until this is over."

Graham blew out an ironic laugh. "Oh, right. As if I'd want to drop that bomb a second before I have to!"

Castle Lohengrin

Durand would give Li-Hua one thing: She was never short of nerve. She'd taken the news of the bungling of the Fitz Clare girl's capture as coolly as he'd reported it.

"It's my responsibility," he said, standing—literally—on the carpet in the gilded black and crimson room. This had been the old duke's study. Like the rest of the castle, it had come with its furnishings, including a substantial ebony writing table with ivory inlay. The grandeur of Durand's surroundings didn't uncoil his nerves. He remembered being called before his father in rooms like this when he was mortal, wondering if he or one of his brothers-in-arms would feel the whip that time. The memory made him square his shoulders determinedly. "I'm the one who trained the men and assigned them to this mission."

"So you are," Li-Hua said.

She stood behind Manuel, the leader of the ill-fated team. Manuel sat in her desk chair, a thronelike affair of carved wood and red velvet. He wasn't chained there, but he might as well have been. Like many of Durand's men, he regarded Li-Hua with more awe than Frank. Though she was younger, her temper was the more vicious of the pair, a trait that earned her much admiration—as long as the admirer wasn't on the receiving end of it.

Now she stroked Manuel's shoulders with her long scarlet nails, a gentle, erotic gesture that her victim had no trouble recognizing as a bad sign. Pink sweat popped out on his forehead and rolled down, causing him to blink painfully. His right eye wasn't healing like the rest of his bruises. When Li-Hua trailed one finger beside the seeping mess, the three remaining members of Manuel's team— who had lined up stiff and silent before a wall of bookcases—winced in an unusual display of sympathy.

"One would think," Li-Hua observed to the room at large, "that Captain Durand was being overly cautious in assigning four *upyr* to abduct one small human."

"She fought like a hellcat," the Spaniard said. "I couldn't shut her up in time. And then those others came to help her. They were stronger than mortals should be. I think Fitz Clare did something to them."

Li-Hua looked at Durand.

"It's possible," he said to her unspoken question. "Some elders can share their power with humans. And it might explain why the girl inflicted a lasting injury."

"Well, *someone* has to pay for this blunder," Li-Hua said, "and thank you for your noble offer, Captain Durand, but *you* are too valuable to me."

One of Manuel's teammates gasped as she pulled a .45 Colt semiautomatic from the waistband at the back of her black trousers. The thing looked like a cannon in her petite hand.

"We're already short of men," Durand pointed out, acting as if the appearance of this weapon needn't mean anything. He ignored how many times he'd done the same—to no avail—with regard to his father's whip. "It seems likely Manuel will work all the harder to compensate for failing."

"Yes, it does," Li-Hua agreed, after which she lifted her arm, cocked the pistol, and shot one of the other three through the heart.

Her marksmanship was so good the *upyr* didn't have time to do more than widen his eyes. The instant the iron projectile reached his vulnerable center, he disappeared in a burst of light.

As he did, Li-Hua licked her lips and smiled. The book that had sat on the shelf behind him spat out a little rain of pulverized paper.

"There," she said, thumbing the safety on and tucking the gun away at the small of her back. "Now we're ready to move on . . ."

Schloss Oberbad

Having to sleep made Graham feel like an idiot.

Everyone needed rest; he accepted that, but normal people slept when they chose to, not because the sun came up. Though he didn't dream—he'd learned *upyr* seldom did—he woke up as grumpy as if he'd endured nothing but nightmares.

His family had been attacked, the stupid castle Estelle had identified as Edmund's prison was better guarded than the crown jewels, and Pen had such a ramrod up her arse she wouldn't let him heal her broken nose. He stumped around the empty bedroom, pulling on his skulking clothes. It took an effort to make noise in his new condition, but it satisfied. The note Ben left on the hotel's stationery told him he and the girls were having dinner in Estelle's room. That reminded Graham of what he'd learned regarding Ben and Sally. Graham had thought his suspicions about the pair were a product of his mental turmoil after discovering Edmund's secret. He should have been so lucky. Now Graham's whole family was bollixed up.

He positively hated that Pen was witnessing it.

When he opened the door to his room, he found the woman herself sitting on the carpet in the passageway, leafing through that morning's *Zürcher Zeitung*. The date of *sechs Januar* startled him. The world moved on no matter what personal dramas one was embroiled in. He noticed Pen was dressed in a slightly more feminine version of the rough clothes he wore. The bandage that taped her nose was as white as the circles under her eyes were dark. Only one of those circles could be blamed on a blackened eye. She looked like hell: too skinny, too mannish, too obstinate. And still his body stirred and heated when she pushed to her booted feet.

"You're up," she said, smacking the folded newspaper on her thigh. "Good. Now we can go."

"You're not going anywhere."

She curled her lip, about to argue, then shifted in discomfort as something occurred to her. "Do you, um, need to have breakfast first?"

Her words streaked from his ears to his groin, hardening him so fast he felt like his cock had punched his trousers from the inside.

"Christ," he said and yanked her into his room. He shoved her to the wall and kissed her, grinding his groin against hers as her thighs wasted no time locking around his hips. God, she was strong, and she tasted like a feast he'd been starving for. The newspaper thumped to the floor, forgotten. Her hands slid down his back to grip his bum— as if he weren't already exerting enough pressure. With a growl he couldn't muffle, he grabbed her hair in his fist and tugged her neck to the side. Pen's erotic preferences being what they were, his roughness earned him a hungry moan.

She smelled too good not to run his tongue slowly up her throat.

"Yes," she groaned, her spine flexing. "Oh, Graham, yes."

He bit her, and she spasmed, her trousers going damp against his hardness. Loving that, he thrust his hand behind her zip and shot one finger into the heat of her. As he drank, her body clamped around it, and again—even harder—when his thumb found the slippery, silken bud of her clit. He rubbed the swelling in a circle against her pubic bone. She was his slave then, writhing and mewling with her desire to be driven to one more peak—making up for the years she'd done without, he supposed. He didn't come himself, ruthlessly reining in his body's responses. He had other pleasures, in any case.

The strength of her blood coursed through him, his elation at imbibing it out of proportion with the crudeness of the act they were engaged in. Doing this with her shouldn't have been so easy, shouldn't have felt so wonderful and right. It was only blood he was drinking, the same as any human had.

His triumph had taken on an edge of resentment by the time he released her neck.

Pen blinked rapidly and swallowed, temporarily bereft of speech. Her legs unlocked from his hips as her gaze slid down him, the huge bulge at his groin declaring him unvanquished. *Her* knees were wobbling. Graham smirked at her, which naturally she couldn't stand.

"Get your hand out of my pants," she ordered, once she was able to.

"I healed your nose," he said, determined to enjoy his revenge, "and took down the swelling in your eye."

Pen's hand flew to each in turn. "Damn it, Graham, I told you not to do that!"

"If anyone asks, just say you're good with makeup."

She glared at him. "I'm still coming with you tonight. This little . . . stunt didn't distract me."

"Then perhaps I should remind you I need you to look out for my family."

"Estelle can fight. And presumably so can Ben."

"Maybe so," Graham agreed, "but you're the one whose eyes are sharp enough to keep them out of trouble in the first place. I'm counting on you, Pen. I'm trusting you with the safety of the people I care most about."

"Bull," she retorted, her tone so reminiscent of her plain-speaking father that he had to smile. "You just want me out of your way."

"You can't deny it makes sense for you to stay. They're easy targets otherwise."

"What will you be doing while I'm guarding your near and dear?"

"Taking a second crack at Castle Lohengrin. There's got to be some way in. Some weakness in their security."

"The longer you take to find it, the more precarious everyone's safety is."

"I know," he said. The dubious thrill of besting her drained away. He put his hand on her lean shoulder. That felt uneasily right as well. "If I don't find a way in tonight, I'll ask you and Ben to make a round of the shops tomorrow during the day. Maybe someone in the village will know something."

Pen narrowed her eyes, set her jaw, then gave him a reluctant nod.

"Good," he said and walked out the door with her watching him.

How much he did trust Pen surprised him—at least in regard to this. Asking her to guard his family was no ploy. In Estelle's accounts of the attack on Sally, her respect for Pen's abilities had been clear. If Estelle thought Pen knew what she was about, Graham didn't see how he could continue to question it.

Two hours later, Graham was hunkered down on the dark and icy terrace of a traditional Swiss-style restaurant called Theobald's. It was probably the same establishment Estelle had dreamed about, because its view of Castle Lohengrin was dead-on. It felt eerie to think of Li-Hua walking around in there. She'd been the one who started him on this journey, pretending to be his handler at MI5, telling him the truth of what Edmund was. She'd also been the first vampire to bite him, though she'd thralled him into forgetting it at the time.

That stirred a shiver he'd have preferred to deny. In the process, she'd also given him his first taste of the darker side of sex.

Ignoring the reaction, Graham kept his field glasses on his nose. He was trying something new with his glamour, pulling shadows around him rather than a more human look. The technique seemed to be working. Thus far, none of the diners had glanced out the windows to where he was. He only wished he could trust the trick to fool his own kind.

He'd been watching the castle from different angles in the village. There was only one approach anyone less than an expert climber could scale: a twisting road the vampires used for deliveries of food for their servants and other supplies. Graham could have scaled the mountain almost anywhere, but once he reached the castle grounds, he'd have been stuck. He couldn't find a hole in their defenses. Every viable entry was barred or watched. Nor was stowing away an option. It might be dark, but the delivery people's faces were verified with torches and their wagons searched. The nearest residence to the castle was a sled dog farm at the mountain's base, probably geared toward entertaining tourists who were tired of tobogganing. Graham didn't see how its presence helped. He had a better view from up here.

"Sodding hell," he muttered, his fist balling on his thigh.

And then he saw the big gray tomcat trotting happily down the switchback.

The reason for its sprightly pace wasn't hard to identify.

It had what looked like the back end of a fish dangling from its mouth: a baked and fileted fish, if Graham's eyes didn't deceive him. A baked fish suggested this cat had found its way into the castle's kitchen, invited or otherwise. Ideas began to bubble in Graham's mind. He was young to try them, but they weren't beyond the realm of possibility.

He made up his mind between the cat's heartbeats, streaking down into the valley and up the track at a velocity no human could have perceived.

No doubt if the cat had sensed him coming, it would have bolted. Instead, when Graham grabbed it from behind, it squeaked in surprise and dropped its dinner. Both cat and meal smelled atrocious, but Graham stooped to retrieve the fish anyway. Reunited with its prize, the cat left off trying to rip him up with its claws. It even purred a little when Graham ventured to scratch it beneath its chin.

As far as Graham was concerned, its contentment was to the good. This stinky feline might be his ticket to redemption.

Let me get this straight," Sally said. "You want to turn yourself into a pussycat. This pussycat, to be precise."

The pussycat in question was curled up in Sally's lap. She sat cross-legged on the floor of her and Estelle's room, her back resting on the bed between Estelle and Ben's legs. Sally had taken one whiff of the creature Graham had smuggled in beneath his coat and had snatched it away for a bath.

Fortunately, the stray was not a yowler. There had been some low growls, a great deal of splashing, and a yelp or two from Sally, but in relatively short order the deed was done. The cat had forgiven her more readily than Graham would have thought, probably due to her drying and petting it with a towel until its gray pelt shone like satin between its various pale fight scars. Now it blinked at Graham with inscrutable yellow eyes, purring loudly enough to be audible across the room.

"Robin and Edmund's line of *upyr* are shapechangers," Graham explained. "They can join with the soul of any animal, but, traditionally, they choose wolves. If I show up as a cat, I shouldn't raise alarms."

"Are you certain you can pull it off?" Estelle asked. "You're very new to your powers."

She sat on the edge of the bed with Ben. Her tone was careful, as if she didn't want to discourage Graham but felt obliged to ask.

"I spoke with Robin," he said. "He explained the process and said there would be no harm in attempting it. Lucius's get, which Robin is, have all been powerful. There's a chance Robin passed that advantage along to me."

"It's worth a try," Pen said, turning her head briefly from the window where she'd been holding the curtain gapped. "It would be extremely handy to get into that castle unnoticed."

Her support surprised him—warmed him even. Graham stared at her shoulders, slim and straight beneath the dark blue ski sweater she was wearing. She was looking out at the grounds again, keeping watch for them all.

Ben drew Graham's attention back by clearing his throat. "You sure you won't forget how to take human form? I'm not ready to have a brother who's furry."

"Robin says that's never happened. The *upyr*'s soul is always dominant over the animal."

Sally petted the rumbling feline between its chewed-looking ears. Clearly, this cat was used to fending for itself. "What happens to the cat?"

"Er," Graham said, because her expression had turned suspicious. "Robin says it poofs."

"Poofs?"

"Disappears in a flash of light. The same thing happens whenever one of my sort . . . expires."

"So you kill it," Sally said bluntly. The cat swiveled its head back at her change in mood.

"Not kill it," Graham corrected. "Just separate its spirit from its body and take it inside of me. After that, its spirit will live as long as I do. According to Robin, on some level, the familiar has to agree to the arrangement or it won't work."

"It's a cat!" Sally exclaimed. "How can it agree?"

"It's a living being. It has a consciousness. A soul. Some people claim pets have their own heaven."

The words called up a memory of his mother tucking him in at night when he was a boy. A puppy of his had been run over by a motorcar. *He's with the angels, Graham*, she had promised. *Playing fetch with them. They love him just like you did.* He could see her face as she said it, could hear her soft, soothing voice as she brushed his boyish tears away. When he thought of his parents, it was usually to remember losing them in the Great War. How thoroughly he'd forgotten what his mother had been like when she was alive shocked him now.

He had sound foundations, strengths that went back even farther than the ones Edmund and Robin instilled in him.

"Give me the cat," he said gently to Sally. "I want to talk to it in the other room."

Sally looked at his face and sighed.

Luckily, the tom didn't object to being handed over.

"Talk to it good," Sally warned. "Even cats deserve a choice."

"I'll go with you," Pen said. "I can watch just as well from the window in the sitting room."

Graham hesitated, then jerked his head in agreement. Someone looking out for him, just in case, sounded like a smart idea.

*   *   *

More than curiosity drove Pen to offer to go with Graham. The Fitz Clares were so darn cliquish she could have spit. Never had that been more obvious than *after* Pen helped save Sally's life. To be fair, Sally had warmed up a bit, but Ben continued to treat her like a stranger, polite to her because she suited his neck-biting big brother's convenience. Estelle remained the nicest, but even she tended to stop discussing "family" business when Pen drew near. Pen had heard more whispering in the past twenty-four hours than she had in all four years of female boarding school.

Did the Fitz Clares think she couldn't figure out what was up with Sally? Or miss the rather obvious identity of the daddy? Amazingly, Pen wasn't certain Estelle knew. She was treating Ben the same as she always had.

Pen reminded herself of one of her father's sayings, that sometimes it was better to keep your savvy under your hat. Negotiations were lost by men who thought the other guy was an idiot. The Fitz Clares' opinion of her didn't matter. She'd made up her mind to help them, and she was darn well going to stick to that.

To her relief, Graham didn't do anything too silly after they'd shut the adjoining door. His idea of "talking" to the cat involved sitting in a chair with it in his lap and petting it until both of their eyes closed. Once the pair was settled into their mental communion, Pen felt free to prop her shoulder on the window and gaze at them. Graham looked different when he was relaxed. His skin glowed a little as his glamour fell, but the biggest change was that his features were peaceful. Watching them, peace seeped into Pen as well. Being with Graham like this was nice. Not arguing. Not wishing they could jump into bed and do whatever they'd done the last time for twice as long . . . although, to be truthful, she might have felt just a smidge of that. Mostly, though, she experienced a degree of contentment she'd rarely known.

Stupid as it sounded, Graham's company suited her.

The big gray tom seemed to share her opinion. It rolled over in Graham's lap, exposing its furry belly to his scratches. As Graham obeyed the invitation, all four of its paws went limp.

"That's settled then," Graham said aloud, startling her.

She barely had time to catch her breath before Graham and the cat disappeared in a burst of light. Pen's skin prickled violently. She took a step toward the chair where they'd been sitting, then stopped herself. The light was still there, a sparkly, starry phosphorescence that seemed to be ringing like a distant chorus of bells. Pen and her father were haphazard churchgoers. Belief was more habit than conviction to her. Nonetheless, she knew, with a certainty that exhilarated, that the sparkly light she saw was Graham's essence. She was actually seeing and hearing a person's soul. The phenomenon was absolutely unexpected. Pen was afraid to blink, almost to breathe.

Could Graham blow away if she stepped wrong when he was like this?

The sparkles began to move faster, swirling above the empty chair in a small cyclone. Some were blue, some silver, some a pink so deep it approached ruby. Suddenly, all the colors drew together in a compact ball. As they coalesced, light flashed again, blinding her. Her ears popped at a change in air pressure. When her vision cleared, a giant cat crouched on the seat where Graham had been.

The tom had been a big feline, but Graham's version of it was huge, more backwoods cougar than house kitty. Whatever Graham had done to join his soul with it, the process had erased his familiar's scars. The cat gleamed with health and vitality. Seeming a little surprised to find itself where it was, it blinked and stretched—its needlelike claws digging in for purchase. Pen could not suppress a shiver of instinctive dread as its long pink tongue swept around its teeth. Possibly, the cat sensed her reaction. It shook itself and looked at her.

A spark of shock ran through Pen's awareness. She'd never seen eyes like that on an animal. They were a mix of brown and yellow, the colors striated and jewel-like. Their pupils narrowed vertically, just as a house cat's should. The intelligence behind them, however, the knowledge and consciousness, couldn't have been more human.

Oh, Lordy, she thought, too breathless to make a sound.

The cat let out an inquiring *mrrp* and jumped off the chair. Given its size, it should have thumped to the floor, but every paw landed silently. It padded to her to butt her leg, tall enough that its head had no trouble reaching her knee. Evidently, the cat that was Graham liked the texture of her wool trousers. He tilted his head and scraped the scent glands of his cheek over them.

Pen wondered if Graham knew he was marking her.

The bubble of humor that rose at that restored function to her lungs.

"Heavens, Graham!" she laughed. "Whatever kitchen window you sneaked out of, I hope it wasn't too small!"

Graham braced his paws on her thighs, the better to look at her. The way his nose twitched was the cutest thing she had ever seen. "Mrow?" he said, a definite note of complaint in it.

Pen couldn't help it. Her laugh became a snort and then a guffaw. The door burst open, the others' gasps of surprise causing tears to run from her eyes.

"Good Lord," Sally exclaimed in her inimitable way. "Graham, you're an elephant!"

Reaching for the cat's mind had been peculiar, like trying to speak to someone who only understood emotions and images. Graham had done his best to convey his wishes in the same fashion. He'd known when he succeeded because he'd sensed pleasure from the cat, satisfaction that it would have an ally from now on. Never again would it long for lost littermates. Never again would it lick wounds alone. In fact, if Graham could prevent it, it would never again be beaten.

The blending itself had been like slipping into a pool of stars. Warm. Sweet. The purest and most selfless peace he had ever known. The cat and he were one, as if they'd come from the same stream of energy in the first place.

Graham knew he'd never forget the feeling. He also knew it wasn't the sort of state a person could stay in long.

He'd been happy with the ease of his accomplishment until Pen began to laugh. Then his desire to snap back at her with human speech caused him to return to human form before he intended to.

"Graham!" Sally gasped, covering her eyes.

Ben began to snicker.

"Your clothes," Pen said, waving at him as she fought back amusement. "They seem to have 'poofed' along with the cat."

Graham looked down at himself. "Hell," he said, for he was indeed stark naked.

Estelle was kind enough to hand him the coverlet from her bed, though her eyes were also twinkling suspiciously.

"I couldn't have been *that* big," he protested.

Estelle and Pen both convulsed, which made him realize what he'd said could be taken more than one way.

"Have your fun then," he snarled, as he snatched the coverlet around him. "Ha ha. Isn't Graham a fool?"

"You're not a fool," Estelle soothed. "Just a little, er, more substantial than we expected."

"Robin didn't warn me! I thought I'd be the same size as it."

Pen patted his shoulder, almost succeeding in keeping her mouth from twitching. "You should still be able to sneak in as long as the vampires don't look at you too closely. Maybe they'll mistake you for a mountain lion."

"And Lord knows *that* wouldn't be suspicious!" Graham sighed, then rubbed his hands down his weary face. "I have to do it. We don't have another choice."

"You'll be fine," Ben assured him. "Don't forget you managed to do what even Robin didn't think you could."

"Your cat was really pretty," Sally added, clearly trying to make up for her elephant comment. "Much better looking than it was before."

She drew a laugh from him without meaning to.

"Very well," he said. "If you can make the best of this, so can I."

Castle Lohengrin

Because the night was young and none of them were feeling patient, Graham decided to make his rescue attempt that night. After some debate, cut short by Pen reminding them the clock was ticking, Graham agreed to let Ben accompany him as far as the mountain's base. There wasn't much Ben could do from there if anything went wrong, but at least he could guard Graham's clothes.

"I'll watch over the others," Pen promised.

Graham looked past her shoulder toward Sally and Estelle. Estelle was crying just a little, her emotions overcoming her as the possibility of Edmund's freedom drew so near.

"Good luck," she said, swiping impatiently at her cheeks. Despite her tears, she was impossibly beautiful, her smooth skin flushed and her gray eyes bright.

To Graham's surprise, he didn't feel the pang of longing he once would have.

Sally bit her lip and waved, and then—as if their bodies

had agreed to do it at the same time—both brothers turned to leave.

They took a sheltered path from the hotel to the castle's mountain, one hikers used in warm weather. Graham stopped inside a circle of snow-encrusted pines to strip off his clothes.

"Brr," Ben said, watching him.

The chuckle that vibrated in Graham's throat was welcome. No one could accuse his family of giving in to depression. He handed the folded pile to Ben. "I'm not cold, but if you start feeling the chill too much, go back to the Oberbad. To paraphrase what a wise man once said to me, you getting frostbite isn't going to help anyone."

"What if you couldn't find your things again without me? Surely you wouldn't stroll into the hotel naked."

"I'd climb the wall. And hopefully crawl in the right window."

Ben considered his brother's amused expression. "You aren't minding this as much as before. Being a vampire, I mean."

"No," Graham said after a pause to realize it was true. "It's turning out to suit me better than I thought."

He might have begged to differ with his own opinion after he changed back into a cat again. It wasn't the physical transformation that was hard, but the one that—unexpectedly—happened in his brain. He butted Ben's leg in parting and bounded off, trying to act as if all was well while every thought that ran through his head seemed to have a slightly skewed shadow. He had to force himself to follow the brush beside the winding road up the mountain. The portion of him that was cat wanted to prowl after interesting scents and skitter away from rustles. Oddly, Graham was seeing in shades of blue and green with no red at all, but what he saw was extremely clear. In his cat form, his vision was even more enhanced than before.

Despite Graham countermanding its less-convenient urges, the tom seemed happy enough. It noticed it was stronger and didn't mind the cold. For his part, Graham found he rather liked running on four legs. Apparently, it would be a while before his cat form was capable of vampire speed. All the same, the cat had amazing control over its body. As long as Graham relaxed and let it happen, every one of its many muscles moved fluidly.

Robin had said his experience of his familiar being separate from himself would fade. Graham wondered if he'd conclude he'd always liked chasing mice.

For now, as he reached the summit and the castle's turrets towered over him, Graham tried to give the cat its head. He was glad the tom stuck naturally to the shadows, thus avoiding the patrols, though it did stop to sniff more spots than Graham would ever have wanted to. Finally, they reached the window that was the cat's favored entry point.

The cat would have continued, but Graham stopped and sat on his haunches. Without thinking, he flicked his tail in dismay.

The window was *small*, an incredibly narrow rectangle in the cellar level's stone. Its glass had been popped out long ago. Smells poured out of it, and steam, suggesting that this was—as he had presumed—an entrance to the kitchen.

The joke Pen had found so hilarious came uncomfortably back to him.

People said if a cat could squeeze its head through a space, the rest of it would follow. At least, Graham thought it was the head. Maybe the saying referred to a cat's shoulders.

It looked like he was going to find out. The cat was urging him on, and he truly didn't have a choice. Cautiously, he laid his ears back and pressed his head inside. Whatever the room was, it was dark—a pantry maybe, he thought.

His hindquarters nearly stuck, but by scrabbling on the icy ground behind him, he made it through.

He landed more heavily than he liked, his whiskers prickling at the difference in the air currents. Shelves rose above him, stacked with dimly glinting mason jars. He slunk around the slightly open door—

And found a drunken cook waiting with a broom.

The cat knew her all too well.

"Scat!" she cried, swiping at him with the harsh bristles. "I told you not to come back, you rascal. You're getting as big as a horse stealing my scraps!"

Graham clamped his mouth on the yowl that wanted to break from him and leaped out of the way. Fortunately, he was faster than the cook and was able to streak around her and out the kitchen door without being hit. The corridor outside was blissfully dark and empty, and the cook was too inebriated to pursue him there. As he heard her collapse back into the chair she'd been dozing in, he took a moment to let the cat's wildly thudding heart settle.

Calming allowed him to pick up a scent that really interested him, a smell he'd memorized as a human and not a cat: a cool, woodsy fragrance he hadn't known he could identify. Experienced through the filter of the cat's perceptions, he realized the scent meant safety to him, meant love and trust and the freedom to let down his guard and play. Never had his own feelings been so clear to him. They filled him with so much emotion that for a moment he couldn't move.

Edmund was here, and not far from where he stood.

He trotted toward the scent as fast as he dared, around a corner and down a long, stony passage lit here and there by bare electric bulbs. Since this castle only pretended to be medieval, modern pipes stretched along it, too. Graham could hear water running through them, the sound intermittent and sluggish. His tail was up with excitement, his ears pricked forward. Finally, he reached the room he knew housed Edmund.

Its door was riveted steel with dents in its lower half, as if someone strong had been kicking it in anger. Bars blocked its small window. Looking up at the nearby wall, Graham spied a key ring hanging from a hook.

The cat wanted to jump for it, to grab it in its teeth or claws. Much as Graham appreciated its desire to help, Graham knew this was a break he couldn't exploit to its fullest in feline form. He made himself long to be human and did it a bit too well. The transition was so swift his head whirled momentarily. He steadied himself on the clammy wall, then slid the key into the lock and turned.

Though he'd braced for something bad, he still sucked in his breath on catching sight of Edmund lying on the surgical table. He was naked, and his eyes were closed. He looked like a starving person but also strangely beautiful: a golden-haired, fairytale prince sleeping under a witch's curse. His skin was shining with the faintest light, his bones as lovely as ivory. He wasn't dimming himself with glamour. This was simply all the energy he had left.

"Father," Graham said, laying his hand ever so gently on Edmund's arm. His wrists were bound with iron and looked raw, so Graham avoided touching him there. "Father, open your eyes. Estelle sent me to bring you home."

Edmund wasn't dreaming. Graham's voice was too real for that—though it wasn't the voice he'd been expecting. Durand must have been seeing to other business, or Graham couldn't have gotten in. The guard on Edmund had been unpredictable lately.

"What are you doing here?" Edmund asked as he forced his heavy eyelids up. "Where's Robin?"

"Robin took over X Section. Hold still for a moment. I'm going to get these cuffs off you."

Holding still Edmund could handle. What he didn't understand was why Graham seemed inexplicably different—

and never mind why he was rescuing him in the nude. Was this a dream, after all? Keys clinked, and pain stabbed briefly through his wrists. Immediately, as the iron was drawn away, Edmund felt more awake.

"*Jesu*," he said, squinting at Graham's face. It was as handsome as a statue of some long-dead Greek general, still rough but perfectly so. Graham's shoulders were broader than he remembered, his height an inch or two increased. He was the ideal version of himself, what nature and God had written into his genes as their ultimate potential. Edmund knew only one act that wrought such a change. "Son, what have you done to yourself?"

A muscle in Graham's cheek twitched as he freed Edmund's ankles, too. He moved quickly, smoothly, making Edmund's conclusion ever-more impossible to deny.

"I only did what I had to. What you would have done in my shoes."

"Graham . . ." Edmund tried to sit up, then discovered he was too weak.

"Here." Graham slipped an arm behind him. "Let me help you. Do you know if there's an exit we can break out of? I don't think you can fit through the hole I came in, even as a wolf."

That made no sense to Edmund. Graham was bigger than Edmund's wolf.

"The kitchen, maybe," he said, focusing on what seemed to matter. "I think it's near here, and there must be an entrance for deliveries. It will be guarded, but maybe we can take whoever is watching it by surprise."

His stomach clenched at the thought of humans who might be there, of the warm, rich blood coursing through their veins. His hunger had been quiescent, but now it roared back to life. He clenched his jaw as his fangs tried to lengthen. He wasn't going to lose control in front of Graham, not after he'd held off from hurting anyone this long.

"Can you change?" Graham asked as if he knew where

his head had gone. "If you can, there's food in the kitchen your wolf could eat."

Edmund gasped as Graham swung him effortlessly off the table and helped him stand. The pain of holding even a fraction of his own weight was incredible.

"I don't know," he said when the first wave of agony passed. "Maybe after I've been away from the iron longer."

"Can you drink from me?" Graham asked. "I don't think we have time to spare."

Edmund gazed into the eyes of his adopted son, which were glowing just a little with anxiety. Though he was an immortal now, the arm that held him was shaking. Awe fought with anger inside Edmund. Graham had done this for him, had changed his life forever for him.

"You might have to force me to stop," Edmund said. "I'm not certain, but I might be hungry enough to hurt you."

Graham's jaw hardened in the same stubborn manner that it had when he was human. "I can stop you. I wouldn't let you do anything you'd regret."

Edmund wasn't sure he believed that, but a moment later it was moot anyway.

"No, no, *no*," scolded a silky voice from the door. "This isn't what's supposed to happen."

It was Li-Hua, and Frank was right behind her.

"He's a vampire already," she complained to Frank. "He won't serve our purposes at all."

Graham did the only thing he could have. The instant Li-Hua's attention shifted, he dropped Edmund and rushed the pair. He would have had a chance to take them if his old fake handler hadn't pinned him with her eyes.

"*Stop*," she commanded, the word ringing like a gong through the cell's dank air.

Light flared in an acid yellow thread between her and Graham as she activated her dormant thrall. She'd been the first *upyr* to bite him, and her claim still compelled. Though Graham fought against it, her order slowed his rush just enough. Already running to meet his charge, Li-Hua's greater momentum slammed him back into the wall. Graham shook his head as if it were ringing and kneed her in the gut. Li-Hua doubled over, but flashed up an instant later with a length of iron chain between her gloved hands—the same iron Edmund had been bound with.

Graham was strong, but he was young, and Li-Hua had an edge in both speed and bloodthirstiness. Edmund could see where this would end if he didn't act. He struggled to his knees, only to have Frank catch hold of him from behind. He pulled Edmund's arms back so sharply they screamed with pain.

"I don't think so, Fitz Clare," he sneered next to Edmund's ear. "This is my sweetheart's show."

His sweetheart used the chain as a lever against Graham's throat, smashing his skull into the stone, over and over, until his eyes rolled back, and he passed out.

Naturally, she kicked him when he was down.

"Take that," she snarled at his fallen body, putting her thrall into it. "You just take that!"

Edmund was so incensed he actually found the strength to drive his elbow into Frank's face.

"Enough," Frank said, lazily backhanding him.

I'm going to kill you, Edmund thought from his helpless sprawl on the floor, his fangs running out with rage. *I'm going to fucking cut you and your lover into pieces before this is over.*

"You can try," Frank said, casting Edmund an amused smile.

Li-Hua dropped the chain and strode back to Frank. He slung his arm around her shoulders as they gazed at their two victims. Li-Hua was breathing hard but not winded.

"What now?" she asked her lover.

"Now we lock them both up and wait. If they keep running true to pattern, it shouldn't be long before the next heroic Fitz Clare appears."

* * *

Durand returned to take charge of chaining them, this time to rings in the wall, thankfully with enough play in the links to allow Edmund to sit on the floor. The mercenary brought them clothes—trousers anyway—which he gave them a chance to step into before securing their ankles. Graham was so groggy from the repeated blows to his skull that he couldn't fasten the garment. Cursing, Durand did up the front for him, despite Graham having tried to fight him when he first woke up. Edmund had no idea why the mercenary allowed them this dignity. His entire manner was frostily furious.

Once Graham and Edmund were secured, Durand carried Li-Hua's Hollywood-style camera in on its tripod. His careful positioning of the spotlights seemed ominous, and for the first time he also set up a microphone on a stand. Because Edmund had shared Estelle's dream-walk of Otto Teudt, the reason for this wasn't mysterious. Clearly, Frank intended to record every detail of subsequent events for his goose-stepping German friends.

Edmund thought Durand would leave without speaking, but he paused at the door. His eyes were narrowed slits of black ice.

"You could have spared yourself this," he said. "You should have done what I offered when you had the chance."

For two hours Ben paced a patch of snow under the ring of evergreens at the mountain's foot, beating his arms against his torso to combat the cold. More lights came on in the upper levels of the castle, until it glowed like a party was in full swing. To his frustration, he wasn't close enough to make out more than the windows' shapes. Something was going on up there. Something he didn't think boded well.

Shortly into the third hour, not wanting to give up, Ben

took off his coat and pulled Graham's shirt on top of his own. It warmed him more than he expected even before he tugged his coat back on, as if Graham's vampiric hardiness had suffused the cloth. He remembered borrowing Graham's clothes when they were boys, not long after Edmund adopted them. Back then he'd idolized Graham too much to care how stupid he looked with Graham's sleeves hanging past his hands. Graham was who Ben had wanted to be: big and fearless and absolutely reliable.

For God's sake, Graham, he thought, staring hard at the castle's lights. *Be reliable now.*

"It's time to come back," Pen said from a meter behind him.

He spun, taking a second to note she carried a wool blanket. His teeth were chattering so hard he could barely get his question out.

"Why aren't you with the girls?"

"Estelle and Sally are fine. You're the one who's going to freeze to death."

Her quiet eyes said she knew. Though he'd known himself for some time, Ben's stomach sank to his boots. "Graham didn't make it."

"He's alive," she said, after which she pulled a crooked face. "Estelle took a little nap and saw him get caught. I volunteered to come out here. They're both worried about you."

When she held the blanket out to him, Ben stepped back as if it would burn. "I can't wear that. I took his shirt."

"Okay," she said. "We'll leave the blanket here for Graham."

She dropped it onto the ground, where they both knew it would likely stay until some hiker stumbled over it next spring. She was humoring him like a child, but Ben didn't care. Despair was threatening to swallow him. Determined not to let it, he set his jaw and waved for her to precede him back along the path.

"I have a plan," she said after a minute of walking. Her voice was slightly hesitant. "For you and me. First thing tomorrow after it's light."

Was he supposed to ask what it was? Did it even matter? If Graham had failed, how could mere mortals hope to fare better?

Pen turned her head to look at him over her shoulder. "Estelle says some of the vampires will be asleep, and all of them will be tired. Graham didn't have that advantage. Plus, they won't be expecting what I've got in store. I picked up a few goodies from an old boyfriend in Zurich."

"All right," Ben said as politely as he was able to. He couldn't think about tomorrow. He only had energy for now.

She paused to stare at him—measuring him, he thought—after which she nodded and walked on.

After a moment, he remembered to say thank you.

Castle Lohengrin

$\sim\!\!\!\sim\!\!\!\sim\!\!\!\sim\!\!\!\sim$

Ben could not believe what Pen had in her steamer trunk. He'd helped her heave it onto her bed a minute ago. Had he known what was in it, he would have used a great deal more care.

"Pen," he said, his voice gone ragged. "Those are sticks of dynamite."

Pen wrinkled her nose sheepishly. "I know. I would have mentioned them earlier, but I thought it would be better, and quieter, to let Graham try to rescue your dad his way. Generally speaking, for most ops, low profiles are preferable."

"Pen, it's *dynamite*." Ben knew it was, because the eight-inch tubes were very clearly labeled. "You've had high explosives bumping around with your woolies since Zurich."

"Oh, that's all right. Dynamite is very stable without the blasting cap. You could actually set a match to it the way it is. It'd burn pretty well, mind you, but it wouldn't explode."

She grinned and handed him one of two light rucksacks. "I'll carry it if it bothers you."

Ben accepted the sack numbly. "Your 'old boyfriend' gave you explosives?"

"Well, I paid him," she said as if it were a trifling matter. "He's not *that* good of an old boyfriend."

"And you know how to use them?"

"I wouldn't have bought the stuff if I didn't." Pen squatted, reached under her bed, and pulled out a gun. For a second, Ben thought he might have a heart attack. It was a handgun, but it was big. With her finger outside the trigger, Pen pointed it at the floor. "Know how to handle one of these?"

"Er." Ben eyed it warily. "I've gone target shooting with friends."

Pen narrowed her eyes at him before shrugging. "That'll have to do, I guess." She balanced the dull silver monster sideways across her hands. "What you have here is a .45-caliber Colt pistol. Good stopping power. Reliable. Relatively slight recoil. You have to cock it before you pull the trigger the first time, but once you do, it automatically chambers the next round. Automatically ejects the spent one, too. You'll be carrying it hammer cocked, safety on."

Ben's palms broke into a sweat as she showed him how this was done. He nodded to indicate he'd understood. Indeed, his natural mechanical aptitude wouldn't have allowed him to be confused.

"Good," Pen said. "Now you've got seven rounds in the magazine, and I have extras ready that you can stow in your pockets. After they're empty, you'll have to reload. I didn't have time to special order iron bullets, so the best we can hope for is to slow down the bad vampires. Once that's done, these guys ought to finish the job."

From her trunk, she pulled out a pair of narrow bladed, metal handled fighting knives. They looked like the sort of weapons old-fashioned Italian bravos used. "Here's a sheath for fastening one on your thigh. Don't get fancy and try to throw it, because I only found these two with the iron. Just put the tip over the heart and shove." She threw a policeman's cosh onto the growing pile on the coverlet. "This is for any humans we come across. Unless they're trying to kill us, we should stick to knocking them out."

"Right," Ben said faintly.

Pen looked up at him in surprise. "Don't tell me you haven't been in fights. I'd have believed that of Graham, but not you."

"I've been in fights," he said. He didn't mention that most had happened when he was drunk. "Too often, probably. But—" He wet his lips. "Isn't there a gun for you?"

She laughed, soft and low, and he suddenly was reminded why she might appeal to Graham. That was the sort of laugh women saved for bed. "There's a gun for me, Ben. Don't you worry your pretty head."

He should have taken insult, but his nerves were too strained. With an effort, he refrained from sharing his theories on Americans and violence. Prohibition lay at fault, was his opinion. It had turned her whole country into a culture of gangsters.

Then again, a person who thought like a gangster might be just the thing right now.

"We're agreed then," Pen said, blissfully unaware of the talking-to she'd been spared. "Let's pack up and tell Sally and Estelle where we're off to."

With their curt and not entirely satisfactory leave-taking behind them, Pen was happy to inform Ben that her gun was a Suomi KP/-31 submachine gun.

Ben wondered if this was her idea of distracting him from the memory of Sally shouting like a fishwife. It wasn't Ben's departure she'd objected to; it was being ordered to remain at the hotel with Estelle.

Be quiet, Ben had snapped, *or I'll let her slap you like she's been itching to.*

Her was Pen, of course, and this threat had so outraged Sally that she'd gone icily silent. He and Pen left soon after, getting while the getting was good. They were now crawling from to cover to cover up the vampires' lightly forested mountain.

"The Suomi is as accurate as a rifle," Pen was gloating in a barely audible whisper. "And shoots more rounds per minute than a Thompson. I only wish it fired .45s, but it does have fantastic muzzle velocity. The Finns knew what they were doing when they built this baby."

She wore the "baby" slung around her back on a strap, allowing her to scoot along on elbows and knees. Ben didn't understand half of what she said but took her word for it. The only time he'd heard a woman wax that rhapsodic was when Sally cooed over a pair of shoes.

"Shh," Pen said, halting suddenly.

Ben didn't have to shush, because he hadn't been talking. His mouth did drop open when Pen rose up, took out her cosh, and hid behind a tree. A second later, he heard footsteps approach—a human, he gathered from the fact that the man was striding without wincing through a sunbeam. Pen stepped out and caught him behind the head as he passed, her downswing so forceful she grunted with the effort. Thankfully, the guard dropped without a cry.

He fell forward onto the gun he'd been carrying.

"What luck!" Pen said, easing the big weapon out from under him. To Ben's eyes, it looked even scarier than hers. "This is a Thompson. It might be too much for you to handle without instruction, but you can carry it in case I need backup."

She handed the thing to Ben. Then, when her victim stirred, she gave his skull another solid whack.

"Lord, Pen," he breathed. "Were you raised by wolves?"

Her expression cooled. "I was not, but as it happens, you

were. Perhaps you'd like to remember that and not get us killed?"

He sucked in a breath, but managed to bite back his response. He guessed he'd hit a nerve with his crack about her family.

"This isn't a game," she reminded him. "If this fellow regains consciousness, he's going to tell his friends we're here. It's all very well to fight fair and be gentlemen, but it's even better to stay alive."

"I understand," he said, trying not to show how nervous her words made him. "You might want to give the cosh to me. I have more upper body strength."

Pen's broad mouth curved in an unexpectedly sweet smile. "When I know you can creep up on the enemy as stealthily as I do, then you can have my toy."

She made him laugh in spite of himself. To his relief, the burst of humor steadied his resolve.

"Come on," she said. "The castle grounds are right through those firs."

Estelle must have been correct about patrols being thinner during the day. They darted across the open area without raising an alarm. Pen gestured for him to stick close to the castle wall, where Ben assumed any lookouts behind the windows would have blind spots.

Castle Lohengrin was huge, a little town with turrets. It was not, however, curtain-walled the way authentic fortresses were. He and Pen were up against the residence itself. Ben couldn't get over how postcard pretty the castle was, though the brick and stone seemed solid enough. Pen found the spot she wanted to one side of the grandiose arch of the main entrance. Crouching down, she shouldered off her rucksack.

"You keep watch," she said. "I'm going to set the charges."

Ben drew the Colt and took the safety off.

As he scanned the grounds around them, he heard Pen

chiseling through the mortar to make holes. The stuff must have been brittle, because her hammering didn't last long.

"Okay," she said in a tone so serious the back of his neck tightened. "I'm going to explain what happens next before I light the fuses.

"There's going to be a big damn boom when these sticks go off, and the castle of the swans is going to have a new front door. You and I will run through it with our heads covered, because a chunk of the wall will be raining down. Places like this invariably have a few slab-of-wood tables in their entry hall, something to stick flower arrangements on. We're going to grab one, turn it on its side, and use it as a barricade. When the vamps come scampering to find out what happened, you and I will pick them off. I'll take out whoever's guarding the door as we first go in. After that, if it moves, you shoot it—no ifs, ands, or buts—unless you think it's me. Don't take a shot that wouldn't be fatal if the target were human. Aim for the head or heart. Remember, a vampire without a weapon can still kill you. If it keels over, you use your knife on it. We want to thin their ranks as much as we can before we try to break your father out."

"What if the attacker is human?"

"If it's human and it's armed, you kill it. If it's not armed, do your best to make a judgment call."

Doing his best suggested she would condone him making a mistake. Sensing his shock, Pen looked up. She'd been sitting on her heels, and the new position had her squinting against the sun, her irises turned to gold.

"Your life or theirs," she said. "For that matter, your family's life or theirs. If you freeze up, you lose your opportunity to save them."

She didn't mention her own life, though that was surely also on the line. It struck Ben, with the force of a speeding train, that she was risking everything to help them. Everything she was. Everything she ever would be. Decision clicked inside him as decidedly as a tumbler dropping in the lock to a safe.

It didn't matter that Pen was a stranger who had pushed her way into this. Ben would fight as hard to defend her as he would for his family.

"I won't hesitate," he said.

She held his gaze a moment longer, then turned to light the fuses.

They ran maybe twenty meters, after which Pen pulled him flat to the snowy ground. Ben didn't have to be told to cover his head. The blast came seconds later, with a percussion that shook the earth under them.

"Go, go, go!" Pen urged, grabbing his arm.

Ben's ears were ringing, but he stumbled up after her. He knew she didn't want to lose the advantage of surprise. A gray-black cloud obscured the lorry-sized hole the dynamite had made, debris showering down on them as they ran through it. The space inside was positively Turkish in its luxury, a barrel-roofed assault on the senses, with multiple tiers of columns in colored stone stretching upward on either side. Even through the smoke, the sheer expanse of gold leaf glowed. Fully half the surfaces he saw appeared to have been dipped in it, and what wasn't gold was either precious inlay or rich frescoes. An incredible marble stairway led up to a gallery on the next level.

Pen jolted him back to the present by opening fire on a pair of shadows behind the door. The rat-a-tat blaze of bullets lit up the dissipating fog. Shaking himself, Ben spotted a heavy table just like Pen had described. He hurried to drag it across the floor to a more defensible position under the rightward gallery's overhang. Two more flashes, brighter than the bullets, told him Pen had "poofed" the vampires she'd shot.

He supposed he should be grateful regular ammo could knock them out.

"Lordy," she murmured, running back to settle beside

him at their barricade. "Those things disappear as clean as a whistle."

Ben didn't have a chance to reply. The next vampires showed up, with their own "Tommy" guns.

At first they were too fast for him to hit, even with the trail of their fire giving them away. Then something funny happened in his brain. It relaxed somehow and slowed, a bit like the moment when he understood what was wrong with a car's engine. The steady ping of bullets hitting far too close stopped distracting him. He realized he knew where the vampires were going to be before they got there. Maybe their muscle tension told him, or maybe it was just a thing that happened in battle. Whatever the reason, if he pointed the gun ahead of them, the bullet would meet them when they arrived.

"Good shot!" Pen praised as he hit one who'd been leaping for a bronze chandelier—no doubt hoping to swing down at them like a swashbuckler from a film.

Candles fell along with the stunned vampire, but the tapers weren't burning. Since the vampire was too close to simply leave lying, Ben unsheathed his knife and slipped out low to finish him. As he did, Pen laid down quick bursts of covering fire.

The instant the tip of Ben's blade reached flesh, the creature awoke.

Its eyes were blue and startled.

"Sven!" someone shouted from the wide marble stairs.

Pen cut down Sven's friend before the shout faded.

He must have been more powerful than the others they'd come up against. Riddled with bullets and separated from his gun, the vampire still had sufficient strength to drag his bloodied self farther up the steps, pretty much by his fingernails, past two of his less-lively, comatose colleagues.

"Finish yours," Pen said, already edging out from cover with her Suomi and her knife ready. "I'll take care of these jokers."

Ben knew he couldn't justify being any less practical.

Pen was right about the poofing. As soon as Ben shoved the iron deep enough, the vampire disappeared like he'd never been, without leaving a single ash. Despite the cleanness of the death, Ben's stomach rolled. He might be glad that their opponents had all been vampires—which was a strange thing to be glad for when you thought about it. Nonetheless, ending a life of any sort wasn't the same as knocking down tin cans.

The death shook him enough that he was lucky the shooting seemed to have stopped.

"Got them," Pen said, trotting back to him from the stairs. When Ben looked, the bodies that had been lying there were gone. The damage the firefight had inflicted on the formerly sumptuous space was jaw-dropping: frescoes shredded, columns knocked awry; it was worse than Viking marauders. Ben couldn't even think what he felt about the destruction.

Pen herself looked pale as she surveyed the area, her face streaked with cordite and sweat. A splinter from the table had pierced her arm deeply enough to cause bleeding. Ben reach over to tug it out, a service she scarcely seemed to notice. The huge entry hall was quiet but for the clink of spent brass rolling on the fancy, rubble-strewn floor. Ben watched her cock her head to the side.

"I don't hear any more coming, and I think we took more than a dozen out of the game. You want to go after your father?"

"You know how to get to the cells?"

"I think so," Pen said. "This place is famous. Lots of people visited when the mad duke's family had possession. I got a good description from my boyfriend."

Her preparedness no longer came as a surprise, though he thought her boyfriend story was a load of guff. Ben shoved a fresh magazine into his pistol and gestured for her to take the lead. Yes, he was the man and ought to protect her, but the way things were going, he reckoned danger could come at them from either direction.

With the hurdle of the fight surmounted, Pen was more optimistic about their odds. She'd gotten through her first real battle—the others having been training exercises with plenty of protective gear—and neither she nor Ben had been shot. Vampires might be super fast and strong, but an aptitude for hitting the side of a barn must not have come with the deal. Ben, on the other hand, had proved to be a freakishly good shot, as good as any professional marksman. He hadn't lost his nerve, either, which was definitely helping Pen keep hers. She was—in essence—the senior officer here. She couldn't afford to fall apart in front of her subordinate.

Fortunately, her contact's information about the castle's layout was reliable. As predicted, the formal state dining room had a paneled staging area on one end, for servers to organize the platters. It was here she'd been promised the door to the kitchen and cellar was.

"Damn," she said when she tried the knob. "It's locked."

She dug her picking tools from a pocket in her rucksack. To her dismay, the firefight must have shaken her more than she realized. Her normally deft fingers wouldn't cooperate.

"Let me," Ben said, laying a gentle hand on hers.

Pen blew out her breath and stepped back. When he hunkered down and peered into the keyhole, he seemed to know what he was doing. Even so, it rankled that his hands were steady.

"Misspent youth?" she suggested.

"I work in a garage. People are always locking themselves out of things."

A satisfying click told her he'd succeeded. He turned

to her, grinning and about to speak, when a look of horror washed over his face.

"Pen!"

She'd let down her guard; forgotten to watch their backs in this little room. She knew a vamp was behind her even as the submachine gun butt smashed into her skull. Her last thought before everything went black was that if she didn't die, her father would kill her.

Her return to consciousness some time later didn't contradict that fear.

She was lying on cold cement, half curled up on her side, with her wrists bound behind her back. Her head ached worse than one of her mother's migraines—or so she imagined; she'd never actually had one. She was trying to breathe through the pain when two small hands gripped her shoulders and hauled her upright, startling her eyes into opening.

The space was so brightly lit that tears blurred her view of it. When her vision cleared, she saw she was in a stone-lined cell about twelve feet square. A gag had been shoved into her mouth, making swallowing difficult. Ben was already sitting up, similarly trussed a foot away from her. Directly opposite them, a tall, pale man in nothing but a pair of trousers sat on the floor. He was staring at his bare white feet—determinedly so, she thought. His wrists and ankles had been secured to bolts in the wall, though the chains were long enough for him to hug his knees.

It took a moment for her to identify him as a vampire. *Upyr* were strong and healthy, and this man was ungodly thin. He was hard to look away from, his wasted state both horrifying and weirdly attractive. Only when the chains beside him rattled did she spy Graham standing next to him. Graham's eyes flared as they met hers, sending a strange, hot tingle streaking down her spine.

That reaction, she thought, wasn't quite appropriate.

The sound of a woman's voice coming from her right tore her gaze away.

"Here we have it," she said, as if continuing a conversation whose beginning Pen had missed. "The classic moment of choice beloved by philosophers. Who shall the hungry vampire feed on? The stranger's child or his own? I don't know about you, but I'm on tenterhooks waiting to find out!"

This was when Pen realized the starving vampire must be Graham's father.

She looked at the woman who had spoken in such arch British tones. She hadn't been born in England, Pen didn't think. Her voice held the slightest shadow of the Orient. As petite as she was lovely, she was dressed in a red-and-white-striped top that made her look like a miniature French sailor. Well-worn denim clad her slender legs, and a jaunty black beret perched atop her straight, shining hair. Odd fashion choices aside, she was a vampire, without a doubt, as were the two tall males who stood behind her. The blond vamp in the double-breasted suit was larger, but the lean, dark one struck her as the more lethal. The blond was smirking. The other had a face that could have been carved from ice. He wore a soldier's black uniform.

As if to emphasize how alien they were, all three of them were glowing.

"Well?" said the female, addressing Edmund. "We did what you asked and brought someone older. Now which of these two morsels looks tastier to you?"

Graham's father was breathing harder than he'd been before, his hands fisted white-knuckled on his chains. Pen became uncomfortably aware of the blood that stained her shirtsleeve. Nostrils flaring, Graham's father shook his head silently.

"Can't choose?" chided his tormentor. "Maybe we should let your prospective victims plead for their lives."

Pen didn't think she liked the sound of that. Graham

had never harmed her when he fed, but his father's condition was clearly desperate. His head came up slowly to face her. Pen's heart jumped into her throat. Now that she saw his face, he resembled the sort of angel who gathers souls: a beautiful death's head. She shuddered, and he did, too. The consciousness that gleamed behind his sapphire eyes wasn't human. His fangs were already extended, shining white and sharp in his parted mouth. In spite of the spotlights filling the room with glare, his pupils swelled with a predator's eagerness. Pen couldn't keep her pulse from accelerating. When he licked his lips, she knew she wouldn't live out the hour.

The professor had a choice: kill his own son or her. By no stretch of the imagination could she expect to be spared.

"No, Father," Ben said.

The female vampire had removed Ben's gag. His father swiveled only his head toward him, a motion that was oddly mechanical. For one brief second, something like despair flickered behind his extremely intent expression.

"I'm willing," Ben said, as if his father were staring at him normally. "Everything I am I owe to you. There's no need to take from her what I give freely."

"I'll kill you," his father warned hoarsely.

"Even so," Ben answered.

"Oh, how touching!" the vampiress exclaimed, her little hands clapping. "Frank, why don't you facilitate their arrangement while I get the film going."

Pen hadn't noticed the motion picture camera on its tripod in the corner. The blond man, the one the female had called Frank, had been blocking it with his body. He moved to help Ben onto his feet, scorn clear in the twist of his handsome mouth.

Pen hadn't been the only one who'd assumed her heartbeats were numbered.

"Help your father to his feet," Frank ordered Graham.

Graham did so haltingly, his gaze sliding uneasily to Pen. Pen's stomach clenched. Did Graham wish the professor had chosen her? Would Pen have felt the same in his shoes?

"It's all right," Ben said, drawing Graham's attention back. "This is the right thing to do."

The female vampire, now stationed behind the camera, began to laugh throatily. "My God, they're all too precious for words!"

"Ben," said the professor, ignoring her.

Standing now, he held Ben's arms above the elbows, his bare, thin chest going in and out with his breathing. Except for his expression, which bore the anguish of ages, he looked no older than his son.

Plainly fascinated, the vampiress turned the camera's crank, the clicking of the film distinctive and steady. Ben looked into his father's eyes. The hair on Pen's arms lifted. His father was behind his face again, a thinking person rather than a starving animal. Pen had the distinct impression that silent messages were passing between the two of them.

"Yes," Ben said, and in a flash too fast to follow, his father's teeth struck his neck.

Edmund had never known such terror or such pride as when Ben volunteered to feed him. The love he was demonstrating, the protective instincts not only toward Edmund but to this woman who had come with him, overwhelmed him with emotion. Ben was a son any father would have been honored to call his own.

He wanted more than anything to wrestle his immortal drive for survival into submission. Ben seemed to sense him trying. *Don't be afraid*, Ben said straight into his mind. *Once my blood makes you strong, you can save the rest.*

Edmund wavered half a second too long. *You're sure?* he asked, quite without meaning to.

"Yes," Ben said.

That was all it took for Edmund's nature to overrule his will.

It was the darkest moment of his existence, drinking from his own son to save himself. He'd never used his children for food. He was their nurturer, not they his. The strength of his shame began to tear him away, but as Ben's hot blood ran into his mouth, an utterly unexpected awareness dawned.

Frank and Li-Hua had made a serious mistake.

Like all his adopted children, Ben was a little more than human. He'd been absorbing Edmund's energy, Edmund's love, bit by bit all his life. Now he acted as a supernatural battery, freely returning everything Edmund had given him. Barriers gone, their auras lapped together the way Edmund had seen infants do with their mothers while in the womb. The sensation of connection was incredible. Every thought and feeling Ben had ever had was bared to him. Good or bad, to Edmund they were beautiful, as if his organs of judgment had been removed. Only Estelle had ever felt so close to him. Edmund wanted to shelter Ben forever, to never let him feel less loved than this, despite which—at that moment—Ben seemed his absolute equal. Mortal or immortal didn't matter. The spiritual stuff in which Ben lived and moved and had his being was exactly as important, and as potent, as the stuff that powered Edmund.

In less time than he would have thought possible, Edmund returned to full master strength.

The whole world seemed to sparkle, washed clean, charged up with the pure, basic force of life. Edmund healed Ben's neck with a thought, then pulled back to smile at the baffled wonderment in his face. This was not the fatal ordeal his son had been girding for, though he had in truth been altered. Edmund saw he had nearly changed him, without even trying to. Ben's aura danced, the faintest blue-white fire flickering above his still human skin.

"Dad," Ben breathed. "What did you do to me?"

"*Scheiss*," Frank murmured, and Edmund knew his smile had turned feral.

I made you stronger, he thought, his hands on Ben's shoulders. *Go help your brother break out of those iron chains.*

"Hey!" Li-Hua protested a second before Edmund snapped his own cuffs.

She'd started forward when Ben moved, but Frank caught her back by the arm, swifter than she to recognize what was going on.

Durand was the quickest of them all. He was no longer in the room. Edmund didn't care about that as long as the rabid lovebirds remained in reach.

"Now," he said, his rage rising up like joy, "you two are going to get yours."

They ran and he roared with pleasure, his wolf exulting at the prospect of a chase. Down the corridor his captors blurred, through the smoky kitchen and up the stairs to the cavernous dining room.

There, Durand turned up again, slowing Edmund with a fusillade of submachine gun fire. Happily, the bullets weren't iron. Frank and Li-Hua weren't about to supply their little army with ammunition that could kill them.

Edmund pushed through the barrage like it was a wind.

"Still defending your charming employers?" he sneered, watching Durand's eyes go white as he kept coming. "How admirable."

Durand's gun ran out of bullets. Edmund was on him in a single bound, grabbing his arms and throwing him. The mercenary sailed above the length of the giant table, not even touching it. It took the carved stone mantel of the walk-in fireplace to stop his flight. He hit so hard one of the caryatids lost its head. A lesser *upyr* would have been concussed. Durand caught himself as he fell and took off running.

Though Edmund had every intention of pursuing, his knees surprised him by giving out and dropping him to the floor. Bullets were pushing from him, dozen upon dozen. He panted as they hit the Turkey carpet in a little metallic rain.

"Dad!" Ben cried, catching up and grabbing him.

Ben must have succeeded in freeing Graham, because Edmund's other son came up a moment later with the human woman hugged to his side. What she was doing here Edmund didn't know, though there did appear to be a bond between her and Graham.

"Pen destroyed the film Li-Hua took," Graham informed him, as if he wanted Edmund to admire her presence of mind. His profile turned from side to side. "Which way did they go? We mustn't let them escape."

Graham's fangs were run out like Edmund's, but he was speaking clearly enough. Robin had changed him, he realized. The stamp of Edmund's blood son was all over him.

"Um," Pen interrupted before he could speak. "Am I the only one who's bothered that it's dusk?"

She waved at the room's high clerestory windows, causing all of them to glance up.

"Shit," Ben said. "We were knocked out longer than I'd guessed."

"My thoughts exactly," Pen agreed. "Which means the vampires we didn't kill this morning will be waking up."

Schloss Oberbad

◆══════════◆

Jesus buggering Christ," Graham swore, shocking Pen. "We have to get these two to safety before we go after Frank and Li-Hua."

Pen had been secretly enjoying the way Graham had taken her under his muscular wing, but this was more coddling than she had any desire for.

"No," she objected, shoving at his chest. "You can't let them get away! Not after everything they've done. Ben and I can take care of ourselves."

"Not against vampires," Graham said grimly. "Not after dark."

"Tell them we'll be fine," she begged Ben, but her former partner didn't look as confident as before. He should have. He'd held his own this morning, and he'd been strong enough to help his brother free himself from his chains. So what if whatever his father had done had rocked him? Now was not the time to lose their momentum.

Graham's father let out a sigh. "He's right, Miss—"

"Anderson," she snapped, "but for God's sake, call me Pen."

Nothing could have made her more aware of Graham's father's otherworldly nature than the change in him since he'd bitten Ben. He looked a different man now: his flesh filled out, his breathtakingly beautiful face shining. His vampire glow, which he had tamped down, almost seemed to hum. He opened his perfect mouth to speak, then shut it and listened.

"I hear them," he said. "At least two dozen, converging on the entry hall."

Two dozen vampires were enough to give Pen pause, but she was convinced Edmund and Graham didn't need to abort their mission. If worse came to worse, she and Ben could hide out of the way somewhere.

The professor turned to Graham before she could say so.

"Take care of Ben," he said. "I'll get Miss Anderson out the front before they reach us."

Then he simply picked her up and ran.

If she hadn't lost her breath, she would have yelled in protest. It didn't feel like a person was carrying her. The muscles of his chest were absurdly hard, his skin impossibly smooth and cool. The only time she'd moved this fast was in an aeroplane, and for that she'd been high above the ground. Wind tore through her hair and clothes, pushing her back against Graham's father as the corridor and entry hall whizzed by. They were outside, under the fading sky, before she had a chance to even look for coming attackers.

"Here!" a voice cried somewhere to the left of them. "Edmund, stop!"

Edmund halted so abruptly her brain took a moment to catch up to the rest of her. To her amazement, they were halfway down the mountain in a scattered stand of evergreens. A dogsled, of all things, sat beside their path. Estelle and Sally stood in its back, waving. It was Estelle who'd hailed them, Estelle whose no-longer-quite-human eyes had determined that the blur of motion coming toward them was Edmund.

When Edmund's gaze met his fiancée's, the skin that had been cool a moment earlier turned sultry. His grip on Pen tightened, preventing her from squirming down the way she wanted to.

"We couldn't wait any longer," Sally explained, oblivious to the little drama playing out between her father and her friend. "We had to see if we could help. Oh, Daddy, you look all right!"

"I am all right," he said, sounding slightly dazed. He set Pen absently on her feet, using his now hot hands to steady her. "You came for us with *dogs*?"

Sally started to babble about the lack of automobiles in Schloss Oberbad, but then Graham and Ben appeared. Ben was clinging piggyback to Graham's shoulders.

"Jesus," Ben said, tottering for a few steps after he got off.

Whatever else anyone might have said was drowned out by all five of the sled dogs suddenly going wild. They'd been quiet in Edmund's presence: polite, Pen might have said. Now, with their curling tails wagging madly, they leaped and barked and strained at their harnesses—as if Graham were their dearest friend and they couldn't wait another instant to get to him. A bit smaller than huskies, the sled dogs' coloring ranged from wolflike to cream. At their very enthusiastic welcome, Graham flushed faintly and looked startled.

Pen began to laugh as she realized what was happening.

"Graham," she said. "They want to chase you. They must sense you've got a cat inside you, and they want to play."

"Hm," Edmund said. "If they're going to chase you, you might as well change form and help pull the sled. Four grown humans is a lot for them to carry."

"Wait," Graham said, catching his father's arm. "I'm not letting you go back alone."

There was something in Edmund's face when he looked at Graham that hadn't been there before—a kind of caution, or maybe it was evasion. He'd learned something, Pen thought, suspected something, that he was hiding from his son. Graham's forehead creased as his father's gaze cut away.

"This is my fight," Edmund said to his still bare feet. "I want you to stay with them."

"But they'll be safe here."

"Look!" Sally interrupted, pointing at the sky. "A hot air balloon."

They all looked, and both Graham and Edmund snarled like beasts at the dark blue teardrop gliding swiftly eastward toward Austria. Apart from the little flame that heated the air, the balloon was almost the same color as the sky. Already the thing was too distant to make out what figures the basket held.

At least it was too distant if you were human.

"It's them," Graham said, his voice so guttural and angry a shiver tripped down Pen's vertebrae. His fangs had run out again. "Goddamn it, they're escaping."

Edmund was silent, his hands curled into fists at his sides. His neck was bowed, and jagged bolts of red sizzled around his head like a halo for a hell demon. The light show was too bright for Pen to believe she'd imagined it. Had he not been turned away, she suspected his expression would have been terrifying. He'd been tortured by these people, driven to the very brink of doing things that would have destroyed him. In truth, by biting Ben he might have been driven over it.

And now—because he'd wanted to ensure the safety of the people who had rescued him—his enemies were getting away.

At that moment, Pen wouldn't have been surprised to see him grab a giant fir and tear it up by the roots.

Not even Sally spoke while he struggled visibly to control himself.

"There's still the nest to clear out," he said at last, the words as rough as if his throat had been sanded raw. "And probably any number of humans whose memories need erasing. I can meet up with you in St. Moritz."

"Edmund," Estelle said. Her tone was soft with love and worry—and perhaps just a hint of scold. "There isn't anything so important that you have to do it alone."

He didn't turn back to them, didn't move except to grow more rigid. "I can handle this. I need to handle this. It will . . . help. Book rooms at the Grand, and I'll find you there."

He flashed away before Estelle could protest, inspiring her to let out her own irate growl.

"He's strong again," Pen reassured her. "He'll be all right."

Estelle's shining gray eyes narrowed on the spot he had disappeared. "Very likely," she said thinly. "At least until *I* get my hands on him."

Durand had known they were in trouble the instant Fitz Clare released his son. Power had thrummed from their captive, filling the cell like a growl too low for *upyr* ears to discern. It had been a sound better suited to the depths of the sea, the vibration shaking the marrow in Durand's bones. Fitz Clare was an elder, a leviathan to outdo Nim Wei. Unlike her, Fitz Clare was enraged with him. Durand had run because his instincts had forced him to. Then, in the dining hall, he'd tried to stand and fight for practically the same reason.

He might as well be dead without his courage.

Much good as it had done him.

Once Fitz Clare had routed him, he'd tried to organize his men, to give them some chance—however futile—to defend themselves. He'd known Fitz Clare would come after them.

Li-Hua had found him in one of the towers where the men were housed and had screamed at him. *You work for us*, she'd shrieked. *Frank and I pay you. You defend us, Captain Durand, not these idiots. I order you to honor your contract!*

And so he found himself swaying in a wicker basket with his half-panicked employers, tethered to the star-dotted sky by a big balloon. He knew his men would die with or without him; knew, too, that they had not regarded him with love. He'd trained them harder than they wished; made them work when they would have slept, despite which he felt quite ill not to be sinking in the ship with them.

Unlike Fitz Clare, he would not have regretted leaving this world behind.

"I can't believe we lost the film," Li-Hua cursed for the dozenth time. "He did something to that boy. I know he did."

It was all she knew—all Frank knew, to judge by his murmurs as he tried to soothe his precious pear blossom. They hadn't perceived what Durand did, hadn't *understood*. Nothing Fitz Clare had done to his son could be captured by a camera, because changing humans into *upyr* had nothing to do with blood. Rituals could not force it, nor mystic words. The secret lay, utterly and completely, in opening one's soul. Durand was just old enough, just close enough to master status that he had seen the truth.

The question was, could he do the deed himself?

He gripped the lip of the basket, his mind tormented from a hundred different directions. He'd sought the key to the change for nearly four centuries. He'd signed on with Frank and Li-Hua to discover it. Finally having the answer gave him a reason to go on living.

Assuming he wanted one.

Castle Lohengrin

Edmund could barely hold human form long enough for the rest to leave. The things he felt were too primitive. When he finally released control, his shift to beast was explosive, the change actually hurting. He welcomed the pain, the power it lent his gathering anger.

His mate had betrayed him, with his own son. Ben's memories hadn't lied. Edmund could see the mark of Graham's bite still glowing on Estelle's skin.

His outrage wasn't that different from when he'd seen his enemies escaping.

The remaining rebels at the castle fled in terror from the flame-eyed avenging monster he had become. Vampires though they were, he had too much speed and power for them to elude his claws. One by one he cornered them and attacked. His wolf's jaws made short work of their helpless necks. Heads flew through the air as, snarling, he tore them off. In minutes, his fur was matted with the blood that showered from their bodies before they dematerialized.

He didn't use his *upyr* gifts to throw off the gore. He

would have bathed in their deaths were it possible. He wanted more of them to kill. Hundreds. Thousands. But it wasn't long until there was only one.

Edmund found the last cowering in a closet. He was young—no more than a decade past being turned. He didn't fight even when Edmund broke down the door with his wolf's shoulder.

"Please," the rebel begged through chattering fangs. He tossed a long kitchen knife out onto the floor. "Don't kill me. I surrender."

The very idea infuriated Edmund. He clamped his teeth on the coward's ankle, dragging him forcibly from his hiding place.

"Please," the man repeated, eyes wild with fear. "I gave you my weapon!"

Edmund changed into human form and crouched, seizing the vampire's neck with one hand, while using the other to retrieve the blade. The kitchen knife was steel, but the edge appeared sharp enough to sever this young idiot's spinal cord.

"You went rogue," he said, his human voice almost as harsh a growl as his wolf's. "You participated in a plot to overthrow the mistress of your line. Your leaders' actions exposed our kind to dangerous mortals. If I don't kill you tonight, Nim Wei or Aimery will."

"I'm sorry," the vampire pleaded.

"Not good enough," Edmund said.

St. Moritz

In addition to serving dinner, the observation lounge at the Grand Hotel St. Moritz offered a panoramic view of the Bernina glacier and the tops of the jagged mountains it had swallowed. One nearby ski slope was lit all along its length, allowing diners to watch tiny figures ribbon down the trail. A lot of guests appeared to like doing that. Though the hour was late, the lounge was thronged with well-heeled tourists. St. Moritz, it seemed, grew livelier after dark.

Estelle stabbed her fork into a tomato and wished they'd all go to bed.

Sally had ordered raclette for the five of them, a traditional Swiss meal she swore would satisfy her longing for cheese and pickles. The dish came to the table with a little grill for melting the cheese, plus a supply of potatoes and fresh-baked bread. It was all very cozy and convivial—assuming one weren't waiting for the head of one's family to kill a bunch of vampires and catch up to the party. To make matters more surreal, no one mentioned they all knew why Sally had cravings.

Sometimes Estelle thought the gift Sally had absorbed from her father was a preternaturally thick skin.

"He didn't want us to take the sled out ourselves," Sally was saying, regaling the others with her and Estelle's adventures. Her tone was too bright to be natural, probably due to her resentment over Ben's rather more dramatic exploits with Pen. "Estelle couldn't budge him, so I batted my eyes and told him my cousin Jack had raced at Lake Placid in the last Olympics. Wouldn't you know there was some Jack or other who did pretty well, and the sled dog man believed me. Didn't you think he believed me, Estelle?"

"I think he wanted to rescue you if you fell off," she said absently.

Estelle scraped some bubbling cheese onto a crusty round of bread, deaf to what Sally said in return. Graham had taken Estelle aside earlier, to fill her in on Ben being the father of Sally's child. She'd hardly had the energy to be shocked, except at herself for not seeing it.

She wondered what would happen to those two now that Edmund had done, well, whatever he'd done to Ben.

Father knows, Graham had said. *When Ben fed him, I could feel Edmund in his head. If he wants to talk about their . . . situation, you shouldn't be in the dark.*

Estelle shoved the toasted bread and cheese into her mouth. Edmund couldn't talk about anything until he showed up. She could have smacked him, she truly could: running off to play hero after they'd finally saved him. Didn't he know how much she'd missed him? Couldn't he guess how deeply she'd worried? Surely cleaning out Frank and Li-Hua's nest could have waited long enough for him to give her a hug!

"*Men*," she muttered darkly to her plate.

"They can be trying," Pen agreed. "Always wanting to run everything."

"Ha," Ben said. "That sounds more like you to me."

"You *were* a good little soldier," Pen complimented him simperingly.

Ben's good-natured laugh had Sally staring hard at him. Estelle couldn't begrudge him a distraction from his worries, so only Graham looked grimmer than his sister over the pair's repartee. Pen wore her rope of pearls and slinky evening gown tonight, fitting in here better than the rest of them. Appearances aside, she had exposed some extraordinary—and possibly suspicious—talents today.

Who the hell are *you?* Estelle heard Graham think with her funny ear.

Graham's head jerked up as he sensed her catching the thought. Both of them were getting better at this.

Sorry, she sent back experimentally. *Accident.*

He smiled so sweetly she feared she'd cry. He was her friend—always and no matter what. Through everything, that had remained unchanged. If anyone understood how angry she was with Edmund, it was Graham. He hadn't wanted to leave without his father any more than she had.

Estelle's nape prickled without warning, followed by an unexpected full body flush. She rose from her chair automatically. Edmund was here. Though the lounge was bustling, her gaze homed in on him standing at the entrance. His stillness made him stand out, his absolute unshakable maleness. Another wave of heat flooded her. He wore fancy dinner dress, likely purchased from the hotel's overpriced shops. His eyes just barely flared at her, his expression inscrutable but searingly intense. He wasn't walking toward them. He was waiting for her to come to him.

Estelle forgot her anger. It had been far too long since they'd been alone in anything but dreams.

"Excuse me," Estelle said. "I have to go."

"It's Daddy!" Sally jumped up, only to have Ben tug her down again.

"Let them have some time together," he said.

If Sally argued, Estelle didn't hear. She was moving between the crowded tables, her gaze never leaving his. Lord, he was gorgeous: tall, lean, his broad shoulders squaring as she approached. When he rolled his lips together, she knew he hadn't been able to stop his fangs from lengthening.

Knowing her simple presence got him excited washed her with heat again.

He caught her hand as soon as he was able, carrying it to his mouth. His hold was possessive, even a little hard—understandable, she supposed, considering their time apart. As he pressed his lips to her knuckles, she spied a faint red line trailing down his sculpted right cheekbone. Given that the scar hadn't finished healing, the initial wound must have been ghastly. Edmund shook his head when she would have exclaimed over it.

The light in his eyes was so fiery she couldn't wonder her face felt burned.

"I booked a suite," he said, "just for us."

An ache pulsed between her legs, as if he'd already stroked her there. Questions could wait, she decided, and so could the others. After all they'd been through, propriety seemed beside the point.

"Take me there," she said huskily.

"My pleasure," he growled back.

She didn't think she could have found the suite again afterward. She walked to it in a dream, every drop of her attention focused on Edmund. He only held her hand as he led the way, but his fingers caressed and squeezed her palm. Each nerve he brushed found a hungry terminus in her sex. She was trembling by the time he shut the door quietly behind them, her body wracked by waves of need.

Seeming to know, he framed her face and let his glamour fall. The sight of his naked beauty was a blow she didn't try to evade. He was staring at her like he meant to search the depths of her soul. Whatever he found made him shake himself.

"Love," he said roughly, "you've no idea how desperately I missed you."

He had tears in his sapphire eyes, which robbed her of the power to speak. She pulled off his scarf and jacket, and began to unbutton his boiled white shirt.

"God," he breathed, his head falling back as her hands reached skin.

They both loved what her heat did to his.

She pushed the shirt off his shoulders and down his arms, kissing him where his heart had started to beat harder. Edmund cursed and tore from the sleeves, his cuff links popping off and scattering. His torso bare, she moved upward, kiss by kiss, to the pulsing hollow of his throat. The pads of her thumbs found his pointed nipples, which grew hard as marble when she circled them. His hands came to rest behind her shoulder blades.

"Estelle," he said, unable to control a shudder. "I have all this power inside me, all these passions. I'm so afraid I'm going to hurt you."

She nipped his chin with a growl that was more than play. "That's what started this, Edmund—you being afraid you'd hurt the people you love. You ran, despite never having hurt any of us. Don't you think it's time you learned to trust yourself?"

He gripped her shoulders, pushing her back so he could see her eyes. "You're angry with me."

"Yes," she admitted. "I truly am."

He blinked at her and then laughed softly. "Estelle. My sensible, honest Estelle. You bring me back to myself without even trying. I swear, I love you more than words can say."

She slid her hands down his alabaster chest and ridged belly, to the hard, thick arch that strained the front of his trousers. Her fingers measured it, encouraged it, then squeezed it hard enough to pull a gasp from him.

"Prove it," she said boldly.

He smiled, fangs gleaming, a hint of the predator in his expression. Her breath caught in primal reaction as he tilted his head to kiss her. She liked being just a little frightened of him.

His conquering of her mouth began slowly—a nip and tug of her lower lip, a long, deep penetration of his tongue. She groaned and pressed her body close to his. He'd never used his fangs this purposefully on her, teasing her with their hardness, sipping her where they nicked.

Little gushes of excitement spurted from her sex, each quick drink a jolt of sensation that flirted with orgasm. She could hardly wait to have one of those with him.

"Edmund," she pleaded, to which he responded by languorously pulling off her clothes.

She wanted him to tear them, to ravish her. Instead, he draped her garments, one by one, on a chair. The air was cool on her heated body, which somehow seemed more naked than it had ever been before. He laid her on a long, streamlined couch, his touch smoothing worshipfully down her legs. He had to see the dampness of her tangled curls, but he didn't hasten his deliberate pace. His eyes were glowing, his breath ragged. She knew what that meant for one of his kind, who barely had to breathe at all. Her gaze followed, fascinated, when his hands shifted to the bulging front of his trousers. He didn't open them, but slid his fingertips over the arch of himself, blatantly displaying the wonders he had to offer her. The outline of his shaft and head grew more delineated. He seemed to want her to watch that, to see how big he was, to imagine how much he liked the light friction.

Very much, she concluded. The instant he freed the metal catch, the cloth that held his zip together tore.

The sound of it ripping was unbearably seductive. She reached for the erection that had sprung so impressively through the shreds, but he caught her wrist mere inches from touching him. This need of his to assert his power titillated her. Helpless not to, she licked her lips. His cock stood out from his groin like a phallus on a rude statue: outrageously thick, perfectly formed, with only its vibration to prove it was alive.

Well, that and the tiny diamondlike drops of pre-come that winked and disappeared at the tip—vampire magic at its most irresistible.

"Edmund . . ." Driven by a compulsion she could not repress, she sat up and bent forward to suck him, balancing herself by wrapping her fingers around his hips. This time, he didn't stop her. She suspected he didn't quite have the self-discipline.

She was glad he didn't. To her mouth and tongue, he was living satin around a core of steel—hot and smooth and faintly tinged with salt. His fingers forked through her hair as she sank on him, causing him to rumble out a groan. Slowly, carefully, he began to thrust into her suckling. His thigh muscles worked as he pushed and pulled between her tongue and palate, their corded state signaling his increased tension. She let one hand drift to his knee and up again, using it to cup his balls. The strength of her caresses on the drawn-up sac heated him until he felt fevered. Adoring that reaction, she tightened the ring of her lips.

"Estelle," he whispered. "You're going to make me spend."

She wanted to, badly enough to taste it. She flicked the flat of her tongue over the flaring head. He shuddered and shoved, and then he pulled one of his vampire tricks. With no transition, she found herself flat on her back with him crouched completely naked between her legs. Her calves were crooked over the hardness of his shoulders, and a nearby lamp now wore his trousers. In the intervening millisecond, he'd spread her thighs wide and stripped himself.

"I want to kiss you here," he said, a growl behind it. "I want to nick you with my teeth and drink."

She couldn't doubt where he meant. He had her clitoris

between his thumb and fingers, gently rotating the tender, sensitive swell of flesh. She should have been nervous, but she didn't know how to not trust him. Moisture ran help-lessly from her sex. He licked it, his tongue as strong and agile as his fingers. Estelle groaned and shoved up at him.

"May I?" he asked, with a force of need she didn't quite understand. "May I bite you here?"

She couldn't answer. Her throat was closed with antici-pation, her spine arched with desire. She fisted his thick golden hair and pulled him closer.

He understood this was permission.

He nicked her, just as he'd said, the lick of pain so brief she could hardly separate it from the ecstasy of him suck-ing up the tiny drop of blood. That ecstasy shoved her to the edge of coming before backing off to a deliciously frustrated throb. He knew precisely what she was feeling, because he groaned and did it again, suckling her with such delicacy that—no matter how she squirmed—she could never quite go over. Her knees tightened on him, her nails digging in as he repeated the diabolic tease.

It was as if he thought he needed to prove something. Luckily, the exercise in restraint had an equal effect on him. His yearning came from him in hair-raising, basso growls. Every time she heard one, she grew wetter.

"Do you want me to beg?" she finally pleaded as he yanked her thighs wide again. "Is that what you're waiting for?"

Her questions startled him. He looked up her body, his lips pulled back from his sharpened fangs. His eyes glowed like two blue coals. They flared brighter and, for just a moment, she thought he was angry.

"I want you desperate," he said.

She touched his face, trying to read what lay behind his expression. "I've been desperate since you went missing. Please, I want you inside me now."

He flashed up her, then hesitated at her neck. She

couldn't imagine what held him back. His breath panted, hot and hard above her strongest pulse.

"Yes," she said, gently stroking his nape. "I want you to drink from me, too."

His lashes lifted, his gaze rising from her throat. He hadn't fed from her many times. He hadn't let himself. He'd feared he'd betray his nature or lose control. Neither of those issues mattered now—which must have occurred to him. His swelling pupils darkened his eyes, while his cock throbbed hot and hard on her thigh.

"I'll enter you first," he said roughly. "I'm too close now. I've had too much of your blood. The second I bite you in earnest, I'm going to come."

He cared about that more than she did, but she was learning what proud creatures male *upyr* were. Without protest, she lifted her knees and drew her hand down his spine. He was sweating, shaking just a tiny bit, the muscles of his buttocks tensed. He grasped his shaft and placed the head against her, the curve of it wide and sleek. Because she loved him, she wanted to do something equally intimate. She put her hand between them and spread her folds for him. He seemed to like the feel of her fingers around his crown.

"Estelle," he gasped. "Remember I love you, no matter what happens."

She wasn't worried, and couldn't think why he was. With a moan of pleasure, she pushed her sex up him.

Oh, that was lovely, that slow, deep joining of flesh to flesh. He glided in, simply glided, his fullness oiled by her arousal. When he was all the way inside her, his body writhed as if he couldn't bear not to rub every inch of his skin on hers. His hands fisted on the cushion beside her head, and then he began to thrust.

In an instant, he betrayed the effects of his involuntary abstinence. He didn't ease into motion; he went flat out, grunting with his need to go deep and hard. It was what she'd wanted from the beginning, all the force, all the unbridled lust. His lips were pulled back uninhibitedly from his fangs. They both cried out at how good what he was doing felt.

"Yes," she urged, every muscle she had intensifying his drive and pull. "Yes, Edmund, like that."

He didn't need a second invitation. He went faster, harder; the sofa creaked ominously from the strain. He gripped the arm above her and accidentally broke it off.

"Floor," he gasped, shifting her in a flash to it. They landed with a thump that seemed to drive his cock to her throat. The strangled sound she made begged him to do it again.

"*Jesu*," he moaned, clamping her buttocks to repeat the effect.

She came with a violence she could not control, her cries inhuman, her body tightening and straining to get closer. Wetness spurted from her. He mouthed her neck as she thrashed, licked up its length to her chin . . .

"Stay still," he said.

The order was harsh, but she couldn't do it. The continued pumping of his hips was driving her insane. If he couldn't stop, she didn't see why she should.

"Still," he repeated, putting his thrall in it. "I want us both to feel this."

She stilled, though her sex continued to spasm wildly around his girth. He watched her face as if to ensure his command would take. His thrusting slowed, allowing her to back off from the lunatic orgasm.

"I'm still," she panted, almost truthfully. She wanted more than breath what was coming next. "Please go ahead."

He went, but it wasn't fast. He sank his teeth in as slowly as he'd initially sunk his cock. Her fingers clenched at the odd, hot pain of the penetration, but she'd be damned if she wanted to call a halt. She absolutely loved what this was doing to him. He was shuddering with desire, his breath panting from his nose, his body shoving up against hers as close as it could get. She wrapped her arms around him, her fists bunched in the sweating small of his back. She could tell this strange way of biting her was significant to him.

He moaned and hitched closer with his hips. Lord, he was big—and swelling even more as his fangs went in. Their energy began to twine together, their awareness. He'd bonded with her more closely the night he ran, but this softer connection was also sweet, like rubbing noses before a fire. His scent surrounded her—forest, earth—and she thought nothing could have comforted her more. The pain of his bite diminished, then rose again as his jaw clamped down. He was marking her, she realized, a claim no other *upyr* could erase. The insight calmed her.

I'm yours, she thought to him. *I've been yours since the day we met.*

He made a sound low in his throat, his lips tightening on her skin as he drew his first good swallow. He hadn't been mistaken about how close he was. His entire body jerked as his climax burst and, naturally, she went with him. Her pleasure snapped the last of his control. He pistoned madly into her, pumping through both their spasms, milking them, heightening them until she choked back a kind of scream.

To be stimulated so intensely was almost more than she could handle.

She blinked, and she was on her belly with him taking her just as vigorously from behind. Her legs were bent to either side of her, her bottom raised. She slapped her hands on the rug for purchase, wanting to help him get plenty of leverage. Intense or not, this was wonderful. She also couldn't forget how much his wolf liked this position. To arouse both sides of his nature was incredibly exciting.

"Again," he growled, yanking her hips up into his groin.

Despite having just come, he was thick and urgent, his tip rubbing the most sensitive spot inside her. Their bodies smacked together fervently. "Go over for me again."

Obeying was not a problem, especially when he repeated that strange, slow bite, this time on the other side of her neck. Her sensation peaked, and she felt him slam into her hard and spurt. The release seemed not to calm him. Maybe he'd been storing it up too long.

"The feel of you . . ." he moaned even as he sped up another fraction. "Oh, God, the feel of you, really here, around me."

She didn't know what to give him, how to ease this seemingly frantic need, no more than she knew how to ease her own.

"Turn me," she begged. "Turn me around and let me bite you."

She must have picked the right request. He cried out, raw and sharp, the room blurring until she found herself in the doorway to the suite's bedroom. He was standing then, her legs caught around his waist, thumping her into the solid wood of the frame. His chest muscles strained as if he was both trying and not trying to drive her through. She bit him on the neck, not able to draw blood, but more than able to make him shudder and plunge desperately into her. He was fucking her like a berserker. He grabbed the molding, twisting his neck in mute encouragement to bite down more.

Her compliance had him groaning, driven past the state where he could form words. Eyes blind with pleasure, he lost control and jetted into her, his hips and shaft shoving her strongly up the door. His seed was running from her, so copious it hadn't had a chance to evaporate. Nor was it going to get a chance to soon. His ejaculation went on and on, as if a dam had burst inside him. She had a feeling she was going to have his palm prints on her bum for days, though with the way she was climaxing, she could hardly mind. Finally, he sighed, low and melodic, obviously feeling relieved at last. Murmuring her name, and still hard inside her, he carried her gently to the bed.

They didn't speak the last time, or not with words. They touched each other instead, making love with their eyes as well as their bodies, showing tenderness and care with every means they had. He stroked her hair and kissed her, biting her so sweetly it didn't hurt at all. He healed each little wound as soon as he made it, the tingle of his power lingering afterward. His *upyr* glow was their only illumination, their shadows moving sensually on the walls. It was a dance, one she never wanted to end. His hands molded her breasts, savoring their fullness, his hips surging hypnotizingly in and out. When she came, that happened slowly, too, a luxuriant coiling and uncoiling of surfeited nerves. He went over with a little gasp that said the peak surprised him, his eyes almost but not quite closing.

Perhaps he'd thought this time would only be for her.

Though he softened, he stayed where he was, propped above her on his forearms. She slid her hands up his chest to feel his heart calming. Her heartbeat shook her body like she had a drum inside, the pulse of it pleasantly erotic. She didn't know what to say—which was silly, but there it was. He began to smile, and she did, too. He lowered his head to rest his cool brow on hers. Though she felt strangely shy, she couldn't resist hugging him.

"*Now* I'm saved," he said.

Now I *am,* she thought.

Edmund didn't want to talk. If he were honest, he barely wanted to move. Estelle lay snuggled against him under the sheet, her hand stroking along his ribs. She was warm and soft and smelled better sweaty than she ever would have guessed. The wolf in him whined silently with bliss. Mates belonged together. That meant safety in the wild. Because

Edmund was with his, this was the first truly peaceful moment he'd had since he'd been captured. He only wished it didn't feel so precarious.

He told himself what had happened between Estelle and Graham wasn't important. Estelle had fed his son because she was the best choice for it. She'd enjoyed it because that was the nature of their beasts. Edmund would have had no reason to even know she'd done it if Ben's concern over the incident hadn't been flapping like a flag in his mind.

Marking Estelle, biting her slowly enough to hurt, had been an instinct too compelling for him to fight. Edmund wasn't proud of doing it, but he understood why he'd needed to—just as he understood why he'd made love to her so aggressively. Whether the threat from another male was real or imaginary, he'd needed to restake his claim. Estelle hadn't objected, which was what mattered.

When she hummed companionably against his collarbone, he fought the urge to drop all his barriers and let her in. He wasn't ready for that yet. His thoughts remained too disturbed. Instead, he drew his fingers through her hair, his energy effortlessly smoothing the tousled waves. He knew it was too much to hope that she'd fall asleep. Five and a half centuries of experience had taught him about women.

Sure enough, Estelle squirmed up until her breasts rested softly atop his chest.

The brands he'd placed on either side of her throat glowed gold, invisible to anyone but an *upyr*. One of her slender fingers trailed down the healing cut on his cheek.

"Edmund," she said, "how did you get this scar?"

"One of Frank and Li-Hua's vampires caught me by surprise."

She pressed her full lips together, her lashes dropping to hide her eyes as she considered how much detail she wanted about the fight. "Are they all dead?"

Forcing himself not to stiffen defensively took an act of

will. Though he knew the rebels' deaths had been necessary, the bloodthirsty way he'd destroyed them didn't sit easily. "They swore an oath to respect either Nim Wei or Aimery's rule. The sentence for breaking that has always been severe. My brother tends to be merciful, but even he could not have pardoned the acts they took part in."

"Was it—" She hesitated, forced herself to go on. "Was it very awful, having to kill them?"

Faces flicked through his mind, last expressions before his victims disappeared in a burst of light. Anger. Fear. Disbelief that their supposedly immortal lives had truly drawn to a close. Most especially, he remembered his own exultation at all of it. Even now, the madness behind him, he wasn't certain he felt remorse. Troubled by that, Edmund rubbed his scar.

"Someone had to end them," he said.

"But you're the one who did."

"I had the power to." He looked at Estelle, knowing she was thinking the slaughter must have been hard on him. She had no idea what he really was struggling with. He went on with the sense that he was lying, though the words he spoke were the truth. "I gave them a quick death. I contained the risk of exposure. I don't think even my sainted brother could complain about my results."

"You didn't want Graham to kill them, did you?"

He fought against the pang her words pulled from him. Even hearing her say Graham's name . . . But the hurt was irrational, and he shouldn't give in to it.

"No," he agreed: truth again, just not all of it. "Graham is no killer. I don't doubt he would have done it, but it would have haunted him afterward."

"Were there humans among the nest?"

"A few." His neck relaxed a fraction, his conscience easier here. "Most had been thralled into helping the rebels against their will. That's a violation of our laws as well. I was able to erase their memories and leave them unharmed. I did the same to Teudt. He won't be a threat to us again."

"Teudt? The man from the Nazis' occult bureau? I think—" Her lips curved crookedly. "I think I would have been tempted to kill him."

"He'll tell his colleagues it was all a load of gammon. That will be more useful."

Estelle watched her fingers draw a tickling circle on his chest. Her lower lip was caught between her teeth. He sensed the question that was coming. "You know about Sally and Ben?"

"Yes."

She lifted her gaze at his simple answer, a wealth of worry behind those beautiful gray eyes.

"It's done," he said, "and it can't be undone. Ben loved her from the first. As a boy that love was different, but his feelings for Sally always were intense."

"It's not him I'm concerned about," she confessed. "I don't think he'd ever let Sally down. She's just so young, and she's had so many boys fall in love with her. I'm afraid she's going to hurt him."

"If she is, you and I can't stop it."

Estelle smiled, tears welling brilliantly in her eyes. "I forgot how wise you are, how good and understanding to everyone. I'm so grateful you're back with us."

She buried her face against his chest to hide that she was crying. Edmund's heart rose to his throat as he embraced her. He didn't want to close his eyes. He knew he didn't deserve her admiration, but if he woke and this wasn't real, if he was actually in that cell, he thought it might kill him.

"I'm grateful, too," he said hoarsely.

St. Moritz

Their dinner finished, Pen drifted to the observation windows to pretend to watch the night skiers. Now that the Fitz Clares were reunited, she felt like a guest who'd stayed too long at a house party. Watching Edmund and Estelle practically set the air ablaze between them had only increased her sense of being an outsider.

No one had thanked her, not even Estelle.

You didn't help them so they'd thank you, she scolded herself. She pushed her thoughts away from why she *had* done it. That was seeming murkier all the time.

To make matters worse, neither of her personas was fitting well tonight—not the woman of action and certainly not the bright young toast of society. This wasn't her crowd in St. Moritz, though her crowd had come here before. Pen wondered if she'd have felt any more herself if Coretta and Binky and the rest had been there with her. Somehow, she doubted it.

She hadn't quite wiped the frown from her face when Graham joined her at the wall of glass. Her muscles tight-

ened. Graham held himself with a hint of his old awkwardness, but she didn't know if the effect was real or glamour.
Had Graham Fitz Clare ever been awkward? Had she ever
known the real him? She was becoming more and more
convinced that the answer to that was no.

"Ben and Sally are going up," he said. "I thought you
and I could talk."

He was scowling slightly as he looked down at her, a bit
too tall for comfort. Though his hands were shoved harm-
lessly in his pockets, the width of his shoulders in his dinner
jacket intimidated all by itself. Pen took in his new handsomeness, forcing herself to acknowledge it, to remember
how much she'd enjoyed him overpowering her when they
had sex. He was a man to be reckoned with: big, strong,
with an imposing physical presence no one could ignore.
The sight of him stripping that presence naked before turning into a large gray cat was burned into her brain. True, the
sight of him—in harness—leading five deliriously excited
sled dogs down a snowy slope was burned there, too, but
somehow the humor of that image didn't cool her blood.
Pen's female friends were going to go into raptures when
they got a gander at the improved Graham—assuming, of
course, that she ever saw him again.

Resenting how the thought of not doing so annoyed her,
she leaned her mostly bare back against the window. She
ran one hand down her rope of pink South Sea pearls. Graham's gaze followed the motion. She thought, just maybe,
he might have snuck a look at her breasts.

"There *is* plenty to talk about," she agreed mildly.
"For instance, what do you suppose your father did to Ben
when he fed from him? Will he be like Estelle now, with a
'funny' pinkie that can lift a car?"

"I don't know," Graham said.

He looked into her eyes, and the very arousal she'd been
fighting ran like a brush fire over her skin. Her nipples bud-

ded beneath the pale green satin of her gown, their heat a noticeable contrast to the smooth, cool cloth. Pen ordered herself not to grit her teeth. "Would it bother you if your father made Ben a vampire?"

"Bother me?" Graham appeared genuinely perplexed.

"Because, before last night, you were the only one of his adopted children who was like him."

Graham furrowed his brows at her. "Is that how you think, Pen? That the people you love are your competition?"

Clearly, this wasn't how he thought. Pen crossed her arms the way she'd been wanting to and stared at him. Graham broke before she did, rubbing the back of his neck as if his rudeness had been lodged there.

"I'm sorry," he apologized. "I shouldn't have said that. I imagine you had to compete for your father's attention as a child, since he was so caught up in business."

Pen snorted to herself. Her father's attention hadn't been the problem. It was her mother's that was the lost cause. But that was just as well. Any daughter would have been better off without Livonia Anderson's languid influence.

"Seriously, Graham," she said, preferring attack to feeling pitiful. "Aren't you worried about how this will affect your family?"

He shrugged his stevedore's shoulders. "Worrying won't help."

It might not help, but she didn't doubt he was doing it. She also didn't doubt that if Estelle had been the person expressing her concern, Graham would have responded gratefully. At that painful bit of knowledge, she finally looked away, a tiny betrayal of weakness that seemed to give Graham whatever cue he'd needed to pursue his own line of questioning.

"Listen," he said, lowering his voice and stepping closer. His hushed tone was hardly necessary. The late night crowd was giving him a wide berth, as if some primordial part of their brains knew he was a predator. "I need to ask you something, Pen, and I need you to be honest with me."

Pen tightened her crossed arms. "Can't your vampire powers tell you if I lie?"

He cocked his brows, not answering. Pen cocked her brows back at him.

"Pen," he said, his tone half amused and half exasperated. His chest lifted with a breath, and he put one hand on her upper arm. Pen wished he hadn't done that. The reach of his fingers felt absolutely huge. "I need to know if you're working for the intelligence community in the States. Is that who trained you to set explosives and handle guns? Is that why you pushed so hard to help us? Does someone in your country suspect the existence of the *upyr*?"

Her mouth had fallen open. She managed to shut it but had less luck tugging her arm away from him.

"I *pushed* so hard to help you, as you put it, because I didn't want you in over your head. I didn't want to see you hurt."

He grimaced—probably irritated by her protectiveness—then shook off the reaction. "You're sure it had nothing to do with getting close enough to learn our secrets?"

She didn't let him make her blanch. "A girl's allowed to be curious. Anyway, I didn't know you had a secret *that* big until you bit me."

She flushed at the reminder, or maybe because he was searching her eyes so insultingly. She was telling the truth . . . mostly.

"I believe you," he said at last.

"Flattered, I'm sure," she drawled.

"Pen . . ."

"You have my answer. You can let go of me."

He didn't, though. He put his other hand on her, too. With both her arms caught in his grip, she felt as if a low-grade electric current were warming her, one that pooled as a hot,

prickling awareness between her thighs. The effect intensi-
fied as his thumbs swept back and forth. She clenched her
jaw, dead set on concealing how much he affected her.

"You have to keep this to yourself," he said, his gravity oddly erotic. "You can't tell . . . whoever you work for
about the *upyr*. I know you probably think they have a
right, even a need to know, but there simply aren't many
humans who can be trusted with the truth. They'd want to
kill us, or use us, or lock us away in labs."

Pen tossed her head angrily. "The people in my government aren't Nazis. In any case, it was your kind who
abducted your father."

"The *upyr* police themselves."

"And maybe they'd kill a human they thought was going
to blab."

They were nose to nose, as close as lovers about to kiss.
All around them, all unknowing, St. Moritz's hoi polloi
chattered and postured for each other. As far as they knew,
their world held nothing more dangerous than falling stock
prices. Perhaps agreeing that he and Pen were too close,
Graham backed off a few inches.

"Some of them would prefer to eliminate that kind of
threat," he concurred.

"Are you one of them?"

She'd whispered the question. She didn't want to believe
it, but she had to ask. Graham stroked her wavy bob from
her face, his golden brown eyes gone sad. Pen wondered
if he really were as sorry as he looked. Couldn't he lie to
her as easily as she had to him? Or more easily, given his
changed nature?

"I'd tell you I believed in killing," he said, "if I thought
it would scare you into keeping quiet. Since I know better, all I'll do is beg. Please, Pen. Please keep what you've
learned to yourself. The safety of my family and a lot of
other perfectly nice vampires depends on it."

She didn't smile at his attempt at humor, nor could she

answer him. Her mind wasn't made up and, for some reason, she found she couldn't give him the empty promises any sensible spymaster would have advised.

"I don't want to see you hurt, either," he went on softly. "I don't want you in over your head."

As he looked straight at her, straight *into* her, she had the most awful urge to fling her arms around him, to have him comfort her and hold her close. It was one thing to want to have sex with him again. Considering how spectacular that had been, she could hardly blame herself. It was quite another kettle of fish, however, to simply crave his embrace. She realized, with some dismay, that it wasn't the vampires she was in over her head with. It was Graham himself.

"I'm tired," she said, easing carefully back from him. "I'm going up to my room."

His gaze followed her as she strode away, a tingling weight on her back and legs. His feet, by contrast, remained exactly where they were.

Pen concluded he'd be seeking out a different source of sustenance tonight.

Sally was packing. She'd shaken out her things when they first arrived in St. Moritz, and now she was returning them to their trunks. The pointlessness of her actions wasn't lost on her, but she'd needed to keep busy. Better to feel stupid, she reasoned, than to go insane.

A tap on the door had her turning with a fluffy angora cardigan clutched to her breast. Was it her father? Had he unearthed the secret she'd been trying so hard to hide?

Ben opened the door before she mustered the power to speak. Then her mouth went dry for different reasons. Ben was just a little prettier since Daddy had bitten him, a little smoother and brighter eyed. Since he'd been plenty pretty before, this scarcely seemed fair. Her breasts seemed to swell within her ruffled cotton sleeping gown—the most modest one she owned.

"You shouldn't be here," she squeaked.

"Sally." His smile was crooked but sweet. "Do you honestly think Estelle is going to be sharing this room with you tonight?"

"That doesn't mean you can."

He stepped into the room, the solemn look in his eyes causing her heart to skip. "He knows, sweetheart. The professor knows what you and I have done."

"He doesn't! Not yet. Maybe we can tell him later, when the baby's farther along."

He took her shoulders between his beautiful hands. One corner of her brain gave a start. The old scars and bruises from his garage work were gone. "He knows now, Sally. He read it from my mind when I was feeding him."

Sally bit her lip to keep it from shaking. Her eyes locked on his, searching them for what she needed to know.

"He doesn't hate us, sweetheart. I didn't read his thoughts as clearly as he did mine, but I promise you, all I felt from him was love."

"That can't be right," Sally quavered. "No one could just forgive us for what we did."

Ben pulled her to his chest, his hand smoothing up and down her back through the thin nightgown. "He forgives us, love. Our friends may be a different story. I expect we'll have to brace ourselves for them being shocked."

"Oh, pooh for what they think," Sally scoffed into his sweater-vest.

Ben laughed into her curls. "I know you don't truly mean that, but together it won't be as hard to face them. I think—" He hesitated. "Sally, I'd like for us to get married as soon as we're home."

"Married?" Sally said when she'd found her breath.

They'd pushed back to look into each other's faces. A

war seemed to be going on behind Ben's: worry, hope, a guardedness she'd never wanted him to feel with her.

"I know it's a big step. I know maybe neither of us have let ourselves think about it, but it makes sense for the baby. Hell, it makes sense for us. I'm never going to love another woman the way I love you. I adore you, Sally, even when you're driving me batty. We fit each other. We love each other. We belong together every bit as much as Father and Estelle."

The war had left his expression, determination replacing it. Wonder expanded in Sally's breast.

"You're not afraid?"

"I'm ruddy terrified!" His amusement perfectly apparent, he cupped her face in his hands. "Keeping you safe has been enough of a challenge. Add a baby, and I'm sure to be a nervous wreck in no time."

"Don't I get to help protect it?"

"Oh, Lord," he said, but he laughed again. "Do you want to, Sally? Do you want to marry me?"

She thought of her childish daydreams: princes on white horses and glamorous movie stars. To her surprise, she realized Ben put all of them in the shade. He was better than a prince. He was a real hero.

"No more blowing things up with Pen," she warned. "At least, not without my permission."

He hugged her and rocked her and kissed her hair. "Can I confess I enjoy you being jealous of her?"

"You don't!" she cried, shoving him.

He didn't let her budge him. "It's only fair, considering all those schoolboys I've watched pining over you."

"They're just boys. You're the man I look up to. The man I love."

His hold tightened around her, and she knew she'd moved him with what she said. Content, she settled her cheek over his heart. It was beating more slowly than she expected, almost like Daddy's had sometimes when he forgot to speed it up. She slid her hands under the back of Ben's shirt to feel it thumping from the other side of him.

"Daddy changed you," she murmured, "like he did Estelle."

When she tipped her head back to look at him, Ben's expression held a trace of anxiety. "I'm not sure what he did. I've felt different ever since he bit me, like someone put a better grade of petrol in my engine. I thought, maybe, it would wear off, but it hasn't yet."

"Are you experiencing an urge to bite me?"

He grinned, hearing both the trepidation and the interest in her tone. "Are you offering to let me try?"

She knew what that teasing glint meant—and so did certain parts of her body. She became aware of his hips resting on her belly, of a decided stirring in his trousers and its answer between her thighs.

"The baby . . ."

His face and eyes darkened. "I'll be careful," he promised. "Oh, God, I'll be so careful."

Ben put the chain on the door, his sole concession to Sally's fear that someone might walk in. He doubted they'd need it. They had a night together, he and Sally—naked, uninterrupted, with no one and nothing to stop them.

Breathing harder at the thought, he pulled his vest and shirt together over his head. He threw them into a corner and watched her smile.

"Ben," she said, her fingers pressed to her curving mouth, "your hair is still spiky."

He didn't know why this was worth noting; he only knew he had to have her now. His bones wanted to get inside her, to meld them into one being. The strength of the craving stole his breath. He was hard as iron, his blood boiling with longing.

"Take that off," he said, his voice guttural.

Sally began to unbutton the neck of her sweet night-gown, instantly enthralling him. She nodded at his trousers. "You, too," she reminded him.

He thought he'd never gotten out of his clothes so fast—not that he cared so much about himself. Seeing her ripe little body naked, from head to toe, was like Christmas morning come again. Speechless, he held out his hands to her. She took them, standing at the end of their reach to look him thoroughly up and down. The time her perusal took was embarrassing. Her lower lip was caught between her teeth, her cheeks and breasts getting pinker by the second as she studied him. The tightening of her rosy nipples made him feel as if a vise were squeezing his chest. He was gasping for air by the time she spoke.

"You're shaking," she said. She freed one hand to touch the aching jut of his cock. "Your penis is shaking."

He groaned as the feathery skating of her fingertips made him stretch longer. Her thumb circled the strongly pulsing tip.

"I think it's bigger, too," she said.

Oh, she knew how to get him going. He wanted to be big for her, to be the malest male she knew. "Maybe it's just more swollen because it's been a while," he managed to rasp. "Maybe it's you having the time to look at me in the light."

Both of them had stepped closer. His hands went to her gorgeous little breasts as if they were magnetized, surrounding and squeezing them. Her nipples fascinated him. He thought they might be redder than they'd been before, maybe because of the baby. He'd heard pregnant women's breasts were more sensitive. Unable to resist, he stretched their peaks gently out between his fingers. He could tell she liked that. Her breath caught in her throat before coming out as a sigh.

She put her hands on his wrists, her fingers fanning the bones as she encouraged his touch to stay where it was.

"Your calluses are gone," she said.

He hoped that was a good thing. His hands did seem more . . . perceptive as they took in the incredible soft, smooth lushness of her breasts. Aside from that, he couldn't really concentrate on what she was saying. She wet her lips, and all thought ended. He had to kiss her, had to send his tongue in deep to play with hers. She moaned into his mouth, her arms coming tightly around him. Her skin was hot, her curves a bounty he couldn't help running his palms over. Needing more, he gripped her bottom and hiked her up. His heart gave one great bound as she scissored both her legs around one of his and rolled her mound up his thigh muscle.

Her sweet, juicy pussy was wet enough to slide.

Excitement stabbed through his cock like a warning bell.

"Sally." He pulled free of her hungry kisses even as her hands clutched his head. "I think I need to take you now. If I wait any longer, I'm going to be rough."

She tugged his hair with a muffled groan. "Don't be too gentle."

He had to, though. He had to for their tiny baby's sake. He walked her toward the bed and watched her scoot back and lie down. A heap of pillows propped up her shoulders, her curls gleaming around her head like a halo. The red bow of her lips was swollen from kissing him.

"I'm not turning off the light," he warned.

She smiled like a wicked angel and spread her thighs.

He crawled up and over her with his heart pounding, his sense that he was stalking prey both odd and arousing. She was his and no one else's. He was going to slide his cock inside her. He was going to mark her as his own.

"I love you," he said as her slender arms twined around his neck. "Lord, Sally, I love you."

Her knees rubbed slowly up his sides. "I think you'd better show me how much."

He was so hard he had to pull his prick down from his belly to enter her. She was very wet and eager enough to moan as his crown squeezed in. The instant it did, goose bumps broke across his skin. Something had changed, unmistakably. As he pushed inside her—his determination to be gentle nearly killing him—his nerves all seemed to go insane at once.

Maybe he *was* bigger, as she'd claimed, because she sure felt tighter to him.

"Hell," he breathed when her inner muscles flickered over him. The subtle motion was almost enough to blow off his head.

He'd wanted her before, and he'd certainly experienced her touch as powerful. This, however, this nerve-jangling, cell-jolting sensitivity was an altogether different order of affairs. He sank another inch and had to gasp for air. The rippling of her sheath around his hardness simply felt too good.

Sally tugged his shoulders in complaint. "Ben," she groaned. "That's too slow."

His hands were tightening on her upper arms, his grip whitening the skin. Alarmed, he forced his fingers to relax.

"You do it," he said, pulling carefully out and rolling onto his back. His prick stuck up like a shuddering tree. "You do it for both of us."

He bit his lip as she straddled him, hardly able to keep himself in check. She was so pretty, so flushed, and her hint of shyness as she tipped him to the needed angle maddened him. She settled gently, taking him into her bit by bit. Groans tore from him at the pleasure, his hands curling into fists. It seemed like years instead of weeks since they'd done this. When her thighs tensed to ride him, he found he couldn't leave the rest to her. He had to take her hips and guide her, had to control what she was doing.

He was the man. This was up to him.

"Not hard," he said as his nerves' insanity started up again. "Just fast, Sally. Just go fast."

She went fast enough to drive the air from his lungs. He cursed with what breath remained, struggling against the urge to slam into her. She was tightening on him, her lashes fluttering as her head fell back. He fought the sensation that the world was going to shatter.

"Sally," he said, shocked that he was asking this already. "Can you—*hell*—can you go over soon?"

She gave a little growl and dropped forward onto her elbows. The position put her breasts against him, those warm and silky female globes of flesh. Since she was moving just as fast as before, they bounced against him. She was nipping him—his chin, his lip—each sting of sensation racheting him higher, as if his arousal were being jacked up on hydraulics. Helpless sounds of enjoyment broke in his chest. He was starting to go. He could feel the dammed-up pressure inside his balls. He shoved a thumb between their hips, hooking the pad over her clitoris. He massaged the sensitive organ as if his life depended on it.

He'd found the spot she liked best. Sally stiffened and let out a gasp, rocketing over the edge just as he began to ejaculate. Fire blazed from him, needs he could not define compelling him to wrap his free hand behind her nape. Her heartbeat thudded in his ear, but he wanted her still closer. He mouthed her neck, sucking it where the flesh was meltingly tender. Tighter he sucked her, and tighter, until her blood rose up beneath her skin, subtly changing her taste. He was so excited he was shaking. The pleasure of his climax grew excruciating. Then—contrary to the laws of physiology—a second orgasm barreled over his first, this one so white-hot and molten it felt like it was turning him inside out.

He grunted but couldn't let her go. Sally was still coming. She shook against him, her pelvis grinding against his hard. Of the same mind as her, he clamped his free hand around her buttocks. He didn't think this could hurt her; his cock wasn't really stone, but he had the sense that he impaled her, that no one had ever gone into a woman as deep as he, that no one had ever shot his seed this hard. She breathed his name, their panted exhalations mingling as she held him.

His madness receded like the aftermath of a storm.

He pushed her gently up to look at her. When she braced herself on his shoulders, his hands slid instinctively to her belly. She seemed to be feeling nothing but pleasure. Her sweet blue eyes were slumbrous, lit with mischievous laughter.

"Ben," she said, "that was some love bite you gave me!"

He touched the bruise he'd left on her throat, a perfect imprint of his human teeth. He realized his gums were throbbing, exactly where fangs would have been if he'd had them. Fear closed like a fist on his vocal cords.

Evidently, the professor had done more to him in that cell than erasing his calluses.

London

They were a somber group pulling into Victoria Station two days later. Sally had sat next to Edmund for the last portion of their journey, claiming a queasiness only his proximity could ease. Graham's energy would have served her nearly as well, but Edmund knew it wasn't her stomach that required soothing.

She wanted to be reassured that he still loved her.

He did this as well as he was able, hugging her gently to him as the train trundled by the wintry orchards of Kent, past the ever-expanding suburbs, and the steam-spouting chimneys of the Battersea Power Station.

Estelle didn't seem to mind sharing his company. She sat across from him next to Pen, a book lying open and unread on her lap. Graham slept until sunset, his head bumping Ben's shoulder. Edmund couldn't blame him for his exhaustion. Even bundled, Edmund was tired to his bones.

Ironically, returning to familiar scenes made him feel less like his old self.

Could he put those weeks in that cell behind him? Could he forget how close he'd come to losing what mattered most—not only his loved ones, but his soul? Frank and Li-Hua were still out there. He'd destroyed their nest but not them. Graham would never be the man he was before. Sally and Ben's relationship was forever changed, not because of his abduction—though he imagined the strain of that hadn't helped. Edmund had told Estelle that what had happened between his children couldn't be undone. He might have said the same about the rest of it.

For all his power, he couldn't turn back one second of what had unfolded in his absence.

Frustration simmered inside him, strengthening as the sky darkened. He was glad for the business there was to handle at the station: coats and scarves to gather, trunks to arrange to have transported to Bedford Square. Without those mundane tasks to occupy him, he might have noticed his rising temper felt a bit too good.

Robin was waiting for them in the main concourse, standing still and quiet in front of the departures board. Edmund hadn't seen his son since Robin had become an elder. To human eyes, he looked more ordinary than ever: a tall, pleasant-faced man in a good wool overcoat and fedora. To Edmund's *upyr* sight, he was nothing like before. His power was a silent lake, spreading out from him through the girders of the station and the earth below. The change shocked Edmund and—illogically, perhaps—angered him.

He strode toward his son with his fingers curling like pincers.

"Father," Robin said, subtly straightening.

Edmund's fist flashed out and socked him straight in the nose.

Robin hadn't seen it coming; Edmund barely had himself. If he hadn't pulled the punch at the last fraction of a second, Robin would have flown across the concourse. As it was, he skidded into a nearby newsagent's stand, smashing its display and inspiring gasps and cries that Edmund ignored—despite a number of them coming from his own family.

Too cautious to rise, Robin sprawled where he was and gaped up at his father.

"You could have come for me yourself," Edmund said, his voice so fierce and low he doubted any human could have heard. "You didn't have to change Graham."

Robin used the back of his hand to wipe a brief stream of blood from his nose. A soft crackling sound signaled that the broken bone was knitting itself.

"You're the one who always talks about letting your human children live out their lives, about their right to make their own choices."

"Damn you," Edmund snarled. "Don't throw my words in my face."

"What should I throw then, Father?" Robin asked, the edge in his question suggesting that—son or not, public place or not—he wasn't going to meekly accept another attack. He pushed the fallen newspapers from his body, rising with both wariness and grace. "Graham wanted to do this. He *needed* to."

"And that was enough for you? You agreed to change him because he felt guilty?"

Robin shook his coat straight and met the challenge in his father's gaze. "You, of all people, know the power guilt can wield. More to the point, are you certain he didn't do a better job than I would have? He pulled a whole team together, from what I hear."

Edmund stared at Robin, unable to believe he wasn't ashamed. "He was *human*. You took that away from him."

"I took his humanness away from *you*. He offered it willingly. In any case, that isn't really why you're angry at me, is it?"

Rage poured through Edmund in a burning flood. He

had to fight the growl that tried to rise in his throat. The truth burst out as if it were exploding. "You told him to feed from *her*. You told him Estelle was the safest choice."

"She was." Robin took his shoulders, grimacing at the prickling contact of their warring master energy. When Edmund stiffened like a statue, his son actually shook him. "He was green, Dad. I barely had time to train him. Don't you remember what you were like when you first were changed? How would Graham—and you—have felt if he'd accidentally killed someone? For that matter, how would you have felt if Estelle had refused to help? She's not that small, Dad, and she doesn't think you are, either."

Edmund had to look away. He couldn't face the understanding in Robin's eyes.

"Don't punish her," Robin said softly. "Don't punish yourself."

"Edmund." Estelle had stepped into his line of sight, her hand gently cupping his averted face. He saw her flick a look at Robin. "Is everything all right?"

He blew a ragged breath, then pulled out some of the money he'd withdrawn from his account when they were in Zurich. The motion effectively shook her off, but he told himself he couldn't help that. The newsagent needed to be reimbursed for the damage Edmund's fit of rage had done.

"Everything's fine," he said, waving for the man to approach. "Let's just take care of this and go home."

To Pen's surprise, Graham got into a taxicab with her. At first, she wondered if this meant he intended to continue their relationship, but the cool, stiff silence in which he sat soon put that fantasy to rest.

More than capable of being cool herself, Pen looked out the window rather than at him. Green Park swept by, a dark, tree-filled darkness to the right of them. The streets of Mayfair surrounded them in quiet elegance, fancy hotels and residences that never quite felt like homes. Pen's veins were admirably chilly by the time they rolled beneath the broad metal awning in front of Claridge's Hotel, where she and her father always took apartments in London. For good or ill, Claridge's was as familiar to her as their New York brownstone.

Pen's brows rose when Graham paid the cabby and got out with her.

"You didn't have to do that," she said.

Graham was watching the taxi pull away. "I wanted to make sure you arrived safely."

"Graham, you being nice isn't going to shut my mouth any tighter on your secrets."

Graham turned his head back to her. She knew she'd been sharp, but she refused to blush. "I got out to say good-bye, Pen. And thank you. Like any decent person would who owed their life to you."

Pen pulled her collar closer to her neck. It was freezing here on the sidewalk, and her breath was coming out in clouds.

"Yeah, well," she said. "I know you didn't ask for my help."

Her grudging admission made him smile, which Pen wasn't sure she liked. He glanced at the doorman and back to her.

"Do you want me to come up with you? If your father's here . . ." He rolled his eyes with rare expressiveness.

"I'm not a coward," she said crisply.

"You don't have to be a coward to dread facing Arnold Anderson alone. Remember, I used to work for him. Knowing him, he's probably figured out you weren't watch shopping in Zurich."

As Pen recalled, she'd told him she was traveling to Paris to purchase clothes. Graham was right, though. Her father would know she'd lied to him. She'd missed his birthday, after all, an event they almost always celebrated together.

Fighting a twinge of guilt at the reminder, she forced her shoulders to stay straight.

"I can handle it," she said.

She didn't say she could handle him. No one *handled* Arnold Anderson.

"Well, then . . ." Graham scuffed his shoe on the sidewalk. "I guess this is goodbye. Take care, Pen. Thanks for helping my family."

For helping you, she thought. *I was helping you.*

He offered his hand, and she shook it, his hard bare fingers swallowing her soft gloved ones. She sensed him being careful not to use too much force, and yet she thought there was—just at the end—an extra smidgen of tightening to his grip.

You're imagining things, she told herself as he let go. A little leftover lust was all that was. She wouldn't let it sway her. She'd decide, all on her own, where her loyalty ought to lie.

"Go home, Graham," she said. "Maybe—" Her throat threatened to close, so she swallowed. "Maybe I'll see you around."

Edmund's residence in Bedford Square was as it always had been. The same dark Georgian brick, the same orderly march of white-framed windows. The pattern of the Coade stone door surround had not changed, nor the leaded fanlight that would let in the morning sun. Edmund had cursed that fanlight a time or two. Now he supposed Graham would.

The idea was quite surreal to him.

As the shiny black taxicab ground to a complete halt, Graham materialized from the shadows beside the stoop. His feet were faster than the vehicle that had brought the rest of his family here. Edmund's son didn't fidget as he waited for them to emerge, but he looked restless, as if his goodbye to his friend had not completely satisfied. Though Graham hadn't mentioned possible concerns, Edmund suspected he might have to pay the woman a visit. Penelope Anderson knew more about them than she should, without any particular incentive to keep that knowledge under her hat.

Deciding which memories could be left and which needed erasing was a delicate task. The thought of performing it on one more human wearied him. Edmund had enough unpleasantness rattling in his brain.

Still, weary for a vampire wasn't the same as weary for a human. He stepped out of the cab and offered Estelle his hand. Robin—who seemed to have forgiven his recent outburst—was paying the driver. Sally and Ben directed the unloading of the arriving trunks.

"There's been some repair work in the entryway," Estelle warned, her arm tucked through his elbow. "Nothing to worry about. Graham and Ben took care of it."

He recognized Nim Wei's cool, bookish scent as soon as he stepped into his home. The smell was faint but unexpected. London's queen had been here, had used her power here not too long ago. He wondered if she'd come to help or hinder, but didn't have the energy to ask. Probably both, if she'd been running true to form.

"Oh, look!" Sally exclaimed from the door to the library-parlor. "Mrs. Mackie straightened up." She turned to Edmund, her pretty little face painfully alight. "I sent her a telegram from Zurich, so she'd know you were all right and that we were on our way. I wasn't sure she'd have time to come in and freshen things."

"She took down the Christmas decorations," Estelle observed.

The housekeeper had indeed done so, though she'd left a small pile of wrapped presents on one of the side tables.

His presents, Edmund realized. Presents his family had bought for him while he was gone.

Sally noted where his startled gaze had stopped. "When you feel better, you can open them."

He must have looked as if he wasn't well, which he hadn't meant to do. He turned his eyes around the room where he'd raised his family, where he'd watched Estelle become a part of them. The throw pillows were plumped, and a fire was laid in the grate, awaiting only a match to crackle merrily. His stacks of books were tidied but not shelved. Mrs. Mackie had left everything the way he liked it. As he took this in, something funny happened in his chest. It hitched and tightened, and then he began to cry.

He pressed his hands to the tears leaking silently down his cheeks. "I'm sorry," he said. "I don't know what's wrong with me."

Estelle put her arms around him, letting him hide his face in her hair. "You're all right. You've simply been through a lot."

"Should we go, Daddy?" Sally asked. "Leave you alone for a while?"

Part of him wanted that, but he pushed straight and shook his head. His tears were drying: *upyr* tears that would disappear without a trace. He looked at his children, at Sally and Ben and Graham and even Robin standing in the doorway. Though all of them were grown—now more than ever—he knew Sally wasn't the only one who longed to know he was truly back.

"Sit with me," he said. "I just want to be with all of you now."

He walked to his favorite leather wing chair on legs that didn't feel like they belonged to him—much less to some powerful master vampire. As if Estelle knew he needed something to hold on to, she slid quietly onto his lap. The rest sat as well, awkward but *there*, home again, all of them safe and sound.

A moment later, Robin popped up from his chair.

"I'll open your presents for you," he volunteered, giving them his sweetest, most boyish grin, the one that hadn't altered since he was ten. "That way none of us has to burst with curiosity!"

Bedford Square,
January 24, 1934

The building on Bedford Square didn't resemble the lair of a master vampire—or, rather, Durand's view of it from the mews did not. From the front, where the windows faced the well-groomed park, the house was stately. From the rear . . . Durand squinted doubtfully up the four-story height. From the rear, the dwelling seemed ordinary, standing cheek by jowl with the narrow houses next to it.

Durand couldn't fathom how Fitz Clare tolerated sharing walls with humans.

But Fitz Clare's living arrangements, however repellent to himself, weren't relevant to his business here. Durand drew in and blew out a breath, the better to climb the house's brick silently. Appearances could be deceiving. It was too soon to conclude he'd misidentified his target, and Durand was not an *upyr* who rushed into things. He'd taken two weeks to sever ties with Frank and Li-Hua, and that was after the fiasco at Castle Lohengrin.

He found a window to the attic that was unlatched. His heart rate did not accelerate when he opened it. This was merely a job—a job he'd set himself, but that made no difference. Eyes absorbing every scrap of light, he swung his whip-lean body through the casement without so much as brushing the piles of paper teetering near the sill. The room appeared to be a study or an office. A desk sat in one corner, sharing the space with a jumble of old furniture. Durand recalled that Fitz Clare's cover in the human world was that of a professor.

He tried to imagine needing such a cover, but could not. He preferred not being known to humans at all.

The clutter in the room turned it into an obstacle course. Durand sidestepped a wooden mallet and sent his senses questing through the house. He registered three sleeping mortals, but that was all. This troubled him. Wasn't Fitz Clare here? The neighbor he'd thralled for information had only seen the older son leaving. But perhaps Fitz Clare's skill at glamour was better than he'd known. Perhaps, to the human, Fitz Clare had been invisible.

He focused harder, wondering if a master vampire were capable of cloaking from his own kind. Even if he could, he'd leave signs Durand was too experienced to miss. Satisfied the garret was empty, he strode for the door. He projected his energy into the hinges, spelling them not to squeak.

Then he opened it.

His eyes told him a figure stood on the landing, a bare-chested male in pajama bottoms. His heart jumped, but his brain insisted he was dreaming. *No one here*, it soothed. *No one here at all.*

"No one" rushed him, slammed its rock-hard hands around his neck, and knocked him back to the floor.

The abandoned croquet mallet splintered beneath his skull.

"What are you doing here?" Fitz Clare hissed. "Why are you in my home?"

Durand was perfectly willing to answer, but Fitz Clare's

grip on his throat was squeezing it shut. He wrenched at
Fitz Clare's wrists, futilely trying to pull them away. Fitz
Clare's aura was swamping his somehow, taking it over so
that he couldn't operate at full strength. Durand used his
legs, his weight, but couldn't wrestle the other *upyr* over.
Stacks of paper fell as he kicked out uselessly.

Fitz Clare's hold on him tightened.

The elder wanted to kill him. Their essences were so
entwined Durand could feel the hot desire as if it welled
out of his own heart. To erase it all would have been sweet:
the helplessness, the anger, the soul-sickening fear that he
could be a prisoner again. Fitz Clare had not conquered,
he had been saved. With his iron knife and his cold pity,
Durand was a reminder of the weakness lurking inside
him. Resenting that, Fitz Clare's energy joined his fingers
in constricting his former guard's windpipe.

Fear rose in Durand, odd, pale lights dancing before his
eyes. This should not have happened. *Upyr* his age didn't
need that much oxygen.

I came to ask for your help, Durand thought to Fitz
Clare as clearly as he could. *Don't kill me.*

Fitz Clare released him with a muffled sound of disgust.

"My *help*!" he spat. "You honestly believe I owe you
my help?"

Durand rubbed his throat, waiting for the sensation
that its muscles had been pulverized to subside. He wasn't
entirely sure they hadn't been.

"Oh, to Hades with it," Fitz Clare said. He clambered
off Durand to sit on the floor, an old brown sofa serving to
prop his back. "I'm too tired to kill you tonight."

If this was Fitz Clare tired, Durand didn't want to see
him "in the pink," as the British said. He attempted speaking and found he could.

"The help I'm requesting is in your interest to give."

"And you couldn't, oh, knock on the front door?"

"I didn't think you'd let me in."

"Well, that makes perfect sense," Fitz Clare said sarcastically. "I mean, it's not as if I'd be within my rights to turn you away."

"Are you going to?" Durand asked.

"No, indeed." Fitz Clare tipped his head back onto the cushion and closed his eyes. "Can't wait to hear the whole story."

Durand's lips thinned with disapproval. Did Fitz Clare think he'd come here on a whim? "Frank and Li-Hua have the List."

Fitz Clare's head came up at this curt announcement, his eyes flaring sharp and clear in the dark. "What *list* would you be referring to?"

Fitz Clare had to know already, but Durand answered nonetheless. "The one your sister-in-law has been compiling. The directory to the identity and last known location of every shapechanging *upyr* in existence. There are some non-shapechangers on it, too, which should please London's queen no end."

"Gillian would never let that out of her hands."

Fitz Clare's words weren't a denial, though chances were they were meant to be. Durand pressed his advantage.

"Your brother's wife kept a backup copy in a spot she must have thought was undiscoverable, a ruined monastery outside Rome. My former employers dug up another prize at the same time, a portion of a manuscript written by a monk called Brother Kenelm. They believed it contained the secret to turning humans into *upyr*. They kidnapped you because Kenelm's instructions were incomplete."

"Kenelm was mine." Fitz Clare rubbed his face, his skin outright glowing now. He *did* look weary as he dropped his hands to his thighs. "Kenelm served the chapel on my estate when I was mortal. He and Gillian and another female cooked up that manuscript together. It was designed to misinform humans, so they wouldn't learn the truth about how to destroy us. I expect your employers discovered the original. Once, there were other copies, left in places where they would be found. That's how the stories about us fearing garlic and crosses got started."

"And is the List misinformation, too?"

Fitz Clare sighed. "Regrettably, no."

He pushed to his feet and gazed out the window, as if he could see through the leagues of darkness to all those *upyr* whose places of safety were now at risk. After a weighted moment, he returned his attention to Durand.

"When did you find out Frank and Li-Hua had this document?"

"They didn't tell me until after we'd run from Schloss Oberbad."

"What do they intend to do with it?"

Durand offered a microscopic shrug. "When I left, that was under debate. They spoke of resurrecting their plan to sell vampires to the Germans—either for study or as assassins—though, clearly, their credibility with their would-be allies isn't what it was. In addition to which, it's difficult to control *upyr* you don't create. You foiled their hope of discovering how to do that, so I rather suspect they'll start killing the List's members, one by one, for as long as they can get away with it. Maybe they expect your brother will pay them off. Maybe they don't give a damn. Neither of their tempers is known for its evenness."

This was more than Durand was used to saying at one time, and he was glad to fall silent. Fitz Clare's chest went up and down with a breath. It wasn't easy to remain sitting with the elder staring down at him, but Durand stayed where he was. He knew he was safer there.

"Do you know where they are now?" Fitz Clare asked.

"I only know they're not where they were, which was Hungary. They were leery of sharing too much of their plans with me. I think, toward the end, they suspected my heart wasn't in working for them. They could be anywhere in the world tonight."

"You reneged on your contract to tell me this."

The obviousness of that statement hardly required a response.

"I want to help you stop them," Durand said instead.

Fitz Clare snorted. "You helped them torture me."

"It was my job."

Fitz Clare shook his head disbelievingly.

"They offered me a chance to be independent, to steer my own ship for the first time in four hundred years. I'm not like you, Fitz Clare. I don't like humans. I don't want to protect England or any-damn-where else."

"Then why help at all? Why break your precious oath over this?"

Durand ordered his gaze not to waver. He'd been asking himself that exact question. Why not give Fitz Clare the information and be done with it? Durand had what he wanted from this debacle, regardless of whether he could turn the key to it yet.

"Frank and Li-Hua are just smart enough to be dangerous. They're going to cause trouble for the rest of us."

"Oh, come on," Fitz Clare sneered. "You're not even a shapechanger. What do you care if a few of my line die? No matter what those two do, you're forewarned. There'll be some cozy hole for you to hide in."

Durand drew a sharp breath. "I don't like them," he burst out.

Fitz Clare's smile was slow, his fangs more than half run out. He looked strangely beautiful wearing that lethal expression. Despite the peril of his position, Durand refused to shiver.

"Well," Fitz Clare said, "you and I *do* have something in common."

No matter how abjectly Edmund's world had just gone to hell, the pleasure of returning to his room and finding

Estelle there was undeniable. He stood in the doorway to watch her slumber, worn out from their earlier lovemaking. He was glad she was strong, because ever since they'd been reunited, he couldn't get enough of her. Her scent, her skin, her warmth were medicines he was starving for. If he hadn't been so tired from overcoming Durand, he would have woken her again.

As it was, his grip tightened on the door frame to support his weight. He was more than exhausted now. He thought he'd felt something snap when he used his aura to dominate Durand's, some crucial fuse he'd blown out by overloading it with his own power. He'd been in no state to hold back when he'd destroyed Frank and Li-Hua's nest, nor had he spared himself when he rooted through the minds of seemingly half the humans in Schloss Oberbad. He was probably lucky the mercenary hadn't needed killing. God knew what he'd have damaged inside himself if he'd attempted that.

Being a master might be new to him, but Edmund knew he wasn't recovering as quickly as he ought. As hard as he tried to hide that from his family, he suspected they sensed it, too.

Everyone was waiting for Edmund to be himself again.

Though he didn't think he'd made a sound, Estelle stirred under the covers. She sat up, naked and pink with sleep, her goddess gorgeousness on full display. In spite of everything, Edmund grinned. As Ben would have put it, Estelle had quite a front grill on her.

She pushed her tangled hair from her lovely face. "What is it, Edmund? Why are you up?"

He came to the bed, sat beside her, and took her hand. "Durand broke into the house. I thought he might want to harm one of you. I stopped him before he could get farther than the attic."

"Did you—" *Kill him?* he heard her think. She cleared her throat and began again. "*Did* he want to harm us?"

Edmund squeezed her fingers, more thankful than he could say that she wasn't giving in to alarm. "He claims he wants to help us. Frank and Li-Hua got their hands on a document, a list of names and locations for all my sort of *upyr.*"

"They can't be allowed to keep it!"

"No, they can't." Too weary to resist, Edmund slid under the sheets and pulled Estelle close. She hummed with pleasure and snuggled into his side. Edmund hoped he'd never take such welcomes for granted. "I'll have to tell my brother what's happened."

"The one who heads your Council?"

He nodded and stroked her hair. "I don't know if Aimery can stop them. Frank and Li-Hua have been planning their rebellion for a while. They have resources. Supporters. They've proven the lengths they're willing to go to. This could get ugly."

"Graham will want to help."

"If I tell him."

"Edmund."

"I know. I can only shelter him so much. I just want everyone to be safe. I want everything to be as it was. Stupid, I suppose."

Estelle raised her head. "You're not stupid. Human, maybe. What I want isn't that different."

"What do you want?"

"To be happy we're all together. To appreciate how good it is to be home."

"It is good. Rare and wonderful and fine."

He tipped his head to kiss her, a tender brush of his mouth on hers. As natural as breath, his hand slipped to cup the silken weight of her breast. Her heart began to beat faster beneath his hold, her hardening nipple causing his sex to stir.

Maybe he wasn't as tired as he thought.

"Estelle," he murmured, deepening the incursion of his

tongue. Her palms were roaming up his back, her long, strong legs closing around one of his. When they tightened, heat flashed through him like a summer storm. His fangs began to extend—

And then a rhythmic thumping from the floor below jerked their heads back from each other. Flushed and breathless from the kiss, Estelle pressed her hand to her mouth. She appeared to be stifling an embarrassed laugh.

"Oh, Lord," she said. "I think that's Sally and Ben."

"Hm," Edmund said, wondering what protocol covered this particular state of affairs. "I don't know that we can complain, seeing as they're married now, but if we're all going to stay together, we may need a bigger house!"

Edmund flopped onto his back, the moment broken by the interruption. Following him, Estelle giggled into his shoulder. His now thickly rigid cock stretched up his abdomen, pulsing with annoyance. Estelle's touch slid down to pet it. Naturally, this was useless for calming him—not that he minded. Her hand was wonderfully warm and smooth as it roved his skin. "Perhaps we need a house with separate wings. Getting married seems to have increased their . . . enthusiasm for each other."

Their enthusiasm couldn't be doubted. They'd all witnessed Ben and Sally's simple civil wedding: Edmund, Robin, Graham, and Estelle. Ben and Sally had been so patently delighted with each other that it had been difficult for their audience to remember any reason why they shouldn't be delighted on their behalf. They had a road ahead of them, Edmund knew, but for the present Ben and Sally were simply two very happy young people.

"Graham's lucky he's out with Robin," Estelle said. "I don't think the world contains enough pillows to shield *his* ears."

"Pity mine instead." He bunted his head back against the bed. "This is all so wrong."

"I know," Estelle commiserated teasingly, her fingers

now walking up his chest. "None of your children were supposed to grow up."

Edmund tightened his arms around her, awed and a little frightened by her ability to read him even when he didn't mean to let her into his thoughts. Estelle was so much more than the bed partner of his dreams.

"You've become this family's rock," he said, needing to share what he felt. "I could see that at the wedding, could sense the bonds you'd formed. The way the four of you pulled together humbles me. As terrible as this ordeal was, it hasn't broken even one of you. You're all surer of yourselves, together and apart.

"And you—" He kissed her brow before his voice gave out. "You're my children's dearest friend and defender."

"They're mine as well," Estelle said as huskily. Her hand was patting his pectoral muscle, soothing both him and her. "This family may be the best gift you've given me."

He closed his eyes and rocked her, no longer able to speak. His lust for her had not abated, but his gratitude for what he'd found momentarily held it back.

My love, he whispered to her mind. *My heart and soul.*

He didn't know if she heard him; he'd been afraid to forge too strong a link. Still, hope welled in him, as sweet and clean as the rising of the night's first star. She was his gift, the treasure he'd given himself the day he fell in love with her. All the years that came before gained meaning because they'd led to that miracle. As for the days to come, he had her to help sort them out, didn't he?

As he rolled her beneath him, as she wrapped him in her arms and sighed a welcome for his slow entry, Edmund could think of worse fates than facing the future with Estelle by his side.

Kissing Midnight

THE FIRST BOOK IN THE FITZ CLARE CHRONICLES
BY *USA TODAY* BESTSELLING AUTHOR

EMMA HOLLY

Edmund Fitz Clare has been keeping secrets he can't afford to expose. Not to the orphans he's adopted. Not to the lovely young woman he's been yearning after for years, Estelle Berenger. He's an *upyr*—a shape-shifting vampire—desperate to redeem past misdeeds.

But deep in the heart of London a vampire war is brewing, a conflict that threatens to throw Edmund and Estelle together—and to turn his beloved human family against him…

M413T0209